3-16-2016

20.0

HL770L

Red Queen #2

F/R

GLASS SWORD

RED QUEEN

GLASS SWORD

VICTORIA AVEYARD

THORNDIKE PRESS

A part of Gale, Cengage Learning

GALE
CENGAGE Learning·

Farmington Hills, Mich • San Francisco • New York • Waterville, Maine
Meriden, Conn • Mason, Ohio • Chicago

Recommended for Young Adult Readers.
Copyright © 2016 by Victoria Aveyard.
Red Queen.
Thorndike Press, a part of Gale, Cengage Learning.

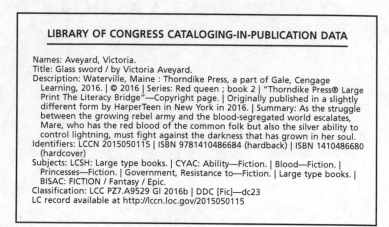

LIBRARY OF CONGRESS CATALOGING-IN-PUBLICATION DATA

Names: Aveyard, Victoria.
Title: Glass sword / by Victoria Aveyard.
Description: Waterville, Maine : Thorndike Press, a part of Gale, Cengage
   Learning, 2016. | © 2016 | Series: Red queen ; book 2 | "Thorndike Press® Large
   Print The Literacy Bridge"—Copyright page. | Originally published in a slightly
   different form by HarperTeen in New York in 2016. | Summary: As the struggle
   between the growing rebel army and the blood-segregated world escalates,
   Mare, who has the red blood of the common folk but also the silver ability to
   control lightning, must fight against the darkness that has grown in her soul.
Identifiers: LCCN 2015050115 | ISBN 9781410486684 (hardback) | ISBN 1410486680
   (hardcover)
Subjects: LCSH: Large type books. | CYAC: Ability—Fiction. | Blood—Fiction. |
   Princesses—Fiction. | Government, Resistance to—Fiction. | Large type books. |
   BISAC: FICTION / Fantasy / Epic.
Classification: LCC PZ7.A9529 Gl 2016b | DDC [Fic]—dc23
LC record available at http://lccn.loc.gov/2015050115

Published in 2016 by arrangement with HarperCollins Children's Books,
a division of HarperCollins Publishers

Printed in Mexico
1 2 3 4 5 6 7 20 19 18 17 16

To my grandparents, here and there.
You are always home.

ONE

I flinch. The rag she gives me is clean, but it still smells like blood. I shouldn't care. I already have blood all over my clothes. The red is mine, of course. The silver belongs to many others. Evangeline, Ptolemus, the nymph lord, all those who tried to kill me in the arena. I suppose some of it is Cal's as well. He bled freely on the sand, cut and bruised by our would-be executioners. Now he sits across from me, staring at his feet, letting his wounds begin the slow process of healing naturally. I glance at one of the many cuts on my arms, probably from Evangeline. Still fresh, and deep enough to leave a scar. Part of me delights in the thought. This jagged gash will not be magically wiped away by a healer's cold hands. Cal and I are not in the Silver world anymore, with someone to simply erase our well-earned scars. We have escaped. Or at least, I have. Cal's chains are a firm reminder of his captivity.

Farley nudges my hand, her touch surprisingly gentle. "Hide your face, lightning girl. It's what they're after."

For once, I do as I'm told. The others follow, pulling red fabric up over their mouths and noses. Cal is the last uncovered face, but not for long. He doesn't fight Farley when she ties his mask into place, making him look like one of us.

If only he was.

An electric hum sets my blood on fire, reminding me of the pulsing, screeching Undertrain. It carries us inexorably forward, to a city that was once a haven. The train races, screaming over ancient tracks like a Silver swift running over open ground. I listen to the grating metal, feel it deep in my bones where a cold ache settles in. My rage, my *strength* back in the arena seem like faraway memories, leaving behind only pain and fear. I can scarcely imagine what Cal must be thinking. He's lost everything, *everything* he ever held dear. A father, a brother, a kingdom. How he's holding himself together, still but for the rocking of the train, I do not know.

No one needs to tell me the reason for our haste. Farley and her Guardsmen, tense as coiled wire, are enough explanation for me. *We are still running.*

Maven came this way before, and Maven will come again. This time with the fury of his soldiers, his mother, and his new crown. Yesterday he was a prince; today he is king. I thought he was my friend, my betrothed, now I know better.

Once, I trusted him. Now I know to hate him, to fear him. He helped kill his father for a crown, and framed his brother for the crime. He knows the radiation surrounding the ruined city is a lie — a trick — and he knows where the train leads. The sanctuary Farley built is no longer safe, not for us. *Not for you.*

We could already be speeding into a trap.

An arm tightens around me, sensing my unease. *Shade.* I still can't believe my brother is here, alive and, strangest of all, like me. Red and Silver — and stronger than both.

"I won't let them take you again," he murmurs, so low I can barely hear him. I suppose loyalty to anyone but the Scarlet Guard, even family, is not allowed. "I promise you that."

His presence is soothing, pulling me backward in time. Past his conscription, to a rainy spring when we could still pretend to be children. Nothing existed but the mud, the village, and our foolish habit of ignoring the future. Now the future is all I think of, wondering what dark path my actions have set us upon.

"What are we going to do now?" I direct the question at Farley, but my eyes find Kilorn. He stands at her shoulder, a dutiful guardian with a clenched jaw and bloody bandages. To think he was a fisherman's apprentice not so long ago. Like Shade, he seems out of place, a ghost of a time before all this.

"There's always somewhere to run," Farley replies, more focused on Cal than anything else.

She expects him to fight, to resist, but he does neither.

"You keep your hands on her," Farley says, turning back to Shade after a long moment. My brother nods, and his palm feels heavy on my shoulder. "She cannot be lost."

I am not a general or a tactician, but her reasoning is clear. I am the little lightning girl — living electricity, a lightning bolt in human form. People know my name, my face, and my abilities. I am valuable, I am powerful, and Maven will do anything to stop me from striking back. How my brother can protect me from the twisted new king, even though he is like me, even though he's the fastest thing I've ever seen, I do not know. But I must believe, even if it seems a miracle. After all, I have seen so many impossible things. Another escape will be the least of them.

The click and slide of gun barrels echo down the train as the Guard makes ready. Kilorn shifts to stand over me, swaying slightly, his grip tight on the rifle slung across his chest. He glances down, his expression soft. He tries to smirk, to make me laugh, but his bright green eyes are grave and afraid.

In contrast, Cal sits quietly, almost peaceful. Though he has the most to fear — chained, surrounded by enemies, hunted by his own brother — he looks serene. I'm not surprised. He's a soldier born and bred. War is something he understands, and we are certainly at war now.

"I hope you don't plan to fight," he says, speaking for the first time in many long minutes. His eyes are on me, but his words bite at Farley. "I hope you plan to run."

"Save your breath, Silver." She squares her shoulders. "I know what we have to do."

I can't stop the words from bursting out. "So does he." The glare she turns on me burns, but I've dealt with worse. I don't even flinch. "Cal knows how they fight, he knows what they'll do to stop us. Use him."

How does it feel to be used? He spit those words at me in the prison beneath the Bowl of Bones and it made me want to die. Now it barely stings.

She doesn't say anything, and that is enough for Cal.

"They'll have Snapdragons," he says grimly.

Kilorn laughs aloud. "Flowers?"

"Airjets," Cal says, his eyes sparking with distaste. "Orange wings, silver bodies, single pilot, easy to maneuver, perfect for an urban assault. They carry four missiles each. Times one squadron, that's forty-eight missiles you're going to have to outrun, plus light ammunition. Can you handle that?"

He's met only with silence. *No, we can't.*

"And the Dragons are the least of our worries. They'll just circle, defend a perimeter, keep us in place until ground troops arrive."

He lowers his eyes, thinking quickly. He's wondering what he would do, if he were on the other side of this. If he were king instead of Maven. "They'll surround us and present terms. Mare and I for your escape."

Another sacrifice. Slowly, I suck in a breath. This morning, yesterday, before all this madness, I would have been glad to give

12

myself over to save just Kilorn and my brother. But now . . . now I know I am special. Now I have others to protect. Now I cannot be lost.

"We can't agree to that," I say. A bitter truth. Kilorn's gaze weighs heavy, but I don't look up. I can't stomach his judgment.

Cal is not so harsh. He nods, agreeing with me. "The king doesn't expect us to give in," he replies. "The jets will bring the ruins down on us, and the rest will mop up the survivors. It will be little more than a massacre."

Farley is a creature of pride, even now when she's terribly cornered. "What do you suggest?" she asks, bending over him. Her words drip disdain. "Total surrender?"

Something like disgust crosses Cal's face. "Maven will still kill you. In a cell or on the battlefield, he won't let any of us live."

"Then better we die fighting." Kilorn's voice sounds stronger than it should, but there's a tremble in his fingers. He looks like the rest of the rebels, willing to do anything for the cause, but my friend is still afraid. Still a boy, no more than eighteen, with too much to live for, and too little reason to die.

Cal scoffs at Kilorn's forced but brazen declaration, yet he doesn't say anything else.

He knows a more graphic description of our impending death won't help anyone.

Farley doesn't share his sentiment and waves a hand, dismissing both of them outright. Behind me, my brother mirrors her determination.

They know something we don't, something they won't say yet. Maven has taught us all the price of trust misplaced.

"We are not the ones who die today," is all she says, before marching toward the front of the train. Her boots sound like hammer falls on the metal flooring, each one smacking of stubborn resolve.

I sense the train slow before I feel it. The electricity wanes, weakening, as we glide into the underground station. What we might find in the skies above, white fog or orange-winged airjets, I do not know. The others don't seem to mind, exiting the Undertrain with great purpose. In their silence, the armed and masked Guard looks like true soldiers, but I know better. They're no match for what is coming.

"Prepare yourself." Cal's voice hisses in my ear, making me shiver. It reminds me of days long past, of dancing in moonlight. "Remember how strong you are."

Kilorn shoulders his way to my side, separating us before I can tell Cal my strength and my ability are all I'm sure of now. The electricity in my veins might be the only thing I trust in this world.

I want to believe in the Scarlet Guard, and certainly in Shade and Kilorn, but I won't let myself, not after the mess my trust, my *blindness* toward Maven got us into. And Cal is out of the question altogether. He is a prisoner, a Silver, the enemy who would betray us if he could — if he had anywhere else to run.

But still, somehow, I feel a pull to him. I remember the burdened boy who gave me a silver coin when I was nothing. With that one gesture he changed my future, and destroyed his own.

And we share an alliance — an uneasy one forged in blood and betrayal. We are connected, we are united — against Maven, against all who deceived us, against the world about to tear itself apart.

Silence waits for us. Gray, damp mist hangs over the ruins of Naercey, bringing the sky down so close I might touch it. It's cold, with the chill of autumn, the season of change and death. Nothing haunts the sky yet, no jets to rain destruction down upon an already destroyed city. Farley sets a brisk pace, leading up from the tracks to the wide, abandoned avenue. The wreckage yawns like a canyon, more gray and broken than I remember.

We march east down the street, toward the shrouded waterfront. The high, half-collapsed structures lean over us, their windows like eyes watching us pass. Silvers could be waiting in the broken hollows and shadowed arches, ready to kill the Scarlet Guard. Maven could make me watch as he struck rebels down one by one. He would not give me the luxury of a clean, quick death. *Or worse,* I think. *He would not let me die at all.*

The thought chills my blood like a Silver shiver's touch. As much as Maven lied to me, I still know a small piece of his heart. I remember him grabbing me through the bars of a cell, holding on with shaking fingers. And I remember the name he carries, the name that reminds me a heart still beats inside him. *His name was Thomas and I watched him die.* He could not save that boy. But he can save me, in his own twisted way.

No. I will never give him the satisfaction of such a thing. I would rather die.

But try as I might, I can't forget the shadow I thought him to be, the lost and forgotten prince. I wish that person were real. I wish he existed somewhere other than my memories.

The Naercey ruins echo strangely, more quiet than they should be. With a start, I realize why. *The refugees are gone.* The woman sweeping mountains of ash, the children hiding in drains, the shadows of my Red brothers and sisters — they have all fled. There's no one left but us.

"Think what you want of Farley, but know she isn't stupid," Shade says, answering my question before I get a chance to ask. "She gave the order to evacuate last night, after she escaped Archeon. She thought you or Maven would talk under torture."

She was wrong. There was no need to torture Maven. He gave his information and his mind freely. He opened his head to his mother, letting her paw through everything she saw there. The Undertrain, the secret city, *the list.* It is all hers now, just like he always was.

The line of Scarlet Guard soldiers stretches out behind us, a disorganized rabble of armed men and women. Kilorn marches directly behind me, his eyes darting, while Farley leads. Two burly soldiers keep Cal on her heels, gripping his arms tensely. With their red scarves, they look like the stuff of nightmares. But there are so few of us now, maybe thirty, all walking wounded. So few survived.

"There's not enough of us to keep this rebellion going, even if we escape again," I whisper to my brother. The low-hanging mist muffles my voice, but he still hears me.

The corner of his mouth twitches, wanting to smile. "That's not your concern."

Before I can press him, the soldier in front of us halts. He is not the only one. At the head of the line, Farley holds up a fist, glaring at the slate-gray sky. The rest mirror her, searching for what we cannot see. Only Cal keeps his eyes on the ground. He already knows what our doom looks like.

A distant, inhuman scream reaches down through the mist. This sound is mechanical and constant, circling overhead. And it is not alone. Twelve arrow-shaped shadows race through the sky, their orange wings cutting in and out of the clouds. I've never seen an airjet properly, not so close or without the cover of night, so I can't stop my jaw from dropping when they come into view. Farley barks orders at the Guard, but I don't hear her. I'm too busy staring at the sky, watching winged death arc overhead. Like Cal's cycle, the flying machines are beautiful, impossibly curved steel and glass. I suppose a magnetron had something to do with their construction — how else can metal *fly*? Blue-tinged engines spark beneath their wings, the telltale sign of electricity. I can barely feel the twinge of them, like a breath against skin, but they're too far away for me to affect. I can only watch — in horror.

They screech and twist around the island of Naercey, never breaking their circle. I can almost pretend they're harmless, nothing but curious birds come to see the obliterated remnants of a rebellion. Then a dart of gray metal sails overhead, trailing smoke, moving almost too fast to see. It collides with a building down the avenue, disappearing through a broken window. A bloom of red-orange explodes a split second later, destroying the entire floor of an already crumbling building. It shatters in on itself, collapsing onto thousand-year-old supports that snap like toothpicks. The entire structure tips, falling so slowly the sight can't be real. When it hits the street, blockading the way ahead of us, I feel the rumble deep in my chest. A cloud of smoke and dust hits us head-on, but I don't cower. It takes more than that to scare me now.

Through the gray-and-brown haze, Cal stands with me, even while his captors crouch. Our eyes meet for a moment, and his shoulders droop. It's the only sign of defeat he'll let me see.

Farley grabs the nearest Guardsman, hoisting her to her feet. "Scatter!" she shouts, gesturing to the alleys on either side of us. "To the north side, to the tunnels!" She points to her lieutenants as she speaks, telling them where to go. "Shade, to the park side!" My brother nods, knowing what she means. Another missile careens into a nearby building, drowning her out. But it's easy to tell what she's shouting.

Run.

Part of me wants to hold my ground, to stand, to fight. My purple-and-white lightning will certainly make me a target and draw the jets away from the fleeing Guard. I might even take a plane or two with me. But that cannot be. I'm worth more than the rest, more than red masks and bandages. Shade and I must survive — if not for the cause, then for the others. For the list of hundreds like us — hybrids, anomalies, freaks, Red-and-Silver impossibilities — who will surely die if we fail.

Shade knows this as well as I do. He loops his arm into mine, his grip so tight as to be bruising. It's almost too easy to run in step with him, to let him guide me off the wide avenue and into a gray-green tangle of overgrown trees spilling into the street. The deeper we go, the thicker they become, gnarled together like deformed fingers. A thousand years of neglect turned this little plot into a dead jungle. It shelters us from the sky, until we can only hear the jets circling closer and closer. Kilorn is never far behind. For a moment, I can pretend we're back at home, wandering the Stilts, looking for fun and trouble.

Trouble is all we seem to find.

When Shade finally skids to a stop, his heels scarring the dirt beneath us, I chance a glance around. Kilorn halts next to us, his rifle aimed uselessly skyward, but no one else follows. I can't even see the street anymore, or the red rags fleeing into the ruins.

My brother glares up through the boughs of the trees, watching and waiting for the jets to fly out of range.

"Where are we going?" I ask him, breathless.

Kilorn answers instead. "The river," he says. "And then the ocean. Can you take us?" He glances at Shade's hands, as if he could see his ability plain in his flesh. But Shade's strength is buried like mine, invisible until he chooses to reveal it.

My brother shakes his head. "Not in one

jump, it's too far. And I'd rather run, save my strength." His eyes darken. "Until we really need it."

I nod, agreeing. I know firsthand what it is to be ability-worn, tired in your bones, barely able to move, let alone fight.

"Where are they taking Cal?"

My question makes Kilorn wince.

"Hell if I care."

"You should," I fire back, even as my voice shakes with hesitation. *No, he shouldn't. Neither should you. If the prince is gone, you must let him go.* "He can help us get out of this. He can fight *with* us."

"He'll escape or kill us the second we give him the chance," he snaps, tearing away his scarf to show the angry scowl beneath.

In my head, I see Cal's fire. It burns everything in its path, from metal to flesh. "He could've killed you already," I say. It's not an exaggeration, and Kilorn knows it.

"Somehow I thought you two would outgrow your bickering," Shade says, stepping between us. "How silly of me."

Kilorn forces out an apology through gritted teeth, but I do no such thing. My focus is on the jets, letting their electric hearts beat against mine. They weaken with each second, getting farther and farther away. "They're flying away from us. If we're going to go, we need to do it now."

Both my brother and Kilorn look at me strangely, but neither argue. "This way," Shade says, pointing through the trees. A small, almost invisible path winds through them, where the dirt has been swept away to reveal stone and asphalt beneath. Again, Shade links his arm through mine, and Kilorn charges ahead, setting a swift pace for us to follow.

Branches scrape against us, bending over the narrowing path, until it's impossible for us to run side by side. But instead of letting me go, Shade squeezes even tighter. And then I realize he's not squeezing me at all. It's the air, the *world*. Everything and anything tightens in a blistering, black second. And then, in a blink, we're on the other side of the trees, looking back to see Kilorn emerge from the gray grove.

"But he was ahead," I murmur aloud, looking back and forth between Shade and the pathway. We cross into the middle of the street, with the sky and smoke drifting overhead. "You —"

Shade grins. The action seems out of place against the distant scream of jets. "Let's say I . . . jumped. As long as you're holding on to me, you'll be able to come along," he says, before hurrying us into the next alley.

My heart races with the knowledge that I just *teleported,* to the point where it's almost possible to forget our predicament.

The jets are quick to remind me. Another missile explodes to the north, bringing down a building with the rumble of an earthquake. Dust races down the alley in a wave, painting us in another layer of gray. Smoke and fire are so familiar to me now that I barely smell it, even when ash begins to fall like snow. We leave our footprints in it. Perhaps they will be the last marks we make.

Shade knows where to go and how to run. Kilorn has no trouble keeping up, even with the rifle weighing him down. By now, we've circled back to the avenue. To the east, a swirl of daylight breaks through the dirt and dust, bringing with it a salty gasp of sea air. To the west, the first collapsed building lies like a fallen giant, blocking any retreat to the train. Broken glass, the iron skeletons of buildings, and strange slabs of faded white screens rise around us, a palace of ruins.

What was this? I dimly wonder. *Julian would know.* Just thinking his name hurts, and I push the sensation away.

A few other red rags dart through the ashen air, and I look for a familiar silhouette. But Cal is nowhere to be seen, and it makes me so terribly afraid.

"I'm not leaving without him."

Shade doesn't bother to ask who I'm talking about. He already knows.

"The prince is coming with us. I give you my word."

My response cuts my insides. "I don't trust your word."

Shade is a soldier. His life has been anything but easy, and he is no stranger to pain. Still, my declaration wounds him deeply. I see it in his face.

I'll apologize later, I tell myself.

If later ever comes.

Another missile sails overhead, striking a few streets away. The distant thunder of an explosion doesn't mask the harsher and more terrifying noise rising all around.

The rhythm of a thousand marching feet.

TWO

The air thickens with a cloak of ash, buying us a few seconds to stare down our oncoming doom. The silhouettes of soldiers move down the streets from the north. I can't see their guns yet, but a Silver army doesn't need guns to kill.

Other Guardsmen flee before us, sprinting down the avenue with abandon. For now, it looks like they might escape, but to where? There's only the river and the sea beyond. There's nowhere to go, nowhere to hide. The army marches slowly, at a strange shuffling pace. I squint through the dust, straining to see them. And then I realize what this is, what Maven has done. The shock of it sparks in me, *through* me, forcing Shade and Kilorn to jump back.

"Mare!" Shade shouts, half-surprised, half-angry. Kilorn doesn't say anything, watching me wobble on the spot.

My hand closes on his arm and he doesn't

flinch. My sparks are already gone — he knows I won't hurt him. "Look," I say, pointing.

We knew soldiers would come. Cal told us, *warned us,* that Maven would send in a legion after the airjets. But not even Cal could have predicted this. Only a heart so twisted as Maven's could dream up this nightmare.

The figures of the first line are not wearing the clouded gray of Cal's hard-trained Silver soldiers. They are not even soldiers at all. They are servants in red coats, red shawls, red tunics, red pants, red shoes. So much red they could be bleeding. And around their feet, clinking against the ground, are iron chains. The sound scrapes against me, drowning out the airjets and the missiles and even the harsh-barked orders of the Silver officers hiding behind their Red wall. The chains are all I hear.

Kilorn bristles, growling. He steps forward, raising his rifle to shoot, but the gun shudders in his hands. The army is still across the avenue, too far for an expert shot even *without* a human shield. Now it's worse than impossible.

"We have to keep moving," Shade mutters. Anger flares in his eyes, but he knows what must be done, what must be *ignored,* to stay alive. "Kilorn, come with us now, or we'll leave you."

My brother's words sting, waking me up from my horrified daze. When Kilorn doesn't move, I take his arm, whispering into his ear, hoping to drown out the chains.

"Kilorn." It's the voice I used on Mom when my brothers went to war, when Dad had a breathing attack, when things fell apart. "Kilorn, there's nothing we can do for them."

The words hiss through his teeth. "That's not true." He glances over his shoulder at me. "You have to do *something*. You can save them —"

To my eternal shame, I shake my head. "No, I can't."

We keep running. And Kilorn follows.

More missiles explode, faster and closer with each passing second. I can barely hear over the ringing in my ears. Steel and glass sway like reeds in the wind, bending and breaking until biting silver rain falls down upon us. Soon, it's too dangerous to run, and Shade's grip tightens on me. He grabs Kilorn too, jumping all three of us as the world collapses. My stomach twists every time the darkness closes in, and every time, the falling city gets closer. Ash and concrete dust choke our vision, making it difficult to breathe. Glass shatters in a bright storm, leaving shallow cuts across my face and hands, shredding my clothes. Kilorn looks worse than I do, his bandages red with fresh blood, but he keeps moving, careful not to outpace us. My brother's grip never weakens, but he begins to tire, paling with every new jump. I'm not helpless, using my sparks to deflect the jagged metal shrapnel that even Shade can't jump us away from. But we're not enough, not even to save ourselves.

"How much farther?" My voice sounds small, drowned out by the tide of war. Against the haze, I can't see farther than a few feet. But I can still *feel*. And what I feel are wings, engines, *electricity* screaming overhead, swooping closer and closer. We might as well be mice waiting for hawks to pluck us from the ground.

Shade stops us short, his honey-colored eyes sweeping back and forth. For one frightening second, I fear he might be lost. "Wait," he says, knowing something we don't.

He stares upward, at the skeleton of a once great structure. It's massive, taller than the highest spire of the Hall of the Sun, wider than the great Caesar's Square of Archeon. A tremor runs down my spine when

I realize — it's *moving.* Back and forth, side to side, swaying on twisting supports already worn by centuries of neglect. As we watch, it starts to tip, slumping slowly at first, like an old man settling into his chair. Then faster and faster, falling above us and around us.

"Hold on to me," Shade shouts over the din, adjusting his grip on us both. He wraps his arm around my shoulders, crushing me to him, almost too tight to bear. I expect the now unpleasant sensation of jumping, but it never comes. Instead, I'm greeted by a more familiar sound.

Gunfire.

Now it isn't Shade's ability saving my life, but his flesh. A bullet meant for me catches him in the meat of his upper arm, while another strafes his leg. He roars in anguish, almost falling to the cracked earth beneath. I feel the shot through him, but I have no time for pain. More bullets sing through the air, too fast and numerous to fight. We can only run, fleeing both the collapsing building and the oncoming army. One cancels out the other, with the twisted steel falling between the legion and us. At least, that's what should happen. Gravity and fire made the structure fall, but the might of magnetrons stop it from shielding us. When I look back, I can see them, with silver hair and black armor, a dozen or so sweeping away every falling beam and steel support. I'm not close enough to see their faces, but I know House Samos well enough. Evangeline and Ptolemus direct their family, clearing the street so the legion can press on. So they can finish what they started and kill us all.

If only Cal had destroyed Ptolemus in the arena; if only I had shown Evangeline the same level of kindness she showed me. Then we might have a chance. But our mercy has a cost, and it might be our lives.

I hold on to my brother, supporting him as best I can. Kilorn does most of the heavy lifting. He takes the bulk of Shade's weight, half dragging him toward a still smoking impact crater. We gladly dive into it, finding some refuge from the storm of bullets. But not much. Not for long.

Kilorn pants and sweat beads on his brow. He rips off one of his own sleeves, using it to bandage up Shade's leg. Blood stains it quickly. "Can you jump?"

My brother furrows his brow, feeling not his pain but his strength. I understand that well enough. Slowly he shakes his head, his eyes going dark. "Not yet."

Kilorn curses under his breath. "Then what do we do?"

31

It takes me a second to realize he's asking me and not my older brother. Not the soldier who knows battle better than us. But he's not really asking me either. Not Mare Barrow of the Stilts, the thief, his friend. Kilorn is looking to someone else now, to who I became in the halls of a palace and the sands of an arena.

He's asking the lightning girl.

"Mare, what do we do?"

"You leave me, that's what you do!" Shade growls through clenched teeth, answering before I can. "You run to the river, you find Farley. I'll jump to you as soon as I can."

"Don't lie to a liar," I say, trying my best to keep from shaking. My brother was only just returned to me, a ghost back from the dead. I won't let him slip away again, not for anything. "We're getting out of here together. *All* of us."

The legion's march rumbles the ground. One glance over the edge of the crater tells me they're less than a hundred yards away, advancing fast. I can see the Silvers between the gaps in the Red line. The foot soldiers wear the clouded gray uniforms of the army, but some have armor, the plates chased with familiar colors. Warriors from the High Houses. I see bits of blue, yellow, black, brown, and more. Nymphs and telkies and silks and strongarms, the most powerful fighters the Silvers can throw at us. They think Cal the king's killer, me a terrorist, and they'll bring the whole city down to destroy us.

Cal.

Only my brother's blood and Kilorn's uneven breathing keeps me from vaulting out of the crater. I must find him, I *must.* If not for myself then for the cause, to protect the retreat. He's worth a hundred good soldiers. He's a golden shield. But he's probably gone, escaped, having melted his chains and run when the city began to crumble.

No, he wouldn't run. He would never run from that army, from Maven, or from me.

I hope I'm not wrong.

I hope he isn't already dead.

"Get him up, Kilorn." In the Hall of the Sun, the late Lady Blonos taught me how to speak like a princess. It is a cold voice, unyielding, leaving no room for contest.

Kilorn obeys, but Shade still has it in him to protest. "I'll only slow you down."

"You can apologize for that later," I reply, helping him hop to his feet. But I'm barely paying attention to them, my concentration elsewhere. "Get moving."

"Mare, if you think we're leaving you —"

When I turn on Kilorn, I have sparks in my hands and determination in my heart. His words die on his lips. He glances past me, toward the army advancing with every passing second. Telkies and magnetrons scrape debris out of the street, opening the obliterated way with resounding scrapes of metal on stone.

"Run."

Again, he obeys and Shade can do nothing but limp along, leaving me behind. As they clamber out of the crater, scrambling west, I take measured steps east. The army will stop for me. They must.

After one terrifying second, the Reds slow, their chains clinking as they halt. Behind them, Silvers balance black rifles on their shoulders, as if they were nothing at all. The war transports, great machines with treaded wheels, grind to a screeching stop somewhere behind the army. I can feel their power thrum through my veins.

The army is close enough now that I hear officers bark orders. "The lightning girl!" "Keep the line, stand firm!" "Take aim!" "Hold your fire!"

The worst comes last, ringing out against the suddenly quiet street. Ptolemus's voice is familiar, full of hatred and rage.

"Make way for the king!" he shouts.

I stagger back. I expected Maven's armies, but not Maven himself. He is not a soldier like his brother, and he has no business leading an army. But here he is, stalking through the parting troops, with Ptolemus and Evangeline on his heels. When he steps out from behind the Red line, my knees almost buckle. His armor is polished black, his cape crimson. Somehow he seems taller than he did this morning. He still wears his father's crown of flames, though it has no place on a battlefield. I suppose he wants to show the world what he's won with his lies, what a great prize he's stolen. Even from so far away, I can feel the heat of his glare and his roiling anger. It burns me from inside out.

Nothing but the jets whistle overhead; it is the only sound in the world.

"I see you're still brave," Maven says, his voice carrying down the avenue. It echoes among the ruins, taunting me. "And foolish."

Like in the arena, I will not give him the satisfaction of my anger and fear.

"They should call you the little quiet girl." He laughs coldly, and his army laughs with him. The Reds remain silent, their eyes fixed on the ground. They don't want to watch what's about to happen. "Well, quiet girl, tell your rat friends it is over. They are surrounded. Call them out, and I will give them the gift of good deaths."

Even if I could give such an order, I never would. "They're already gone."

Don't lie to a liar, and Maven is the grandest liar of all.

Still, he looks unsure. The Scarlet Guard has escaped so many times already, in Caesar's Square, in Archeon. Perhaps they might escape even now. What an embarrassment that would be. What a disastrous start to his reign.

"And the traitor?" His voice sharpens, and Evangeline moves closer to him. Her silver hair glints like the edge of a razor, brighter than her gilded armor. But he moves away from her, batting her aside like a cat would a toy. "What about my wretched brother, the fallen prince?"

He never hears my answer, for I have none.

Maven laughs again and this time it stabs through my heart. "Has he abandoned you too? Did he run away? The coward kills our father and tries to steal my throne, only to slink off and hide?" He bristles, pretending for the sake of his nobles and soldiers. For them, he must still seem the tragic son, a king never meant for a crown, who wants nothing more than justice for the dead.

I raise my chin in challenge. "Do you think Cal would do such a thing?"

Maven is far from foolish. He is wicked but not stupid, and he knows his brother better than anyone else alive. Cal is no coward and never will be. Lying to his subjects will never change that. Maven's eyes betray his heart and he glances side-long, at the alleys and streets leading away from the war-torn avenue. Cal could be hiding in any one, waiting to strike. I could even be the trap, the bait to draw out the weasel I once called my betrothed and my friend. When he turns his head, his crown slips, too big for his skull. Even the metal knows it does not belong to him.

"I think you stand alone, Mare." He speaks softly. Despite all he's done to me, my name in his mouth makes me shiver, thinking of days gone by. Once he said it with kindness and affection. Now it sounds like a curse. "Your friends are gone. You have lost. And you are an abomination, the only one of your wretched kind. It will be a mercy to remove you from this world."

More lies, and we both know it. I mirror his cold laugh. For a second, we look like friends again. Nothing is further from the truth.

A jet overhead sweeps by, its wings almost scraping the tip of a nearby ruin. It's so close. *Too close.* I can feel its electric heart, its whirring engines somehow keeping it aloft. I reach for it as best I can, like I have so many times before. Like the lights, like the cameras, like every wire and circuit since I became the lightning girl, I take hold of it — and *shut it off.*

The airjet dips, nose down, gliding for a moment on heavy wings. Its original trajectory meant to take it above the avenue, high over the legion to protect the king. Now it dives headfirst into them, sailing over the Red line to collide with hundreds of Silvers. The Samos magnetrons and Provos telkies aren't quick enough to stop the jet as it plows into the street, sending asphalt and bodies flying. The resounding boom as it explodes nearly knocks me off my feet, pushing me farther away. The blast is deafening, disorienting, and painful. *No time for pain* repeats in my head. I don't bother to watch the chaos of Maven's army. I am already running, and my lightning is with me.

Purple-and-white sparks shield my back, keeping me safe from the swifts trying to run me down. A few collide with my lightning, trying to break through. They fall back in piles of smoked flesh and twitching bone. I'm grateful I can't see their faces, or else I might dream of them later. Bullets come next, but my zigzagging sprint makes me a difficult target. The few shots that get close shriek apart in my shield, like my body was supposed to when I fell into the electric net at Queenstrial. That moment seems so long ago. Overhead, the jets scream again, this time careful to keep their distance. Their missiles are not so polite.

The ruins of Naercey stood for thousands of years, but will not survive this day. Buildings and streets crumble, destroyed by Silver powers and missiles alike. Everything and everyone has been unleashed. The magnetrons twist and snap steel support beams, while telkies and strong-arms hurl rubble through the ashen sky. Water bleeds up from the sewers as nymphs attempt to flood the city, flushing out the last of the Guardsmen hiding in the tunnels below us. The wind howls, strong as a hurricane, from the windweavers in the army. Water and rubble sting my eyes, the gusts so sharp they are nearly blinding. Oblivions' explosions rock the ground beneath me and I stumble, confused. I never used to fall. But now my face scrapes against the asphalt, leaving blood in my wake. When I get back up, a banshee's glass-shattering scream knocks me down again, forcing me to cover my ears. More blood there, dripping fast and thick between my fingers. But the banshee who flattened me has accidentally saved me. As I fall, another missile blasts over my head, so near I feel it ripple the air.

It explodes too close, the heat pulsing through my hasty lightning shield. Dimly, I wonder if I'll die without eyebrows. But instead of burning through me, the heat stands constant, uncomfortable but not unbearable. Strong, bruising hands wrench me to my feet, and blond hair glints in the firelight. I can just make out her face through the biting windstorm. *Farley.* Her gun is gone, her clothes torn, and her muscles quiver, but she keeps holding me up.

Behind her, a tall, familiar figure cuts a black silhouette against the explosion. He holds it back with a single, outstretched hand. His shackles are gone, melted or cast away. When he turns, the flames grow, licking at the sky and the destroyed street, but never us. Cal knows exactly what he's doing, directing the firestorm around us like water around rock. As in the arena, he forms a burning wall across the avenue, protecting us from his brother and the legion beyond.

But now, his flames are strong, fed by oxygen and rage. They leap up into the air, so hot the base burns ghostly blue.

More missiles drop, but again, Cal contains their power, using it to feed his own. It's almost beautiful, watching his long arms arc and turn, transforming destruction into protection with steady rhythm.

Farley tries to pull me away, overpowering me. With the flames defending us, I turn to see the river a hundred yards away. I can even see the hulking shadows of Kilorn and my brother, limping toward supposed safety.

"Come on, Mare," she growls, half dragging my bruised and weakened body.

For a second, I let her pull me along. It hurts too much to think clearly. But one glance back and I understand what she's doing, what she's trying to make *me* do.

"I'm not leaving without him!" I shout for the second time today.

"I think he's doing fine on his own," she says, her blue eyes reflecting the fire.

Once, I thought like her. That Silvers were invincible, gods upon the earth, too powerful to destroy. But I killed three just this morning; Arven, the Rhambos strongarm, and the nymph lord Osanos. Probably more with the lightning storm. And they almost killed me, and Cal, for that matter. We had to save each other in the arena. And we must do so again.

Farley is bigger than me, taller and stronger, but I'm more agile. Even banged up and half-deaf. One flick of my ankle, one well-timed shove, and she stumbles backward, letting go. I turn in the same motion, palms outstretched, feeling for what I need. Naercey has far less electricity than Archeon or even the Stilts, but I don't need to leach power from anything now. I make my own.

The first blast of nymph water pounds against the flames with the strength of a tidal wave. Most of it flash boils into vapor, but the rest falls on the wall, extinguishing the great tongues of fire. I answer the water with my own electricity, aiming for the waves curling and crashing in midair. Behind the wave, the Silver legion marches forward, lunging for us. At least the chained Reds have been pulled away, relegated to the back of the line. Maven's doing. He won't let them slow him down.

His soldiers meet my lightning instead of open air, and behind it, Cal's fire jumps back up from the embers.

"Move back slowly," Cal says, gesturing with an open hand. I mirror his measured steps, careful not to look away from the oncoming doom. Together we alternate back and forth, protecting our own retreat. When his flame falls, my lightning rises, and so on. Together, we have a chance.

He mutters little commands: when to step, when to raise a wall, when to let it drop. He looks more exhausted than I've ever seen him, his veins blue-black beneath pale skin, with gray circles rimming his eyes. I know I must look worse. But his pacing keeps us from giving out entirely, allowing little bits of our strengths to return just when we need.

"Just a little farther," Farley calls, her voice echoing from behind. But she's not running off. She's staying with us, even though she's just human. *She's braver than I gave her credit for.*

"Farther to what?" I growl through gritted teeth, tossing up another net of electricity. Despite Cal's commands, I'm getting slower, and a bit of rubble flies through. It breaks a few yards away, crumbling into dust. We are running out of time.

But so is Maven.

I can smell the river, and the ocean beyond. Sharp and salty, it beckons, but to what end, I have no idea. I only know that Farley and Shade believe it will save us from Maven's jaws. When I glance behind me, I see nothing but the avenue, dead-ending at

43

the river's edge. Farley stands, waiting, her short hair stirring in the hot wind. *Jump,* she mouths, before plunging off the edge of the crumbled street.

What is it with her and leaping into an abyss?

"She wants us to jump," I tell Cal, turning back just in time to supplant his wall.

He grunts in agreement, too focused to speak. Like my lightning, his fires grow weak and thin. We can almost see through them now, to the soldiers on the other side. Flickering flame distorts their features, turning eyes into burning coals, mouths into smiling fangs, and men into demons.

One of them steps up to the wall of fire, close enough to burn. But he doesn't. Instead, he draws the flames apart like a curtain.

Only one person can do that.

Maven shakes embers from his silly cape, letting the silk burn away while his armor holds firm. He has the gall to smile.

And somehow, Cal has the strength to turn away. Instead of tearing Maven apart with his bare hands, he takes my wrist in his searing-hot grip. We sprint together, not bothering to defend our backs. Maven is no match for either of us, and he knows it. Instead, he screams. Despite the crown and the blood on his hands, he is still so young.

"Run, murderer! Run, lightning girl! Run fast and far!" His laughter echoes off the crumbling ruins, haunting me. "There is nowhere I won't find you!"

I'm dimly aware of my lightning failing, giving out as I get farther away. Cal's own flame crumbles with it, exposing us to the rest of the legion. But we're already jumping through midair, to the river ten feet below.

We land, not with a splash but the resounding clang of metal. I have to roll to keep from shattering my ankles, but still feel a hollow, aching pain run up my bones. *What?* Farley waits, knee-deep in the cold river, next to a cylindrical metal tube with an open top. Without speaking she clambers into it, disappearing into whatever lies beneath us. We have no time to argue or ask questions, and follow blindly.

At least Cal has the good sense to close the tube behind us, shutting out the river and the war above. It hisses pneumatically, forming an airtight seal. But that won't protect us for long, not against the legion.

"More tunnels?" I ask breathlessly, whirling to Farley. My vision spots with the motion and I have to slump against the wall, my legs shaking.

Like she did on the street, Farley puts one arm under my shoulder, supporting my weight. "No, this isn't a tunnel," she says with a puzzling smirk.

And then I feel it. Like a battery humming somewhere, but bigger. Stronger. It pulses all around us, down the strange hallway swimming with blinking buttons and low, yellow lights. I glimpse red scarves moving down the passage, hiding the faces of the Guardsmen. They look hazy, like crimson shadows. With a groan, the whole hall shudders and *drops,* angling downward. *Into the water.*

"A boat. An underwater boat," Cal says. His voice is faraway, shaky, and weak. Just like I feel.

Neither of us makes it more than a few feet before we collapse against the sloping walls.

THREE

In the past few days, I've woken up in a jail cell and then on a train. Now it's an underwater boat. *Where will I wake up tomorrow?*

I'm beginning to think this has all been a dream, or a hallucination, or worse. But can you feel tired in dreams? Because I certainly do. My exhaustion is bone-deep, in every muscle and nerve. My heart is another wound entirely, still bleeding from betrayal and failure. When I open my eyes, finding cramped, gray walls, everything I want to forget comes rushing back. It's like Queen Elara is in my head again, forcing me to relive my worst memories. As much as I try, I can't stop them.

My quiet maids were executed, guilty of nothing but painting my skin. Tristan, speared like a pig. Walsh. She was my brother's age, a servant from the Stilts, my friend — *one of us.* And she died cruelly, by her own hand, to protect the Guard, our

47

purpose, and me. Even more died in the tunnels of Caesar's Square, Guardsmen killed by Cal's soldiers, killed by our foolish plan. The memory of red blood burns, but so does the thought of silver. Lucas, a friend, a protector, a Silver with a kind heart, executed for what Julian and I made him do. Lady Blonos, decapitated because she taught me how to sit properly. Colonel Macanthos, Reynald Iral, Belicos Lerolan. Sacrificed for the cause. I almost retch when I remember Lerolan's twin boys, four years old, killed in the explosion that followed the shooting. Maven told me it was an accident — a punctured gas line, but now I know better. His evil runs too deep for such co-incidence. I doubt he minded throwing a few more bodies on the blaze, if only to convince the world the Guard was made of monsters. He'll kill Julian too, and Sara. They're probably dead already. I can't think of them at all. It's too painful. Now my thoughts turn back to Maven himself, to cold blue eyes and the moment I realized his charming smile hid a beast.

The bunk beneath me is hard, the blankets thin, with no pillow to speak of, but part of me wants to lie back down. Already my headache returns, throbbing with the electric pulse of this miracle boat. It is a firm reminder — there is no peace for me here. Not yet, not while so much more must be done. *The list. The names. I must find them. I must keep them safe from Maven and his mother.* Heat spreads across my face, my skin flushing with the memory of Julian's little book of hard-won secrets. A record of those like me, with the strange mutation that gives us Red blood and Silver abilities. The list is Julian's legacy. And mine.

I swing my legs over the side of the cot, almost thwacking my head on the bunk above me, and find a neatly folded set of clothing on the floor. Black pants that are too long, a dark red shirt with threadbare elbows, and boots missing laces. Nothing like the fine clothes I found in a Silver cell, but they feel right against my skin.

I barely have the shirt over my head when my compartment door bangs open on great iron hinges. Kilorn waits expectantly on the other side, his smile forced and grim. He shouldn't blush, having seen me in various stages of undress for many summers, but his cheeks redden anyway.

"It's not like you to sleep so long," he says, and I hear worry in his voice.

I shrug it off and stand on weak legs. "I guess I needed it." An odd ringing in my ears takes hold, piercing but not painful. I shake my head back and forth, trying to get rid of it, looking like a wet dog in the process.

"That'll be the banshee scream." He crosses to me and takes my head in gentle but callused hands. I submit to his examination, sighing in annoyance. He turns me sideways, glancing at ears that ran red with blood however long ago. "You're lucky it didn't hit you head-on."

"I'm a lot of things, but I don't think lucky is one of them."

"You're alive, Mare," he says sharply, pulling away. "That's more than many can say." His glare brings me back to Naercey, when I told my brother I didn't trust his word. Deep in my heart, I know I still don't.

"I'm sorry," I mutter quickly. Of course I know others have died, for the cause and for me. But I've died too. Mare of the Stilts died the day she fell onto a lightning shield. Mareena, the lost Silver princess, died in the Bowl of Bones. And I don't know what new person opened her eyes on the Undertrain. I only know what she has been and what she has lost, and the weight of it is almost crushing.

"Are you going to tell me where we're going, or is that another secret?" I try to keep the bitterness from my voice but fail miserably.

Kilorn is polite enough to ignore it and leans back against the door. "We left Naercey five hours ago, and we're headed northeast. That's honestly all I know."

"And that doesn't bother you at all?"

He only shrugs. "What makes you think the higher-ups trust me, or you, for that matter? You know better than anyone how foolish we've been, and the high cost we've paid." Again, I feel the sting of memory. "You said yourself, you can't even trust Shade. I doubt anyone's going to be sharing secrets anytime soon."

The jab doesn't hurt as much as I expected it to. "How is he?"

Kilorn tosses his head, gesturing out to the hallway. "Farley carved out a nice little medical station for the wounded. He's doing better than the others. Cursing a lot, but definitely better." His green eyes darken a bit, and he turns his gaze away. "His leg —"

I draw in a startled breath. "Infected?" At home in the Stilts, infection was as bad as a severed arm. We didn't have much medicine, and once the blood went bad, all you could do was keep chopping, hoping to outrun fever and blackened veins.

To my relief, Kilorn shakes his head. "No, Farley dosed him good, and the Silvers fight with clean bullets. So that's big of them." He laughs darkly, expecting me to join him. Instead, I shiver. The air is so cold down here. "But he'll definitely be limping for a while."

"Will you take me to him or do I have to figure out the way myself?"

Another dark laugh and he extends his arm. To my surprise, I find that I need his support to help me walk. Naercey and the Bowl of Bones have certainly taken their toll.

Mersive. That's what Kilorn calls the strange underwater boat. How it manages to sail *beneath* the ocean is beyond both of us, though I'm sure Cal will figure it out. He's next on my list. I'll find him after I make sure my brother is still breathing. I remember Cal being barely conscious when we escaped, just like me. But I don't suppose Farley will set him up in the medical station, not with injured Guardsmen all around. There's too much bad blood and no one wants an inferno in a sealed metal tube.

The banshee's scream still rings in my head, a dull whine that I try to ignore. And with every step, I learn about new aches and bruises. Kilorn notes my every wince and slows his pace, allowing me to lean on his arm. He ignores his own wounds, deep cuts hidden beneath yet another set of fresh bandages. He always had battered hands, bruised and cut from fishing hooks and rope, but they were familiar wounds. They meant he was safe, employed, free from conscription. If not for one dead fish master, little scars would be his only burden.

Once that thought would have made me sad. Now I feel only rage.

The main passage of the mersive is long but narrow, divided by several metal doors with thick hinges and pressurized seals. To close off portions if need be, to stop the entire vessel from flooding and sinking. But the doors give me no comfort whatsoever. I can't stop thinking about dying at the bottom of the ocean, locked in a watery coffin. Even Kilorn, a boy raised on water, seems uncomfortable. The dim lights set into the ceiling filter strangely, cutting shadows across his face to make him appear old and drawn.

The other Guardsmen aren't so affected, coming and going with great purpose. Their red scarves and shawls have been lowered, revealing faces set in grim determination.

They carry charts, trays of medical supplies, bandages, food, or even the occasional rifle down the passage, always hurrying and chattering to each other. But they stop at the sight of me, pressing back against the walls to give me as much room as possible in the narrow space. The more daring ones look me in the eye, watching me limp past, but most stare at their feet.

A few even seem afraid.

Of me.

I want to say thank you, to somehow express how deeply indebted I am to every man and woman aboard this strange ship. *Thank you for your service* almost slips past my lips, but I clench my jaw to keep it back. *Thank you for your service.* It's what they print in the notices, the letters sent to tell you your children have died for a useless war. How many parents did I watch weep over those words? How many more will receive them, when the Measures send even younger children to the front?

None, I tell myself. *Farley will have a plan for that, just like we will come up with a way to find the newbloods — the others like me. We will do something. We* must *do something.*

The Guardsmen against the wall mutter among themselves as I pass. Even the ones

54

who can't stand to look at me whisper to one another, not bothering to mask their words. I suppose they think what they're saying is a compliment.

"The lightning girl" echoes from them, bouncing off the metal walls. It surrounds me like Elara's wretched whispers, ghosting into my brain. *Little lightning girl. It's what she used to call me, what* they *called me.*

No. No, it isn't.

Despite the pain, I straighten my spine, standing as tall as I can.

I am not little anymore.

The whispers follow us all the way to the medical station, where a pair of Guardsmen keeps watch at the closed door. They're also watching the ladder, a heavy metal thing reaching up into the ceiling. The only exit and only entrance in this slow bullet of a ship. One of the guards has dark red hair, just like Tristan, though he's nowhere near as tall. The other is built like a boulder, with brown skin, angled eyes, a broad chest, and massive hands better suited to a strongarm. They bow their heads at the sight of me but, to my relief, don't spare me much more than a glance. Instead, they turn their attentions to Kilorn, grinning at him like school friends.

"Back so soon, Warren?" The redhead

chuckles, waggling his eyebrows in suggestion. "Lena's gone off her shift."

Lena? Kilorn tenses beneath my arm, but says nothing to betray his discomfort. Instead, he laughs along, grinning. But I know him better than any, enough to see the force behind his smile. To think, he's been spending his time *flirting* while I've been unconscious and Shade lies wounded and bleeding.

"The boy's got enough on his plate without chasing pretty nurses," the boulder says. His deep voice echoes down the passage, probably carrying all the way to Lena's quarters. "Farley's still making rounds, if you're after her," he adds, jabbing a thumb at the door.

"And my brother?" I speak up, disentangling myself from Kilorn's supporting grip. My knees almost buckle, but I stand firm. "Shade Barrow?"

Their smiles fade, stiffening into something more formal. It's almost like being back in the Silver court. The boulder grips the door, spinning the massive wheel lock so he doesn't have to look at me. "He's recovering well, miss, er, my lady."

My stomach drops at the title. I thought I was done with such things.

"Please call me Mare."

56

"Of course," he replies without any kind of resolve. Though we are both part of the Scarlet Guard, soldiers together in our cause, we are not the same. This man, and many others, will never call me by my given name, no matter how much I want them to.

He swings open the door with a tiny nod, revealing a wide but shallow compartment filled with bunks. Sleeping quarters at one time, but now the stacked beds are full of patients, the single aisle buzzing with men and women in white shifts. Many have clothes spattered with crimson blood, too preoccupied setting a leg or administering medication to notice me limping into their midst.

Kilorn's hand hovers by my waist, ready to catch me should I need him again, but I lean on the bunks instead. If everyone's going to stare at me, I might as well try to walk on my own.

Shade props up against a single thin pillow, supported mostly by the sloping metal wall. He can't possibly be comfortable, but his eyes are closed, and his chest rises and falls in the easy rhythm of sleep. Judging by his leg, suspended from the ceiling of his bunk by a hasty sling, and his bandaged shoulder, he's surely been medicated a few times. The sight of him so broken, even

57

though I thought him dead just yesterday, is shockingly hard to bear.

"We should let him sleep," I murmur to no one in particular, expecting no answer.

"Yes, please do," Shade says without opening his eyes. But his lips quirk into a familiar, mischievous smile. Despite his grim, injured figure, I have to laugh.

The trick is a familiar one. Shade would pretend to sleep through school or our parents' whispered conversations. I have to laugh at the memory, remembering how many little secrets Shade picked up in this particular way. I may have been born a thief, but Shade was born a spy. No wonder he ended up in the Scarlet Guard.

"Eavesdropping on nurses?" My knee cracks as I sit on the side of his bunk, careful not to jostle him. "Have you learned how many bandages they've got squirreled away?"

But instead of laughing at the joke, Shade opens his eyes. He draws Kilorn and me closer with a beckoning hand. "The nurses know more than you think," he says, his gaze flickering toward the far end of the compartment.

I turn to find Farley busying herself over an occupied bunk. The woman in it is out cold, probably drugged, and Farley monitors her pulse closely. In this light, her scar stands out rudely, twisting one side of her mouth into a scowl before cutting down the side of her neck and under her collar. Part of it has split open and was hastily stitched up. Now the only red she wears is the swath of blood across her white nurse's shift and the half-washed stains reaching to her elbows. Another nurse stands at her shoulder, but his shift is clean, and he whispers hurriedly in her ear. She nods occasionally, though her face tightens in anger.

"What have you heard?" Kilorn asks, shifting so that his body blocks Shade entirely. To anyone else, it looks like we're adjusting his bandages.

"We're headed to another base, this time off the coast. Outside Nortan territory."

I strain to remember Julian's old map, but I can't think of much more than the coastline. "An island?"

Shade nods. "Called Tuck. It must not be much, because the Silvers don't even have an outpost there. They've all but forgotten it."

Dread pools in my stomach. The prospect of isolating myself on an island with no means of escape scares me even more than the mersive. "But they know it exists. That's enough."

"Farley seemed confident in the base there."

Kilorn scoffs aloud. "I remember her thinking Naercey was safe too."

"It wasn't her fault we lost Naercey," I say. *It's mine.*

"Maven tricked everyone, Mare," Kilorn replies, nudging my shoulder. "He got past me, you, *and* Farley. We all believed in him."

With his mother to coach him, to read our minds and mold Maven to our hopes, it's no wonder we were all fooled. And now he is king. Now he will fool — and control — our whole world. *What a world that will be, with a monster for its king, and his mother holding his leash.*

But I push through such thoughts. They can wait. "Did Farley say anything else? What about the list? She still has it, doesn't she?"

Shade watches her over my shoulder, careful to keep his voice low. "She does, but she's more concerned with the *others* we're meeting in Tuck, Mom and Dad included." A rush of warmth spreads through me, an invigorating curl of happiness. Shade brightens at the sight of my small but genuine smile, and he takes my hand. "Gisa too, and the lumps we call brothers."

A cord of tension releases in my chest but

is soon replaced by another. I tighten my grip on him, one eyebrow raised in question. "*Others? Who? How can that be?*" After the massacre beneath Caesar's Square and the evacuation of Naercey, I didn't think anyone else existed.

But Kilorn and Shade don't share my confusion, electing to exchange furtive glances instead. Yet again, I'm in the dark, and I don't like it one bit. But this time, it's my own brother and best friend keeping secrets, not an evil queen and scheming prince.

Somehow, this hurts more. Scowling, I glare at them both until they realize I'm waiting for answers.

Kilorn grits his teeth and has the good sense to look apologetic. He gestures to Shade. *Passing the blame.* "You know more than I do."

"The Guard likes to play things close to the chest, and rightfully so." Shade adjusts himself, sitting up a little more. He hisses at the motion, clutching at his wounded shoulder, but waves me off before I can help him. "We want to look small, broken, disorganized —"

I can't help but snort, eyeing his bandages. "Well, you're doing a terrific job."

"Don't be cruel, Mare," Shade snaps

back, sounding very much like our mother. "I'm trying to tell you that things aren't so bad as they seem. Naercey was not our only stronghold and Farley is not our only leader. In fact, she's not even true Command. She's just a captain. There are others like her — and even more above her."

Judging by the way she orders around her soldiers, I would think Farley was an empress. When I chance another glance at her, she's busy redoing a bandage, all while scolding the nurse who originally set the wound. But my brother's conviction can't be ignored. He knows much more than I do about the Scarlet Guard, and I'm inclined to believe what he says about them is true. There's more to this organization than what I see here. It's encouraging — and frightening.

"The Silvers think they're two steps ahead of us, but they don't even know where we stand," Shade continues, his voice full of fervor. "We seem weak because we want to."

I turn back quickly. "Maven tricked you, trapped you, slaughtered you, and ran you out of your own house. Or are you going to try and tell me that was all part of another plan?"

"Mare —" Kilorn mumbles, putting his shoulder against mine in a display of comfort. But I shove him away. He needs to hear this too.

"I don't care how many secret tunnels and boats and bases you have. You're not going to win against him, not like this." Tears I didn't know I still had sting my eyes, prickling at Maven's memory. It's hard to forget him as he was. *No.* As he pretended to be. The kind, forgotten boy. The shadow of the flame.

"Then what do you suggest, lightning girl?"

Farley's voice shocks through me like my own sparks, setting every nerve on edge. For a brief, blistering second, I stare at my hands knotted in Shade's sheets. Maybe she'll leave if I don't turn around. Maybe she'll let me be.

Don't be such a fool, Mare Barrow.

"Fight fire with fire," I tell her as I stand. Her height used to intimidate me. Now glaring up at her feels natural and familiar.

"Is that some kind of Silver joke?" she sneers, crossing her arms.

"Do I look like I'm joking?"

She doesn't reply, and that's answer enough. In her silence, I realize the rest of the compartment has gone quiet. Even the injured stifle their pain to watch the lightning girl challenge their captain.

"You thrive on looking weak and striking hard, yes? Well, they do everything they can to look strong, to seem invincible. But in the arena, I proved they are not." *Again, stronger, so everyone can hear you.* I call on the firm voice Lady Blonos brought to life in me. "They are *not* invincible."

Farley isn't stupid and finds it easy to follow my train of thought. "You're stronger than they are," she says, matter-of-fact. Her eyes stray to Shade, lying tense in his bunk. "And you're not the only one who is."

I nod sharply, pleased that she already knows what I want. "Hundreds of names, hundreds of Reds with abilities. Stronger, faster, better than they are, with blood as Red as the dawn." My breath catches, as if it knows it stands on the edge of the future. "Maven will try to kill them, but if we get to them first, they could be —"

"The greatest army this world has ever seen." Farley's eyes glass at the thought. "An army of newbloods."

When she smiles, her scar strains against its stitches, threatening to split open again. Her grin widens. She doesn't mind the pain.

But I certainly do. I suppose I always will.

FOUR

Farley's not as tall as Kilorn, but her steps are faster, more deliberate, and harder to keep up with. I do my best, almost jogging to match her pace through the mersive corridor. Like before, the Guardsmen jump out of our way, but now they salute her as we pass, clasping hands to their chest or fingers to their brow. I must say Farley cuts an impressive figure, wearing her scars and wounds like jewels. She doesn't seem to mind the blood on her shift, absently wiping her hands against it. Some of it belongs to Shade. She dug the bullet out of his shoulder without blinking.

"We didn't lock him up, if that's what you think," she says lightly, as if talk of imprisoning Cal is casual gossip.

I'm not stupid enough to rise to that bait, not now. She's feeling me out, testing my reaction, my *allegiance.* But I'm no longer the girl who begged for her help. I'm not so easily read anymore. I've lived on a razor wire, balancing lie after lie, hiding myself. It's nothing to do the same now and bury my thoughts deep down.

So I laugh instead, pasting on the smile I perfected in Elara's court. "I can tell. Nothing's been melted," I reply, gesturing to the metal walls.

I read her as she tries to read me. She masks her expression well, but surprise still flickers in her eyes. Surprise and *curiosity*.

I haven't forgotten the way she treated Cal on the train — with shackles, armed guards, and disdain. And he took it like a kicked dog. After his brother's betrayal and his father's murder, he had no fight inside him. I didn't blame him. But Farley doesn't know his heart — or his strength — like I do. She doesn't know how dangerous he really is. *Or how dangerous I am, for that matter.* Even now, despite my many injuries, I feel power deep inside, calling out to the electricity pulsing through the mersive. I could control it if I wanted. I could shut this whole thing down. I could drown us all. The lethal idea makes me blush, embarrassed by such thoughts. But they are a comfort all the same. I'm the greatest weapon of all on a ship full of warriors, and they don't seem to know it.

We seem weak because we want to. Shade was talking about the Guard when he said that, explaining their motives. Now I wonder if he wasn't also trying to convey a message. Like words hidden in a letter long ago.

Cal's bunk room is at the far end of the mersive, tucked away from the bustle of the rest of the vessel. His door is nearly hidden behind a twist of pipes and empty crates stamped with *Archeon, Haven, Corvium, Harbor Bay, Delphie,* and even *Belleum* from Piedmont to the south. What the crates once held, I can't say, but the names of the Silver cities send a twinge down my spine. *Stolen.* Farley notices me staring at the crates but doesn't bother to explain. Despite our shaky agreement over what she calls "newbloods," I still haven't entered her inner circle of secrets. I suppose Cal has something to do with that.

Whatever powers the ship, a massive generator by the feel of it, rumbles beneath my feet, vibrating into my bones. I wrinkle my nose in distaste. Farley might not have locked Cal up, but she's certainly not being kind either. Between the noise and the shaking sensation, I wonder if Cal was able to sleep at all.

"I suppose this is the only place you could

put him?" I ask, glaring at the cramped corner.

She shrugs, banging a hand on his door. "The prince hasn't complained."

We don't wait long, though I'd very much like the time to collect myself. Instead, the wheel lock spins in seconds, clanking round at great speed. The iron hinges grate, screaming, and Cal pulls open the door.

I'm not surprised to see him standing tall, ignoring his own aches. After a lifetime preparing to be a warrior, he's used to cuts and bruises. But the scars within are something he doesn't know how to hide. He avoids my gaze, focusing on Farley, who doesn't notice or doesn't care about the prince with a shattered heart. Suddenly my wounds seem a bit easier to bear.

"Captain Farley," he says, as if she's disturbed him at dinnertime. He uses annoyance to mask his pain.

Farley won't stand for it and tosses her short hair with a sniff. She even reaches to close the door. "Oh, did you not want a visitor? How rude of me."

I'm quietly glad I didn't let Kilorn tag along. He'd be even worse to Cal, having hated him since they first met back in the Stilts.

"Farley," I tell her through gritted teeth.

My hand stops the door short. To my delight — and distaste — she flinches away from my touch. She flushes horribly, embarrassed with herself and her fear. Despite her tough exterior, she's just like her soldiers. Afraid of the lightning girl. "I think we're fine from here."

Something twitches in her face, a twinge of irritation as much with herself as with me. But she nods, grateful to be out of my presence. With one last daggered glance at Cal, she turns and disappears back down the corridor. Her barked orders echo for a moment, indecipherable but strong.

Cal and I stare after her, then at the walls, then at the floor, then at our feet, afraid to look at each other. Afraid to remember the last few days. The last time we watched each other across a doorway, dancing lessons and a stolen kiss followed. That might as well be another life. *Because it was. He danced with Mareena, the lost princess, and Mareena is dead.*

But her memories remain. When I walk past, my shoulder brushing one firm arm, I remember the feel and smell and taste of him. Heat and wood smoke and sunrise, but no longer. Cal smells like blood, his skin is ice, and I tell myself I don't want to taste him ever again.

"They've been treating you well?" I speak first, reaching for an easy topic. One glance around his small yet clean compartment is answer enough, but I might as well fill the silence.

"Yes," he says, still hovering by the open door. Debating whether to shut it.

My eyes land on a panel in the wall, pried back to reveal a tangle of wires and switches beneath. I can't help but smile softly. Cal's been tinkering.

"You think that's smart? One wrong wire . . ."

That draws a weak but still comforting smile from him. "I've been fooling with circuitry for half my life. Don't worry, I know what I'm doing."

Both of us ignore the double meaning, letting it slide past.

He finally decides to shut the door, though he leaves it unlocked. One hand rests on the metal wall, fingers splayed, looking for something to hold on to. The flame-maker bracelet still winks on his wrist, bright silver against dull, hard gray. He notes my gaze and pulls down one stained sleeve; I guess no one thought to give him a change of clothes.

"As long as I stay out of sight, I don't think anyone will bother with me," he says, and goes back to fiddling with the open panel. "It's kind of nice." But the joke is hollow.

"I'll make sure it stays that way. If that's what you want," I add quickly. In truth, I have no idea what Cal wants now. *Beyond vengeance. The one thing we still have in common.*

He quirks an eyebrow at me, almost amused. "Oh, is the lightning girl in charge now?" He doesn't give me a chance to respond to the jibe, closing the distance between us in a single long step. "I get the feeling you're just as cornered as me." His eyes narrow. "Only you don't seem to know it."

I flush, feeling angry — and embarrassed. "Cornered? I'm not the one hiding in a closet."

"No, you're too busy being put on parade." He leans forward, and the familiar heat between us returns. *"Again."*

Part of me wants to slap him. "My brother would *never* —"

"I thought my brother would *never,* and look where that got us!" he thunders, throwing his arms wide. The tips of his fingers touch either wall, scraping up against the prison he's found himself in. *The prison I put him in.* And he's caged me in with him,

71

whether he knows it or not.

Blazing heat flares from his body, and I have to step back a little. He doesn't miss the action and deflates, letting his eyes and arms drop. "Sorry," he bites out, brushing a lock of black hair off his forehead.

"Never apologize to me. I don't deserve it."

He glances at me sidelong, his eyes dark and wide, but he doesn't argue.

Heaving a breath, I lean back against the far wall. The space between us gapes like open jaws. "What do you know about a place called Tuck?"

Grateful for the change in conversation, he pulls himself together, retreating into a prince's persona. Even without a crown, he seems regal, with perfect posture and his hands folded behind his back. "Tuck?" he repeats, thinking hard. A crease forms between his thick, dark brows. The longer it takes him to speak, the better I feel. If he doesn't know about the island, then few else will. "Is that where we're going?"

"It is." *I think.* A cold thought ripples through me, remembering Julian's lessons hard learned in the court and the arena. *Anyone can betray anyone.* "According to Shade."

Cal lets my uncertainty hang in the air,

kind enough not to prod at it. "I think it's an island," he finally says. "One of several off the coast. It's not Nortan territory. Nothing to warrant a settlement or base, not even for defense. It's just open ocean out there."

A bit of the weight on my shoulders lifts. We'll be safe for now. "Good, good."

"Your brother, he's like you." It's not a question. "Different."

"He is." What else is there to say?

"And he's all right? I remember he was injured."

Even without an army, Cal is still a general, caring for the soldiers and the wounded. "He's fine, thank you. Took a few bullets for me, but he's recovering well."

At the mention of bullets, Cal's eyes flicker over me, finally allowing himself to look at me fully. He lingers on my scraped face and the dried blood around my ears. "And you?"

"I've had worse."

"Yes, we have."

We lapse into silence, not daring to speak further. But we still continue to stare at each other. Suddenly his presence is difficult to stand. And yet I don't want to go.

The mersive has other ideas.

Beneath my feet, the generator shudders,

its pounding pulse changing rhythm. "We're almost there," I mutter, sensing electricity flow or ebb to different parts of the craft.

Cal doesn't feel it yet, unable to, but he doesn't question my instincts. He knows my abilities firsthand, better than anyone on the ship. Better than my own family. For now, at least. Mom, Dad, Gisa, the boys, they're waiting for me on the island. I'll see them soon. They're here. They're *safe.*

But how long I'll be with them, I don't know. I won't be able to stay on the island, not if I want to do something for the new-bloods. I'll have to go back to Norta, use whatever and whoever Farley can give me, to try and find them. It already seems impossible. I don't even want to think about it. And yet my mind buzzes, trying to form a plan.

An alarm sounds overhead, synchronizing with a yellow light that starts to flash over Cal's door. "Amazing," I hear him mutter, distracted for a moment by the great machine all around us. I don't doubt he wanted to explore, but there's no room for the inquisitive prince here. The boy who buried himself in manuals and built cycles from scratch has no place in this world. *I killed him, just as I killed Mareena.*

Despite Cal's mechanically inclined mind

and my own electrical sense, we have no idea what comes next. When the mersive angles, nosing up out of the depths of the ocean, the whole room tips. The surprise of it knocks us both off our feet. We collide with the wall and each other. Our wounds bang together, drawing pained hisses from us both. The feel of him hurts more than anything else, a deep stab of memory, and I scramble away quickly.

Wincing, I rub one of my many bruises. "Where's Sara Skonos when you need her," I grumble, wishing for the skin healer who could mend us both. She could chase away the aches with a single touch, returning us both to fighting form.

More pain crosses Cal's face, but not from his injuries. *Well done, Mare. Wonderful job, bringing up the woman who knew his mother was murdered by the queen. The woman no one believed.* "Sorry, I didn't mean —"

He waves me off and finds his feet, one arm pressed against the wall for balance. "It's fine. She's —" The words are thick, stilted. "I chose not to listen to her. I didn't *want* to listen. That was my fault."

I met Sara Skonos only once, when Evangeline almost exposed me to our entire training session. Julian summoned her — Julian, who *loved* her — and watched as she mended my bloody face and bruised back. Her eyes were sad, her cheeks hollow, her tongue missing entirely. Taken for words spoken against the queen, for a truth no one believed. *Elara killed Cal's mother, Coriane the Singer Queen. Julian's own sister, Sara's best friend. And no one seemed to mind. It was so much easier to look away.*

Maven was there too, hating Sara with every breath. I know now that was a crack in his shield, revealing who he truly was beneath practiced words and gentle smiles. Like Cal, I didn't see what was right in front of me.

Like Julian, she is probably dead already.

Suddenly the metal walls and the noise and the popping of my ears are too much.

"I need to get off this thing."

Despite the strange angle of the room and the persistent ringing in my head, my feet know what to do. They have not forgotten the mud of the Stilts, the nights spent in alleys, or the obstacle courses of Training. I wrench the door open, gasping for breath like a girl drowned. But the stale, filtered air of the mersive offers me no respite. I need the smell of trees, water, spring rains, even summer heat or winter snow. *Something* to remind me of the world beyond this suffocating tin can.

Cal gives me a head start before following, his footsteps heavy and slow behind me. He's not trying to catch up, but give me space. If only Kilorn could do the same.

He approaches from farther down the corridor, using handholds and wheel locks to ease himself down the angled craft. His smile fades at the sight of Cal, replaced not by a scowl but by cold indifference. I suppose he thinks ignoring the prince will anger him more than outright hostility. Or perhaps Kilorn doesn't want to test a human flamethrower in such close quarters.

"We're surfacing," he says, reaching my side.

I tighten my grip on a nearby grate, using it to steady myself. "You don't say?"

Kilorn grins, leaning against the wall in front of me. He plants his feet on either side of mine, a challenge if there ever was one. I feel Cal's heat behind me, but the prince seems to be taking the indifferent path as well, and says nothing.

I won't be a piece in whatever game they're playing. I've done that enough for a lifetime. "How's what's-her-name? Lena?"

The name hits Kilorn like a slap. His grin slackens, one side of his mouth drooping. "She's fine, I guess."

"That's good, Kilorn." I give him a

friendly, if condescending, pat on the shoulder. The deflection works perfectly. "We should be making friends."

The mersive levels out beneath us, but no one stumbles. Not even Cal, who has nowhere near my balance or Kilorn's sea legs, hard earned on a fishing boat. He's taut as a wire, waiting for me to take the lead. It should make me laugh, the thought of a prince deferring to me, but I'm too cold and worn to do much of anything but carry on.

So I do. Down the corridor, with Cal and Kilorn in tow, to the throng of Guardsmen waiting by the ladder that brought us down here in the first place. The wounded go first, tied onto makeshift stretchers and hoisted up into the open night. Farley supervises, her shift even bloodier than before. She makes for a grim sight, tightening bandages, with a syringe between her teeth. A few of the worse off get shots as they pass, medication to help with the pain of being moved up the narrow tube. Shade is the last of the injured, leaning heavily on the two Guardsmen who teased Kilorn about the nurse. I would push through to him, but the crowd is too tight, and I don't want any more attention today. Still too weak to teleport, he has to fumble on one leg and blushes furiously when Farley straps him onto a stretcher. I can't hear what she says to him, but it calms him somewhat. He even waves off her syringe, instead gritting his teeth against the jarring pain of being hoisted up the ladder. Once Shade is safely carried up, the process goes much faster. One after the other, Guardsmen follow one another up the ladder, slowly clearing the corridor. Many of them are nurses, men and women marked by white shifts with varying degrees of bloodstains.

I don't waste time waving others ahead, faking politeness like a lady should. We're all going to the same place. So when the crowd clears a little, the ladder opening to me, I hurry forward. Cal follows, and his presence combined with mine parts the Guardsmen like a knife. They step back quickly, some even stumbling, to give us our space. Only Farley stands firm, one hand around the ladder. To my surprise, she offers Cal and me a nod. *Both* of us.

That should've been my first warning.

The steps on the ladder burn in my muscles, still strained from Naercey, the arena, and my capture. I can hear a strange howling up above, but it doesn't deter me in the slightest. I need to get out of the mersive, as fast as possible.

My last glimpse of the mersive, looking back over my shoulder, is strange, angling over Farley and into the medical station. There are wounded still in there, motionless beneath their blankets. *No, not wounded,* I realize as I pull myself up. *Dead.*

Higher up the ladder, the wind sounds, and a bit of water drips down. Nothing to bother with, I assume, until I reach the top and the open circle of darkness. A storm howls so strongly that the rain pelts sideways, missing most of the tube and ladder. It stings against my scraped face, drenching me in seconds. *Autumn storms.* Though I cannot recall a storm so brutal as this. It blows through me, filling my mouth with rain and biting, salty spray. Luckily, the mersive is tightly anchored to a dock I can barely see, and it holds firm against the roiling gray waves below.

"This way!" a familiar voice yells in my ear, guiding me off the ladder and onto the mersive hull slick with rain and seawater. Through the darkness, I can barely see the soldier leading me, but his massive bulk and his voice are easy to place.

"Bree!" I close my hand on his, feeling the calluses of my oldest brother's grip. He walks like an anchor, heavy and slow, helping me off the mersive and onto the dock.

It's not much better, metal eaten with rust, but it leads to land and that's all I care about. Land and *warmth,* a welcome respite after the cold depths of the ocean and my memories.

No one helps Cal down from the mersive, but he does fine on his own. Again, he's careful to keep some distance, walking a few respectable paces behind us. I'm sure he hasn't forgotten his first meeting with Bree back in the Stilts, when my brother was anything but polite. In truth, none of the Barrows cared for Cal, except Mom and maybe Gisa. But they didn't know who he was then. Should be an interesting reunion.

The storm makes Tuck difficult to see, but I can tell the island is small, covered in dunes and tall grass as tumultuous as the waves. A crack of lightning out on the water illuminates the night for a moment, showing the path in front of us. Now out in the open, without the cramped walls of the mersive or the Undertrain, I can see we number less than thirty, including the wounded. They head for two flat, concrete buildings where the dock meets land. A few structures stand out on the gentle hill above us, looking like bunkers or barracks. But what lies beyond them, I can't say. The next bolt of lightning, closer this time, shivers delightfully in my nerves. Bree mistakes it for cold, and draws me closer, draping one heavy arm across my shoulders. His weight makes it hard to walk, but I endure.

The end of the dock cannot come fast enough. Soon I'll be inside, dry, on solid ground, and reunited with the Barrows after far too long. The prospect is enough to get me through the bustle of wet activity. Nurses load the wounded onto an old transport, its storage bed covered in water-proof canvas. It was certainly stolen, as was everything else. The two buildings on land are hangars, their doors ajar enough to reveal more transports waiting inside. There's even a few boats anchored to the dock, bobbing in the gray waves as they ride out the storm. Everything is mismatched — outdated transports in varying sizes, sleek new boats, some painted silver, black, one green. Stolen or hijacked or both. I even recognize the clouded gray and blue, the Nortan navy colors, on one boat. Tuck is like a much larger version of Will Whistle's old wagon, packed with bits and pieces of trade and thievery.

The medical transport putters off before we reach it, fighting through the rain and up the sandy road. Only Bree's nonchalance keeps me from quickening my pace. He isn't worried about Shade, or what lies at the top of the hill, so I try not to be too.

Cal doesn't share my sentiment and finally speeds up so he can walk next to me. It's the storm or the darkness, or maybe simply his silver blood making him look so pale and afraid. "This can't last," he mutters, low enough so only I can hear.

"What's that, Prince?" Bree says, his voice a dull roar. I nudge him in the ribs, but it doesn't do much more than bruise my elbow. "No matter, we'll know soon enough."

His tone is worse than his words. Cold, brutal, so unlike the laughing brother I used to know. The Guard has changed him too. "Bree, what are you talking about?"

Cal already knows and stops in his tracks, his eyes on me. The wind musses his hair, pasting it to his forehead. His bronze eyes darken with fear, and my stomach churns at the sight. *Not again,* I plead. *Tell me I haven't walked into another trap.*

One of the hangars looms behind him, its doors opening wide on strangely quiet hinges. Too many soldiers to count step forward in unison, as regimented as any legion, their guns ready and eyes bright in the rain. Their leader might as well be a shiver, with almost white-blond hair and an icy disposition. But he's red-blooded as I am — one of his eyes is clouded crimson, bleeding beneath the lens.

"Bree, what is this?!" I yell, rounding on my brother with a visceral snarl. Instead, he takes my hands in his, and not gently. He holds me firm, using his superior strength to keep me from pulling away. If he were anyone else, I would shock him good. But this is my brother. I can't do that to him, I *won't*.

"Bree, *let me go!*"

"We won't hurt him," he says, repeating it over and over. "We're not going to hurt him, I promise you."

So this isn't my cage. But that doesn't calm me at all. If anything, it makes me more angry and desperate.

When I look back, Cal's fists are aflame, his arms stretched wide to face the blood-eyed man. "Well?" he growls in challenge, sounding more like an animal than a man. *A cornered animal.*

Too many guns, even for Cal. They'll shoot him if they must. It might even be what they want. An excuse to kill the fallen prince. Part of me, most of me, knows they would be justified in this. Cal was a hunter of the Scarlet Guard, essentially guaranteeing Tristan's death, Walsh's suicide, and

Farley's torture. Soldiers killed at his orders, wiping out most of Farley's rebel force. And who knows how many he's sent to die on the war front, trading Red soldiers for a few measly miles of the Lakelands. He owes no allegiance to the cause. He is a danger to the Scarlet Guard.

But he is a weapon as well as I am, one we can use in the days to come. For the newbloods, against Maven, a torch to help lift the darkness.

"He can't fight out of this, Mare." That's Kilorn, choosing the worst of moments to sidle back. He whispers in my ear, acting like his closeness can influence me. "He'll die if he tries."

His logic is hard to ignore.

"On your knees, Tiberias," the blood-eyed man says, taking bold steps toward the flaming prince. Steam rises from his fire, as if the storm is trying to stamp him out. "Hands behind your head."

Cal does neither, and he flinches at the mention of his birth name. He stands firm, strong, proud, though he knows the battle is lost. Once he might have surrendered, trying to save his own skin. Now he believes that skin worthless. Only I seem to think otherwise.

"Cal, do as he says."

The wind carries my voice so that the whole hangar hears. I'm afraid they can hear my heart too, hammering like a drum in my chest.

"Cal."

Slowly, reluctantly, a statue crumbling to dust, Cal sinks to his knees and his fire sputters out. He did the same thing yesterday, kneeling next to his father's decapitated corpse.

The blood-eyed man grins, his teeth gleaming and straight. He stands over Cal with relish, enjoying the sight of a prince at his feet. Enjoying the *power* it gives him.

But I am the lightning girl, and he knows nothing of true power.

FIVE

They try to convince me it's for the best, but their poor excuses fall on unsympathetic ears. Kilorn and Bree quickly use every argument they've been told to say.

He's dangerous, even to you. But I know better than any that Cal would never hurt me. Even when he had reason to, I feared nothing from him.

He's one of them. We can't trust him. After what Maven's done to his legacy and reputation, Cal has nothing and no one but us now, even if he refuses to admit it.

He is valuable. A general, a prince of Norta, and the most wanted man in the kingdom. That one gives me pause, and strikes a chord of fear deep down. If the blood-eyed man decides to use Cal as leverage against Maven, to trade him or sacrifice him, it will take all I have to stop him. All my influence, all my *power* — and I don't know if it will be enough.

So I do nothing but nod along with them, slowly at first, pretending to agree. Pretending to be controlled. Pretending to be *weak.* I was right. Shade was warning me before. Once again, he saw the turn of the tide long before it rolled in. Cal is power, fire made flesh, something to be feared and defeated. And I am lightning. What will they try to do to me if I don't play my part?

I have not stepped into another jail, not yet, but I can feel the key in the lock, threatening to turn. Luckily, I have experience in this kind of thing.

The blood-eyed man and his soldiers march Cal into the hangar, not stupid enough to try and bind his hands. But they never lower their guns or their guard, careful to keep their distance lest one of them be burned for their boldness. I can only watch, eyes wide but mouth shut, when the hangar door slides closed again, separating the two of us. They won't kill him, not until he gives them a reason. I can only hope Cal behaves.

"Go easy on him," I whisper, leaning into Bree's warmth. Even in the cold autumn rain, he feels like a furnace. Long years fighting on the northern front have made him immune to wet and cold. I think back to Dad's old saying. *The war never leaves.*

Now I know it firsthand, though my war is very different from his.

Bree pretends not to hear me, hurrying us both from the docks. Kilorn follows close behind, his boots catching my heels once or twice. I resist the urge to kick him, and focus on climbing the wooden steps leading to the barracks on the hill above. The steps are worn down, beaten by too many feet to count. *How many came this way?* I wonder. *How many are here now?*

We crest the hill and the island stretches out before us, revealing a military base larger than I expected. The barracks on the ridge was one of at least a dozen I see now, organized in two even rows separated by a long, concrete yard. It's flat and well-maintained, not like the steps or the dock. There's a white line painted down the middle of the yard, perfectly straight, leading away into the stormy night. What it goes to, I have no idea.

The whole island has an air of stillness, momentarily frozen by the storm. Come the morning, when the rain breaks and the darkness lifts, I suppose I'll see the base in all its glory — and finally understand the people I'm dealing with. I'm developing a bad habit of underestimating others, particularly where the Scarlet Guard is concerned.

And like Naercey, Tuck is far more than it seems.

The cold I felt on the mersive and in the rain persists, even when I'm ushered into the doorway of the barracks marked with a painted black "3." I'm cold in my bones, in my heart. But I can't let my parents see that, for their sake. I owe them this much. They must think me whole, unbroken, unaffected by Cal's imprisonment and my own ordeals in a palace and an arena. And the Guard must think I'm on their side — relieved to be "safe."

But aren't I? Didn't I swear an oath to Farley and the Scarlet Guard?

They believe as I do, in an end to Silver kings and Red slaves. They sacrificed soldiers *for* me, *because* of me. They are my *allies,* my brethren, brothers and sisters in arms — but the blood-eyed man gives me pause. He is not Farley. She might be gruff and single-minded, but she knows what I've been through. She can be reasoned with. I doubt reason lives in the heart of the blood-eyed man.

Kilorn is strangely quiet. This silence is not like us at all. We're used to filling the space with insults, with teasing, or in Kilorn's case, with utter nonsense. It's not in our nature to be quiet around each other, but now we have nothing to say. He knew what they planned to do to Cal and agreed with it. Worse, he didn't even tell me. I would feel angry but for the cold. It eats at my emotions, dulling them into something like the electrical hum in the air.

Bree doesn't notice the strangeness between us, not that he would. Besides being pleasantly foolish, my oldest brother left when I was a gangly thirteen-year-old who thieved for fun, not necessity, and wasn't so cruel as I've become. Bree doesn't know me as I am now, having missed almost five years of my life. But then, my life has changed more in the last two months than ever before. And only two people were with me through it. The first is imprisoned and the second wears a crown of blood.

Any sensible person would call them my enemies. Strange, my enemies know me best, and my family doesn't know me at all.

Inside the barracks is blissfully dry, humming with lights and wires bundled along the ceiling. The thick concrete walls turn the corridor into a maze, with no markers to guide the way. Every door is shut, steel gray and unremarkable, but a few bear the signs of life within. Some woven beach grass adorning a knob, a broken necklace strung across a doorway, and so on. This place holds not just fearsome soldiers but the refugees of Naercey and who knows where else. After the enactment of the Measures, commanded from my own lips, many Guardsmen and Reds alike fled the mainland. How could they stay, threatened by conscription and execution? *But how did they manage to get away? And how did they make it here?*

Another question joins my steadily growing list.

Despite my distraction, I keep careful notice of the twists and turns my brother takes. Right here, one, two, three corners, left by the door with "PRAIRIE" carved into it. Part of me wonders if he's taking a roundabout route on purpose, but Bree isn't smart enough for that. I guess I should be thankful. Shade would have no problems playing the trickster, but not Bree. He's brute strength, a rolling boulder easy to dodge. He's a Guardsman too, freed from one army just to join another. And based on how he held me on the docks, he owes his allegiance to the Guard and nothing else. Tramy will probably be the same, always eager to follow, and occasionally guide, our older brother. Only Shade has the good sense to keep his eyes open, to wait and see what fate awaits us *newbloods.*

The door ahead of us stands ajar, as if waiting. Bree doesn't need to tell me this is our family's bunk, because there's a purple scrap of fabric tied around the doorknob. It's frayed at the edges and clumsily embroidered. Lightning bolts of thread spark across the rag, a symbol that is neither Red nor Silver, but *mine*. A combination of the colors of House Titanos, my mask, and the lightning that surges inside of me, my shield.

As we approach, something wheels behind the door, and a bit of warmth moves through me. I would know the sound of my father's wheelchair anywhere.

Bree doesn't knock. He knows everyone's still awake, waiting for me.

There's more room than in the mersive, but the bunk is still small and cramped. At least there's space to move, and plenty of beds for the Barrows, with even a bit of living space around the doorway. A single window, cut high in the far wall, is closed tight against the rain, and the sky seems a bit lighter. Dawn is coming.

Yes it is, I think, taking in the overwhelming amount of red. Scarves, rags, scraps, flags, banners, red on every surface and hanging from every wall. I should've known it would come to this. Gisa sewed dresses for Silvers once; now she painstakingly makes flags for the Scarlet Guard, decorating whatever she can find with the torn sun of resistance. They aren't pretty, with uneven stitches and simple patterns. Nothing compared to the art she used to weave. That's my fault too.

She sits at the little metal table, frozen with a needle in her half-healed claw of a hand. For a moment, she stares, and so do the rest. Mom, Dad, Tramy, staring but not knowing the girl they're looking at. The last time they saw me, I couldn't control myself. I was trapped, weak, confused. Now I am injured, nursing bruises and betrayals, but I know what I am, and what I must do.

I have become more, more than we could ever have dreamed. It frightens me.

"Mare." I can barely hear my mother's voice. My name trembles on her lips.

Like back in the Stilts, when my sparks threatened to destroy our home, she is the first to embrace me. After a hug that isn't nearly long enough, she pulls me to an empty chair.

"Sit, baby, sit," she says, her hands shaking against me. *Baby.* I haven't been called that in years. Strange that it returns now, when I'm anything but a child.

Her touch ghosts over my new clothes, feeling for the bruises beneath like she can see right through the fabric. "You're hurt," she mutters, shaking her head. "I can't believe they let you walk, after — well, after all that."

I'm quietly glad she doesn't mention Naercey, the arena, or before. I don't think I'm strong enough to relive them, not so soon.

Dad chuckles darkly. "She can do as she pleases. There's no *let* to it." He shifts and I notice more gray in his hair than ever. He's thinner too, looking small in the familiar chair. "Just like Shade."

Shade is common ground, and easier for me to talk about. "You've seen him?" I ask, letting myself relax against the cold metal seat. It feels good to sit.

Tramy gets up from his bunk, his head nearly scraping the ceiling. "I'm going to the infirmary now. Just wanted to make sure you're —"

Okay is no longer a word in my vocabulary.

"— still standing."

I can only nod. If I open my mouth, I might tell them about everything. The hurt, the cold, the prince who betrayed me, the prince who saved me, the people I've killed. And while they might already know, I can't bring myself to admit what I've done. To

95

see them disappointed, disgusted, *afraid* of me. That would be more than I can bear tonight.

Bree goes with Tramy, patting me gruffly on the back before following our brother out the door. Kilorn remains, still silent, leaning against the wall as if he wants to fall into it and disappear.

"Are you hungry?" Mom says, busying herself at a tiny excuse for a cabinet. "We saved some dinner rations, if you want."

Though I haven't eaten in I don't even know how long, I shake my head. My exhaustion makes it hard to think of anything but sleep.

Gisa notes my manner, her bright eyes narrowed. She pushes back a piece of rich, red hair the color of our blood. "You should sleep." She speaks with so much conviction I wonder who the older sister really is. "Let her sleep."

"Of course, you're right." Again, Mom pulls me along, this time out of the chair and toward a bunk with more pillows than the rest. She nannies, fussing with the thin blankets, putting me through the motions. I only have the strength to follow, letting her tuck me in like she never has before. "Here we are, baby, sleep."

Baby.

I'm safer than I've been in days, surrounded by the people I love most, and yet I've never wanted to cry more. For them, I hold back. I curl inward and bleed alone, inside, where no one else can see.

It isn't long before I'm dozing, despite the bright lights overhead and the low murmurs. Kilorn's deep voice rumbles, speaking again now that I'm out of the equation.

"Watch her" is the last thing I hear before I sink into darkness.

Sometime in the night, somewhere between sleep and waking, Dad takes my hand. Not to wake me up, but just to hold on. For a moment, I think he is a dream, and I'm back in a cell beneath the Bowl of Bones. That the escape, the arena, the executions were all a nightmare I must soon relive. But his hand is warm, gnarled, familiar, and I close my fingers on his. He is real.

"I know what it is to kill someone," he whispers, his eyes faraway, two pinpricks of light in the blackness of our bunk. His voice is different, just as he is different in this moment. A reflection of a soldier, one who survived too long in the bowels of war. "I know what it does to you."

I try to speak. I certainly try.

Instead, I let him go, and I drift away.

■ ■ ■ ■

The tang of salt air wakes me the next morning. Someone opened the window, letting in a cool autumn breeze and bright sunlight. The storm has passed. Before I open my eyes, I try to pretend. This is my cot, the breeze is coming from the river, and my only choice is whether to go to school. But that is not a comfort. That life, though easier, is not one I would return to if I could.

I have things to do. I must see to Julian's list, to begin preparations for that massive undertaking. And if I request Cal for it, who are they to refuse me? Who could say no in the face of saving so many from Maven's noose?

Something tells me the blood-eyed man might, but I push it away.

Gisa sprawls in the bunk across from me, using her good hand to pick loose a few threads from a piece of black cloth. She doesn't bother to watch as I stretch, popping a few bones when I move.

"Good morning, *baby,*" she says, barely hiding a smirk.

She gets a pillow to the face for her trouble. "Don't start," I grumble, secretly glad for the teasing. If only Kilorn would do that, and be a little bit of the fisher boy I remember.

"Everyone's in the mess hall. Breakfast is still on."

"Where's the infirmary?" I ask, thinking of Shade and Farley. For the moment, she's one of the best allies I have here.

"You need to eat, Mare," Gisa says sharply, finally sitting up. "Really."

The concern in her eyes stops me short. I must look worse than I thought, for Gisa to treat me so gently. "Then where's the mess?"

She huffs as she stands, tossing her project down on the bunk. "I knew I'd get stuck babysitting," she mutters, sounding very much like our exasperated mother.

This time she dodges the pillow.

The maze of the barracks goes by quicker now. I remember the way, at least, and mentally note the doors as we pass. Some are open, revealing empty bunk rooms or a few idling Reds. Both tell the tale of Barracks 3, which seems to be the designated "family" structure. The people here don't look like soldiers of the Guard, and I doubt most of them have ever been in a fight. I see evidence of children, even a few babies, who fled with their families or were taken to Tuck. One room in particular overflows with old or broken toys, its walls hastily painted a sickly yellow in an attempt to brighten the concrete. There's nothing written on the door, but I understand who the room is for. *Orphans.* I quickly avert my eyes, looking anywhere but the cage for living ghosts.

Piping runs the length of the ceiling, carrying with it a slow but steady pulse of electricity. What powers this island, I don't know, but the deep hum is a comfort, reminding me of who I am. At least that is something no one can take away, not here, so far from the silencing ability of the now dead Silver Arven. Yesterday he almost killed me, stifling my ability with his own, turning me back into the Red girl with nothing but the dirt beneath her fingernails. In the arena, I barely had time to be frightened of such a prospect, but now it haunts me. My ability is my most prized possession, even though it separates me from everyone else. But for power, for my *own* power, it is a price I am willing to pay.

"What's it like?" Gisa says, following my gaze to the ceiling. She focuses on the wiring, trying to feel what I can, but comes back empty. "The electricity?"

I don't know what to tell her. Julian would

explain quite easily, probably debating himself in the process, all while detailing the history of abilities and how they came to be. But Maven told me only yesterday that my old teacher never escaped. He was captured. And knowing Maven, not to mention Elara, Julian is most likely dead, executed for all he gave to me, and for crimes committed long ago. For being the brother of the girl the old king truly loved.

"Power," I finally say, wrenching open the door to the outside world. Sea air presses against me, playing in my ratty hair. "Strength."

Silver words, but true all the same.

Gisa is not one to let me off the hook so easily. Still, she falls silent. She understands her questions are not any I want to answer.

In the daylight, Tuck seems both less and more ominous. The sun shines bright overhead, warming the autumn air, and past the barracks, the sea grass gives way to a sparse collection of trees. Nothing like the oaks and pines of home, but good enough for now. Gisa leads us across the concrete yard, navigating through the bustle of activity. Guardsmen in their red sashes unload mobiles, stacking more crates like the ones I saw on the mersive. I slow a little, hoping to get a glance of their cargo, but strange

101

soldiers in new uniforms give me pause. They wear blue, not the bright color of House Osanos, but something cold and dark. It's familiar but I can't place it. They look like Farley, tall and pale, with bright blond hair cut aggressively short. *Foreign,* I realize. They stand over the cargo piles, rifles in hand, guarding the crates.

But guarding them from who?

"Don't look at them," Gisa mutters, grabbing onto my sleeve. She tugs me along, eager to get away from the blue soldiers. One in particular watches us go, his eyes narrowed.

"Why not? Who are they?"

She shakes her head, tugging again. "Not here."

Naturally, I want to stop, to stare at the soldier until he realizes who and what I am. But that is a foolish, childish need. I must maintain my mask, must seem the poor girl broken by the world. I let Gisa lead on and away.

"The Colonel's men," she whispers as soon as we're out of earshot. "They came down with him from the north."

The north. "Lakelanders?" I reply, almost gasping in surprise. She nods, stoic.

Now the uniforms, the color of a cold lake, make sense. They are soldiers of another army, *another* king, but they're here, with us. Norta has been at war with the Lakelands for a century, fighting over land, food, and glory. The kings of fire against the kings of winter, with both red and silver blood in between. But the dawn, it seems, is coming for them all.

"The Colonel's a Lakelander. After what happened in Archeon" — her face pains, though she doesn't know the half of my ordeal there — "he came to 'sort things out,' according to Tramy."

There's something wrong here, tugging at my brain like Gisa tugging on my sleeve. "Who is the Colonel, Gisa?"

It takes me a moment to realize we've reached the mess, a flat building just like the barracks. The din of breakfast echoes behind the doors, but we don't pass through. Even though the smell of food makes my stomach rumble, I wait for Gisa's answer.

"The man with the bloody eye," she finally says, pointing to her own face. "He's taken over."

Command. Shade whispered the word back on the mersive, but I didn't think much of it. Is this what he meant? Is the Colonel who he was trying to warn me about? After his sinister treatment of Cal last night, I have to think so. And to know such a man is in charge of this island, and everyone on it, is no particular comfort.

"So Farley's out of a job."

She shrugs. "Captain Farley failed. He didn't like that."

Then he'll hate me.

She reaches for the door, one small hand outstretched. The other has healed better than I thought it would, with only her fourth and fifth fingers still oddly twisted, curled inward. Bones gone wrong, in punishment for trusting her sister in a time long ago.

"Gisa, where did they take Cal?" My voice is so low I'm afraid she doesn't hear me. But then her hand stills.

"They talked about him last night, when you went to sleep. Kilorn didn't know, but Tramy, he went to see him. To watch."

A sharp pain shoots through my heart. "Watch *what*?"

"He said just questions for now. Nothing that would hurt."

Deep inside, I scowl. I can think of many questions that would hurt Cal more than any wound. "Where?" I ask again, putting a bit of steel in my voice, speaking like a Silver-born princess should.

"Barracks One," she whispers. "I heard

them say Barracks One."

As she opens the door to the mess, I look past her, to the line of barracks marching toward the trees. Their numbers are clearly painted, black against sun-bleached concrete: *2, 3, 4 . . .*

A sudden chill runs down my spine.

There is no Barracks 1.

Six

Most of the food is bland, gray porridge and lukewarm water. Only the fish is good, cod taken straight from the sea. It bites of salt and ocean, just like the air. Kilorn marvels at the fish, idly wondering what kind of nets the Guard uses. *We're in a net, you idiot,* I want to shout, but the mess is no place for such words. There are Lakelanders in here as well, stoic in their dark blue. While the red-uniformed Guardsmen eat with the rest of the refugees, the Lakelanders never sit, constantly on the prowl. They remind me of Security officers, and I feel a familiar chill. Tuck is not so different from Archeon. Different factions vie for control, with me right in the middle. And Kilorn, my friend, my oldest friend, might not believe this is dangerous. Or worse, he could understand — and not care.

My silence persists, broken only by steady bites of fish. They're watching me closely, as instructed. Mom, Dad, Kilorn, Gisa, all pretending not to stare, and failing. The boys are gone, still at Shade's bedside. Like me, they thought him dead, and are making up for lost time.

"So how did you get here?" The words stick in my mouth, but I force them out. Better I ask the questions before they start in on me.

"Boat," Dad says gruffly around a slurp of porridge. He chuckles at his joke, pleased with himself. I smile a little, for his sake.

Mom nudges him, clucking her tongue in exasperation. "You know what she means, Daniel."

"I'm not stupid." He grumbles, shoveling back another spoonful. "Two days ago, round midnight, Shade popped up on the porch. I mean actually popped." He gestures with his hands, snapping his fingers. "You know about that, don't you?"

"I do."

"Near gave us all a heart attack, what with the popping and him being, well, alive."

"I can imagine," I murmur, remembering my own reaction to seeing Shade again. I thought us both dead, in some place far beyond this madness. But like me, Shade had merely become someone — *something* — else to survive.

Dad continues, on a roll now, literally. His chair rocks back and forth on squeaky wheels, moving with his wild gestures. "Well, after your mom stopped crying over him, he got down to it. Started throwing stuff in a bag, useless stuff. The porch flag, the pictures, your letter box. Didn't make no sense, really, but it's hard to ask anything of a son come back to life. When he said we had to leave, now, *right* now, I could tell he wasn't joking. So we did."

"What about the curfew?" The Measures are still sharp in my head, nails in my skin. How could I forget them, when I was forced to announce them myself? "You could've been killed!"

"We had Shade and his . . . his . . ." Dad struggles for the right word, gesturing again.

Gisa rolls her eyes, bored with our father's antics. "He calls it jumping, remember?"

"That's it." He nods. "Shade jumped us past the patrols and into the woods. From there, we went to the river and a boat. Cargo's still allowed to travel at night, you see, so we ended up sitting in a crate of apples for who knows how long."

Mom cringes at the memory. "*Rotten* apples," she adds. Gisa giggles a little. Dad almost smiles. For a moment, the gray porridge is Mom's bad stew, the concrete walls become rough-hewn wood, and it's the Barrows at dinner. It's home again, and I'm just Mare.

I let the seconds tick by, listening and smiling. Mom jabbers about nothing so I don't have to speak, letting me eat in quiet peace. She even chases away the stares of the mess hall, meeting every eye that swings my way with a vicious glare I know firsthand. Gisa plays her part too, distracting Kilorn with news of the Stilts. He listens intently, and she bites her lip, pleased by his attention. I guess her little crush hasn't gone away just yet. That leaves only Dad, glopping through his second bowl of porridge with abandon. He stares at me over the rim of his bowl, and I glimpse the man he was. Tall, strong, a proud soldier, a person I barely remember, so far from what he is now. But like me, like Shade, like the Guard, Dad is not the ruined, foolish thing he seems. Despite the chair, the missing leg, and the clicking contraption in his chest, he's still seen more battles and survived longer than most. He lost the leg and lung only three months before a full discharge, after near twenty years of conscription. How many make it that far?

We seem weak because we want to. Perhaps those are not Shade's words at all, but our father's. Though I've only just come into my own strength, he's been hiding his since he came home. I remember what he said last night, half-hidden in dreams. *I know what it is to kill someone.* I certainly don't doubt it.

Strange, it's the food that reminds me of Maven. Not the taste, but the act of eating itself. My last meal was at his side, in his father's palace. We drank from crystal glasses and my fork had a pearl handle. We were surrounded by servants, but still very much alone. We couldn't talk about the night to come, but I kept stealing glances at him, hoping I wouldn't lose my nerve. He gave me such strength in that moment.

I believed he had chosen me, and my revolution. I believed Maven was my savior, a blessing. I believed in what he could help us do.

His eyes were so blue, full of a different kind of fire. A hungry flame, sharp and strangely cold, tinged with fear. I thought we were afraid together, for our cause, for each other. I was so wrong.

Slowly, I push the plate of fish away, scraping the table. *Enough.*

The noise draws Kilorn's eye like an alarm, and he swings back around to face me.

"All done?" he asks, glancing at my half-eaten breakfast.

In response, I stand up, and he jumps to his feet along with me. Like a dog following commands. *But not mine.* "Can we go to the infirmary?"

Can, we. The words are carefully chosen, a smoke screen to make him forget who and what I am now.

He nods, grinning. "Shade's doing better by the second. Well, Barrows, care for a trip?" he adds with a glance toward the closest thing he has to a family.

My eyes widen. I need to speak to Shade, to find out where Cal is and what the Colonel plans for him. As much as I missed my family, they'll only get in the way. Luckily, Dad understands. His hand moves swiftly beneath the table, stopping Mom before she can speak, communicating without words. She shifts, adopting an apologetic smile that doesn't reach her eyes. "We'll come along later, I think," she says, meaning much more than those few words. "About time for a battery change, isn't it?"

"Bugger," Dad grumbles loudly, tossing his spoon into his bowl of muck.

Gisa's eyes flicker to mine, reading what I need. *Time, space, an opportunity to start untangling this mess.* "I've got more banners to sort out," she sighs. "You lot go through them pretty fast."

Kilorn shrugs off the good-natured jab with a laugh and a crooked smile, like he's done a thousand times. "Suit yourselves. It's this way, Mare."

Condescending as it may be, I let him lead me through the mess. I'm careful to make a show of it, playing up a limp, keeping my eyes downcast. I fight the urge to stare back at everyone watching, the Guardsmen, the Lakelanders, even the refugees. My time in the dead king's court serves me just as well on a military base, where once again I must hide who I am. Then I pretended to be Silver, unflinching, unafraid, a pillar of strength and power called Mareena. But that girl would be right next to Cal, confined in the missing Barracks 1. So I must be Red again, a girl named Mare Barrow, a girl no one should fear or suspect, reliant on a Red boy and not herself.

Dad and Shade's warning has never been so clear.

"Leg still bothering you?"

I'm so focused on faking the limp, I barely hear Kilorn's concern. "It's nothing," I finally respond, pressing my lips into a thin line of forced pain. "I've had worse."

"Jumping off Ernie Wick's porch comes to

mind." His eyes glitter at the memory.

I broke my leg that day, and spent months in a plaster cast that cost both of us half our savings. "That wasn't my fault."

"I believe you chose to do it."

"I was *dared.*"

"Now who would've done such a thing?"

He laughs outright, pushing us both through a set of double doors. The hallway on the other side is obviously a new addition. The paint still looks wet in places. And overhead, the lights flicker. *Bad wiring,* I know instantly, feeling the places where the electricity frays and splits. But one cord of power remains unbroken, flowing down the passage to the left. To my chagrin, Kilorn takes us right.

"What's that?" I ask, gesturing the opposite way.

He doesn't lie. "I don't know."

The Tuck infirmary isn't so grim as the medical station on the mersive. The high, narrow windows are thrown open, flooding the chamber with fresh air and sunlight. White shifts shuttle back and forth between patients, their bandages blissfully clean of red blood. Soft conversation, a few dry coughs, even a sneeze fill the room. Not a single yelp of pain or crack of bone interrupts the gentle noise. No one is dying here. *Or they have simply died already.*

Shade isn't hard to find, and this time, he isn't pretending to sleep. His leg is still elevated, held up by a more professional sling, and his shoulder bandage is fresh. He angles to the right, facing the bed next to him with a stoic expression. Who he's addressing, I can't tell yet. A curtain surrounds the bed on two sides, hiding the occupant from the rest of the infirmary. As we approach, Shade's mouth moves quickly, whispering words I can't decipher.

He stops short at the sight of me, and it feels like a betrayal.

"You just missed the brutes," he calls out, adjusting himself so there's room for me on the bed. A nurse moves to help, but Shade waves him off with a bruised hand.

The brutes, his old nickname for our brothers. Shade grew up small, and was often Bree's punching bag. Tramy was kinder, but always followed in Bree's lumbering footsteps. Eventually Shade grew smart and quick enough to evade them both, and taught me to do the same. I don't doubt he sent them from his bedside, allowing him enough privacy to talk with me — and whoever it is behind the curtain.

"Good, they're on my nerves already," I

reply with a good-natured smile.

To outsiders, we look like jawing siblings. But Shade knows better, his eyes darkening as I reach the foot of his bed. He notes my forced limp and nods infinitesimally. I mirror the action. *I got your message, Shade, loud and clear.*

Before I can even hint at asking him about Cal, another voice cuts me off. I grit my teeth at the sound of her, willing myself to keep calm.

"How do you like Tuck, lightning girl?" Farley says from the secluded bed next to Shade. She swings her legs over the side, facing me fully, with both hands clenched in her bedsheets. Pain streaks across her pretty face ruined by a scar.

The question is easy to dodge. "I'm still deciding."

"And the Colonel? How do you like him?" she continues, dropping her voice. Her eyes are guarded, unreadable. There's no telling what she wants to hear. So I shrug, busying myself with arranging Shade's blankets instead.

Something like a smile twists her lips. "He makes quite a first impression. Needs to prove he's in control with every breath, especially next to people like you two."

I round Shade's bed in an instant, planting myself between Farley and my brother. In my desperation, I forget to limp. "Is that why he took Cal away?" The words come sharp and fast. "Can't have a warrior like him running around, making him look bad?"

She lowers her eyes, as if ashamed. "No," she murmurs. It sounds like an apology, but for what, I don't know yet. "That's not why he took the prince."

Fear blossoms in my chest. "Then why? What has he done?"

She doesn't get the chance to tell me.

A strange quiet descends on the infirmary, the nurses, my heart, and Farley's words. Her curtains hide the door from us, but I hear the stomp of boots marching in quick time. No one speaks, though a few soldiers salute from their beds as the boots close in. I can see them through the gap between the curtain and floor. Black leather, caked in wet sand, and getting closer by the second. Even Farley shivers at the sight, digging her nails into the bed. Kilorn draws closer, half concealing me with his bulk, while Shade does his best to sit up.

Though this is a medical ward filled with Red wounded and my so-called allies, a little piece of me calls to the lightning. Electricity flares in my blood, close enough to reach for if I need it.

The Colonel rounds the curtain, his red eye fixed in a constant glare. To my surprise, it lands on Farley, forsaking me for the moment. His escorts, Lakelanders by their uniforms, look like pale, grim versions of my brother Bree. Hewn of muscle, tall as trees, and obedient. They flank the Colonel in practiced motion, taking up positions at the end of Shade's and Farley's beds. The Colonel himself stands in between, boxing in Kilorn and me. *Proving he's in control.*

"Hiding, Captain?" the Colonel says, fingering the curtain around Farley's bed. She bristles at the name and the insinuation. When he tsks aloud, she visibly cringes. "You're smart enough to know an audience won't protect you."

"I tried to do all you've asked, the difficult and the impossible," she fires back. Her hands quiver in the blankets, but with rage, not fear. "You left me a hundred soldiers to overthrow Norta, an entire country. What did you expect, Colonel?"

"I expected you to return with more than twenty-six of them." The retort lands hard. "I expected you to be smarter than a seventeen-year-old *princeling.* I expected you to protect your soldiers, not throw them to a den of Silver wolves. I expected much and more from you, Diana, much and more than what you gave."

Diana. The name is his killing blow. *Her real name.*

Her shivers of rage turn to shame, reducing Farley to a hollow shell. She stares at her feet, fixating on the floor below. I know her look well, the look of a shattered soul. If you speak, if you move, you'll collapse. Already, she's starting to crumble, leveled by the Colonel, his words, and her own name.

"I convinced her, Colonel."

Part of me wishes my voice would shake, to make this man think I fear him. But I've faced worse than a soldier with a bloody eye and a bad temper. Much, much worse.

Gently, I push Kilorn to the side, moving forward.

"I vouched for Maven and his plan. If not for me, your men and women would be alive. Their blood is on my hands, not hers."

To my surprise, the Colonel only chuckles at my outburst. "Not everything revolves around you, Miss Barrow. The world does not rise and fall at your command."

That's not what I meant. It sounds foolish, even in my own head.

"These mistakes are her own and no one else's," he continues, turning back to face

Farley. "I strip you of your command, Diana. Do you challenge this?"

For a brief, simmering moment, it looks like she might. But she drops her head and her gaze, retreating inward. "I do not, sir."

"Your best choice in weeks," he snaps, turning to go.

But she isn't finished. She looks up once more. "What of my mission?"

"Mission? What mission?" The Colonel seems more intrigued than angry, his one good eye darting in its socket. "I was not made aware of any new orders."

Farley turns her gaze back to me and I feel an odd kinship to her. Even defeated, she's still fighting. "Miss Barrow had an interesting proposition, one I plan to pursue. I believe Command will agree."

I almost grin at Farley, emboldened by her declaration in the face of such an opponent.

"What proposition is this?" the Colonel says, squaring his shoulders to me. From this close, I see the distinct swirls of blood in his eye, moving slowly, clouds on the wind.

"I was given a list of names. Of Reds like my brother and me, born with the mutation that enables our own . . . abilities." I must convince him, I *must.* "They can be found, protected, *trained.* Red like us but strong as Silvers, able to fight them in the open. Maybe even powerful enough to win the war." A shaky breath rattles in my chest, quivering with thoughts of Maven. "The king knows about the list, and will surely kill them all if we don't find them first. He won't let so strong a weapon go."

The Colonel is silent for a moment, his jaw working as he thinks. He even fidgets, playing with a fine chain necklace hidden in his collar. I glimpse links of gold between his fingers, revealing a fine prize no soldier should carry. I wonder who he stole it from.

"And who gave you these names?" he finally asks, his voice level and hard to read. For a brute, he's surprisingly good at hiding his thoughts.

"Julian Jacos." Tears well in my eyes at the name, but I will not let them fall.

"A Silver." The Colonel sneers.

"A sympathizer," I fire back, bristling at his tone. "He was arrested for *rescuing* Captain Farley, Kilorn Warren, and Ann Walsh. He *helped* the Scarlet Guard, he sided with *us.* And he's probably dead for it."

The Colonel settles back on his heels, still scowling. "Oh, your Julian is alive."

"Alive? Still?" I gasp, shocked. "But

Maven said he would kill him —"

"Strange, isn't it? For King Maven to leave such a traitor still breathing?" He revels in my surprise. "The way I see it, your Julian was never with you at all. He gave you the list to pass on to us, to send the Guard on a goose chase ending in another trap."

Anyone can betray anyone. But I refuse to believe that about Julian. I understand enough of him to know where his true loyalties lie — with me, Sara, and anyone who would oppose the queen who killed his sister.

"And even if, *if,* the list is true, and the names do lead to other" — he searches for the word, not bothering to be gentle — "*things* like you, then what? Do we dodge the worst agents of the kingdom, hunters better and faster than us, to find them? Do we attempt a mass exodus of the ones we *can* save? Do we found the Barrow School for Freaks, and spend years training them to fight? Do we ignore everything else, all the suffering, the child soldiers, the executions, for *them*?" He shakes his head, making the thick muscles on his neck strain. "This war will be over and our bodies cold before we gain a single bit of ground with your proposition." He glances at Farley, heated. "The rest of Command will say the same, Diana, so unless you wish to play the fool yet again, I suggest you keep quiet about this."

Each point feels like the blow from a hammer, smashing me down to size. He's right about some things. Maven will send his best to hunt down and kill the list. He'll try to keep it secret, which will slow him down, but not by much. We'll certainly have our work cut out for us. But if there's even a chance for another soldier like me, like Shade, isn't it worth the cost?

I open my mouth to tell him just that, but he holds up a hand. "I will hear no more of it, Miss Barrow. And before you make a snide comment about me trying to stop you, remember your oath. You swore to the Scarlet Guard, not your own selfish motives." He gestures to the room of injured soldiers, all harmed fighting for me. "And if their faces are not enough to keep you in line, then remember your friend and his own position here."

Cal. "You wouldn't dare hurt him."

His bloody eye darkens, swirling with deep crimson the color of rage.

"To protect my own, I certainly would." The corners of his eyes lift, betraying a smirk. "Just as you did. Make no mistake, Miss Barrow, you have hurt people to serve your own ends, the prince most of all."

For a moment, it's like my own eyes have clouded with blood. All I see is red, a livid anger. Sparks rush to my fingertips, dancing just beneath my skin, but I clench my fists, holding them back. When my vision clears, the lights flicker overhead, the only indication of my fury. And the Colonel is gone, having left us to simmer alone.

"Easy there, lightning girl," Farley murmurs, her voice softer than I've ever heard it. "It's not all bad."

"Isn't it?" I bite out through gritted teeth. I want nothing more than to explode, to let my true self out and show these weak men exactly who they're dealing with. But that would get me a cell at best, a bullet at worst. And I would have to die with the knowledge that the Colonel is correct. I've done so much damage already, and always to the people closest to me. *For what I thought was right,* I tell myself. *For the better.*

Instead of commiserating, Farley straightens her spine and sits back, watching me seethe. The shamed child she was disappears with shocking ease. *Another mask.* Her hand strays to her neck, pulling out a gold chain to match the Colonel's. I don't have time to wonder about the connection — because something dangles from the neck-

123

lace. A spiky iron key. I don't need to ask where the corresponding lock is. *Barracks 1.*

She tosses it to me blithely, a lazy smile on her face.

"You'll find I'm remarkably good at giving orders, and particularly awful at following them."

SEVEN

Kilorn grumbles all the way out of the infirmary and into the concrete yard. He even walks slowly, forcing *me* to slow down for him. I try to ignore him, for Cal's sake, for the cause, but when I catch the word *foolish* for the third time, I have to stop short.

He collides with my back. "Sorry," he says, not sounding at all apologetic.

"No, I'm sorry," I spit back, spinning to face him. A little bit of the anger I felt toward the Colonel spills over and my cheeks flush with heat. "I'm sorry you can't stop being an ass for *two minutes* so you can see exactly what's going on here."

I expect him to shout at me, to match me blow for blow in the usual way. Instead, he sucks in a breath and steps back, working furiously to calm himself.

"You think I'm so stupid?" he says. "Please, Mare, educate me. Show me the light. What do you know that I don't?"

The words beg to fall out. But the yard is too open, filled with the Colonel's soldiers, Guardsmen, and refugees hustling back and forth. And while there are no Silver whispers to read my mind, no cameras to watch my every move, I won't go soft now. Kilorn follows my gaze, eyeing a troop of Guardsmen who jog within a few yards of us.

"You think they're spying on you?" he all but sneers, dropping his voice to a mocking whisper. "C'mon, Mare. We're all on the same side here."

"Are we?" I ask, letting the words sink in. "You heard what the Colonel called me. A *thing.* A *freak.*"

Kilorn blushes. "He didn't mean that."

"Oh, and you know the man so well?"

Thankfully, he has no retort for that.

"He looks at me like I'm the enemy, like I'm some kind of *bomb* about to go off."

"He's —" Kilorn stumbles, unsure of the words even as they leave his lips. "He's not entirely wrong though, is he?"

I spin so fast the heel of my boot leaves black skid marks in the concrete. Would that I could leave a similar bruise on Kilorn's stupid, sputtering face.

"Hey, c'mon," he calls after me, closing the distance in a few quick steps. But I keep walking, and he keeps following. "Mare, stop. That came out wrong —"

"You *are* stupid, Kilorn Warren," I tell him over my shoulder. The safety of Barracks 3 beckons, rising up ahead of me. "Stupid and blind and cruel."

"Well, you're no picnic either!" he thunders back, finally becoming the argumentative twit I know he is. When I don't reply, nearly sprinting for the barracks door, his hand closes on my upper arm, stopping me cold.

I try to twist out of his grasp, but Kilorn knows all my tricks. He pulls, dragging me away from the door, and into the shaded alley between Barracks 3 and 4. "Let go of me," I command, indignant. I hear a little bit of Mareena come back to life in the cold, royal tone of my voice.

"There it is," he growls, pointing a finger in my face. "That. *Her.*"

With a mighty shove, I push him back, breaking his grip on me.

He sighs, exasperated, and runs a hand through his tawny hair. It sticks up on end. "You've been through a lot, I know that. We *all* know that. What you had to do to stay alive with *them,* all while helping us, finding out what you are, I don't know how you came out on the other side. But it changed you."

So perceptive, Kilorn.

"Just because Maven betrayed you doesn't mean you have to stop trusting people altogether." He drops his eyes, fiddling with his hands. "Especially me. I'm not just something for you to hide behind, I'm your friend, and I'm going to help you with whatever you need, however I can. Please, trust me."

I wish I could.

"Kilorn, grow up" comes out instead, so sharp it makes him flinch. "You should've told me what they were planning. But you made me an accomplice, you made me *watch* when they marched him away at *gunpoint,* and now you tell me to trust you? When you're in so deep with these people who are just waiting for an excuse to lock *me* up? How stupid do you think *I* am?"

Something stirs in his eyes, the vulnerability hidden inside the relaxed persona he tries so hard to maintain. This is the boy who cried beneath my house. The boy he was, resisting the call to fight and die. I tried to save him from that and, in turn, pushed him closer to danger, the Scarlet Guard, and doom.

"I see," he says finally. He takes a few

quick steps back, until the alley yawns between us. "It makes sense," he adds, shrugging. "Why would you trust me? I'm just the fish boy. I'm nothing compared to you, right? Compared to Shade. And *him* —"

"Kilorn Warren." I scold him like I would a child, like his mother did before she abandoned him. She would shriek when he skinned his knees or spoke out of turn. I don't remember much else of her, but I remember her voice, and the withering, disappointed glares she saved for her only son. "You know that's not true."

The words come out hard, a low, visceral growl. He squares his shoulders, fists balled at his sides. "Prove it."

To that, I have no answer. I have no idea what he wants from me. "I'm sorry," I choke out, and this time I mean it. "I'm sorry for being —"

"Mare." A warm hand on my arm stops my stumbling. He stands above me, close enough to smell. Thankfully the scent of blood is gone, replaced by salt. *He's been swimming.*

"You don't need to apologize for what they did to you," he mumbles. "You never have to do that."

"I — I don't think you're stupid."

"That might be the nicest thing you've ever said to me." He chuckles after a long moment. He pastes on a grin, ending the conversation. "I take it you've got a plan?"

"Yes. Are you going to help?"

Shrugging, he spreads his arms wide, gesturing at the rest of the base. "Not much else for the fish boy to do."

I shove him again, drawing a genuine smile from him. But it doesn't last.

Along with the key, Farley gave me detailed directions to Barracks 1. As on the mainland, the Scarlet Guard still favors their tunnels, and Cal's prison is, of course, located underground.

Technically, underwater. *The perfect prison for a burner like Cal.* Built beneath the dock, hidden by the ocean, guarded by blue waves and the Colonel's blue uniforms. It's not only the island prison but also the armory, the Lakelander bunks, and the Colonel's own headquarters. The main entrance is a tunnel leading from the beach hangars, but Farley assured me of another way. *You might get wet,* she warned with a wry smile. While the prospect of diving into the ocean unsettles me, even so close to the beach, Kilorn is annoyingly calm. In fact, he's probably excited, happy to put his long years on the river to good use.

The protection of the ocean dulls the usually alert Guard, and even the Lakelanders soften as the day wears on. Soldiers focus more on the cargo loads and storage hangars rather than patrolling. The few who keep their posts, pacing the length of the concrete yard with guns against their shoulders, walk slowly, easily, often stopping to talk to each other.

I watch them for a long while, pretending to listen to Mom or Gisa as they chatter over their work. Both sort blankets and clothing into separate piles, unloading a collection of unmarked crates along with several other refugees. I'm supposed to help, but my focus is clearly elsewhere. Bree and Tramy are gone, back with Shade in the infirmary, while Dad sits by. He can't unload, but still grumbles orders all the same. He's never folded clothes in his life.

He catches my eye once or twice, noting my twitching fingers and darting glances. He always seems to know what I'm up to, and now is no different. He even rolls his chair back, allowing me a better view of the yard. I nod at him, quietly thankful.

The guards remind me of the Silvers back in the Stilts, before the Measures, before Queenstrial. They were lazy, content in my quiet village, where insurrection was rare. How wrong they were. Those men and women were blind to my thieving, to the black market, to Will Whistle and the slow creep of the Scarlet Guard. And these Guardsmen are blind too, this time to my advantage.

They don't notice me watching, or Kilorn when he approaches with a tray of fish stew. My family eats gratefully, Gisa most of all. She twists her hair when Kilorn isn't looking, letting it curl over one shoulder in a ruby fall of red.

"Fresh catch?" she says, indicating the bowl of stew.

He wrinkles his nose and pretends to grimace at the gray glops of fish meat. "Not from me, Gee. My old master, Cully, would never sell this. Except to the rats, maybe."

We laugh together, me out of habit, following a half second later. For once, Gisa is less ladylike than I am and she giggles openly, happily. I used to envy her practiced, perfect ways. Now I wish I wasn't so trained and could shed my forced politeness as easily as she has.

While we force down the lunch, Dad pours out his bowl when he thinks I'm not looking. No wonder he's getting thin. Before I — or, worse, Mom — can scold him he runs a hand over a blanket, feeling the fabric.

"These are Piedmont made. Fresh cotton. Expensive," he mutters when he realizes I'm standing next to him. Even in the Silver court, Piedmont cotton was considered very fine, a common alternative to silk, reserved for high-ranking Security, Sentinel, and military uniforms. I remember Lucas wore it, up until the moment he died. I realize now I never saw him out of uniform. I can't even picture it. And his face is already fading. A few days and I'm forgetting him, a man I sent to his death.

"Stolen?" I wonder aloud, running a hand over the blanket, if only for distraction.

Dad continues his investigation and runs a hand down the side of a crate. Sturdy, wide planks of wood, freshly painted white. The only distinguishing mark is a dark green triangle, smaller than my hand, stamped in the corner. What it means, I don't know.

"Or given," Dad says.

He doesn't need to speak for me to know we're thinking about the same thing. If there are Lakelanders with us here, on this very island, then the Scarlet Guard could easily have friends elsewhere, in different nations and kingdoms. *We seem weak because we want to.*

With a stealth I didn't know he possessed, Dad takes my hand quickly and quietly. "Be careful, my girl."

But while he is afraid, I feel hope. The Scarlet Guard has deeper roots than I knew, than any Silver could imagine. And the Colonel is only one of a hundred heads, just like Farley. An opposition definitely, but one I can overcome. After all, he's not a king. Of those, I've had my fair share.

Like Dad, I pour my stew into a crack in the concrete. "I'm finished," I say, and Kilorn jumps up. He knows his cues.

We're going to visit Shade, or at least that's what we say out loud, for the benefit of the others close by. My family knows better, even Mom. She blows me a kiss as I walk away, and I tuck it close to my heart.

When I pull up my collar, I become just another refugee, and Kilorn is no one at all. The soldiers pay us no mind. It's easy to walk the length of the concrete yard, away from the docks and the beach, following the thick white line.

In the light of midday, I see the concrete extends toward gentle, sloping hills, looking very much like a wide road to nowhere. The painted line continues ahead, but a thinner, more worn line branches off at a right angle. It connects the central line to another structure, located at the end of the barracks, towering over everything else on the island. It looks like a larger version of the hangars on the beach, tall and wide enough to fit six transports stacked on top of one another. I wonder what it holds, knowing the Guard does their own share of thieving. But the doors are shut fast, and a few Lakelander men idle in the shade. They chat among themselves, keeping their guns close. So my curiosity will have to wait, perhaps forever.

Kilorn and I turn right, toward the gap between Barracks 8 and 9. The high windows of both are dark, abandoned — the buildings are empty. Waiting for more soldiers, more refugees, or worse, more orphans. I shiver as we pass through their shadows.

The beach isn't hard to get to. After all, this is an island. And while the main base is well developed, the rest of Tuck is empty, covered only in dunes, hills swathed in tall grass, and a few pockets of ancient trees. There aren't even paths through the grass, with no animals large enough to make them. We disappear nicely, winding through the swaying plants until we reach the beach. The dock stands a few hundred yards away, a wide knife jutting out into the waves. From this distance, the patrolling Lakelanders are only smudges of dark blue pacing back and forth. Most focus on the cargo ship approaching from the far side of the dock. My jaw drops at the sight of such a large vessel obviously controlled by Reds. Kilorn is more focused.

"Perfect cover," he says, and starts to take off his shoes. I follow suit, kicking off my laceless boots and worn socks. But when he pulls his shirt over his head, exposing familiar, lean muscles shaped by hauling nets, I'm not so inclined to follow. I don't fancy running around a secret bunker shirtless.

He folds his shirt over his shoes, fiddling a bit. "I take it this isn't a rescue mission." *How could it be? There's nowhere to go.*

"I just need to see him. Tell him about Julian. Let him know what's going on."

Kilorn winces, but he nods all the same. "Get in, get out. Shouldn't be too hard, especially since they won't expect anything from the ocean side."

He stretches back and forth, shaking out his feet and fingers to make ready for the swim. All the while, he goes over Farley's whispered instructions. There's a moon pool at the bottom of the bunker, opening up into a research lab. Once used to study marine life, now it serves as the Colonel's own quarters, though he never visits them during the day. It'll be locked from the inside, easy to open, and the corridors are simple to navigate. At this time of day, the bunks will be empty, the passage from the docks sealed, and very few guards will remain behind. Kilorn and I faced worse as children, when we stole a case of batteries for my dad from a Security outpost.

"Try not to splash," Kilorn adds, before wading into the surf. Goose bumps rise on his skin, reacting to the cold autumn ocean, but he barely feels it. I certainly do, and by the time the water reaches my waist my teeth are chattering. With one last glance toward the dock, I dive below a wave, letting it chill me to the bone.

Kilorn cuts through the water effortlessly, swimming like a frog, making almost no noise at all. I try to mimic his movements, following close to his side as we swim farther out. Something about the water heightens my electrical sense, making it easier to feel the piping running out from the shore. I could trace it with a hand if I wanted, noting the path of electricity from the docks, through the water, and into Barracks 1. Eventually Kilorn turns toward it, angling us on a diagonal to the shore, and then parallel. His advance is masterful, with the stolen boats at anchor to hide our approach. Once or twice he touches my arm beneath the waves, communicating with a slight pressure. Stop, go, slow, fast, all of it while he stays fixed on the dock ahead. Luckily, the freighter ship is unloading, drawing the attention of any soldiers who might spot our heads bobbing through the water. More crates, all white, stamped with the green triangle. *More clothes?*

No, I realize as a crate topples, cracking open. Guns spill across the dock. Rifles, pistols, ammunition, probably a dozen in one crate alone. They gleam in the sunlight, newly made. Another gift for the Scarlet Guard, another twist of even deeper roots I never knew existed.

The knowledge makes me swim faster, pushing me past Kilorn even when my muscles ache. I duck under the dock, safe at last from any eyes above, and he follows, keeping pace just behind me.

"It's right below us." His whispers echo oddly, reverberating off the metal dock above and the water all around. "I can just feel it with my toes."

I almost laugh at the sight of Kilorn stretching, his brow set in concentration as he tries to brush a foot against the hidden bunker of Barracks 1. "Something funny?" he grumbles.

"You're so useful," I reply with a mischievous smirk. It feels good to be with him like this, sharing a secret goal again. Although this time we're breaking into a military bunker, not someone's half-locked house.

"Here," he finally says, before his head disappears below the water. He bobs back up again, arms wide to keep himself afloat. "The edge."

Now comes the hard part. The plunge through suffocating, drowning darkness.

Kilorn reads the fear on my face plainly. "Just hold on to my leg, that's all you have to do."

I can barely nod. "Right." *The moon pool is on the bottom of the bunker, only twenty-five feet down.* "It's nothing at all," Farley had said. *Well, it certainly looks like something,* I think, peering at the black water below me. "Kilorn, Maven will be *so* disappointed if the ocean kills me before he can."

To anyone else, the joke would be in poor taste. But Kilorn chuckles lowly, his grin bright against the water. "Well, as much as I'd like to annoy the king," he sighs, "let's try and avoid drowning, shall we?"

With a wink, he dives, end over end, and I

grab hold.

The salt stings my eyes, but it's not so dark as I thought it would be. Sunlight angles through the water, breaking up the shadow cast by the dock above. And Kilorn moves us quickly, pulling us down along the side of the barracks. The water-bent sunlight dapples his bare back, spotting him like a sea creature. I focus mainly on kicking when I can and not getting caught on anything. *This is not twenty-five feet,* my mind grumbles when the twinge of oxygen deprivation sets in.

I exhale slowly, letting the bubbles rise past my face, up to the surface. Kilorn's own breath streams past, the only testament to his strain. When he finds the bottom edge, I feel his muscles tense, and his legs kick along, powering us both beneath the hidden bunker. Dimly, I wonder if the moon pool has a door, and if it'll be closed. What a joke that would be.

Before I know what's happening, Kilorn bursts up and through something, hauling me with him. Stuffy but blissful air hits my face and I gulp it down in deep, greedy gasps.

Already sitting on the edge of the pool, his legs dangling in the water, Kilorn grins at me. "You wouldn't last a morning unknotting nets," he says with a shake of the head. "That was barely a bath compared to what Old Cully used to make me do."

"You really know how to cut me deep," I reply dryly, hoisting myself up and into the Colonel's chambers.

The compartment is cold, lit by low lights, and offensively well organized. Old equipment is pushed neatly against the right wall, gathering dust, while a desk runs the length of the left. Stacks of files and papers crowd the surface in neat rows, dominating the space. At first I don't even see a bed, but it's there, a narrow bunk that rolls out from beneath the desk. Clearly the Colonel doesn't sleep much.

Kilorn was always a slave to his curiosity, and now is no different. He drips his way over to the desk, ready to explore.

"Don't touch anything," I hiss at him while I wring out my sleeves and pant legs. "Get one drop on those papers and he'll know someone was in here."

He nods, pulling his hand back. "You should see this," he says, his tone sharp.

I step to his side in an instant, fearing the worst. "What?"

Careful, he points a finger at the only thing decorating the walls of the compartment. A photograph, warped by age and damp, but the faces are still visible. Four figures, all blond, posing with stern but open expressions. The Colonel is there, barely recognizable without his bloody eye, one arm around a tall, well-boned woman, and his hand on a young girl's shoulder. Both the woman and the girl wear dirt-stained clothes, farmers by the look of it, but the gold chains at their necks say differently. Silently, I remove the gold chain from my pocket, comparing the metal so fine it could be thread to the necklaces in the picture. But for the mismatched key dangling from the end, they are identical. Gently, Kilorn takes the key from my hand, puzzling over what it could mean.

The third figure explains it all. A teenager with a long, golden braid, she stands shoulder to shoulder with the Colonel and wears a smirk of satisfaction. She looks so young, so different without her short hair and scars. *Farley.*

"She's his daughter," Kilorn says aloud, too shocked for much else.

I resist the urge to touch the photograph, to make sure it's real. The way he treated her back in the infirmary, it can't possibly be true. But he called her Diana. He knew her real name. *And they had the necklaces, one from a sister, one from a wife.*

"C'mon," I murmur, pulling him away from the picture. "It's nothing to bother with now."

"Why didn't she say anything?" In his voice, I hear a little bit of the betrayal I've felt for days.

"I don't know."

I keep hold of him, moving us both toward the compartment door. *Left down the stairs, right at the landing, left again.*

The door swings open on oiled hinges, revealing an empty passage quite like the ones on the mersive. Sparse and clean, with metal walls and piping above us. Electricity bleeds overhead, pumping through a wired network of veins. It's coming from the shore, feeding the lights and other machinery.

Like Farley said, there's no one down here. No one to stop us. I suppose, as the Colonel's daughter, she would know first-hand. Quiet as cats, we follow her instructions, mindful of every single step. I'm reminded of the cells beneath the Hall of the Sun, where Julian and I incapacitated a squadron of black-masked Sentinels to free Kilorn, Farley, and the doomed Walsh. It seems so far away, yet that was only days ago. *A week. Just one week.*

I shudder to think where I'll be in seven

143

more days.

At last we come to a shorter passage, a dead end with three doors on the left, three doors on the right, and just as many observation windows set in between. The glass of each is dark, but for the window on the end. It flickers slightly, casting harsh white light through the pane. A fist collides with the glass and I flinch, expecting it to crack beneath Cal's knuckles. But the window holds firm, echoing dully with every *boom boom* of his fists, showing nothing more than smears of silver blood.

No doubt he hears me coming, and thinks I'm one of *them.*

When I step in front of the window, he freezes mid-motion, one clenched and bleeding fist poised to strike. His flame-maker bracelet slides down his thick wrist, still spinning from his momentum. That's a comfort, at least. They didn't know enough to take away his greatest weapon. But then why is he still imprisoned at all? Couldn't he just melt the window and be done with it?

For a single, blazing moment, our eyes meet through the glass, and I think our combined stare might shatter it. Thick, silver blood drips from where he struck his hand, mixing with already-dried stains. He's been at this for a while, beating himself bloody in an attempt to get out — or burn off a little bit of his rage.

"It's locked," he says, his voice muffled behind the glass.

"Couldn't tell," I reply, smirking.

Next to me, Kilorn holds up the key.

Cal starts, as if noticing Kilorn for the first time. He smiles, grateful, but Kilorn doesn't return the gesture. He won't even meet his eyes.

From somewhere down the hall, I hear shouting. Footsteps. They echo strangely in the bunker but grow closer with every heartbeat. Coming for us.

"They know we're here," Kilorn hisses, looking back. Quickly, he jams the key in the lock and turns it. It doesn't budge and I throw my shoulder against the door, slamming into cold, unforgiving iron.

Kilorn forces the key again, twisting. This time I'm close enough to hear the mechanism click. The door swings inward as the first soldier rounds the corner, but my thoughts are only of Cal.

It seems princes make me blind.

The invisible curtain drops the moment Kilorn shoves me into the cell. It's a familiar sensation but I can't place it. I've felt it before, I know I have, but where? I don't have time to wonder. Cal surges past me, a strangled yell erupting from his lips, his long arms outstretched. Not to me, or the window. To the door as it yanks shut.

The click of the lock echoes inside my skull, again and again and again.

"What?" I ask the heavy, stale air. But the only answer I need is Kilorn's face, staring at me from the other side of the glass. The key hangs from one clenched fist, and his face curls into something between a scowl and a sob.

I'm sorry, he mouths, and the first Lakelander soldier appears through the window. More follow, flanking the Colonel. His satisfied smirk matches the one his daughter wore in the photograph, and I begin to understand what just happened. The Colonel even has the audacity to laugh.

Cal hurls himself at the door in vain, driving his shoulder against solid iron. He swears through the pain, cursing Kilorn, me, this place, himself. I barely hear him over Julian's voice in my head.

Anyone can betray anyone.

Without thought, I call for the lightning. My sparks will free me and turn the Colonel's laughter into screams.

But they don't come. There's nothing. Bleak nothing.

Like in the cells, like the arena.

"Silent Stone," Cal says, leaning heavily against the door. He points with one bloody fist to back corners of the floor and ceiling. "They have Silent Stone."

To make you weak. To make you like them.

Now it's my turn to pound my fists against the window, punching at Kilorn's head. But I hit glass, not flesh, and hear only the cracking of my own knuckles instead of his stupid skull. Despite the wall between us, he flinches.

He can barely look at me. He shivers when the Colonel puts one hand on his shoulder, whispering into his ear. Kilorn can only watch as I scream, an indecipherable roar of frustration, and my blood joins Cal's on the glass.

Red running through silver, joining into something darker.

EIGHT

The legs of the metal chair scrape against the floor, the only sound in the square cell. I leave the other chair where it lies, upended and battered after being thrown against the wall. Cal did quite a number on the cell before I got here, hurling both chairs and a now dented table. There's a single chink in the wall, just below the window, where the corner of the table hit home. But throwing furniture is no use to me. Instead of wasting my energy, I conserve it, and take a seat in the center of the room. Cal paces back and forth before the window, more animal than man. Every inch of him yearns for fire.

Kilorn is long gone, having left with his new friend the Colonel.

And I am revealed for exactly what I am — a particularly stupid fish, constantly moving from hook to hook, never learning my lesson. But next to the Hall of the Sun, Archeon, and the Bowl of Bones, this might as well be a vacation, and the Colonel is nothing compared to the queen or a line of executioners.

"You should sit," I tell Cal, finally growing tired of his vengeful intensity. "Unless you plan on wearing your way through the floor?"

He scowls, annoyed, but stops moving all the same. Instead of pulling up a chair, he leans against the wall in a childish act of defiance. "I'm starting to think you like prisons," he says, idly knocking his knuckles against the wall. "And that you have the worst taste in men."

That stings more than I'd like it to. Yes, I cared for Maven, cared for him far more than I want to admit, and Kilorn is my closest friend. They are betrayers both.

"You're not too good at choosing friends either," I fire back, but it glances off him harmlessly. "And I don't have" — the words jumble, coming out wrong and stilted — "*any* taste in men. This has nothing to do with that."

"Nothing." He chuckles, almost amused. "Who were the last two people to lock us in a cell?" When I don't reply, shamed, he presses on. "Admit it, you've got a hard time keeping your heart and your head separated."

I stand so fast the chair falls backward, clanging against the floor. "Don't act like you didn't love Maven. Like you didn't let *your* heart make decisions where he was concerned."

"He is my brother! Of course I was blind to him! Of course I didn't think he would kill our — our father." His voice breaks at the memory, letting me glimpse the ragged and broken child beneath the facade of a warrior. "I made mistakes because of him. And," he adds quietly, "I made mistakes because of *you.*"

So did I. The worst was when I put my hand in his, letting him pull me from my bedroom, into a dance and a downward spiral. I let the Guard kill innocents for Cal, to keep him from going to war. To keep him close to me.

My selfishness had a horrible cost.

"We can't do that anymore. Make mistakes for each other," I whisper, skirting around what I really mean. What I've been trying to tell myself for days now. Cal is not a path I should choose or want. Cal is simply a weapon, something for me to use — or something for others to use against me. I must prepare for both.

After a long moment, he nods. I get the feeling he sees me in the same way.

The damp of the barracks sets in, joining the cold still deep in my bones. Normally I would shiver, but I'm getting used to this feeling. I suppose I should get used to being alone too.

Not in the world, but in here. In my heart.

Part of me wants to laugh at our predicament. Again, I am side by side with Cal in a cell, waiting for whatever fate has in store for us. But this time, my fear is tempered by anger. It won't be Maven coming to gloat, but the Colonel, and for that I'm terribly thankful. Maven's taunts are not ones I ever want to suffer again. Even the thought of him hurts.

The Bowl of Bones was dark, empty, a deeper prison than this. Maven stood out sharply, his skin pale, eyes bright, his hands reaching for mine. In the poisoned memory, they flicker between soft fingers and ragged claws. Both want to make me bleed.

I told you to hide your heart once. You should have listened.

They were his last words to me, before he sentenced us to execution. I wish it hadn't been such good advice.

Slowly, I exhale, hoping to expel the memories with my breath. It doesn't work.

"So what do we do about this, General

Calore?" I ask, gesturing to the four walls holding us prisoner. Now I can see the slight outlines in the corners, the square blocks a bit darker than the rest, fixed right into the panels of the walls.

After a long moment, Cal pulls out of thoughts just as painful as mine. Glad for the distraction, he rights the other chair swiftly, pushing it against a corner. He steps up, almost banging his head on the ceiling, and runs a hand over the Silent Stone. It's more dangerous to us than anything on this island, more damaging than any weapon.

"By my colors, how did they get this?" he mutters, his fingers trying to find an edge. But the stone lies flush, perfectly embedded. With a sigh, he jumps back down and faces the observation window. "Our best chance is breaking the glass. There's no getting around these in here."

"It's weaker, though," I say, staring at the Silent Stone. It stares right back. "In the Bowl of Bones, I felt like I was suffocating. This is nowhere near that bad."

Cal shrugs. "Not as many blocks here. But still enough."

"Stolen?"

"They have to be. There's only so much Silent Stone and only the government can use it, for obvious reasons."

"That's true . . . in Norta."

He tilts his head, perplexed. "You think these came from somewhere else?"

"There are smuggled shipments coming in from all over. Piedmont, the Lakelands, other places too. And haven't you seen any soldiers down here? Their uniforms?"

He shakes his head. "No. Not since that red-eyed bastard marched me in yesterday."

"They call him the Colonel, and he's Farley's father."

"I'd feel sorry for her, but my family's infinitely worse."

I scoff, half-amused. "They're *Lakelanders,* Cal. Farley, and the Colonel, and all his soldiers. Which means there's more where they came from."

Confusion clouds his face. "That — that can't be. I've seen the battle lines myself; there's no way through." He looks at his hands, idly drawing a map in midair. It makes no sense to me, but he knows it intimately. "The lakes are blockaded on both shores; the Choke is out of the question completely. Moving goods and stores is one thing, but not people, not in this magnitude. They'd have to have wings to get across."

My breath rushes inward, as fast as my realization. The concrete yard, the immense hangar at the end of the base, the wide road leading to nowhere.

Not a road.

A runway.

"I think they do."

To my surprise, a wide, genuine grin breaks across Cal's face. He turns to the window, peering out at the empty passage. "Their manners leave a lot to be desired, but the Scarlet Guard are going to cause my brother a lot of headaches."

And then I'm smiling too. If this is how the Colonel treats his so-called allies, I'd love to see what he does to his enemies.

Dinnertime comes and goes, marked only by a grizzled old Lakelander carrying a tray of food. He motions for both of us to step back and face the far wall, so he can slide the tray through a slit in the door. Neither of us responds, stubbornly standing our ground by the window. After a long standoff, he marches away, eating our dinner with a grin. It doesn't bother me in the slightest. I grew up hungry. I can handle a few hours without a meal. Cal, on the other hand, pales when the food saunters off, his eyes following the plate of gray fish.

"If you wanted to eat, you should've told me," I grumble, taking my seat again.

"You're no use if you're starving."

"That's what they're supposed to think," he replies, a bit of a glint in his eye. "I figure I'll faint after breakfast tomorrow, and see how well their medics take a punch."

It's a shaky plan at best, and I wrinkle my nose in distaste.

"Do you have a better idea?"

"No," I say, sullen.

"That's what I thought."

"Hmph."

The Silent Stone has a strange effect on both of us. In taking away what we rely on most, our abilities, the cell forces us to become someone else. For Cal, that means being smarter, more calculating. He can't lean on infernos, so he turns to his mind instead. Although, judging by the fainting idea, he's not the sharpest blade in the armory.

The change in me is not so evident. After all, I lived seventeen years in silence, not knowing what power lingered within me. Now I'm remembering that girl again, the heartless, selfish girl who would do anything to save her own skin. If the Lakelander returns with another tray, he better be ready to feel my hands around his throat and, if we manage to get out of this cell, my lightning in his bones.

"Julian's alive." I don't know where the words come from, but suddenly they're hanging in the air, fragile as snowflakes.

Cal's head jerks up, his eyes suddenly bright. The prospect of his uncle still breathing cheers him almost as much as freedom. "Who told you that?"

"The Colonel."

Now it's Cal's turn to "hmph."

"I think I believe him." That earns a disparaging glare, but I press on. "The Colonel thinks Julian was part of Maven's trap, another Silver to betray me. It's why he doesn't believe in the list."

Cal nods, his eyes faraway. "The ones like you."

"Farley calls them — us — newbloods."

"Well," he sighs, "the only thing they'll be called is dead if you don't get out of here soon. Maven will hunt them all."

Blunt but true. "For revenge?"

To my surprise, he shakes his head. "He's a new king following a murdered father. Not the most stable place to start his reign. The High Houses, Samos and Iral especially, would leap at a chance to weaken him. And the discovery of newbloods, after he publicly denounced you, would certainly do that."

Though Cal was raised to be a soldier, trained in the barracks of a living war, he

156

was also born to be a king. He might not be so conniving as Maven, but he understands statecraft better than most.

"So every person we save will hurt him, not just on the battlefield, but on the throne."

He smirks crookedly, leaning his head back against the wall. "You're throwing 'we' around quite a bit."

"Does that bother you?" I ask, testing the waters. If I can rope Cal into tracking down the newbloods with me, we might actually have a chance of outpacing Maven.

A muscle in his cheek twitches, the only indication of his indecision. He doesn't get a chance to answer before the now familiar march of boots cuts him off. Cal groans to himself, annoyed at the Colonel's return. When he starts to rise, my hand shoots out, pushing him back into his seat.

"Don't stand for him," I mutter, leaning back in my own chair.

Cal does as he's told and settles in, arms crossed over his broad chest. Now instead of beating against the window and tossing tables at the walls, he looks stoic, serene, a boulder of flesh waiting to crush whoever comes too close. If only he could. But for the Silent Stone, he would be a blazing inferno, burning hotter and brighter than the sun. And I would be a storm. Instead, we're reduced to our bones, to two teenagers grumbling in a cage.

I do my best to keep still when the Colonel appears in the window. I don't want to give him the satisfaction of my anger, but when Kilorn appears at his shoulder, his expression cold and stern, my body jolts. Now it's Cal's turn to hold me back, his hand a slight pressure on my thigh, keeping me seated.

The Colonel stares for a moment, as if memorizing the sight of the prince and the lightning girl imprisoned. I'm seized by the urge to spit on the bloodstained glass but refrain. Then he turns away from us, gesturing with long, crooked fingers. They twitch once, twice, beckoning for someone to step forward. Or be brought forth.

She fights like a lion, forcing the Colonel's bodyguards to hold her clean off the ground. Farley's fist catches one of them in the jaw, sending him sprawling, breaking his grip on her arm. She slams the other into the passage wall, crushing his neck between her elbow and the window of another cell. Her blows are brutal, meant to inflict as much damage as she can, and I can see purple bruises already blooming on her captors. But the bodyguards are careful not to hurt her, doing their best to keep her merely restrained.

Colonel's orders, I suppose. He'll give his daughter a cell, but not bruises.

To my dismay, Kilorn doesn't stand idle. When the guards get her up against a wall, each one bracing a shoulder and leg, the Colonel gestures to the fish boy. With shaking hands, he pulls out a dull gray box. Syringes gleam within.

I can't hear her voice through the glass, but it's easy to read her lips. *No. Don't.*

"Kilorn, stop it!" The window is suddenly cold and smooth beneath my hand. I beat against it, trying to catch his attention. "Kilorn!"

But he squares his shoulders, turning his back so I can't see his face. The Colonel does the opposite, staring at me instead of the syringe plunging into his daughter's neck. Something strange flickers deep in his good eye — regret, maybe? No, this is not a man with doubts. He'll do whatever he must, to whoever he must.

Kilorn pulls back after doing the deed, the empty syringe sharp in his hand. He waits, watching Farley thrash against her captors. But her movements slow and her eyelids droop as the drugs take hold. Finally she sags against the Lakelander guards, unconscious, and they drag her to the cell across from mine. They lay her down before locking the door, shutting her in just like Cal — just like me.

When her door clangs shut, the lock in mine clicks open.

"Redecorating?" the Colonel says with a sniff, eyeing the dented table as he enters. Kilorn follows, tucking the box of syringes back into his coat, in warning. *For you, if you step out of line.* He avoids my stare, busying himself with the box while the door locks behind them, leaving the two guards to man the passage on the other side.

Cal glares from his seat, his expression murderous. I don't doubt he's thinking about all the ways he could kill the Colonel, and which would hurt the most. The Colonel knows that too, and draws a short but lethal pistol from its holster. It idles in his hand, a coiled snake waiting to strike.

"Please sit, Miss Barrow," he says, gesturing with the gun.

Obeying his command feels like surrender, but I have no other choice. I take my seat, letting Kilorn and the Colonel stand over us. If not for the gun and the guards in the hall, watching closely, we might have a chance. The Colonel is tall, but older, and Cal's hands would fit nicely around his throat. I would have to take Kilorn myself, relying on my knowledge of his still-healing wounds to bring the traitor down. But once we bested them, the door would still be locked, the guards still watching. Our fight would accomplish nothing at all.

The Colonel smirks, as if reading my thoughts. "Best stay in your chair."

"You need a gun to keep two children in line?" I scoff back at him, angling my chin at the pistol in his hand. There isn't a soul on earth who would dare call Cal a child, even without his abilities. His military training alone makes him deadly, something the Colonel knows well enough.

He ignores the insult and plants his feet in front of me, so his bloody eye bores into mine. "You know, you're lucky I'm a progressive man. There aren't many who would let him live" — he nods toward Cal, before sweeping back to me — "and a few who would kill you as well."

I glance at Kilorn, hoping he realizes what side he's on. He fidgets like a little boy. If we were children again, still the same size, I would punch him squarely in the stomach.

"You're not keeping me around for the pleasure of my company," Cal says, cutting right through the Colonel's dramatics. "So what are you going to trade me for?"

The Colonel's reaction is the only confirmation I need. His jaw clenches, tightening in anger. He wanted to say the words himself, but Cal's taken the wind out of his sails.

"Trade," I murmur, though it comes out more like a hiss. "You're going to trade away one of the best weapons you've got? How stupid *are* you?"

"Not stupid enough to think he'll fight for us," the Colonel replies. "No, I leave that foolish hope to you, lightning girl."

Don't rise to the bait. It's what he wants. Still, it takes everything in me to stare straight ahead, and keep my eyes from Cal. Truthfully, I don't know where his loyalties lie, or who he fights for. I only know who he'll fight against — *Maven.* Some would think that puts us on the same side. But I know better. Life and war are not so simple as that.

"Very well, Colonel Farley." He flinches when I use his last name. His head turns slightly, resisting the urge to look back at his daughter unconscious in her cell. *There's pain there,* I note, filing it away for later use.

But the Colonel responds to my jab in kind. "The king has put forth a bargain," he says, his words pressing like a knife on the verge of drawing blood. "In exchange for

162

the exiled prince, King Maven has agreed to reinstate the traditional age of conscription. Back to eighteen, instead of fifteen years old." He lowers his eyes, his voice dropping with them. For a brief, splintering moment, I catch a glimpse of the father beneath the brutal exterior. His mind wanders to the children sent to die. "It's a good deal."

"Too good," I say quickly, my tone hard and strong enough to hide the fear beneath. "Maven will never honor such a trade. *Never.*"

To my left, Cal exhales slowly. He draws his hands together, fingers steepled, displaying the many cuts and bruises he's earned over the last few days. They twitch in succession, one after the other. A distraction from whatever truth he's trying to avoid.

"But you have no choice," Cal says, his hands finally still. "Turning down the deal dooms them all."

The Colonel nods. "Indeed. Take heart, Tiberias. Your death will save thousands of innocent children. They are the only reason you're still breathing."

Thousands. Certainly they're worth Cal, certainly. But deep in my heart, in the twisted, cold part of myself I'm starting to know all too well, something disagrees. *Cal*

*is a fighter, a leader, a killer, a hunter. And
you need him.*

In more ways than one.

Something glitters in Cal's eye. If not for
the Silent Stone, I know his hands would
shudder with flame. He leans forward
slightly, lips pulling back against his even,
white teeth. It's so aggressive and animalistic
I expect to see fangs.

"I am your rightful king, Silver-born for
centuries," he replies, seething. "The only
reason *you're* still breathing is because I
can't burn the oxygen from this room."

I've never heard such a threat from Cal,
so visceral it cuts my insides. And the
Colonel, usually calm and stoic, feels it as
well. He pulls back too quickly, almost
stumbling into Kilorn. Like Farley, he's
embarrassed by his fear. For a moment, his
complexion matches his bloody eye, making
him look like a tomato with limbs. But the
Colonel is made of sterner stuff, and chases
away his fear in a single, collected moment.
He smooths back his white-blond hair,
pressing it flat to his skull, and holsters his
gun with a satisfied sigh.

"Your boat leaves tonight, Your Royal
Highness," he says with a crack of his neck.
"I advise you to say good-bye to Miss
Barrow. I doubt you'll see her ever again."

My hand closes around the seat of my chair, digging into the cold, rough metal. If only my name was Evangeline Samos. Then I would wrap this chair around the Colonel's throat until he tasted iron and saw blood in both eyes.

"What about Mare?"

Even now, on the heels of his own death sentence, how is Cal stupid enough to worry about me?

"She'll be watched," Kilorn butts in, speaking for the first time since he entered my cage. His voice quivers, as it should. The coward has everything to be afraid of, including me. "Guarded. But not hurt."

Distaste flickers across the Colonel's face. I suppose he wants me dead too. Who could overrule him, I don't know. Farley's mysterious Command, perhaps, whoever they are.

"Is that what you'll do to people like me?" I spit, feeling myself rise from my seat. "The newbloods? Are you going to bring Shade down here next and put him in a cage like some sort of *pet*? Until we learn to obey?"

"That depends on him," the Colonel replies evenly, each word a cold kick in the gut. "He's been a good soldier. So far. Just like your friend here," he adds, putting one flat hand on Kilorn's shoulder. He reeks of fatherly pride, something Kilorn's been without. After so long an orphan, even a father as horrible as the Colonel must feel good. "Without him, I would've never had the excuse, or the opportunity, to lock you up."

I can only glare at Kilorn, hoping my gaze hurts him as much as he's hurt me. "How proud you must be."

"Not yet," the fish boy replies.

If not for our years in the Stilts, our many hours thieving and slinking like alley rats, I would've never seen it. But Kilorn is easy to read, for me at least. When he angles his body, simultaneously arching his back and shrugging his hips, it looks natural. But there's nothing natural about what he's trying to do. The bottom of his jacket sags, outlining the box holding the syringes. It slips dangerously, sliding between the fabric and stomach, faster and faster.

"Oh —" he chokes out, jumping from the Colonel's grasp when the box springs free. It bursts open in midair, spitting needles as it falls. They hit the floor, shattering and spilling fluid across our toes. Most would think them all broken, but my quick eyes notice one syringe still intact, half-hidden by Kilorn's curling fist.

"Dammit, boy," the Colonel says, stooping without a thought. He reaches for the box, hoping to salvage something, but gets a needle in the neck for his trouble.

The surprise of it gives Kilorn the second he needs to squeeze, emptying the syringe into the Colonel's veins. Like Farley, he fights, cracking Kilorn across the face. He goes flying, colliding with the far wall.

Before the Colonel can take another step, Cal explodes out of his chair and slams him against the observation window. The Lakelander soldiers look on helplessly from the other side of the glass, their guns ready but useless. After all, they can't open the door. They can't risk letting the monsters out of their cage.

The combination of the drugs and Cal's dead weight knocks the Colonel out cold. He slides down the window, knees buckling beneath him, and slumps into a very undignified pile. With his eyes closed, he looks much less threatening. Normal, even.

"Ow" sounds from the wall where Kilorn stands, massaging his cheek. Drugged or not, the Colonel packs a mean punch. A bruise has already begun to form. Without thought, I take quick steps toward him. "It's nothing, Mare, don't worry —"

But I'm not coming to comfort him. My fist collides with the opposite cheek, knuckles knocking against bone. He howls, moving with the momentum of my punch, almost losing his balance altogether.

Ignoring the pain in my fist, I brush my hands together. "Now you match." And then I embrace him, arms closing around his middle. He flinches, expecting more pain, but soon relaxes against my touch.

"They were going to catch you down here either way. Figured I'd do more good if I wasn't in the cell next to you." He heaves a sigh. "I told you to trust me. Why didn't you believe it?"

For that, I have no answer.

At the observation window, Cal sighs aloud, drawing the attention back to the task at hand. "I can't fault your bravery, but does this plan go much further than singing this sack of scum a lullaby?" He toes the Colonel's body with a foot while jabbing a thumb at the window, indicating the guards still watching us.

"Just 'cause I can't read doesn't mean I'm stupid," Kilorn says, a bit of an edge to his voice. "Watch the window. Should be any second."

Ten seconds to be exact. We stare for exactly ten seconds before a familiar form appears, blinking into existence. Shade, looking much better than the brother I saw in the infirmary just this morning. He stands on his own two feet, with a brace on his injured leg and nothing more than bandages around his shoulder. He wields a crutch like a club, bashing both the guards before they get a chance to realize what's going on. They drop to the floor like sacks of hammers, stupid looks on their faces.

The lock of the cell opens with a joyous echo, and Cal is at the door in a heartbeat, wrenching it open. He steps out into the air of the passage, breathing deep. I can't follow him fast enough and sigh aloud when the weight of Silent Stone drops away. With a grin, I pull sparks to my fingers, watching them crackle and vein across my skin.

"Missed you," I murmur to my dearest friends.

"You're a strange one, lightning girl."

To my surprise, Farley leans against her open cell door, the picture of calm. She doesn't look at all affected by the drugs — if they had any affect at all.

"The benefit of befriending nurses," Kilorn says, bumping my shoulder. "A nice smile was all it took to distract Lena, and slip something harmless into the box."

"She'll be heartbroken to find you gone," Farley replies, twisting her lips into something akin to a pout. "Poor girl."

Kilorn only scoffs. His eyes flicker to me.

"That's not my problem."

"And now?" Cal says, the soldier in him coming forth. His shoulders tense, firm beneath his threadbare clothes, and he turns his neck back and forth, keeping an eye on every corner of the passage.

Shade puts out his arm in response, palm pointed toward the ceiling. "Now we jump," he says.

I'm the first to put my hand on his arm, holding tight. Even if I can't trust Kilorn, Cal, or anyone else, I can trust in ability. In strength. In power. With Cal's fire, my storm, and Shade's speed, nothing and no one can touch us.

While we are together, I will never suffer a prison again.

NINE

The bunker passes by in flashes of light and color. I catch only glimpses as Shade lets loose, jumping us through the structure. His hands and arms are everywhere, grasping, giving us all enough space to hold on. He must be strong enough to take us all, because no one gets left behind.

I see a door, a wall, the floor tipping toward me. Guards give chase at every turn, shouting, shooting, but we're never in one place long enough. Once, we land in a crowded room blossoming with electricity, surrounded by video screens and radio equipment. I even catch sight of some cameras piled in the corner before the occupants react to us and we jump away. Then I'm squinting in the sunlight of the dock. This time, the Lakelanders get close enough that I can see their faces, pale against the evening light. Then it's sand beneath my feet. Another jump and it's concrete. We jump farther in the open, starting at one end of the runway before teleporting all the way to the hangar. Shade winces with the strain, his muscles tight, the cords of his neck standing out starkly. One last jump takes us inside the hangar, to face cool air and relative quiet. When the world finally stops twisting and pulling, I feel like collapsing. Or throwing up. But Kilorn keeps me standing, holding me up to see what we've come so far for.

Two airjets dominate the hangar, their wings spread wide and dark. One is smaller than the other, built for a single occupant, with a silver body and orange-tipped wings. *Snapdragon,* I remember, thinking back to Naercey and the swift, lethal jets that rained fire down upon us. The bigger one is pitch-black, menacing, with a larger body and no distinguishing colors to speak of. I've never seen anything like it, and dimly wonder if Cal has either. After all, he's going to be the one to fly it, unless Farley has yet another skill in her bag of tricks. Judging by the way she stares at the jet, her eyes wide, I doubt it.

"What are you doing in here?"

The voice echoes strangely in the hangar, bouncing off the walls. The man who appears beneath the wing of the Snapdragon

172

doesn't have the look of a soldier, wearing gray coveralls instead of a Lakelander uniform. His hands are black with oil, marking him as a mechanic. He glances between us, taking in Kilorn's bruising cheeks and Shade's crutch. "I-I'll have to report you to your superiors."

"Report away," Farley barks, looking every inch the captain she was. Next to her scar and the tense cut of her jaw, I'm surprised the mechanic doesn't faint on the spot. "We're on strict orders from the Colonel." She gestures quickly, pointing Cal toward the black jet. "Now get this hangar door open."

The mechanic continues to stammer while Cal leads us to the rear of the jet. As we pass beneath the wing, he reaches up a hand, letting it drag against the cool metal. "A Blackrun," he explains quietly. "Big and fast."

"And stolen," I add.

He nods, stoic, reaching the same conclusion as me. "From the Delphie airfield."

A training exercise, Queen Elara had said at a luncheon long ago. She brushed aside the rumor of stolen jets with a wave of her salad fork, humiliating the now dead Colonel Macanthos in front of her trove of ladies. I thought she was lying then, covering up more of the Guard's actions, but it also seemed impossible — who could steal a jet, let alone two? Apparently the Scarlet Guard could — and did.

The back of the Blackrun, beneath the tail, yawns open like a mouth, creating a ramp for loading and unloading cargo. Namely, us. Shade goes first, leaning heavily on his crutch, his face damp and pale with exertion. So many jumps have taken their toll. Kilorn follows, dragging me along, with Cal right behind us. I can still hear the echo of Farley's voice when we clamber inside, navigating through semidarkness.

Seats line both curved walls, with heavy-duty straps dangling from each one. Enough to transport two dozen men at least. I wonder where this jet flew last, and who it carried. Did they live, did they die? And will we share their fate?

"Mare, I need you up here," Cal says, pushing past me to the front of the jet. He drops heavily into the pilot's seat, facing an unfathomable panel of buttons, levers, and instruments. All the dials and gauges are pointed to zero, and the jet hums with nothing but the beating of our own hearts. Through the thick glass of the cockpit, I can see the hangar door — still closed — and Farley, still arguing with the mechanic.

Sighing, I take the seat next to him and begin to strap myself in. "What can I do?" The buckles click and snap as I tighten each one in turn. If we're going to be flying, I don't want to be bouncing around the inside of the jet.

"This thing's got batteries, but they need a kick, and I don't think that mechanic's going to give it to us," he says with a bit of a glint in his eye. "Do what you do best."

"Right." Determination floods through me, strong as my sparks. *It's just like switching on a lamp, or a camera,* I tell myself. *Only a lot bigger and more complicated —* *and more important.* Briefly I wonder if it can be done, if I'm enough to jump-start the massive Blackrun. But the memory of lightning, purple and white and powerful, streaking out of the sky to strike the Bowl of Bones, tells me I am. If I can start a storm, I can certainly bring this jet to life.

Arms outstretched, I put my hands on the panel. I don't know what to feel for, only that I feel nothing. My fingers dance along the metal, searching for anything to latch on to, anything I might be able to use. My sparks rise in my skin, ready to be called on. "Cal," I mutter through gritted teeth, reluctant to let the cry escape.

He understands and works quickly, reaching under the control panel to something beneath. Metal tears with a biting screech, melted at the edges, as he pries away the panel casing. He reveals a mess of wires, crossing in woven bundles, and I'm reminded of veins beneath skin. I only need to get them pumping. Without thought, I plunge a hand into the wires, letting my sparks pulse out. They search on their own, looking for somewhere to go. When my fingers brush a particularly thick wire, a round, smooth cord that fits my hand perfectly, I can't help but smile. My eyes fall shut, allowing me to concentrate. I push harder, letting my strength flow into the power line. It carries through the jet, splitting and branching along different paths, but I force my sparks on. When they hit the engine and the immense batteries, my grip tightens, nails digging into skin. *Come on.* I can feel myself pour into the batteries, flooding them, until I brush against their own stored energy. My head dips, leaning against the panel, letting the cool metal calm my flushing skin. With one last push, the dam inside the jet breaks, bursting through the walls and wires. I don't see the Blackrun power to life, but I feel it all around.

"Well done," Cal says, sparing a second to

squeeze my shoulder. His touch doesn't linger though, in accordance with our agreement. No distractions, least of all now. I open my eyes to see his hands dancing across the panel controls, flipping switches and adjusting knobs seemingly at random.

When I lean back, another hand takes my shoulder. Kilorn lets his hand rest, but his touch is strangely gentle. He's not even looking at me but the jet, his face torn between awe and fear. With his mouth agape and eyes wide, he looks almost childish. I feel small myself, sitting in the belly of an airjet, about to do what we never dreamed possible. *The fish boy and the lightning girl, about to fly.*

"Does she expect me to ram this thing through a wall?" Cal mutters under his breath, his own smile long gone. He looks over his shoulder, eyes searching, not for me, but my brother. "Shade?"

My brother looks liable to faint, and reluctantly shakes his head. "I can't jump things this big, this — complicated. Even on a good day." It pains him to say such a thing, though he has no reason at all to be ashamed. But Shade is a Barrow, and we do not like to admit weakness. "I can grab Farley, though," he continues, his hands straying to his buckles.

Kilorn knows my brother as well as I do, and pushes him back into his seat. "You're no use dead, Barrow," he says, forcing a crooked grin. "I'll get that door open."

"Don't bother," I spit out, my eyes fixed outside the cockpit. I push my power outward, and with a great screeching groan, the hangar door starts to open, pulling up from the floor in a smooth, steady motion. The mechanic looks puzzled, watching the mechanism controlling the door grind away, while Farley bolts. She sprints out of sight, racing the rising door. A blaze of sunset follows her, cut with streaking, long shadows. Two dozen soldiers stand in silhouette, blocking the opening. Not just Lakelanders, but Farley's own Guardsmen, marked by their red sashes and scarves. Each one has a gun aimed at the Blackrun, but they hesitate, not willing to fire. To my relief I don't recognize Bree or Tramy among them.

One of the Lakelanders steps forward, a captain or lieutenant judging by the white stripes on his uniform. He shouts something, a hand outstretched, his lips forming the word *stop*. But we can't hear him above the growing roar of engines.

"Go!" Farley shouts, appearing at the back of the plane. She hurtles into the closest seat, buckling herself in with shaking hands.

178

Cal doesn't need to be told twice. His hands work double-time, twisting and pressing, as if this is second nature. But I hear him muttering under his breath, like a prayer, reminding himself of what to do. The Blackrun lurches forward, wheels rolling, while the rear ramp rises into place, sealing the interior of the craft with a satisfying pneumatic hiss. *No going back now.*

"All right, let's get this thing moving," Cal says, settling back into his pilot's chair with an almost excited twist. Without warning, he grabs a lever on the panel, pushing it forward, and the jet obeys.

It rolls ahead, on a collision course with the line of soldiers. I grit my teeth, expecting a brutal scene, but they're already running, fleeing the Blackrun and her vengeful pilot. We tear from the hangar, gaining speed with every passing second, to find the runway in chaos. Transports roar past the barracks, heading for us, while a troop of soldiers fires boldly from the roof of the hangar. The bullets *ping* into the metal hull, but never puncture it. The Blackrun is made of stronger stuff and pushes on, turning a hard right that rattles us in our seats.

Kilorn gets the brunt of it, not having fastened his safety belts properly. His head bangs against the curved wall and he curses, cradling his bruised cheeks. "You sure you can fly this thing?" he growls, directing all his anger at Cal.

With a sneer, Cal pushes further, urging the jet to its top speed. Out the window, I see the transports falling away, unable to keep pace. But ahead, the runway, a bland gray road, is steadily coming to an end. Soft green hills and stunted trees have never looked so menacing.

"Cal," I breathe, hoping he hears me over the scream of engines. "Cal."

Behind me, Kilorn fumbles with his belt, but his fingers are shaking too badly to be of any use. "Barrow, you got one last jump in you?" he shouts, glancing at my brother.

Shade doesn't seem to hear him. His eyes stare forward, his face pale with fear. The hills are closing in, seconds away now. I picture the jet driving over them, steady for a moment, before tipping end over end to explode in a fiery wreck. *Cal would survive that, at least.*

But Cal won't let us die. Not today. He leans hard on another lever, the veins in his fist standing out sharply. Then the hills fall away, like a cloth pulled off a table. It's not the island I see anymore but the deep blue autumn sky. My breath disappears with the land, stolen away by the sensation of rising through the air. The pressure pushes me back into my seat and does something almost painful to my ears, *popping* them. Behind me, Kilorn stifles a yelp and Shade curses under his breath. Farley doesn't react at all. She's frozen, her eyes wide in shock.

I've experienced many strange things these last few months, but nothing compares to flying. It's a jarring contrast, feeling the immense thrust of the plane as it ascends, every tick of the engines throwing us skyward, while my own body is so powerless, so passive, so dependent on the craft around me. It's worse than Cal's speeding cycle, but also better. Biting my lip, I make sure not to shut my eyes.

We climb and climb, listening to nothing but roaring engines and our own pounding hearts. Wisps of cloud flit by, breaking across the cockpit like white curtains. I can't stop myself from leaning forward, almost pressing my nose to the glass to get a good look outside. The island wheels below, a drab green against the iron-blue sea, growing smaller by the second, until I can't distinguish the runway or the barracks.

When the jet levels out, reaching whatever height Cal decides on, he turns in his seat. The smug look on his face would make

Maven proud. "Well?" he says, staring at Kilorn. "Can I fly this thing?"

A grumbled "yes" is all he gets, but that's enough for Cal. He turns back to the panel, hands resting on a U-shaped mechanism centered before him. The jet responds to his touch, dipping gently when he turns the U. When he's satisfied, he punches a few more buttons on the console and leans back, seemingly letting the plane fly itself. He even unbuckles his safety belts, shrugging out of them to get more comfortable in his seat.

"So where are we heading?" he asks the silence. "Or are we just winging it now?"

I wince at the pun.

A resounding smack echoes through the jet as Kilorn slaps a stack of papers against his knee. *Maps.* "The Colonel's," Kilorn explains, his eyes boring into mine. *Trying to make me understand.* "There's a landing strip near Harbor Bay."

But Cal shakes his head like an annoyed teacher with an increasingly foolish student. "You mean Fort Patriot?" he scoffs. "You want me to land us in the middle of a Nortan air base?"

Farley is the first out of her seat, almost ripping her buckles apart. She examines the maps with sharp, deliberate motions. "Yes, we are completely stupid, Your Highness," she says coldly. She unfolds one map, before shoving it under his nose. "Not the fort. Nine-Five Field."

Gritting his teeth against a retort, Cal takes the map gingerly and examines the square of lines and color. After a moment, he laughs outright.

"What is it?" I ask, pulling the map from his hand. Unlike the giant, indecipherable ancient scroll in Julian's old classroom, this map displays familiar names and places. The city of Harbor Bay dominates the south, bordering the ocean coast, with Fort Patriot occupying a peninsula jutting out into the water. A thick brown strip around the city, too uniform to be natural, can only be another stretch of barrier trees. As in Archeon, the greenwarden's creation of strange forests protects Harbor Bay from pollution. In this case, probably from New Town, the labeled area hugging the barrier trees like a belt, forming a wall around the outskirts of Harbor Bay.

Another slum, I realize. Like Gray Town, where Reds live and die beneath a sky full of smoke, forced to build transports, light-bulbs, airjets, everything and anything the Silvers themselves can't comprehend. Techies aren't allowed to leave their so-called cities, even to conscript to the army. Their skills are too valuable to lose to war, or their own free will. The memory of Gray Town stings, but knowing it's not the only abomination of its kind cuts even deeper. How many live in the confines of that slum? Or this one? How many *like me,* for that matter?

I taste bile as it rises in my throat, but swallow hard, forcing myself to look away. I search through the surrounding lands, mostly mill towns, the occasional small city, and dense forest dotted with a few dilapidated ruins. But Nine-Five Field doesn't seem to be anywhere on the map. A secret probably, like anything to do with the Scarlet Guard.

Cal notes my confusion and allows himself one last chuckle. "Your friend wants me to land a Blackrun on a damn ruin," he finally says, tapping the map lightly.

His finger lands on a dotted line, the symbol for one of the ancient, massive roads of long ago. I saw one once, when Shade and I got lost in the woods near the Stilts. It was cracked by the ice of a thousand winters and bleached white by centuries of sun, looking more like craggy rocks than an old thoroughfare. A few trees grew straight through it, forcing their way up through asphalt. The thought of landing an airjet on one turns my stomach.

"That's impossible," I stammer, imagining all the ways we could crash and die attempting to touch down on the old road.

Cal nods in agreement, quickly taking the map from my hands. He spreads it wide, his fingers dancing along the different cities and rivers as he searches. "With Mare, we don't need to touch down here. We can take our time, refuel the batteries whenever we need, and fly as long as we want, as far as we want." Then, with a shrug, "Or until the batteries stop holding a charge."

Another bolt of panic streaks through me. "And how long might that be?"

He responds with a crooked grin. "Blackruns went into use two years ago. At worst, this girl's got another two on her cells."

"Don't scare me like that," I grumble.

Two years, I think. *We could circle the world in that time. See Prairie, Tiraxes, Montfort, Ciron, lands that are only names on a map. We could see them all.*

But that is a dream. I have a mission of my own, newbloods to protect, and a kingly score to settle.

"So then, where do we start?" Farley asks.

"We let the list decide. You have it, don't you?" I try my best not to sound afraid. If

Julian's book of names was left back in Tuck, then this little jaunt will be over before it's even begun. Because I'm not going one inch farther without it.

Kilorn responds instead, pulling the familiar notebook from inside his shirt. He tosses it my way, and I catch it deftly. It feels warm in my hands, still holding on to his heat. "Lifted it from the Colonel," he says, trying his best to sound casual. But pride bleeds through, small as it may be.

"His quarters?" I wonder, remembering the austere bunker beneath the ocean.

But Kilorn shakes his head. "He's smarter than that. Kept it locked up in the barracks armory, with the key on his necklace."

"And you . . . ?"

With a satisfied smirk, he pulls on his collar, revealing the gold chain at his neck. "I might not be as good a pickpocket as you, but —"

Farley nods along. "We were planning on stealing it eventually, but when they locked you up, we had to *improvise*. And quickly."

"Oh." So this is what my few hours in a cell paid for. *You can trust me,* Kilorn said before he tricked me into a cage. Now I realize he did it for the list, for the newbloods, and for me. "Well done," I whisper.

Kilorn pretends to shrug it off, but his

grin gives away how pleased he truly is.

"Yes, well, I'll take that now if you don't mind," Farley says, her voice gentler than I've ever heard it. She doesn't wait for Kilorn's response and reaches out to grab the chain in a quick, even motion. The gold glints in her hand but quickly disappears, tucked in a pocket. Her mouth twitches a little, the only indication of how affected she is by her father's necklace. *No, it's not his. Not truly.* The photograph in the Colonel's quarters is proof of that. Her mother or her sister wore that chain, and for whatever reason, she isn't wearing it now.

When she raises her head again, the twitch is gone, her gruff manner returned. "Well, lightning girl, who's closest to Nine-Five?" she asks, jutting her chin at the book.

"We're *not* landing at Nine-Five," Cal says, firm but commanding. On this, I have to agree with him.

Quiet until now, Shade groans in his seat. He's no longer pale, but vaguely green. It's almost comical — he can handle teleporting just fine, but it seems flying does him in. "Nine-Five *isn't* a ruin," he says, trying his very best not to be sick. "Have you forgotten Naercey already?"

Cal exhales slowly, rubbing his chin with a hand. There's the beginning of a beard, a dark shadow across his jaw and cheeks. "You repaved it."

Farley nods slowly and smiles.

"And you couldn't just say that outright?" I curse at her, wiping the self-important grin right off her face. "You know there's no extra points for being dramatic, *Diana*. Every second you waste feeling smug could mean another dead newblood."

"And every second *you* waste questioning me, Kilorn, and Shade on everything down to the air you breathe does the same thing, lightning girl," she says, closing the distance between us. She towers over me, but I don't feel small. With the cold confidence forged by Lady Blonos and the Silver court, I meet her gaze without a hint of a shiver. "Give me reason to trust you and I will."

A lie.

After a moment, she shakes her head and backs away, giving me enough space to breathe. "Nine-Five *was* a ruin," she explains. "And to anyone curious enough to visit, it just looks like a stretch of abandoned road. One mile of asphalt that hasn't broken apart yet."

She starts pointing to other ruined roads on the map. "It's not the only one."

A varied network webs the map, always hidden in the ancient ruins, but close to the smaller towns and villages. *Protection,* she calls them, because Security is minimal, and the Reds of the countryside are more inclined to look the other way. Perhaps less so now, with the Measures in place, but certainly before the king decided to take away even more of their children. "The Blackrun and the Snapdragon are the first jets we've stolen, but more will come," she adds with a quiet pride.

"I wouldn't be sure of that," Cal replies. He's not being hostile, just pragmatic. "After they were taken from Delphie, it'll be even harder to get into a base, let alone a cockpit."

Again, Farley smiles, completely convinced of her own hard-won secrets. "In Norta, yes. But the airfields of Piedmont are woefully underguarded."

"Piedmont?" Cal and I breathe in surprised unison. The allied nation to the south is far away, farther even than the Lakelands. It should be well beyond the reach of Scarlet Guard operatives. Smuggling from that region is easy to believe, I've seen the crates with my own eyes, but outright infiltration? It seems . . . impossible.

Farley doesn't seem to think so. "The Piedmont princes are utterly convinced that the Scarlet Guard is a Nortan problem.

Fortunately for us, they're incorrect. This snake has many heads."

I bite my lip to keep back a gasp, and maintain what little remains of my mask. *The Lakelands, Norta, and now Piedmont?* I'm torn between wonder and fear of an organization large enough and patient enough to infiltrate, not one, but three sovereign nations ruled by Silver kings and princes.

This is not the simple, ragtag bunch of true believers I imagined.

This is a machine, large and well oiled, in motion for longer than anyone thought possible.

What have I fallen into?

To keep my thoughts from welling up in my eyes, I flip open the book of names. Julian's study of artifacts, peppered with the name and location of every newblood in Norta, calms me. If I can recruit them, train them, and show the Colonel that we are not Silver, we are not to be feared, then we might have a chance at changing the world.

And Maven won't have the chance to kill anyone else in my name. I won't carry the weight of any more gravestones.

Cal leans in next to me, but his eyes are not on the pages. Instead, he watches my hands, my fingers, as they sweep through the list. His knee brushes my own, hot even through his ragged pants. And though he says nothing, I understand his meaning. Like me, he knows there's always more than meets the eye, more than we can even begin to comprehend.

Be on your guard, his touch says.

With a nudge, I reply.

I know.

"Coraunt," I say aloud, stopping my finger short. "How close is Coraunt to the Nine-Five landing strip?"

Farley doesn't bother to look for the village on the map. She doesn't need to. "Close enough."

"What's in Coraunt, Mare?" Kilorn asks, sidling up to my shoulder. He's careful to keep his distance from Cal, putting me between them like a wall.

The words feel heavy. My actions could free this man. Or doom him.

"His name is Nix Marsten."

Ten

The Blackrun was the Colonel's own jet, used to skip between Norta and the Lakelands as quickly as possible. It's more than a transport for us. It's a treasure trove, still loaded with weapons, medical supplies, even food rations from its last flight. Farley and Kilorn sort the stores into piles, dividing guns from bandages, while Shade changes the dressings on his shoulder. His leg stretches out oddly, unable to bend in the brace, but he doesn't show any signs of pain. Despite his smaller size, he was always the toughest one in the family, second only to Dad white-knuckling through his constant agony.

My breath suddenly feels ragged, stinging the walls in my throat, stabbing in my lungs. *Dad, Mom, Gisa, the boys.* In the whirlwind of my escape, I've forgotten about them entirely. Just like before, when I first became Mareena, when King Tiberias and Queen

Elara took away my rags and gave me silk. It took me hours to remember my parents at home, waiting for a daughter who would not return. And now I've left them waiting again. They might be in danger for what I've done, subject to the Colonel's wrath. I drop my head into my hands, cursing. *How could I forget them? I only just got them back. How could I leave them like this?*

"Mare?" Cal mutters under his breath, trying not to draw attention to me. The others don't need to see me curling in, punishing myself with every little breath.

You're selfish, Mare Barrow. A selfish, stupid little girl.

The low hum of engines, once a slow, steady comfort, becomes a hard weight. It beats against me like waves on the Tuck beach, unending, engulfing, drowning. For a moment, I want to let it consume me. Then I will feel nothing but the lightning. No pain, no memory, just power.

A hand at the back of my head takes a bit of the edge off, pushing warmth into my skin to meet the cold. The thumb draws slow, even circles, finding a pressure point I didn't know existed. It helps a little.

"You have to calm down," Cal continues, his voice much closer this time. I glance out the corner of my eye to see him leaning down next to me, his lips almost brushing my ear. "Jets are a little sensitive to lightning storms."

"Right." The word is so hard to say. "Okay."

His hand doesn't move, staying with me. "In through the nose, out through the mouth," he coaches, his voice low and calming as if he's talking to a spooked animal. I guess he's not entirely wrong.

I feel like a child, but I take the advice anyway. With every breath, I let another thought go, each one harsher than the last. *You forgot them.* In. *You killed people.* Out. *You let others die.* In. *You are alone.* Out.

The last one isn't true. Cal is proof of that, as are Kilorn, Shade, and Farley. But I can't shake the feeling that, while they stand with me, there's no one *beside* me. Even with an army at my back, I am still alone.

Maybe the newbloods will change that. Maybe not. Either way, I have to find out.

Slowly, I sit back up, and Cal's hand follows. He draws away after a long moment, when he's sure I don't need him anymore. My neck feels suddenly cold without his warmth, but I have too much pride to let him know that. So I turn my gaze outward, focusing on the clouds blurring past, the sinking sun, and the ocean beneath. White-capped waves angle against a long chain of islands, each one connected by alternating strips of sand, marsh, or a dilapidated bridge. A few fishing villages and light towers dot the archipelago, seemingly harmless, but my fists clench at the sight of them. *There could be a watch atop one of them. We could be seen.*

The largest of the islands has a harbor filled with boats, navy judging by their size and the silver-blue stripes decorating their hulls.

"I assume you know what you're doing?" I ask Cal, my eyes still on the islands. Who knows how many Silvers are down there, searching for us? And the harbor, crowded with ships, could hide any number of things. Or people. *Like Maven.*

But Cal doesn't seem concerned with any of that. Again, he scratches his growing stubble, fingers rasping over rough skin. "Those are the Bahrn Islands, and nothing to worry about. Fort Patriot, on the other hand . . ." he says, pointing vaguely northwest. I can just make out the shore of the mainland, hazy in the golden light. "I'm going to stay out of their sensor range as long as I can."

"And when you can't?" Kilorn is suddenly standing over us, leaning on the back of my chair. His eyes dart back and forth, alternating between Cal and the islands below. "You think you can outfly them?"

Cal's face is calm, confident. "I know I can."

I have to hide my smile behind a sleeve, knowing it will only incense Kilorn. Though I've never flown with Cal before today, I have seen him in action on a cycle. And if he's half as good at flying jets as he is at driving that two-wheeled death machine, then we're in very capable hands.

"But I won't have to," he continues, satisfied with Kilorn's silence. "Every jet has a call sign, to let the forts know exactly which bird's going where. When we get in range, I'll send an old one out, and if we're lucky, no one will think to double-check."

"Sounds like a gamble," Kilorn grumbles, searching for anything to poke holes into Cal's plan, but the fish boy finds himself woefully outmatched.

"It works," Farley pipes in from her place on the floor. "That's how the Colonel gets past, if he can't fly between the sensories."

"I suppose it helps that no one expects rebels to know how to fly," I add, trying to alleviate a bit of Kilorn's embarrassment. "They're not looking for stolen jets in the air."

To my surprise, Cal stiffens sharply. He gets up from his seat in a quick, jarring motion, leaving his chair spinning. "Instrument response is sluggish," he mutters in hasty explanation. A lie, poorly made, judging by the dark scowl on his face.

"Cal?" I call, but he doesn't turn around. He doesn't even acknowledge me, and stalks off toward the back of the jet. The others watch him with narrowed eyes, still painfully cautious of him.

I can only stare, perplexed. *What now?*

I leave him to his thoughts and go to Shade, still sprawled on the floor. His leg looks better than expected, supported by the well-made brace, but he still needs the curved metal crutch at his side. After all, he did take two bullets in Naercey and we have no skin healers to put him back together with a simple touch.

"Can I get you anything?" I ask.

"Wouldn't say no to some water," he says begrudgingly. "And dinner."

Happy to be able to do at least something for him, I collect a canteen and two sealed packets of provisions from Farley's stores. I expect her to make a fuss about rationing the food, but she barely spares me a glance. She's taken my seat in the cockpit, and stares out the window, enthralled by the world passing beneath. Kilorn idles next to her, but never touches Cal's empty chair. He doesn't want to be scolded by the prince, and is careful to keep his hands away from the instrument panel. He reminds me of a child surrounded by splintered glass, wanting to touch but knowing he should not.

I almost take a third ration packet, as Cal hasn't eaten since the Colonel locked him up, but one glance toward the back of the jet stills my hand. Cal stands alone, fiddling with an open panel, putting on a show of fixing something that isn't broken. He quickly zips himself into one of the uniforms stored away on board: a black-and-silver flight suit. The tattered clothes of the arena and execution puddle at his feet. He looks more like himself, a prince of fire, a warrior born. If not for the distinctive walls of the Blackrun, I would think us back in a palace, dancing around each other like moths around a candle. There's a badge emblazoned over his heart, a black-and-red emblem flanked by a pair of silver wings. Even from this distance, I recognize the dark points, twisted into the image of flame. *The Burning Crown.* That was his father's, his grandfather's, his birthright. Instead, the crown was taken in the worst way, paid for with his father's blood and his brother's soul. And as much as I hated the king, the throne, and all it stood for, I can't help but feel sorry for Cal. He's lost everything — an entire life, even if that life was wrong.

Cal feels my gaze and looks up from his busywork, still for a moment. Then his hand strays to the badge, tracing the outline of his stolen kingdom. In one sharp twist that makes me flinch, he rips it from the suit and tosses it away. Rage flickers in his eyes, deep beneath his calm exterior. Though he tries to hide it, his anger always bubbles to the surface, glinting between the cracks in his well-worn mask. I leave him to his fussing, knowing the inner workings of the jet can calm him better than anything I might say.

Shade shifts, giving me space next to him, and I plop down without much grace. Silence hangs over us like a dark cloud as we pass the canteen back and forth, sharing a very strange family dinner on the floor of a twice-stolen Blackrun.

"We did the right thing, didn't we?" I whisper, hoping for some kind of absolution. Though he's only a year older than me, I've always relied on Shade's advice.

To my relief, he nods. "It was only a matter of time before they threw me in with you. The Colonel doesn't know how to handle people like us. We scare him."

"He's not the only one," I answer glumly, remembering the averted eyes and whispers of everyone I've encountered thus far. Even in the Hall of the Sun, where I was surrounded by impossible abilities, I was still different. And in Tuck, I was the lightning girl. Respected, recognized, and *feared.* "At least the others are normal."

"Mom and Dad?"

I nod, wincing at the mention of them. "Gisa too, and the boys. They're true Red so he can't — he won't do anything to them." It sounds like a question.

Shade takes a thoughtful bite of his rations, a flaky, dry bar of compacted oats. It leaves crumbs all over him. "If they'd helped us, it'd be a different story. But they didn't know anything about our escape, so I wouldn't worry. Leaving the way we did" — his breath catches, as does mine — "it was better for them. Dad would've helped otherwise, Mom too. At least Bree and Tramy are loyal enough to the cause to escape any suspicion. Not to mention, neither of them is bright enough to pull something like this off." He pauses, thoughtful. "I doubt even the Lakelanders would like throwing an old woman, a cripple, and

200

little Gisa in a cell."

"Good," I reply, relieved ever so slightly. Feeling better, I brush the flakes of his ration bar off his shirt.

"I don't like it when you call them normal," he adds, catching my wrist. His voice is suddenly low. "There's nothing wrong with us. We're different, yes, but not wrong. And certainly not better."

We are anything but normal, I want to tell him, but Shade's stern words kill the thought. "You're right, Shade," I say with a nod, hoping he won't see through my feeble lie. "You always are."

He laughs and finishes his dinner in a massive bite. "Can I get that in writing?" He chuckles, releasing his grip on me. His smile is so familiar I begin to ache. I feign a smile, for his benefit, but Cal's heavy steps quickly wipe it away.

He strides past us, stepping clean over Shade's extended leg, his eyes fixed on the cockpit. "We should be in range soon," he says to no one in particular, but it sends us into action.

Kilorn scrambles away from the cockpit, as if shooed away like a little boy. Cal ignores him completely. His focus is on the airjet, and nothing else. For now, at least, their animosity takes a backseat to the obstacles ahead.

"I'd buckle in," Cal adds over his shoulder, catching my eye as he sinks into his own seat. He fastens his safety belts with detached precision, tightening each one with quick, hard tugs. At his side, Farley does the same, silently claiming my chair for the time being. Not that I mind. Watching the jet take off was terrifying — I can only imagine what landing looks like.

Shade is proud, but not stupid, and lets me help him to his feet. Kilorn takes Shade's other side, and together we make quick work of getting him standing. Once he's up, Shade maneuvers himself easily, getting buckled into his seat with a crutch under one arm. I take the seat next to him, with Kilorn on my other side. This time, my friend buckles himself in tightly, and grips his restraints in grim anticipation.

I focus on my own belts, feeling strangely safe when they tighten against me. *You just strapped yourself to a hurtling piece of metal.* It's true, but, at least for the next few minutes, life and death depend solely on the pilot. I'm just along for the ride.

In the cockpit, Cal busies himself with a dozen switches and levers, preparing the jet for whatever comes next. He squints, averting his eyes from the sunset and its blaze of light. It sets his silhouette on fire, illuminating him with red-and-orange fingers that could be his own flames. I'm reminded of Naercey, the Bowl of Bones, even our Training matches, when Cal ceased to be a prince and became an inferno. Back then I was shocked, surprised every time he revealed his brutal self, but no longer. I can never forget what burns beneath his skin, the rage that fuels him, and how strong they both are.

Anyone can betray anyone, and Cal is no exception.

A touch at my ear makes me jump in my seat, jolting against my restraints. I turn to see Kilorn's hand hanging in midair and his face quirked in an amused smile.

"You still have them," he says, gesturing to my head.

Yes, Kilorn, I still have ears, I want to bite back. But then I realize what he's talking about. Four stones, pink, red, deep purple, and green — my earrings. The first three are from my brothers, part of a single set split between Gisa and me. They were bittersweet gifts, given when they conscripted into the army and left our family, perhaps for good. The last one is from Kilorn, given on the edge of doom, before the Scarlet Guard attacked Archeon, before the betrayal that still haunts us all. The earrings were with me through everything, from Bree's conscription to Maven's treachery, and each stone feels heavy with memory.

Kilorn's gaze lingers on the green earring, the one that matches his eyes. The sight of it softens him, wearing down the hard edge he's gained over the last few months.

"Of course," I reply. "These will be with me to my grave."

"Let's keep the grave talk to a minimum, especially at the moment," Kilorn mutters, eyeing his restraints again.

From this angle, I get a closer look at his bruised face. One black eye from the Colonel, one purpling cheek from me. "Sorry about that," I say, apologizing for both my words and the injury.

"You've given me worse." Kilorn laughs, smiling. He's not wrong.

The harsh, grating hiss of radio static shatters the peaceful moment. I turn to see Cal leaning forward, one hand on the steering instrument, the other clutching the radio mouthpiece.

"Fort Patriot Control, this is BR one eight dash seven two. Origin Delphie, destination Fort Lencasser."

His calm, flat tone echoes down the jet. Nothing about his voice sounds amiss or even slightly interesting. Hopefully Fort Patriot agrees. He repeats the call sign twice more, even sounding bored by the time he finishes. But his body is all nerves and he chews his lip worriedly, waiting for a response.

The seconds seem to stretch into hours as we listen, hearing nothing but the hiss of static on the other end of the radio. Next to me, Kilorn tightens his belts, preparing for the worst. I quietly do the same.

When the radio crackles, heralding a response, my hands clutch the edge of my seat. I might have faith in Cal's flying abilities, but that doesn't mean I want to see them put to the test outrunning an attack squadron.

"Received, BR one eight dash seven two," a stern, authoritative voice finally replies. "Next call in will be Cancorda Control. Received?"

Cal exhales slowly, unable to stop a grin from spreading. "Received, Patriot Control."

But before I can relax, the radio continues hissing, making Cal's jaw clench. His hands stray to the steering instrument, fingers tightening around each prong with steady focus. That action alone is enough to frighten us all, even Farley. In the chair next to him, she watches with wide eyes and parted lips, as if she can taste the words to come. Shade does the same, staring at the radio on the panel, his crutch tucked close.

"Storms over Lencasser, proceed with caution," the voice says after a long, heart-pounding moment. It's bored, dutiful, and completely uninterested in us. "Received?"

This time, Cal's head drops, his eyes half-shut in relief. I can barely stop myself from doing the same. "Received," he repeats into the radio. The hiss of static dies with a satisfying click, signaling the end of the transmission. *That's it. We're beyond suspicion.*

No one speaks until Cal does, turning over his shoulder to flash a crooked grin. "No sweat," he says, before carefully wiping away the thin sheen on his forehead.

I can't help but laugh aloud at the sight — a fire prince, sweating. Cal doesn't seem to mind. In fact, his grin widens before he turns back to the controls. Even Farley allows herself the ghost of a smile and Kilorn shakes his head, disentangling his hand from mine.

"Well done, Your Highness," Shade says, and while Kilorn uses the title like a curse, it sounds entirely respectful in my brother's mouth.

I suppose that's why the prince smiles, shaking his head. "My name is Cal, and that's all."

Kilorn scoffs deep in his throat, low enough for only me to hear, and I dig an elbow into his ribs. "Would it kill you to be a little polite?"

He angles away from me, avoiding yet another bruise. "I'm not willing to risk it," he whispers back. And then, louder, to Cal, "I take it we don't call in at Cancorda, *Your Highness*?"

This time I bring my heel down on his foot, earning a satisfying yelp.

Twenty minutes later, the sun has set and we're beyond Harbor Bay and the slums of New Town, flying lower by the second. Farley can barely stay in her seat, craning her neck to see as much as she can. It's only trees below us now, thickening into the massive forest that occupies most of Norta. It almost looks like home out there, as if the Stilts wait just over the next hill. But home is to the west, more than a hundred miles away. The rivers here are unfamiliar, the roads strange, and I don't know any of the villages huddled against the waterways. The newblood Nix Marsten lives in one of them, not knowing what he is or what kind of danger he's in. *If he's still living.*

I should wonder about a trap but I don't. I can't. The only thing pushing me forward is the thought of finding other newbloods. Not just for the cause but for *me,* to prove I'm not alone in my mutation, with only my brother by my side.

My trust in Maven was misplaced, but not my trust in Julian Jacos. I know him better than most, and so does Cal. Like me, he knows the list of names is real and if the others disagree, they certainly don't show it. Because I think they want to believe, too. The list gives them hope of a weapon, an opportunity, a way to fight a war. The list is an anchor for us all, giving each of us something to hold on to.

When the jet angles toward the forest, I focus on the map in hand to distract myself, but still I feel my stomach drop.

"I'll be damned," Cal mutters, staring out the window at what I assume are the ruins turned runway. He flips another switch and the panels beneath my feet vibrate, coinciding with a distinct *whirr* that echoes through the body of the airjet. "Brace for landing."

"And that means what exactly?" I ask through clenched teeth, turning to see not sky out the window but treetops.

The entire jet shudders before Cal can respond, smacking against something solid.

We bounce in our seats, fingers clenched around our belts, as the momentum of the jet sways us back and forth. Shade's crutch goes flying, hitting the back of Farley's chair. She doesn't seem to notice, her knuckles bone white on the arms of her seat. But her eyes are wide, open, and unblinking.

"We're down," she breathes, almost inaudible over the deafening roar of engines.

Night falls quietly over the so-called ruin, broken by distant birdsong and the low whine of the airjet. Its engines spin slower and slower, shutting down after our journey north. The shocking blue tinge of electricity beneath each wing fades, until the only light comes from inside the jet and the stars above.

We wait, silent, in the hope that our landing has gone unnoticed.

It smells like autumn, the air perfumed by dying leaves and the damp of distant rainstorms. I breathe it deeply at the bottom of the ramp. The silence is punctuated only by Kilorn's distant snores as he catches a few much-needed moments of sleep. Farley has already disappeared, a gun in hand, to scout out the rest of the hidden runway. She took Shade with her, just in case. For the first time in weeks, months even, I'm not under guard or closely watched. I belong to myself again.

Of course, that doesn't last long.

Cal hastens down the ramp, a rifle over his shoulder, a pistol on his hip, and a pack dangling from his hand. With his black hair and dark jumpsuit, he could be made of shadow, something I'm sure he plans to use to his advantage.

"And what are you doing?" I ask, deftly catching his arm. He could break my grip in a second, but doesn't.

"Don't worry, I didn't take much," he says, gesturing to the pack. "I can steal most of what I need anyway."

"You? Steal?" I scoff at the thought of a prince, and a brute of all things, doing anything of the sort. "At best you'll lose your fingers. At worst, your head."

He shrugs, trying not to look concerned. "And that matters to you?"

"It does," I tell him quietly. I do my best to keep the pain from my voice. "We need you here, you know that."

The corner of his mouth twitches, but not to smile. "And that matters to *me*?"

I want to beat some sense into him, but Cal is not Kilorn. He'd take my fist with a smile and keep on walking. The prince must be reasoned with, convinced. *Manipulated.*

"You said yourself, every newblood we save is another strike against Maven. That's still true, isn't it?"

He doesn't agree, but he doesn't argue either. He's listening, at least.

"You know what I can do, what Shade can do. And Nix might be even stronger, *better,* than both of us. Right?"

More silence.

"I know you want him dead."

Despite the darkness, a strange light glimmers in Cal's eyes.

"I want that too," I tell him. "I want to feel my hands around his throat. I want to see him bleed for what he's done, for every person he's killed." It feels so good to say it out loud, to admit what scares me most of all, to the only person who understands. *I want to hurt him in the worst way. I want to make his bones sing with lightning, until he can't even scream.* I want to destroy the monster that Maven is now.

But when I think about killing him, part of my mind wanders back to the boy I believed him to be. I keep telling myself he wasn't real. The Maven I knew and cared for was a fantasy, tailored specifically for me. Elara twisted her son into a person I would love, and she did her job so well.

Somehow, the person who never existed haunts me, worse than the rest of my ghosts.

"He's beyond our reach," I say, both for Cal and for my own benefit. "If we go after him now, he'll bury us both. You *know* this."

Once a general and still a great warrior, Cal understands battle. And despite his rage, despite every fiber of him begging for revenge, he knows this isn't a battle he can win. *Yet.*

"I'm not part of your revolution," he whispers, his voice almost lost in the night. "I'm not Scarlet Guard. I'm *not* part of this."

I almost expect him to stamp his foot in exasperation.

"Then what *are you,* Cal?"

He opens his mouth, expecting an answer to tumble out. Nothing does.

I understand his confusion, even if I don't like it. Cal was raised to be everything I'm fighting against. He doesn't know how to be anything else, even now, alongside Reds, hunted by his own, betrayed by his blood.

After a long, terrible moment, he turns around, retreating into the jet. He casts off his pack and his guns and his resolve. I exhale quietly, relieved by his decision. He'll stay.

But for how much longer, I don't know.

Eleven

According to the map, Coraunt is four miles northeast, sitting at the intersection of Regent's River and the extensive Port Road. It doesn't look like more than a trading outpost, and one of the last villages before the Port Road turns inland, weaving around the flooded, impassable marshlands on its journey to the northern border. Of the four great byways of Norta, the Port Road is the most traveled, connecting Delphie, Archeon, and Harbor Bay. That makes it the most dangerous, even this far north. Any number of Silvers, military or otherwise, could be passing through — and even if they aren't actively hunting us, there isn't a Silver in the kingdom who wouldn't recognize Cal. Most would try to arrest him; some would certainly try to kill him on sight.

And they could, I tell myself. It should frighten me to know this, but instead I feel invigorated. Maven, Elara, Evangeline and

Ptolemus Samos — despite all their power and abilities, all of them are vulnerable. They *can* be defeated. We only need the proper weapons.

The thought makes it easy to ignore the pain of the last few days. My shoulder doesn't ache so badly, and in the quiet of the forest, I realize the ringing in my head has lessened. A few more days and I won't remember the banshee's scream at all. Even my knuckles, bruised from striking Kilorn's cheekbone today, barely hurt anymore.

Shade jumps among the trees, his form flickering in and out of being like starlight through clouds. He keeps close, never appearing out of eyesight, and is careful to pace his teleporting. Once or twice he whispers, pointing out a twist in the deer trail or a hidden ravine, mostly for Cal's benefit. While Kilorn, Shade, and I were raised in the woods, he grew up in palaces and military barracks. Neither prepared him for traversing a forest at night, as evidenced by the loud snapping of branches and his occasional stumbling. He's used to burning a path, forcing his way through obstacles and enemies with strength and strength alone.

Kilorn's teeth gleam every time the prince trips, forming a pointed smile.

"Careful there," he says, yanking Cal away from a boulder hidden in shadow. Cal easily wrenches out of the fish boy's grip, but that's all he does, thankfully. Until we reach the stream.

Branches arc overhead from the trees on either bank, their leaves brushing against one another across the gap of water. Starlight winks through, illuminating the stream as it winds through the forest to join the Regent. It's narrow, but there's no telling how deep it might be. At least the current looks gentle.

Kilorn is probably more comfortable on water than land, and jumps nimbly into the shallows. He tosses a single stone into the middle of the stream, listening to the *plop* of rock on water. "Six feet, maybe seven," he says after a moment. Well over my head. "Should we make you a raft?" he adds, grinning my way.

I first swam the Capital, a true river more than three times as deep and ten times as wide, when I was fourteen. So it's nothing to plunge right into the stream, dipping my head beneath the dark, cold water. This close to the ocean, it tastes faintly of salt.

Kilorn follows without question, his long-practiced strokes taking him across the stream in seconds. I'm surprised he doesn't show off more, turning flips or holding his breath for minutes at a time. When I reach the opposite shore, I realize why.

Shade and Farley perch on the distant bank, eyeing the water below. Both their faces twitch, fighting smirks or smiles as they watch the prince in the shallows. The stream breaks neatly around Cal's ankles, gentle as a mother's touch, but his face goes pale in the moonlight. He rapidly crosses his arms, trying to hide his shaking hands.

"Cal?" I ask aloud, careful to keep my voice low. "What's wrong?"

Already lounging against a tree trunk, Kilorn snorts in the darkness. He zips off his jacket, ringing out the waterlogged material with practiced efficiency. "Come on, Calore, you can fly a jet but you can't swim?" he says.

"I *can* swim," Cal replies hotly. He forces another step into the stream, now up to his knees. "I just don't care for it."

Of course he wouldn't. Cal is a burner, a controller of flame, and nothing weakens him more than water. It makes him helpless, powerless, everything he's been taught to hate, fear, and fight. I remember him in the arena, how he almost died. Trapped by Lord Osanos, surrounded by a floating orb of water even he could not burn away. It must have felt like a coffin, a watery grave.

I wonder if he thinks of it too, if the memory makes the quiet stream look more like a churning, endless ocean.

My first instinct is to swim back, to help him across with my own two hands, but that would send Kilorn into a laughing fit even Cal wouldn't be able to stomach. And a brawl in the middle of the woods is the last thing we need.

"In through the nose, Cal." When he looks up, our eyes locking across the stream, I give him a tiny, supporting nod. *Out through the mouth.* It's just his own advice repeated back, but it soothes him all the same.

He takes another step forward, then another and another, chest heaving with each steadying breath. And then he's swimming, paddling across the stream like a massive dog. Kilorn shakes with silent laughter, one hand over his mouth. I toss a few stones his way. It shuts him up long enough for Cal to reach the shallows again, and he eagerly sprints out of the water. A bit of steam rises from his skin, driven by the heat of his own embarrassment.

"S'cold," he mumbles, shaking his head so he doesn't have to look at us. His black hair sticks, plastered to one side of his silver-flushed face. Without thought, I brush it away, smoothing his hair back into a more dignified style. He holds my gaze all the while, looking pleasantly surprised by the action.

Then it's my turn to blush. *We said no distractions.*

"Don't tell me you're afraid of water too?" Kilorn calls across the stream, his voice too loud and gruff. Farley only laughs in reply, grabbing my brother's wrist. A split second later, they stand next to us, smirking and dry.

They jumped. Of course.

Shade scoffs, squeezing my tail of wet hair. "Idiots," he says kindly.

But for the crutch, I'd push him squarely into the stream.

My hair has almost dried by the time we reach the rise above Coraunt. Clouds roll in, covering the moon and stars, but the lights of the village are enough to see by. From our vantage point, Coraunt looks like the Stilts, built at the mouth of the Regent's River, centered on a crossroads. One, neatly paved and slightly raised above the salt marsh, is clearly the Port Road. The other runs east to west, and turns into a packed dirt road beyond the village. A watchtower on the riverbank points toward the sky, its crown illuminated by a revolving beacon of light. I flinch when it passes over us.

"Think he's down there?" Kilorn breathes, meaning Nix. He eyes the number of squat houses below, huddled in the shadow of the watchtower.

" 'Nix Marsten. Living. Male. Born 12/20/271 in Coraunt, Marsh Coast, Regent State, Norta. Current residence: Same as birth.' That's all the list said," I repeat from memory, seeing the words in my mind. I leave out the last part, the one that sears like a brand. *Blood type: not applicable. Gene mutation, strain unknown.* It follows every name on the list, including my own. It's the marker Julian said he used to find these people in the bloodbase, matching my blood to theirs. Now it's up to me to use that information — and hope that I'm not too late.

I squint against the darkness, trying to see through the night. Fortunately the Regent looks quiet, a black and calm river, and the roads are empty. Even the ocean looks still as glass. Curfew is in full effect, as commanded by the wretched Measures still in place. "No navy ships that I can see. And no traffic on the Port Road."

Cal nods, agreeing, and my heart swells. Surely Maven's hunters would not travel without an entourage of soldiers, making them easy to spot. That leaves two possibilities: they haven't come for Nix yet, or they're long gone.

"Shouldn't be too hard, even with the curfew." Farley's eyes flash over the village, taking in every roof and street corner. I get the feeling she's done this before. "Lazy town, lazy officers. Ten coppers says they don't even bother to secure the town records."

"I'll take you on that," Shade replies, nudging her shoulder.

"We'll meet you over there," Cal says. He points at a grove of trees half a mile away. It's hard to see in the darkness, surrounded by marsh and tall grass. Perfect cover, but I shake my head.

"We're not splitting up."

"You'd rather traipse in there together, with you and me leading the charge? Why don't I just blow up the Security outpost, and you can fry any officer who comes your way?" Cal replies. He does his best to keep calm, but sounds more and more like an exasperated teacher. *Like his uncle Julian.*

"Of course not —"

"Neither of us can set foot in that village, Mare. Not unless you intend to kill every person who sees our faces. *Every person.*"

His eyes bore into mine, willing me to understand. Every *person.* Not just Security, not just soldiers, not even Silver civilians. *Everyone.* Any whisper of us, any rumor, and Maven will come running. With Sentinels, soldiers, *legions,* everyone and everything in his power. Our only defense is staying hidden, and staying ahead. We can't do either if we leave a trail.

"Okay." My voice sounds as small as I feel. "But Kilorn stays with us."

Kilorn's eyes flicker, dancing between me and Cal. "This will go a lot faster if you don't keep nannying me, Mare."

Nanny. I suppose that's what I'm being, even now when he can think, fight, and provide for himself. If only he wasn't so foolish, so dedicated to refusing my protection.

"Maven knows your name," I tell him. "We'd be stupid to think your ID photo hasn't been sent to every officer and outpost in the country."

His lips twist into a scowl. "What about Farley —"

"I'm Lakelander, boy," Farley answers for me. At least we're on the same page.

"Boy?" Kilorn says with a scowl. "You're barely older than me."

"Four years older, to be precise," Shade

221

answers smoothly.

Farley only rolls her eyes at both of them. "Your king has no claim over my records, and he doesn't know my true name."

"I'm only going because everyone thinks I'm dead," Shade pipes in, leaning on his crutch. He puts a calming hand on Kilorn's shoulder, but he shrugs him off.

"Fine," he grumbles under his breath. Without so much as a backward glance, he starts marching toward the grove, quick and quiet as a field mouse.

Cal glares after him, a corner of his mouth twitching in distaste. "Any chance we can lose him?"

"Don't be cruel, Cal," I reply sharply, heading after Kilorn. I make sure to hit the prince as I pass, bumping him with my good shoulder. Not to harm, but to communicate. *Leave him alone.*

He follows me closely, dropping his voice to a whisper. Warm fingers brush my arm, trying to soothe me. "I'm only joking."

But I know that's not true. That's not true at all. And worst of all, I wonder if he's right. Kilorn isn't a soldier, or a scholar, or a scientist. He can weave a net faster than anyone I know, but what good is that when we're catching *people,* not fish? I don't know what kind of training he received in the Guard, but it's little more than a month's worth. He survived the Hall of the Sun because of me, and outlived the massacre of Caesar's Square because of luck. With no ability, little training, and less sense, how can he do anything but slow us down?

I saved him from conscription, but not for this. Not for another war. Part of me wishes I could send him home, back to the Stilts, our river, and the life we knew. He would live poor, overworked, unwanted, but he would *live.* That future, tucked between the woods and the riverbank, is no longer possible for me. But it could be for him. I want it for him.

Is it mad to let him stay here?

But how do I let him go?

I have no answer for either question, and push away all thoughts of Kilorn. They can wait. When I look back, meaning to say good-bye to Shade and Farley, I realize they're already gone. A shiver of fear runs down my spine as I imagine an ambush down in Coraunt. Gunfire echoes in my head, still close in my memory. *No.* With Shade's ability and Farley's experience, nothing can stop them tonight. And without me, without the lightning girl to hide, no one will have to die.

Kilorn is a shadow through the tall grass, parting green stalks with able hands. He hardly leaves a trail, not that it matters. With Cal crashing along behind me, his broad bulk trampling everything in his path, there's no point in masking our presence. And we'll be gone long before morning, hopefully with Nix in tow. If we're lucky, no one will notice a missing Red, allowing us time to get ahead of Maven once he figures out what we're doing.

What is that, exactly? The voice in my head turns strange, a combination of Julian, Kilorn, Cal, and a little bit of Gisa. It needles, poking at what I'm too afraid to admit. *The list is only the first step. Tracking down newbloods — but then what do we do with them? What do I do?*

Frustration makes me walk faster, until I outstrip Kilorn. I barely notice him slowing to let me pass, knowing I want to lead alone. The grove gets closer by the second, shrouded in darkness, and I wish I *was* alone. I haven't had a moment's peace since I woke up alone in the mersive. But even that was fleeting, my silence broken apart by Kilorn. I was glad to see him then, but now, now I wish I had that time to myself. Time to think, to plan, to grieve. To wrap myself around what my life has become.

"We give him a choice." I speak aloud, knowing neither Cal nor Kilorn would stray beyond earshot. "He comes with us or he stays here."

Cal leans against a nearby tree, his body relaxed, but his eyes stay fixed on the horizon. Nothing escapes his gaze. "Do we tell him the consequences of this *choice*?"

"If you want to kill him, you'll have to go through me," I reply. "I won't put a new-blood to death for refusing to join up. Besides, if he wants to tell an officer I was here, he'll have to explain why. And that's as good as a death sentence for Mr. Marsten."

The prince's lip curls. He fights the urge to snarl. But arguing with me will get him nowhere, not now. He's obviously not used to taking any orders but his own. "Do we tell him about Maven? That he'll die if he stays? That *others* will die if Maven tracks you down?"

I dip my head, nodding. "We tell him everything we can, and then we let him decide who and what he wants to be. As for Maven, well . . ." I search for the right thing to say, but those words are scarcer with every passing moment. "We stay ahead of him. I guess that's all we can do."

"Why?" Kilorn pipes in. "Why give him a

choice at all? You said yourself, we need everyone we can get. If this Nix guy is half of what you are, we can't afford to let him go."

The answer is so simple, and it cuts me to bone.

"Because no one ever gave me a choice."

I tell myself that I would still walk this path if I knew the consequences — save Kilorn from conscription, discover my ability, join the Guard, tear lives apart, fight, kill. Become the lightning girl. But I don't know if that's true. I honestly don't know.

Maybe an hour passes in heavy, tense silence. It suits me just fine, giving me time to think, and Cal revels in the quiet. After the past few days, he's just as hungry for rest as I am. Not even Kilorn dares to joke. Instead, he's content to sit on a gnarled root, weaving strands of tall grass into a brittle, useless net. He smiles faintly, enjoying the old, familiar knots.

I think of Nix down in the village, probably pulled from his bed, maybe gagged, definitely ensnared in a net of my own making. Would Farley threaten his wife, his children, to make him come? Or would Shade simply grab his wrist and *jump*, sending them both hurtling through the sicken-

226

ing vise of teleportation until they land in the grove? *Born 12/20/271.* Nix is almost forty-nine, my father's age. Will Nix be like him, wounded and broken? Or is he whole, waiting for us to break him?

Before I can fall into a spiral of dark and damning questions, the tall grass stirs. *Someone is coming.*

It's like flipping a switch in Cal. He pushes off his tree, every muscle taut and ready for whatever might step out of the grass. I half expect to see fire on his fingertips, but after long years of military training, Cal knows better. In the darkness, his flame would be like the watchtower beacon, alerting every officer to our presence. To my surprise, Kilorn looks just as vigilant as the prince. He drops his grass net, crushing it underfoot as he stands. He even pulls a hidden dagger from his boot, a sharp, thick little blade he once used to gut fish. The sight of it sets my teeth on edge. I don't know when the knife became a weapon, or when he started carrying it in his shoe. *Probably around the time people started shooting at him.*

I'm not without my own weapons. The low thrum in my blood is all I need, sharper than any blade, more brutal than any bullet. Sparks vein beneath my skin, ready if I need them. My ability has a subtlety that Cal's lacks.

A birdcall splits the night, hooting through the grass. Kilorn responds in kind, whistling out a low tune. He sounds like the thrushes that nest in the stilt houses at home. "Farley," he murmurs under his breath, pointing at the tall grass.

She is the first to step out of the shadows, but not the last. Two figures follow: one is my brother leaning on his crutch, and the other is squat, with muscled limbs and the round belly men gain with age. *Nix.*

Cal's hand closes around my upper arm, exerting a slight pressure. He pulls gently, moving me back into the deeper shadows of the grove. I go without hesitation, knowing that we can't be too careful. Dimly, I wish for a scrap of scarlet, to mask my face as we did in Naercey.

"Did you have any trouble?" Kilorn says, stepping up to Farley and Shade. He sounds older somehow, more in control than I'm used to. He keeps his eyes on Nix, following every twitch of the round little newblood's fingers.

Farley waves off the question like an annoyance. "Simple. Even with this one limping around," she adds, jabbing a thumb at Shade. Then she turns to Nix. "He didn't put up a fight."

Despite the darkness, I see a deep red blush creep across Nix's face. "Well, I'm not stupid, am I?" He speaks gruffly, directly. A man with no use for secrets. *Though his blood hides the greatest secret of all.* "You're that Scarlet Guard. The officers would string me up for having you in my house. Even uninvited."

"Good to know," Shade mutters under his breath. His bright eyes dim a little as he cuts a meaningful look my way. *Our very presence could doom this man.* "Now, Mr. Marsten —"

"Nix," he grumbles. Something glimmers in his eye and he follows Shade's gaze. He finds me in the shadows and squints, trying to see my face. "But I think you already knew that."

Kilorn steps lightly, shifting so he blocks me from view. The motion seems innocent, but Nix's brow furrows as he understands the deeper meaning. He bristles, standing toe to toe with Kilorn. The younger boy towers over him, but Nix doesn't show an inch of fear. He raises one ruddy finger, pointing at Kilorn's chest. "You pulled me out here after curfew. That's a hanging offense. Now you tell me what for, or else I'll

229

wander on home and try not to die on the way."

"You're different, Nix." My voice sounds too high, too young. *How do I explain? How do I tell him what I wish someone told me? What I don't even truly understand?* "You know there's something about you, something you can't explain. You might even think there's something . . . wrong with you."

My last words find home like arrows. The gruff little man flinches as they land; bits of his anger melt away. He knows exactly what I'm talking about. "Yes," he says.

I don't move from my place deep in the grove, but instead gesture for Kilorn to step aside. He does as asked, letting Nix walk past him. As he approaches, joining me in the shadows, my heartbeat quickens. It pounds in my ears, a nervous, eager drum. This man is a newblood, like me, like Shade. Another who understands.

Nix Marsten looks nothing like my father, but they have the same eyes. Not in color, not in shape, but still, they are the same. They share the hollow look that speaks of emptiness, a loss time cannot heal. To my horror, Nix's hurt runs deeper even than Dad's, a man who can barely breathe, let alone walk. I see it in the droop of his shoulders, in the neglect of his gray hair and clothing. Were I still a thief, a rat, I wouldn't bother to steal from this man. He has nothing left to give.

He returns my stare, eyes flickering over my face and body. They widen when he realizes who I am. "The Lighting Girl." But when he recognizes Cal at my shoulder, his shock quickly gives way to rage.

For an almost fifty-year-old man, Nix is surprisingly fast. In the shadows, I barely see him drop a shoulder and charge, catching Cal around the middle. Though he's half the prince's size, he takes him down like a bull, smashing them both into a sturdy tree trunk. It *crack*s loudly beneath the blow, shaking from roots to branches. After half a heartbeat, I realize that I should probably step in. Cal is Cal, but we have no idea who Nix is, or what he can do.

Nix gets in one bruising punch, hitting Cal's jaw so hard I fear it might be broken, before I manage to get my arms around his neck. "Don't make me, Nix," I rumble in his ear. "Don't make me."

"Do your worst," Nix spits back, trying to elbow me off. But I hold firm, squeezing his neck. The flesh feels rock hard beneath my touch. *Very well.*

I push enough power through me to stun

Nix into submission. The jolt should set his hair on end. My purple sparks hit his skin, and I expect him to drop back, maybe shake a little, and come to his senses. But he doesn't seem to feel my lightning at all. It only annoys him, like a fly would a horse. I shock him again, stronger this time, and again, nothing. In my surprise, he manages to throw me off and I land hard, my back against a tree.

Cal does better, dodging and catching as many punches as he can. But he hisses in pain at the contact, even the blows that glance off his arm. Finally the flame-maker bracelet at his wrist sparks, forming a fireball in his hand. It breaks against Nix's shoulder like water on rock, burning the clothes but leaving the flesh unharmed.

Stoneskin echoes in my head, but this man is no such thing. His skin is still ruddy and smooth, not gray or stony. It is simply *impenetrable.*

"Stop this!" I growl, trying to keep my voice low. But the scuffle, or should I say butchery, continues on. Silver blood pours from Cal's mouth, staining Nix's knuckles black in the shadows.

Kilorn and Farley rush past me, their hurried footsteps pounding in time. I don't know how much use they'll be against this human wrecking ball, and I hold out a hand to stop them. But Shade reaches Nix before they do, jumping into position behind him. He grabs Nix by the neck, like I did, and then they're both gone. They appear ten feet away a split second later, and Nix falls to the ground, his face vaguely green. He tries to get up, but Shade braces his crutch against his neck, pinning him.

"Move and I'll do it again," he says, his eyes alive and dangerous.

Nix raises one silver-stained hand in surrender. The other clutches his stomach, still flipping from the surprise and sensation of being squeezed through thin air. I know it all too well.

"Enough," he pants. A sheen of sweat glints across his forehead, betraying the exhaustion setting in. *Impenetrable, but not unstoppable.*

Kilorn plops back down on his root, snatching up the remnants of his net. He smiles to himself, almost laughing at the sight of Cal beaten and bleeding. "I like this one," he says. "I like him very much."

I fight to my feet, ignoring the old aches setting off across my bones. "The prince is *with us,* Nix. He's here to help, same as me."

That does nothing to assuage him. Nix sits back on his heels, baring yellow teeth.

His breath sounds ragged and visceral. "Help?" he scoffs. "That Silver bastard helped my daughters into an early grave."

Cal does his best to look polite, despite the blood dripping down his chin. "Sir —"

"Dara Marsten. Jenny Marsten," Nix hisses in reply. His glare goes right through me, a knife in the darkness. "The Hammer Legion. Battle of the Falls. They were nineteen years old."

Died in the war. A tragedy, if not a crime, but how is it Cal's fault?

Judging by the look of pure shame crossing his face, Cal agrees with Nix. When he speaks, his voice is thick, choked with emotion. "We won," he murmurs, unable to look Nix in the eye. "We won."

Nix clenches a single fist, but resists the urge to charge. "*You* won. *They* drowned in the river, and their bodies went over Maiden Falls. The grave diggers couldn't even find their shoes. What was it the letter said?" he presses on, and Cal winces. "Ah yes, that my girls 'died for victory.' To 'defend the kingdom.' And there were some very nice signatures at the bottom. From the dead king, the general of the Hammer, and the tactical genius who decided an entire legion should march across the river."

Every eye turns to Cal, and he burns

under our gaze. His face goes white, flushed with blood and disgrace. I remember his room back in the Hall of the Sun, the books and manuals filled to the brim with notes and tactics. They made me sick then and they make me sick now, with Cal *and* myself. Because I've forgotten who he truly is. Not just a prince, not just a soldier, but a murderer. In another life it could've been me he marched to death, or my brothers, or Kilorn.

"I'm sorry," Cal breathes. He forces himself to look up, to meet the eyes of an angry, grieving father. I suppose he was trained to do it. "I know my words mean nothing. Your daughters — *all* the soldiers — deserved to live. And so do you, sir."

Nix's knees crack when he stands, but he doesn't seem to notice. "Is that a threat, boy?"

"A warning," Cal replies, shaking his head. "You're like Mare, like Shade." He gestures to us in turn. "Different. What we call a newblood. Red *and* Silver."

"Don't you ever call me Silver," Nix says through gritted teeth.

It doesn't stop Cal from continuing, rising to his feet. "My brother will be hunting people like you. He plans to kill you all, and pretend you never existed. He plans to erase you from history."

Something sticks in Nix's throat and confusion clouds his eyes. He glances to me, looking for support. "There are . . . others?"

"Many others, Nix." This time when I touch his skin, I have no intention of shocking him. "Girls, boys, old and young. All over the country, waiting to be found."

"And when you find them . . . us? What then?"

I open my mouth to answer, but nothing comes out. *I haven't thought that far ahead.*

Farley steps forward when I can't, extending a hand. She holds a red scarf, ragged but clean. "The Scarlet Guard will protect them, hide them. And train them if they want to be trained."

I almost balk at her words, thinking back to the Colonel. The last thing he seems to want is newbloods around, but Farley sounds so sure, so convincing. Like always, I'm sure she has something else up her sleeve, something I shouldn't question. Yet.

Slowly, Nix takes the scarf from her, turning it over in his stained hands. "And if I refuse?" he asks lightly, but I hear the steel beneath.

"Then Shade will put you right back in bed, and you'll never hear from us again," I tell him. "But Maven *will* come. If you don't want to stick with us, you're better off in the wild."

His grip tightens on the scarlet fabric. "Not much of a choice."

"But you *do* have a choice." I hope he knows I mean it. I hope it for my own sake, for my own soul. "You can choose to stay, or come. You know better than anyone how much has been lost — but you can help us regain something too."

Nix is quiet for a long while after that. He paces, scarf in hand, occasionally glancing through the branches at the watchtower beacon. It revolves three times before he speaks again.

"My girls are dead, my wife's dead, and I'm sick of the marsh stink," he says, stopping in front of me. "I'm with you." Then he glares over my shoulder, and I don't need to turn around to know he's looking at Cal. "Just keep that one far away from me."

Twelve

We trudge back through the woods un-
scathed, chased by nothing except sea
breeze and clouds. But I can't shake the
feeling of dread curling around my heart.

Even though Nix almost split Cal's skull,
recruiting him seemed easy. Too easy. And
if I've learned anything over the past seventeen years, over the past *month,* it's that
nothing is easy. Everything has a price. If
Nix is not a trap, then he is certainly a
danger. *Anyone can betray anyone.*

So even though he reminds me of Dad,
even though he's little more than a gray
beard and grief, even though he's like me, I
close my heart to the man from Coraunt. I
have saved him from Maven, told him what
he was, and let him make his choice. Now I
must carry on, to do the same for another
and another and another. All that matters is
the next name.

The starlight illuminates the woods

enough for a quick glance, and I thumb through the now familiar pages of Julian's list. There are few in the area, clustered around the city of Harbor Bay. Two are listed in the city proper, and one in the New Town slum. How we'll get to any of them, I'm not sure. The city will surely be walled like Archeon and Summerton, while the restrictions on techie slums are even worse than the Measures. Then I remember; walls and restrictions don't apply to Shade. Luckily, he's walking better by the hour, and shouldn't need the crutch after a few more days. Then we'll be unstoppable. Then we might even *win*.

The thought thrills and confuses me in equal measure — what will a world like that look like? I can only imagine where I'll be. At home maybe, certainly with my family, somewhere in the woods where I can hear a river. With Kilorn nearby, of course. But Cal? I don't know where he'll choose to be, in the end.

In the darkness of night, it's easy to let your mind wander. I'm used to forests and don't really need to focus to keep from tripping on roots and leaves. So I dream as I walk, thinking of what might be. An army of newbloods. Farley leading the Scarlet Guard. A proper Red uprising, from the

Choke trenches to the alleys of Gray Town. Cal always said that all-out war was not worth the cost, that the loss of Red and Silver life would be too great. I hope he's right. I hope Maven will see what we are, what we can do, and know he cannot win. Even he is not a fool. Even he knows when he is beaten. *At least, I hope he does.* Because as far as I can tell, Maven has never been defeated. Not when it really counts. Cal won their father, his soldiers, but Maven won the crown. Maven won every battle that truly mattered.

And given time . . . he would've won me too.

I see him in every shadow of every tree, a ghost standing tall against the rainstorm in the Bowl of Bones. Water streams between the points of his iron crown, into his eyes and mouth, into his collar, into the icy abyss that is his wasted heart. It goes red in color, turning from water to my blood. He opens his mouth to taste it, and the teeth within are sharp, gleaming razors of white bone.

I blink him away, blotting out the memory of the traitor prince.

Farley murmurs in the darkness, detailing the true purpose of the Guard. Nix is a smart man, but like everyone else beneath the rule of the Burning Crown, he has been fed lies. *Terrorism, anarchy, bloodlust,* those are the words the broadcasts use when describing the Guard. They show the children dead in the Sun Shooting, the flooded wreckage of the Archeon Bridge, everything to convince the country of our supposed evil. All the while, the real enemy sits on his throne and smiles.

"What about *her*?" Nix whispers, tossing a flint-eyed glance in my direction. "Is it true she seduced the prince into killing the king?"

Nix's question cuts like a blade, so wounding I expect to see a knife sticking out of my chest. But my own pains can wait. Ahead of me, Cal stills, his broad shoulders rising and falling, an indication of deep, steadying breaths.

I put a hand to his arm, hoping to calm him as he calms me. His skin flames beneath my fingers, almost too hot to touch.

"No, it isn't," I tell Nix, pushing all the steel I can into my voice. "That's not what happened at all."

"So the king's head rolled off on its own, then?" He chuckles, expecting a rise of laughter. But even Kilorn has the good sense to stay quiet. He doesn't even smile. He understands the pain of dead fathers.

"It was Maven," Kilorn growls, surprising

us all. The look in his eyes is pure fire. "Maven and his mother, the queen. She can control your mind. And —" His voice falters, not wanting to continue. The king's death was so horrible, even for a man we hated.

"And?" Nix prods, chancing a few steps toward Cal. I stop him with one daggered glare, and thankfully, he halts a few feet away. But his face pulls into a sneer, eager to see the prince in pain. I know he has his reasons to torture Cal, but that doesn't mean I have to let him.

"Keep walking," I murmur, so low only Cal can hear.

Instead, he turns, his muscles taut beneath my touch. They feel like hot waves rolling on a solid sea. "Elara made me do it, Marsten." His bronze eyes meet Nix's, daring him to take another step. "She twisted her way into my head, controlling my body. But she let my mind stay. She let me watch as my arms took his sword, as I separated his head from his shoulders. And then she told the world it's what I wanted all along." And then softer, as if reminding himself, "She made me kill my father."

Some of Nix's malice dies away, enough to reveal the man beneath. "I saw the pictures," he mumbles, as if in apology.

"They were everywhere, on every screen in town. I thought — It looked —"

Cal's eyes flicker, out to the trees. But he's not looking at the leaves. His gaze is in the past, to something more painful. "She killed my true mother as well. And she'll kill all of us if we let her."

The words come out hard and harsh, a rusty blade to saw flesh. They taste wonderful in my mouth. "Not if I kill her first."

For all his talents, Cal is not a violent person. He can kill you in a thousand different ways, lead an army, burn down a village, but he will not enjoy it. So his next words take me by surprise.

"When the time comes," he says, staring at me, "we'll flip a coin."

His bright flame has grown dark indeed.

When we emerge from the forest, a brief shudder of fear runs through me. What if the Blackrun's gone? What if we were tracked? *What if, what if, what if.* But the airjet is exactly where we left it. It's nearly invisible in the darkness, blending into the gray-black runway. I resist the urge to sprint into its safety, and force myself to keep pace next to Cal. Not too close, though. *No distractions.*

"Keep your eyes open," Cal mutters, a

small but firm warning as we approach. He doesn't take his eyes off the jet, watching for any indication of a trap.

I do the same, glaring at the back ramp still lowered against the runway, open to the night air. It looks clear to me, but shadows gather in the belly of the Blackrun, pitch-dark and impossible to see through from this distance.

It took a great amount of energy and focus to power on the entire jet, but the lightbulbs within are another story. Even from ten yards away, it's easy to reach out to their wiring, spark up their charges, and illuminate the inside of the jet with a bright and sudden glow. Nothing moves inside, but the others react, surprised by the burst of light. Farley even frees her pistol from the holster strapped to her leg.

"It's just me," I tell her with a wave of my hand. "The jet's empty."

My pace quickens. I'm eager to be inside, cocooned by the growing charge of electricity that strengthens with my every step. When I set foot on the ramp, climbing up into the craft, it feels like entering a warm embrace. I run a hand along the wall, tracing the outline of a metal panel as I pass by. More of my power flows, bleeding out from the lightbulbs, running along electrical pathways into the massive cell batteries beneath my feet and fixed under each wing. They hum in perfect unison, sending out their own energy, switching on what I haven't. The Blackrun comes to life.

Nix gasps behind me, in awe of the massive, metal jet. He's probably never seen one this close, let alone stepped inside one. I turn around, expecting to find him staring at the seats or the cockpit, but his eyes are firmly fixed on me. He flushes and ducks his head in what could be a shaky bow. Before I can tell him exactly how much that annoys me, he shuffles to a seat, puzzling over the safety belts.

"Do I get a helmet?" he asks the silence. "If we're going to be crashing through the air, I want a helmet."

Laughing, Kilorn takes a seat next to Nix and buckles them both in with quick, agile fingers. "Nix, I think you're the only one here who *doesn't* need one."

They chuckle together, sharing crooked smiles. If not for me, for the Scarlet Guard, Kilorn would've probably turned out just like Nix. A battered old man, with nothing left to give but his bones. Now I hope he gets the chance to grow old, to have aching knees and a gray beard of his own. If only Kilorn would let me protect him. If only he didn't insist on throwing himself in front of every bullet that comes his way.

"So she really is the lightning girl. And this one's a . . ." He gestures across the jet, to Shade, searching for a word to describe his ability.

"Jumper," Shade offers with a respectful nod. He fastens his belts as tightly as he can, already paling at the prospect of another flight. Farley doesn't look so affected, and resolutely stares from her seat, eyes on the windows of the cockpit.

"Jumper. Okay. What about you, boy?" He nudges Kilorn with his elbow, blind to the boy's fading smile. "What can you do?"

I sink into the cockpit seat, not wanting to see any pain in Kilorn's face. But I'm not quick enough. I catch a glimpse of his embarrassed flush, his rigid shoulders, his narrowing eyes and piercing scowl. The reason is shockingly clear. *Jealousy* twists through every inch of him, spreading as quickly as an infection. The intensity of it surprises me. Not once did I ever think Kilorn wanted to be like me, like a *Silver*. He's proud of his blood, he always has been. He even raged at me, back when he first saw what I had become. *Are you one of them?* he growled, his voice harsh and unfamiliar.

He was so angry. But then, why is he angry now?

"I catch fish," he says, forcing a hollow smile. There's a bitterness in his voice, and we let it fester in our silence.

Nix speaks first, clapping Kilorn on the shoulder. "Crabs," he says, wiggling his fingers. "Been a crabber all my life."

A bit of Kilorn's discomfort recedes, pulling back behind a crooked grin. He turns to watch Cal switch his way across the control panel, making the Blackrun ready for another flight. I feel the jet respond in kind, its energy flowing toward the wing-mounted engines. They start to whir, gaining power with every passing second.

"Looks good," Cal says, finally punching a hole in the uncomfortable quiet. "Where to next?"

It takes a second to realize he's asking me. "Oh." I stumble over the words. "The closest names are in Harbor Bay. Two in the city proper, one in the slums."

I expect more of a fuss at the prospect of breaking into a walled, Silver city, but Cal only nods. "That won't be easy," he warns, his bronze eyes flashing with the panel's blinking lights.

"I'm so happy you're here to tell us what we don't already know," I reply dryly.

"Farley, you think we can do it?"

She nods, and there's a crack in her usually stoic mask, revealing emotion beneath. *Excitement.* Her fingers drum on her thigh. I get the sickening sense that she sees part of this as a game. "I've got enough friends in the Bay," she says. "The walls won't be a problem."

"Then to the Bay we go," Cal says. His grim tone is not at all comforting.

Neither is the drop in my stomach as the jet lurches forward, screaming down a mile of hidden runway. This time, when we angle into the sky, I close my eyes tight. Between the comforting thrum of engines and the knowledge that I am not needed, it's frighteningly easy to fall asleep.

I shift between sleep and waking many times, never truly succumbing to the quiet darkness my mind so desperately needs. Something about the jet keeps me suspended, my eyes never opening, but my brain never completely shutting off. I feel like Shade, pretending to be asleep, collecting whispered secrets. But the others are silent and, judging by Nix's sputtering snores, out like snuffed candles. Only Farley stays awake. I hear her unbuckle and move to Cal's side, her footsteps almost inaudible over the jet engines. I doze off then, catching a few needed minutes of shallow rest, before her low voice brings me back.

"We're over the ocean," she murmurs, sounding confused.

Cal's neck cracks as he turns, bone on bone. He didn't hear her coming, too focused on the jet. "Perceptive," he says after he recovers.

"Why are we over the ocean? The Bay is south, not east —"

"Because we've got more than enough juice to circle off the coast, and they need to sleep." Something like fear taints his voice. *Cal hates water. This must be killing him.*

Her scoff grates low in her throat. "They can sleep where we land. The next runway is hidden like the last."

"*She* won't. Not with newbloods on the line. She'll march until she drops, and we can't let her do that."

A long pause. He must be staring, convincing her with eyes instead of words. I know firsthand how persuasive his eyes can be.

"And when do you sleep, Cal?"

His voice lowers, not in volume, but mood. "I don't. Not anymore."

I want to open my eyes. To tell him to turn around, to make as much haste as he can.

We're wasting time out on the ocean, burning precious seconds that could spell life or death for the newbloods of Norta. But my anger is tempered by exhaustion. And cold. Even next to Cal, a walking furnace, I feel the familiar creep of ice in my flesh. I don't know where it comes from, only that it arrives in moments of quiet, when I'm still, when I think. When I remember all I've done, and what has been done to me. The ice sits where my heart should be, threatening to split me open. My arms curl around my chest, trying to stop the pain. It works a little, letting warmth back into me. But where the ice melts, it leaves only emptiness. An abyss. And I don't know how to fill it back up.

But I will heal. I must.

"I'm sorry," he murmurs, almost too low to hear. Still enough to keep me from drifting away. But his words aren't meant for me.

Something jostles my arm. Farley, as she moves closer to hear him.

"For what I did to you. Before. In the Hall of the Sun." His voice almost breaks — Cal carries ice of his own. The memory of frozen blood, of Farley's torture in the cells of the palace. She refused to betray her own, and Cal made her scream for it. "I don't expect you to accept any kind of apology, and you shouldn't —"

"I accept," she says, curt but sincere. "I made mistakes that night as well. We all did."

Even though my eyes are closed, I know she's looking at me. I can feel her gaze, painted with regret — and resolve.

The bump of wheels against concrete jerks me awake, bouncing me in my seat. I open my eyes, only to squeeze them shut again, turning away from the bright stab of sunlight pouring through the cockpit windows. The others are wide awake, talking quietly, and I look over my shoulder to face them. Even though we're tearing across the runway, slowing down but still moving, Kilorn lurches to my side. I guess his river legs are good for something, because the motion of the jet doesn't seem to affect him at all.

"Mare Barrow, if I catch you dozing one more time, I'll report you to the outpost." He mimics our old teacher, the one we shared until he turned seven and left to apprentice with a fisherman.

I look up at him, grinning at the memory. "Then I'll sleep in the stocks, *Miss Vandark,*" I reply, sending him into a bout of chuckles.

As I wake more fully, I realize I'm covered in something. Soft, worn fabric, dark in color. *Kilorn's jacket.* He pulls it away before I can protest, leaving me cold without its warmth.

"Thanks," I mutter, watching him pull it back on.

He just shrugs. "You were shivering."

"It's going to be a haul into the Bay." Cal's voice is loud over the roaring engines, still spooling down from the flight. He never takes his eyes off the runway and guides the jet to a halt. Like Nine-Five Field, this so-called ruin is surrounded by forest and totally deserted. "Ten miles through forest and outskirts," he adds, angling his head toward Farley. "Unless you have something else up your sleeve?"

She laughs to herself, unbuckling her belts. "Learning, are you?" With a snap, she lays the Colonel's map across her knees. "We can cut it to six if we take the old tunnels. And avoid the outskirts altogether."

"Another Undertrain?" The thought fills me with a combination of hope and dread. "Is that safe?"

"What's an Undertrain?" Nix grumbles, his voice faraway. I won't waste my time explaining the rattling metal tube we left behind in Naercey.

Farley ignores him too. "There aren't any stationed in the Bay, not yet, but the tunnel itself runs right under the Port Road. That is, if it hasn't been closed up?"

She glances at Cal, but he shakes his head. "Not enough time to. Four days ago, we thought the tunnels were collapsed and abandoned. They aren't even mapped. Even with every strongarm at his disposal, Maven couldn't possibly have blocked them all by now." His voice falters, heavy with thought. I know what he's remembering.

It was only four days ago. Four days since Cal and Ptolemus found Walsh in the train tunnels beneath Archeon. Four days since we watched her kill herself to protect the secrets of the Scarlet Guard.

To distract myself from the memory of Walsh's glassy, dead eyes, I stretch out of my seat, bend and flex my muscles. "Let's get moving," I say, and it sounds more like a command than I would like.

I've memorized the next batch of names. *Ada Wallace. Born 6/1/290 in Harbor Bay, Beacon, Regent State, Norta. Current residence: Same as birth.* And the other, also listed in Harbor Bay — *Wolliver Galt. Born 1/20/302.* He shares a birthday with Kilorn, identical down to the year. But he is not Kilorn. He is a newblood, another Red-and-

Silver mutation for Kilorn to envy.

Strange then that Kilorn shows no animosity toward Nix. In fact, he seems friendlier than usual, hovering around the older man like an underfoot puppy. They talk quietly, bonding over the shared experience of growing up poor, Red, and hopeless. When Nix brings up nets and knots, a dull topic Kilorn adores, I turn my focus toward getting everything else situated. Part of me wishes I could join them, to debate the value of a good double-bone loop rather than the best infiltration strategy. It would make me feel normal. Because no matter what Shade says, we are anything but.

Farley is already on the move, pulling a dark brown jacket over her shoulders. She tucks her red scarf into it, hiding the color, and starts packing up rations from our stores. They aren't low yet, but I make a mental note to lift anything I can during our journey, if I get the chance. Guns are another matter — we only have six total, and stealing more will be no easy feat. Three rifles, three pistols. Farley already has one of each, the long-barreled rifle across her shoulder and the pistol at her hip. She slept with them attached to her, like they were limbs. So it comes as a surprise when she unlatches them both, returning the guns to the storage locker on the wall.

"You're going in unarmed?" Cal balks, his own rifle in hand.

In response, she pulls up a pant leg, revealing a long knife tucked into her boot. "The Bay's a big city. We'll need the day to find Mare's people, and maybe the whole night to get them out. I won't risk that carrying an unregistered firearm. An officer would execute me on the spot. I'll take my chances with villages, where there's less enforcement, but not the Bay," she adds, hiding the knife again. "Surprised you don't know your own laws, Cal."

He flushes silver, the tips of his ears turning bone white in embarrassment. Try as he might, Cal never had a head for laws and politics. That was Maven's domain, always Maven's.

"And anyways," Farley continues, her eyes slicing at us both, "I consider you and the lightning girl much better weapons than guns."

I can almost hear Cal's teeth grinding together, in anger and frustration. "I told you, we can't —" he begins, and I don't have to listen to his muttered words to know his arguments. *We're the most wanted people in the kingdom, we're dangerous to everyone, we'll jeopardize everything.* And while my first instinct is to listen to Cal, my second, my constant, is not to trust him. Because sneaking is not his specialty — it's *mine.* While he debates with Farley, I quietly prepare myself for the tunnels and Harbor Bay. I remember it from Julian's books, and slide the map away from Farley. She doesn't notice the smooth action, still busy badgering Cal. Shade joins, intervening on her behalf, and the jabbering three leave me to sit silently and plan.

The Colonel's map of Harbor Bay is newer than the one Julian showed me, and more detailed. Just as Archeon was built around the massive bridge the Scarlet Guard destroyed, Harbor Bay, naturally, centers on its famous, bowl-like harbor. Most of it is artificially built, forming a too-perfect curve of ocean against land. Both greenwardens and nymphs helped build the city and the harbor, alternately burying and flooding the ruins of what once stood here. And dividing the ocean circle, jutting straight out into the water, is a straight roadway full of gates, army patrols, and choke points. It separates the civilian Aquarian Port from the aptly named War Port, and leads to Fort Patriot, perched on a flat square of walled land in the middle of the harbor. The fort is considered the most valuable in the country, the only base that services all three branches of the military. Patriot is home to the soldiers of the Beacon Legion, as well as squadrons of the Air Fleet. The water of the War Port itself is deep enough for even the largest of ships, creating an essential dock for the Nortan navy. Even on the map, the fort looks intimidating — hopefully Ada and Wolliver will be found *outside* its walls.

The city itself spreads around the harbor, crowding between the docks. Harbor Bay is older than Archeon, incorporating the ruins of the city that once stood here. The roads twist and split unpredictably. Next to the neat grid of the capital, the Bay looks like a tangle of knotted wire. Perfect for rogues like us. Some of the streets even dip underground, linking up with the tunnel network Farley seems to know so well. While extracting two newbloods from Harbor Bay won't be easy, it doesn't seem so impossible. Especially if a few power outages happen to roll through the city at just the right moment.

"You're welcome to stay here, Cal," I say, lifting my head from the map. "But I'm not sitting this one out."

He stops midsentence, turning to face me. For a moment, I feel like a pile of kindling about to be set ablaze. "Then I hope you're ready to do what you have to."

Ready to kill everyone who recognizes me. Anyone who recognizes me.

"I am."

I'm very good at lying.

THIRTEEN

It's easy to convince Nix to stay behind. Even with his invulnerability, he's still a village crabber who's never gone farther than the salt marshes of his home. A rescue mission inside a walled city is no place for him, and he knows it. Kilorn is not so easily swayed. He agrees to stay on the jet only after I remind him that someone needs to keep an eye on Nix.

When he hugs me tightly, saying good-bye for the moment, I expect to hear a whispered warning, some advice maybe. Instead, I get encouragement, and it's more comforting than it should be. "You're going to save them," he murmurs. "I know you are."

Save them. The words echo in my head, following me down the jet ramp and into the sunlit forest. *I will,* I tell myself, repeating until I believe in myself as much as Kilorn does. *I will, I will, I will.*

The woods here are thinner, forcing us to

be on constant guard. In the daylight, Cal doesn't have to worry about flame, and keeps his fire ready, each fingertip burning like the wick of a candle. Shade is off the ground entirely, jumping himself from tree to tree. He searches the forest with a soldier's precision, his hawk-like gaze sweeping in every direction before he's satisfied. I keep my own senses open, feeling for any burst of electricity that might be a transport or low-flying airship. There's a dull hum to the southeast, toward Harbor Bay, but that's to be expected, just like the ebb and flow of traffic along the Port Road. We're well out of earshot of the byway, but my inner compass tells me we're getting closer with every step.

I feel them before I see them. It's small, the slightest pressure against my open mind. The tiny battery bleeds electricity, probably powering a watch or radio.

"From the east," I murmur, pointing toward the approaching energy source.

Farley whips toward the direction, not bothering to crouch. But I certainly do, dropping to a knee in the foliage, letting the first colors of autumn camouflage my dark red shirt and brown hair. Cal is right beside me, flames close to his skin, controlled so that they don't set the forest on fire. His breathing is even, steady, practiced, as his eyes search through the trees.

I extend a finger, pointing toward the battery. A single spark runs down my hand and disappears, calling out to the electricity drawing near.

"Farley, get down," Cal growls, his voice almost lost among the rustling leaves.

Instead of obeying, she backs against a tree, melting into the shadows of the trunk. Sunlight through the leaves above dapples her skin, and her stillness makes her look like part of the forest. But she is not quiet. Her lips part, and a low birdcall echoes through the branches. The same one she used outside Coraunt, to communicate to Kilorn. *A signal.*

The Scarlet Guard.

"Farley," I hiss through gritted teeth. "What's going on?"

But she isn't paying attention to me and watches the trees instead. Waiting. Listening. A moment later, someone hoots out a trilling reply, similar but not the same. When Shade responds from the tree above us, adding his own call to the strange song, a bit of my fear lifts away. Farley could lead me into a trap, but Shade wouldn't. *I hope.*

"Captain, thought you were stuck on that blasted island," a coarse voice says, filtering

261

out of a thick grove of elms. The accent, hard vowels and missing *r*'s, is thick and distinct — Harbor Bay.

Farley smiles at the sounds, pushing off her tree trunk smoothly. "Crance," she says, beckoning to the figure picking through the underbrush. "Where's Melody? I was supposed to meet her. Since when are you Egan's errand boy?"

When he steps out from the foliage, I do my best to size him up, taking in the little details I taught myself to notice long ago. He leans, compensating for something heavy left behind. A rifle perhaps, or maybe a club. *Errand boy indeed.* He has the look of a dockworker or a brawler, with massive arms and a barrel chest hiding beneath the bulk of worn cotton and a quilted vest. It's heavily patched, creating a motley plaid of discarded fabric, all red in hue. Strange that his vest is so battered, but his leather boots look new, polished to a high sheen. Stolen, probably. *My kind of man.*

Crance shrugs at Farley, a twitch tugging at his dark face. "She's got business on the docks. And I prefer *right-hand man,* if you don't mind." He turns the twitch into a grin, then bows in a smooth, exaggerated motion. "Of course, Boss Egan bids you welcome, Captain."

"It's not Captain anymore," Farley mutters, frowning as she clasps his forearm in some version of a handshake. "I'm sure you've heard."

He merely shakes his head. "You'll find few here who'll go along with that. The Mariners answer to Egan, not your Colonel."

Mariners? Another division within the Scarlet Guard, I suppose.

"Are your friends going to keep hiding in the bushes?" he adds, angling a glance at me. His blue eyes are electrifying, made even sharper by his umber skin. But they aren't enough to distract me from the more pressing issue — I still feel the pulsing watch battery, and Crance isn't wearing a watch.

"What about *your* friends?" I ask him, standing up from the forest floor.

Cal moves in time with me, and I can tell he's scrutinizing Crance, sizing him up. The other man does the same, one kind of soldier to another. Then he grins, teeth gleaming.

"So this is why the Colonel's making such a fuss." He chuckles, taking one daring step forward.

Neither of us flinches, despite his size. We're more dangerous than he is.

He lets out a low whistle, turning his gaze back to me. "The exiled prince and the lightning girl. And where's the Rabbit? I knew I heard him."

Rabbit?

Shade's form appears behind Crance, one arm on his crutch, the other around Crance's neck. But he's smiling, *laughing.* "I told you not to call me that," he chides, shaking Crance's shoulders.

"If the shoe fits," Crance replies, shrugging out of Shade's grasp. He makes a hopping motion with his hand, laughing as he does so. But his grin fades a little at the sight of the crutch and bandages. "You fall down a flight of stairs or something?" Crance keeps his tone light, but darkness clouds his bright eyes.

Shade waves off his concern and grips one broad shoulder. "It's good to see you, Crance. And I guess I should introduce you to my sister —"

"No introductions necessary," Crance says, shoving an open hand my way. I take it willingly, letting him squeeze my own forearm in a hand twice the size of my own. "Good to meet you, Mare Barrow, but I have to say, you look better on the wanted posters. Didn't know that was possible."

The others grimace, just as frightened as I

am of the thought of my face plastered in every door and window. *We should've expected this.*

"Sorry to disappoint," I force out, letting my hand drop out of his. Exhaustion and worry have not been kind to me. I can feel the dirt on my skin, not to mention the tangles in my hair. "I've been a little too busy to look in the mirror."

Crance takes the jibe in stride, grinning wider. "You really do have spark," he murmurs, and I don't miss his eyes straying to my fingers. I fight the urge to show him exactly how much spark he's dealing with, and dig my nails into the flesh of my palms.

The touch of a battery is still there, a firm reminder. "So are you going to keep pretending you don't have us surrounded?" I press, gesturing to the trees crowding in from every angle. "Or are we going to have a problem?"

"No problem at all," he says, raising his hands in mock surrender. Then he whistles again, this one high and keen, like a falcon on the hunt. Though Crance does his best to keep smiling, to seem relaxed, I don't miss the suspicion in his eyes. I expect him to keep close watch of Cal, but it's me he doesn't trust. *Or doesn't understand.*

The crunch of leaves announces the appearance of Crance's friends, also dressed in a combination of rags and stolen finery. It's a uniform of sorts, so mismatched they begin to look alike. Two women and a man, the one with a battered but ticking watch, all seemingly unarmed. They salute Farley, smile at Shade, and don't know how to look at Cal and me. It's better that way, I suppose. I don't need more friends to lose.

"Well, Rabbit, let's see if you can keep up," Crance needles, falling into step.

In response, Shade jumps to a nearby tree, his bad leg dangling and a smile on his lips. But when his eyes meet mine, something shifts. And then he's behind me for a split second, moving so quickly I barely see him.

I hear what he whispers all the same.

"Trust no one."

The tunnels are damp, the curved walls tangled with moss and deep roots, but the floor is clear of rock and debris. For Undertrains, I suspect, if any need to slip into Harbor Bay. But there's no screech of metal on metal, no blinding pound of a train battery screaming toward us. All I feel is the flashlight in Crance's hand, the other man's watch, and the steady pattern of traffic on the Port Road thirty feet above our heads. The heavier transports are the worst, their wires and instruments whining in the back of my skull. I cringe as each one passes overhead, and I quickly lose count of how many rush toward Naercey. If they were clustered together, I would suspect a royal convoy carrying Maven himself, but the machines come and go seemingly at random. *This is normal,* I tell myself, calming my nerves so I don't short out the flashlight and plunge us all into darkness.

Crance's followers bring up the rear, which should put me on edge, but I don't mind. My sparks are only a heartbeat away, and I have Cal at my side if someone makes a bad decision. He's more intimidating than I am, one hand ablaze with red and dancing fire. It casts flickering shadows that morph and change, painting the tunnel in swirls of red and black. *His colors, once. But they're lost to him now, just like everything else.*

Everything but me.

It's no use whispering down here. Every sound carries, so Cal keeps his mouth firmly shut. But I can still read his face. He's uncomfortable, fighting against every instinct as a soldier, a prince, and a Silver. Here he is, following his enemy into the unknown — and for what? To help me? To hurt Maven? Whatever the reasons, one day they won't be good enough to keep going.

One day, he's going to stop following me and I need to prepare myself for it. I need to decide what my heart will allow — and what loneliness I can bear. But not yet. His warmth is with me still, and I can't help but keep it close.

The tunnels aren't on our map — or on any map I've seen — but the Port Road is, and I suspect we're right below it. It leads straight into the heart of the Bay, through Pike Gate, curving around the harbor itself before heading north to the salt marshes, Coraunt, and the frozen borderlands far away. More important than the Port Road is the Security Center, the administrative hub for the entire city, where we can find records and, most important, addresses for Ada and Wolliver. The third name, the young girl in the slums of New Town, might be there as well.

Cameron Cole, I remember, though the rest of her information escapes me at the moment. I don't dare pull out Julian's list to double-check, not with so many unfamiliar faces around. The less who know about the newbloods, the better. Their names are death sentences, and I have not forgotten Shade's warning.

With any luck, we'll have everything we need by nightfall, and be back to the Blackrun by breakfast, with three more new-bloods in tow. Kilorn will grumble, angry at us for being gone so long, but that's the least of my worries. In fact, I look forward to his flushed face and petulant whining. Despite the Guard and his newfound rage, the boy I grew up with still glimmers beneath, and he is just as comforting as Cal's fire or my brother's embrace.

Shade talks to fill the silence, joking with Crance and his followers. "This man's the reason I got out of the Choke alive," my brother explains, gesturing to Crance with his crutch. "Executioners couldn't get me, but starvation almost did."

"You stole a head of cabbage. I just let you eat it," Crance replies with a shake of his head, but his flush betrays his pride.

Shade doesn't let him off so easily. He pastes on a grin that could light the tunnels, but there's no light in his eyes. "A smuggler with a heart of gold."

I watch their back-and-forth with narrowed eyes and open ears, following the conversation like a game. One compliments the other, recalling their journey back from the Choke, eluding Security and the legions alike. And while they might have formed a friendship in those weeks, it doesn't seem to exist anymore. Now, they're just men sharing memories and forced smiles, each one trying to figure out exactly what the other wants. I do the same, coming to my own conclusions.

Crance is a glorified thief, a profession I know well enough. The best part about thieves is you can trust them — to do their worst. If our positions were reversed, and I was my old self escorting a fugitive into the Stilts, would I turn them over for a few tetrarchs? For a few weeks of food or electricity rations? I remember hard winters well enough, cold and hungry days that seemed to have no end. Sicknesses with easy cures, but no money to buy the medicine. Even the bitter ache of simple want, to take something beautiful or useful simply *because.* I have done horrible things in such moments, stealing from people as desperate as I was. *To survive. To keep us all alive.* It's the justification I used back in the Stilts, when I took coins from families with starving children.

I don't doubt that Crance would turn me over to Boss Egan if he could, because it's what I would do. Sell me to Maven for an exorbitant price. But luckily, Crance is hopelessly outgunned. He knows it, so he must maintain his smile. *For now.*

The tunnel curves downward and the Undertrain tracks end suddenly, where the space grows too narrow for a train to pass through. It feels cooler the deeper we go, and the air presses in. I try not to think about the weight of the earth above us. Eventually, the walls become cracked and decrepit, and would probably collapse if not for the newly added supports. Naked wooden beams march into the darkness, each one holding up the tunnel ceiling, keeping us from being buried alive.

"Where do we surface?" Cal says aloud, directing his question at anyone who will answer. Distaste poisons every word. The deeper tunnels have him on edge, just like me.

"West side of Ocean Hill," Farley replies, mentioning the royal residence in Harbor Bay. But Crance cuts her off with a shake of his head.

"Tunnel's closed up," he grumbles. "There's new construction, king's orders. Three days he's been on the throne and he's already a pain in my ass."

From this close, I hear Cal's teeth gnash together. A burst of anger brightens his fire, throwing a blaze of heat through the tunnel that the others pretend to ignore. *King's orders.* Even when he isn't trying, Maven thwarts our progress.

Cal glances at his feet, stoic. "Maven always hated the Hill." His words echo strangely off the walls, surrounding us in his memories. "Too small for him. Too old."

The shadows shift on the walls, distorting our figures. I see Maven in every twisted shape, in every pool of darkness. He told me once he was the shadow of the flame. Now I fear he's becoming the shadow in my mind, worse than a hunter, worse than a ghost. At least I'm not alone in his hauntings. At least Cal feels him too.

"The Fish Market then." Farley's gruff bark brings me back to the mission at hand. "We'll have to circle around, and we'll need a distraction outside the Security Center, if you can manage."

I glance back at the map, brain buzzing. From the looks of it, the Security Center is directly connected to Cal's old palace, or at least is part of the same compound. And the Fish Market, I assume, is a good distance away. We'll have to scramble just to get where we need to be, let alone slip inside. Judging by the scowl on Cal's face, he's not looking forward to it.

"Egan will oblige," Crance says, nodding at Farley's request. "He'll help in any way he can. Not that you'll need much, with the Rabbit on your side."

Shade grimaces kindly, still annoyed by the nickname. "How familiar are you with the Reds of the Bay? Think a few names will ring a bell?"

I have to bite my lips shut to keep from hissing at my brother. The last thing I want to do is tell Crance who we're looking for — especially because he'll wonder why. But Shade glances at me, eyebrows raised, goading me into speaking the names aloud. Next to him, Crance does his best to keep his expression neutral, but his eyes gleam. He's all too eager to hear what I have to say.

"Ada Wallace." It comes out a whisper, like I'm afraid the walls of the tunnel might steal my secret. "Wolliver Galt."

Galt. It sends a spark of recognition across Crance's face, and he has no choice but to nod. "Galt I know. Old family, live off Charside Road. Brewers by trade." He squints, trying to remember more. "Best ale in the Bay. Good friends to have."

My heartbeat quickens in my chest, delighted by the prospect of such luck. But it's tempered by the knowledge that now Crance — and the mysterious Egan — know who we're looking for.

"Can't say I know the Wallace one," he continues. "It's a common enough name, but no one comes to mind."

To my chagrin, I can't tell if he's lying. So I have to push, to keep him talking. Perhaps Crance will reveal something, or give me an excuse to *convince* him to do so.

"You called yourselves the Mariners?" I ask, careful to keep my tone neutral.

He flashes a grin over his shoulder, then lifts a sleeve to reveal a tattoo on his forearm. A blue-black anchor, surrounded by red, swirling rope. "Best smugglers in the Beacon," he says proudly. "You want it, we run it."

"And you serve the Guard?"

That question makes his smile drop away and he rolls down his sleeve again. There's a shadow of a nod, but nothing more convincing than that.

"I take it Egan's another captain." I quicken my pace, until I'm almost stepping on Crance's heels. His shoulders tighten at my closeness, and I don't miss it when the hairs on the back of his neck raise. "And that makes you what? His lieutenant?"

"We don't bother with titles," he replies, dodging my needling. But I'm just getting started. The others look on, confused by my behavior. *Kilorn would understand. Better yet, he would play along.*

"Forgive me, Crance." The words come out sickly sweet. I sound like a court lady, not a sneak thief, and it rankles him. "I'm simply curious about our brothers and sisters in the Bay. Tell me, what convinced you to join the cause?"

Hard silence. When I look back, Crance's friends are just as quiet, their eyes almost black in the dim tunnel light.

"Was it Farley? Were you recruited?" I press on, waiting for some sign of a break. Still he doesn't respond. And a tremor of fear rolls through me. What isn't he telling us? "Or did you seek the Guard out, like I did? Of course, I had a very good reason. I thought Shade was dead, you see, and I wanted vengeance. I joined up because I wanted to kill the people who killed my brother."

Nothing, but Crance's pace quickens. I've touched on *something.*

"Who did the Silvers take from you?"

I expect Shade to scold me for my questions, but he stays quiet. His attention never wavers from Crance's face, trying to see what the smuggler is hiding. Because he is certainly hiding something from us, and we're all beginning to feel it. Even Farley tenses up, though she seemed so friendly moments ago. She's realized something, seen something she didn't see before. Her hand strays into her jacket, closing around what can only be another hidden knife. And Cal never let his guard drop to begin with. His fire burns, a naked threat to split the darkness. Again I think of the tunnel. It starts to feel like a grave.

"Where is Melody?" Farley murmurs, putting out one gentle hand to stop Crance's progress. We halt as well, and I think I hear our hearts pounding against the tunnel walls. "Egan would never send you, not alone."

Slowly, I shift my body, turning so my back faces the wall, so I can see both Crance and his rogues. Cal does the same, mirroring my motions. A bit of fire springs from his empty hand, waiting and ready in his palm. My own sparks dance in and out of my skin, tiny bolts of purple-white. They feel good to hold, little threads of pure strength. Above us, the traffic has increased, and I suspect we're close to the city gates, if not directly below them. *Not a very good place for a battle.*

Because that's what this is about to become.

"*Where* is Melody?" Farley repeats, and her blade sings against the air. It reflects Cal's fire and glints sharply, burning light into Crance's eyes. "Crance?"

His eyes widen despite the blinding glare,

full of true regret. That is enough to send shivers of terror down my spine. "You know what we are, who Egan is. We're *criminals,* Farley. We believe in money — and survival."

I know the life all too well. But I turned from that path. I'm not a rat anymore. I'm the lightning girl, and now I have too many ideals to count. Freedom, revenge, liberty, everything that fuels the sparks within me, and the resolve that keeps me going.

Crance's rogues move as slowly as I do, loosing guns from hidden holsters. Three pistols, each one in an able, twitching hand. I suppose Crance has one too, but he hasn't revealed his weapon yet. He's too busy trying to explain, trying to make us understand exactly what's about to happen. And I certainly do. Betrayal is familiar to me, but it still turns my stomach and freezes my body with fear. I do all I can to ignore it, to focus.

"They took her," he murmurs. "Sent Egan her trigger finger this morning. It's the same all over the Bay, every gang lost someone or something dear. The Mariners, the Seaskulls, even took Ricket's little boy, and he's been out of the game for years. And the payout." He pauses, whistling darkly. "It's nothing to laugh at."

"For what?" I breathe, not daring to take my eyes off the Mariner closest to me. She stares right back.

Crance's voice is a deep, sorrowful croak. "For you, lightning girl. It's not just the officers and the armies looking for you. It's us too. Every smuggling ring, every thief company from here to Delphie. You're being hunted, Miss Barrow, in the sun and in the shadows, by Silvers and by your own. I'm sorry, but that's the way of it."

His apology isn't for me, but Farley and my brother. His friends, now betrayed. My friends, in grave danger because of me.

"What kind of trap did you set?" Shade growls, doing his best to look menacing despite the crutch under one arm. "What are we walking into?"

"Nothing you'll like, Rabbit."

In the strange light of Cal's fire, my sparks, and Crance's flashlight, I almost miss the flicker of his eyes. They dart to the left, landing on the support beam right next to me. The ceiling above it is cracked and splitting, with bits of dirt poking through the shards of concrete.

"You son of a bitch," Shade growls, his voice too loud, his manner exaggerated. He looks liable to throw a punch at any moment — the perfect distraction. *Here we go.*

The three Mariners raise their guns, aiming for my brother. For the fastest thing in existence. When he raises a fist, they pull their triggers — and their bullets cut through nothing but open air. I drop into a crouch, deafened by gunshots so close to my head, but keep all my focus where it must be — the support beam. A blast of lightning splinters the wood like a detonation, charring straight through. It shatters, collapsing, as I throw a second bolt at the cracked ceiling. Cal vaults sideways, toward Crance and Farley, dodging falling slabs of concrete. If I had time, I'd be afraid of getting buried with the Mariners, but Shade's familiar hand closes around my wrist. I shut my eyes, fighting the squeezing sensation, before hitting ground a few yards down the tunnel. Now we're ahead of Crance and Farley, currently helping Cal to his feet. The tunnel on the other side of them is collapsed, filled up with dirt and concrete and three crushed bodies.

Crance spares one last look for his fallen Mariners, then draws his hidden pistol. For one brief, blistering moment, I think he might shoot me. But instead he raises his electrifying gaze, staring down the tunnel as it quakes around us. His lips move, forming a single word.

"Run."

FOURTEEN

Left, right, left again, climb.

Crance's barked orders follow us through the tunnels, guiding our pounding footsteps. The occasional echoing boom of another collapse keeps us moving as fast as we can — we've set off a chain reaction, an implosion within the tunnels. Once or twice, the tunnel collapses so close to us I hear the sharp snap of cracking support beams. Rats run with us, twisting out of the gloom. I shudder when they dash over my toes, naked tails whipping like tiny ropes. We didn't have many rats at home — the river floods would drown them — and the waves of greasy black fur make my skin crawl. But I do my best to swallow my revulsion. Cal isn't keen on them either, and swipes at the ground with one flaming fist, pushing back the vermin every time they get too close.

Dust swirls at our heels, choking the air, and Crance's flashlight is all but useless in the gloom. The others rely on touch, reaching out to feel along the tunnel walls, but I keep my mind fixed on the world above, on the web of electrical wire and rolling transports. It paints a map in my head, fixing over the paper one I've nearly memorized. With it, I feel everything with my growing range. The sensation is overwhelming, but I push through, forcing myself to take in everything I can. Transports scream overhead, rolling toward the initial collapse. A few career through alleyways, probably avoiding sunken roads and twisted debris. *A distraction. Good.*

The tunnels are Farley and Crance's domain, a kingdom made of dust. But it falls to Cal to get us out of the darkness, and the irony is not lost on us both. When we dead-end at a service door, welded shut, Cal doesn't need to be told what to do. He steps forward, hands outstretched, his bracelet sparking — and then white-hot flame springs to life. It dances in his palms, allowing him to grip the door's hinges and heat them until they melt into red globs of iron. The next obstacle, a metal grate clotted with rust, is even easier, and he peels it away in seconds.

Again the collapsing tunnel shudders like a thunderclap, but from much farther away.

More convincing are the rats, now calm, disappearing back into the dark they came from. Their little shadows are a strange, disgusting comfort. We've outrun death together.

Crance gestures through the broken grate, meaning for us to follow. But Cal hesitates, one scalding hand still resting on iron. When he loosens his grip, it leaves behind red metal and the indent of his hand.

"The Paltry?" he asks, glancing down the tunnel. Cal knows Harbor Bay much better than I. After all, he's lived here before, occupying Ocean Hill every time the royal family came to the area. No doubt Cal's done his share of sneaking through the docks and alleys here, just like he was doing the first time he met me.

"Aye," Crance replies with a quick nod. "Close to the Center as I can get you. Egan instructed me to take you through the Fish Market, and has the Mariners ready to grab you, not to mention a squad of Security. He won't expect you to go through Paltry Place, and won't have anyone on lookout."

The way he says it sets my teeth on edge. "Why?"

"The Paltry is Seaskull territory."

The Seaskulls. Another gang, likely branded with tattoos more foreboding than

Crance's anchor. If not for Maven's scheming, they might've helped a Red sister, but instead, they've been turned into enemies almost as dangerous as any Silver soldier.

"That's not what I meant," I continue, using Mareena's voice to hide my fear. "Why are you helping us?"

A few months ago, the thought of three bodies crushed by rubble might've frightened me. Now I've seen much worse, and barely spare a thought for Crance's cohorts and their twisted bones. Crance, despite his criminal nature, doesn't look so comfortable. His eyes glare back into the darkness, after the Mariners he helped kill. They were probably his friends.

But there are friends *I* would trade, lives *I* would forsake, for my own victories. I've done it before. It isn't hard to let people die when their deaths gives life to something else.

"I'm not one for oaths, or Red dawns, or any of the other nonsense your lot goes on about," he mumbles, one fist closing and clenching in rapid succession. "Words don't impress me. But you're doing a hell of a lot more than talking. The way I see it, I can either betray my boss — or my blood."

Blood. Me.

His teeth gleam in the dim light, flashing

284

with every barbed word. "Even rats want to get out of the gutter, Miss Barrow."

Then he steps through the grate, toward the surface that could kill us all.

And I follow.

I square my shoulders, turning to face the echoes and the end of the tunnel's safety. I've never been to Harbor Bay before, but the map and my electrical sense are enough. Together, they paint a picture of roads and wiring. I can feel the military transports rolling toward the fort, and the lights of the Paltry. What's more, a city is something I understand. Crowds, alleys, all the distractions of daily life — these are my kinds of camouflage.

Paltry Place is another market, alive as Grand Garden in Summerton or the square of the Stilts. But it is dirtier, more harried, free of Silver overlords but choked with teeming Red bodies and haggling shouts. *A perfect place to hide.* We emerge on the lowest level, a subterranean tangle of stalls crisscrossed by greasy canvas canopies. But there's no smoke or stink down here — Reds might be poor, but we are not stupid. One glimpse up, through the grated, wide hole in the ceiling, tells me the upper levels sell stinking fish or smoked meat, letting the scents escape into the sky. For now, we're surrounded by peddlers, inventors, weavers, each one trying to foist their wares onto patrons who don't have two tetrarch coins to rub together. The money makes everyone desperate. Merchants want to get it, buyers want to keep it, and it blinds them all. No one notices a few well-trained sneaks slip out from a forgotten hole in the wall. I know I should feel afraid, but being surrounded by my own is strangely comforting.

Crance leads, his muscled swagger morphing into a limp to match Shade's. He pulls a hood from his vest and hides his face in shadow. To the casual eye, he looks like a bent old man, though he's anything but. He even supports Shade a little, one arm braced against his shoulder to help my brother walk. Shade doesn't have to worry about hiding his face, and keeps his focus on not slipping over the uneven ground of the lower Paltry. Farley brings up the rear, and I'm reassured to know she has my back. For all her secrets, I can trust her, not to see a trap, but to weasel her way out of one. In this world of betrayal, it's the best I can hope for.

It's been a few months since I last stole something. And when I slide a pair of charcoal-gray shawls from a stall, my motions are quick and perfect, but I feel an unfamiliar twinge of regret. Someone made these; someone spun and wove the wool into these rough scraps. Someone needs these. *But so do I.* One for me, one for Cal. He takes it quickly, drawing the frayed wool around his head and shoulders to hide his recognizable features. I do the same, and none too soon.

Our first few steps into the crowded, dim market lead us right past a signboard. Usually filled with notices of sale, news scraps, memorials, the Red noise has been covered up by a checkered swath of printings. A few children mill about the signboard, ripping up the bits of paper in reach. They toss the scraps at each other like snowballs. Only one of the kids, a girl with ragged black hair and bare, brown feet, bothers to look at what they're doing. She stares at two familiar faces, each glaring down from a dozen huge posters. They are stark and grim, headlined with big black letters that read "WANTED BY THE CROWN, for TERRORISM, TREASON, and MURDER." I doubt many of the people swarming the Paltry can read, but the message is clear enough.

Cal's picture isn't his royal portrait, which made him appear strong, kingly, and dashing. No, the image of him is grainy but distinct, a frozen still from one of the many cameras that captured him in the moments before his failed execution in the Bowl of Bones. His face is haggard, pulled by loss and betrayal, while his eyes spark with unchecked rage. The muscles stand out as his neck, straining. There might even be dried blood on his collar. It makes him look every inch the murderer Maven wants him to seem. The lower posters of him are torn up or covered in graffiti, in spiky, scratched handwriting almost too violently etched to make out. *The Kingkiller, The Exile.* The titles rip at the paper, as if the words could make the photographed skin bleed. And weaving among the titles — *find him, find him, find him.*

Like Cal, the picture of me is taken from the Bowl of Bones. I know exactly which moment. It was before I walked through the gates of the arena, when I stood and listened to Lucas take a bullet to the brain. In that second, I knew I was going to die, but worse, I knew I was useless. The now-dead Arven was with me, suffocating my abilities, reducing me to nothing. My printed eyes are wide, afraid, and I look small. I am not the lightning girl in this photo. I am only a scared teenager. Someone no one would stand behind, let alone protect. I don't doubt Maven chose this frame himself, knowing exactly what kind of image this would project. But some have not been fooled. Some saw the split second of my strength, my lightning, before the execution broadcast was cut away. Some know what I am, and they have written it across the posters for all to see.

Red Queen. The lightning girl. She lives. Rise, Red as dawn. Rise. Rise. Rise.

Every word feels like a brand, searing hot and deep. But we can't tarry by the wall of wanted posters. I nudge Cal, directing him away from the brutal vision of us. He goes willingly, following Shade and Crance through the swirling crowd. I resist the urge to hold on to him, to try and take a bit of the weight off his shoulders. No matter how much I might want to feel him, I cannot. I must keep my eyes ahead, and away from the fire of a fallen prince. I must freeze my heart to the one person who insists on setting it ablaze.

Winding up the Paltry is easier than it should be. A Red market is of no consequence to anyone important, so cameras and officers are sparse on the lower levels. But I keep my senses open, feeling out the few electrical sight lines that manage to penetrate through the haphazard stalls and storefronts. I wish I could just shut them off, instead of awkwardly avoiding them, but even that is too dangerous. A mysterious outage would surely draw attention. The officers are even more troubling, standing out sharply in the black uniforms of Security. As we climb through the levels of the Paltry, up to the city surface, they grow in number. Most look bored by the rush of Red life, but a few keep their wits. Their eyes dart through the crowd, *searching.*

"Hunch," I whisper, gripping Cal's wrist sharply. The action sends a spark of nerves through my hand and up my arm, forcing me to pull away far too quickly.

Still, he does as I tell him, stooping to hide his height. It might not be enough though. *All of this might not be enough.*

"Worry about *him.* If he bolts, we need to be ready," Cal murmurs back, his lips close enough to brush my ear. He points one finger out from the folds of his shawl, gesturing to Crance. But my brother has the Mariner well in hand, keeping a firm grip on Crance's vest. Like us, he doesn't trust the smuggler further than he can throw him.

"Shade has him. Focus on keeping your head down."

Breath hisses through Cal's teeth, another

exasperated sigh. "Just watch. If he's going to run, he'll do it in about thirty seconds."

I don't need to ask how Cal knows this. Judging by the motion of the crowd, thirty seconds will take us to the top of the twisting, rickety staircase, planting us firmly on the main floor of the Paltry. I can see the hub of the market now, just above us, streaming with midday light that is almost blinding after our time underground. The stalls look more permanent, more professional and profitable. An open kitchen fills the air with the smell of cooking meat. After ration packs and salt fish, it makes my mouth water. Worn wooden arches bow overhead, supporting a patched and torn canvas roof. A few of the arches are damaged, warped by seasons of rain and snow.

"He won't run," Farley whispers, butting in between us. "At least not to Egan. He'll lose his head for betraying the Mariners. If he's going anywhere, it's out of the city."

"Then let him," I whisper back. Another Red to babysit is the last thing I need. "He's fulfilled his use to us, hasn't he?"

"And if he runs right into a jail cell and an interrogation, what then?" Cal's voice is soft, but full of menace. A cold reminder of what must be done to protect ourselves.

"He let three of his people die for me, to

keep me safe." I don't even remember their faces. I can't let myself. "I doubt torture will bother him much."

"All minds can fall to Elara Merandus," Cal finally says. "You and I know that better than anyone. If she gets him, we'll be found. The Bay newbloods will be found."

If.

Cal wants to kill a man based on such a terrible word. He takes my silence as agreement, and to my shame, I realize he's not entirely wrong. At least he won't make me do it, though my lightning can kill as quickly as any flame. Instead, his hands stray inside his shawl, to the knife I know he keeps tucked away. Within the folds of my sleeves, my hands start to shake. And I pray that Crance stays the course; that his steps never falter. That he doesn't get a knife in the back for daring to help me.

The main floor of the Paltry is louder than the depths, an overload of sound and sight. I scale back my senses a little, shutting out what I must to keep my wits about me. The lights whine overhead, ragged with a pulse of uneven currents. Their wiring is faulty, flickering in places. It makes one of my eyes twitch. The cameras are more intense too, focused on the Security post at the center of the marketplace. It's little more than a stall itself, six-sided, with five windows, a door, and a shingled roof. Except the box is full of officers instead of mismatched wares. *Too many officers,* I realize with a steadily growing horror.

"Faster," I whisper. "We must go faster."

My feet find a quicker pace, outstripping Cal and Farley, until I'm almost on Crance's heels. Shade glances over his shoulder, brow furrowed. But his gaze slides past me, past all of us, and fixes on something in the crowd. No, *someone.*

"We're being followed," he mumbles, his grip tightening on Crance's arm. "Sea-skulls."

Instincts be damned, I tip my hood so I can get a glimpse of them. They're not hard to pick out. White ink on shaved heads, tattooed skulls of jagged bone on their scalps. No less than four Seaskulls pick their way through the crowd, following us as rats would a mouse. Two from the left, two from the right, flanking us. If the situation wasn't so dire, I would laugh at their matching tattoos. The crowd knows them by sight, and parts to let them pass, to let them *hunt.*

The other Reds clearly fear these criminals, but I do not. A few thugs are nothing compared to the might of the dozen Security officers milling about their post. They could be swifts, strongarms, oblivions — Silvers who can make us pay in blood and pain. At least I know they're not so dangerous as the Silvers of court, the whispers and silks and silences. Whispers as powerful as Queen Elara don't wear lowly black uniforms. They control armies and kingdoms, not a few yards of marketplace, and they are far away from here. *For now.*

To our surprise, the first blow comes not from behind but from dead ahead of us. A bent old crone with a cane is not who she seems, and hooks Crance around the neck with her gnarled piece of wood. She throws him to the ground and removes her cloak in one motion, revealing a bald head and a skull tattoo.

"Fish Market not enough for you, Mariner?" she snarls, watching as Crance lands on his back. Shade goes down with him, too tangled up in Crance's limbs and his own crutch to stay standing.

I move to help, lunging forward, but an arm grabs me around the waist, pulling me back into the crowd. Others look on, eager for a bit of entertainment. No one notices us melt into the wall of faces, not even the four Seaskulls who followed us. We are not their target — *yet.*

"Keep walking," Cal rumbles in my ear.

But I set my feet. I will not be moved, not even by him. "Not without Shade."

The Seaskull woman smacks Crance as he tries to stand, her cane cracking soundly against bone. She's quick, turning her weapon on Shade, who is smart enough to stay on the ground, his arms raised in mock surrender. He could disappear in an instant, jumping his way to safety, but knows he cannot. Not with every eye watching. Not with the Security post so close by.

"Fools and thieves, the lot of them," a woman grumbles nearby. She seems to be the only one annoyed by the display. Merchants, patrons, and street urchins alike look on in anticipation, and the Security officers do nothing at all, watching with veiled amusement. I even catch a few of them passing coins, making bets on the brewing fight.

Another smack, this time hitting Shade's wounded shoulder. He grits his teeth, trying to hold back a grunt of pain, but it echoes loudly over the Paltry. I almost feel it myself, and wince as he crumples.

"I don't know your face, Mariner," the Seaskull crows. She hits him again, hard enough to send a message. "But Egan certainly will. He'll pay for your safe, if bruised, return."

My fist clenches, wishing for lightning, but I feel flame instead. Hot skin against mine, fingers worming into my grip. *Cal.* I won't be able to spark up without hurting him. Part of me wants to, to push him away and save my brother in a single sweeping motion. But that will get us nowhere.

With a sharp gasp, I realize we could not ask for a better distraction — a better moment to slip away. *Shade is not a distraction,* a voice screams in my head. I bite my lip, almost breaking the skin. I can't leave him, I can't. I can't lose him again. *But we can't stay here. It's too dangerous, and so much more is at stake.*

"The Security Center," I whisper, trying to keep my voice from shaking. "Ada Wallace must be found, and the Center is the only way." The next words taste like blood. "We should go."

Shade lets the next blow knock him sideways, giving him a better angle. His eyes meet mine. I hope he understands. My lips move without sound. *Security Center,* I mouth to him, telling him where to meet us when he gets away. *Because he will get away. He's a newblood like me. These people are no match for him.*

It almost sounds convincing.

His face falls, torn by the knowledge that

I will not save him. But he nods all the same. And then the press of bodies swallows him whole, blocking him from sight. I turn my back before cane hits bone, but I hear the hard, echoing sound. Again I wince, and tears bite my eyes. I want to look back, but I have to walk away, to do what must be done, and forget what must be forgotten.

The crowd cheers and presses forward to see — making it all the easier for us to slip into the street, and deep into the city of Harbor Bay.

The streets surrounding the Paltry are like the market itself — crowded, noisy, stinking of fish and bad tempers. I expect no less from the Red sector of the city, where houses are cramped and leaning out over the alleys, forming shadowed archways half-filled with garbage and beggars. There are no officers that I can see, drawn either to the gang fight in the Paltry or the tunnel collapses far behind us. Cal takes the lead now, moving us steadily south, away from the Red center.

"Familiar territory?" Farley asks, cutting a suspicious glance at Cal when he ducks us down yet another twisting alley. "Or are you just as turned around as I am?"

He doesn't bother to answer, responding only with a quick wave of the hand. We scamper by a tavern, its windows already swarming with shadows of professional drunks. Cal's eyes linger on the door, painted an offensively bright red. One of his old haunts, I suppose, when he could slip out of Ocean Hill undetected to see his kingdom without the sheen of Silver high society. *That's what a good king would do,* he said once. But as I discovered, his definition of a good king was very, very flawed. The beggars and the thieves he's encountered over the years were not enough to convince the prince. He saw hunger and injustice, but not enough to warrant change. Not enough to be worth his worry. That is until his world chewed him up and spit him out — making him an orphan, an exile, and a traitor.

We follow him because we must. Because we need a soldier and a pilot, a blunt instrument to help us achieve our goals. At least, that's what I tell myself as I trail at his heels. I need Cal for noble reasons. To save lives. To *win*.

But like my brother, I too have a crutch. Mine is not metal. It is flesh and fire and bronze eyes. If only I could cast him away. If only I was strong enough to let the prince go and do what he would with his vengeance. To die or live as he saw fit. *But I need him. And I can't find the strength to let him go.*

Though we're far from the Fish Market, a horrible smell permeates through the street. I push my shawl to my nose, trying to block out whatever it is. *Not fish,* I steadily realize, and the others know it too.

"We shouldn't go this way," Cal murmurs, putting out a hand to stop me, but I duck under his arm. Farley is right on my heels.

We emerge from the side street into what was once a modest garden square. Now it is deathly quiet, the windows of the houses and shops shut fast. The flowers are burned, the soil turned to ash. Dozens of bodies swing from the bare trees, their faces purple and bloated, with rope nooses around their necks. Each one has been stripped naked, save for their matching red medallions. Nothing fancy, just carved wooden squares dangling from rough cord. I've never seen necklaces like that, and I focus on them to keep my eyes from so many dead faces.

They've been up for a while, judging by the smell and the buzzing cloud of flies.

I'm not a stranger to death, but these corpses are worse than any I've seen — or made.

"The Measures?" I wonder aloud. Did these men and women break curfew? Speak out of turn? Were they executed for the orders I gave? *Not your orders,* I tell myself reflexively. But that doesn't lessen the guilt. Nothing will.

Farley shakes her head. "They're Red Watch," she mumbles. She starts to step forward, but thinks better of it. "Bigger cities, bigger Red communities, they have their own guards and officers. To keep the peace, to keep our laws, because Security won't."

No wonder the Seaskulls attacked Crance and Shade so openly. They knew no one would punish them. They knew the Red Watch was dead.

"We should cut them down," I say, though I know it's not possible. We don't have the time to bury them, nor do we want the trouble.

I make myself turn away. The sight is an abomination, one I will not forget, but I do not weep. Cal is there, waiting a respectable distance away, as if he doesn't have the right to enter the hanging square. I quietly agree. His people did this. *His people.*

Farley is not so collected as me. She tries to hide the tears gathering in her eyes, and I pretend not to notice them as we walk away.

"There will be a reckoning. They will

answer for this," she hisses, her words tighter than any noose.

The farther we go from the Paltry, the more ordered the city becomes. Alleys widen into streets, curving gently instead of turning at hairpin angles. Buildings here are stone or smoothed concrete, and don't look ready to fall down in a strong breeze. A few homes, meticulously kept but small, must belong to the successful Reds of the city, judging by the red doors and shutters. They are marked by our color, branded, so everyone knows who and what lives inside. The Reds wandering the street are just as clear, mostly servants wearing corded red bracelets. A few have striped badges pinned to their clothes, each one bearing a familiar color order, denoting which family they serve.

The closest one has a badge of red and brown — *House Rhambos.*

My lessons with Lady Blonos come flooding back, a blur of half-remembered facts. Rhambos, one of the High Houses. Governors of this, the Beacon region. Strongarms. They had a girl in Queenstrial, a slip of a thing named Rohr who could tear me in half. I met another Rhambos in the Bowl of Bones. He was supposed to be one of my executioners, and I killed him. I electrified him until his bones shrieked.

I can still hear him screaming. After the hanging square, the thought almost makes me smile.

The Rhambos servants turn west, up a slight incline to a hill that overlooks the harbor. Heading for their master's mansion, no doubt. It's one of many palatial homes dotting the rise, each one boasting pristine white walls, sky-blue roofs, and tall silver spires topped with sharp-pointed stars. We follow, winding our way up, drawing closer to the largest structure of all. It looks crowned in constellations, surrounded by clear, gleaming walls — diamondglass.

"Ocean Hill," Cal says, following my gaze.

The compound dominates the crest of the rise, a fat white cat lazing peacefully behind crystalline walls. Like Whitefire Palace, the edges of the roof are gilded in metal flames, so expertly forged they seem to dance in the sunlight. Its windows wink like jewels, each one gleaming and clean, the product of who knows how many Red servants' toil. The echo of construction scrapes and rumbles from the palace, doing only Maven knows what to the royal residence. Part of me wants to see it, and I have to laugh at such a foolish side of myself. If I ever step inside a palace again, it will be in chains.

Cal can't look at the Hill long. It is a distant memory now, a place he can no longer go, a home to which he cannot return.

I suppose we have that in common.

FIFTEEN

Gulls perch on the stars adorning every roof, watching as we pass through the cool, midday shadows. I feel exposed beneath their gaze, a fish about to be snapped up for dinner. Cal keeps us moving at a brisk pace, and I know he feels the danger too. Even in the back alleys, overlooked only by service doors and servants' quarters, we are still hopelessly out of place in our hoods and threadbare clothing. This part of the city is peaceful, quiet, pristine — and dangerous. The farther in we go, the tenser I feel. And the low pulse of electricity deepens, a steady thrum in every house we pass. It even arcs overhead, carried through wire camouflaged by twisting vines or blue-striped awnings. But I feel no cameras, and the transports stick to the main streets. So far, we have gone unnoticed, protected by a pair of bloody distractions.

Cal guides us quickly through what he

calls the Star Sector. Judging by the thousand stars on a hundred domed roofs, the neighborhood is aptly named. He skirts us down the alleys, careful to give Ocean Hill a wide berth until we circle back to a main road busy with traffic. An offshoot of the Port Road, if I remember the map correctly, connecting Ocean Hill and its outbuildings to the bustling harbor and Fort Patriot below, stretching out into the water. From this angle, the city spreads all around us, a painting of white and blue.

We fall in with the Reds crowding the sidewalks. There, the white flagstones are choked with military transports. They vary in size, ranging from two-man vehicles to armored boxes on wheels, most of them stamped with the sword symbol of the army. Cal's eyes glitter beneath his hood, watching each one pass. I'm more concerned with the civilian transports. They're fewer in number, but they gleam, moving swiftly through the traffic. The more impressive ones fly colored flags, denoting the house they belong to, or the passenger they carry. To my relief, I don't see the red and black of Maven's House Calore, or the white and navy of Elara's House Merandus. At least I won't have to expect the very worst from today.

The jostling crowd forces us to walk huddled together, with Cal on my right and Farley on my left. "How much farther?" I whisper, edging my face back into my hood. The map has gone fuzzy in my head, despite my best efforts. Too many twists and turns to keep straight, even for me.

Cal nods his head in response, gesturing to a bustling throng of people and transports up ahead. I gulp at the sight of what is undoubtedly the beating heart of Harbor Bay. The crown of the city's hill, ringed by white stone and diamondglass walls. I can see the palace gates, bright blue and scaled with silver, but a few starry turrets peek out. It is a beautiful place, but cold, cruel, and razor sharp. Dangerous.

On the map, this looked like nothing more than a plaza in front of the gates of Ocean Hill, connected to the harbor and the gates of Fort Patriot down the gentle slope. The reality is much more complicated. Here, the two worlds of this kingdom seem to mingle, Red and Silver drawn together for a fraction of a moment. Dockworkers, soldiers, servants, and high lords cross beneath the crystal dome arcing over the massive court-yard. A fountain twists in the center, surrounded by white and blue flowers not yet touched by autumn. Sunshine shimmers through the dome, refracting dancing light onto the realm of brightly colored chaos. The fort gates are directly down the avenue from us, dappled by the shifting light of the dome. Like those of the palace, they are artfully crafted. Forty feet high, made of burnished bronze and silver braided into giant, swirling fish. If not for the dozens of soldiers and my sheer terror, I might find the gates magnificent. They hide the bridge beyond, and Fort Patriot farther out to sea. Horns and shouts and laughter add to the overload, until I have to look down at my boots and catch my breath. The thief in me delights at the thought of so much confusion, but the rest is frightened and frayed, a live wire trying to contain its sparks.

"You're lucky it's not the Night of a Single Star," Cal murmurs, his eyes faraway. "The whole city explodes for the festival."

I don't have the strength or the need to respond to him. The Night is a Silver holiday, held in memory of some navy battle decades ago. It means nothing to me, but one glance at Cal and his distracted gaze tells me he doesn't agree. He's seen the Night in this very city, and remembers it fondly. Music and laughter and silk. Maybe fireworks over the water, and a royal feast to end the party. His father's approving smile, jokes with Maven. Everything he's lost.

Now it's my turn to look faraway. *That life is gone, Cal. It shouldn't make you happy anymore.*

"Don't worry," he adds when his expression clears. He shakes his head, trying to hide a sad smile. "We've made it. That's the Security Center there."

The building he indicates stands on the edge of the bustling square, its white walls stark against the tangled traffic below. It looks like a beautiful fortress, with thick-glassed windows, and steps leading up to a terrace surrounded by columns carved into the scaly tails of enormous fish. Patrolled walkways arch over the diamondglass walls of Ocean Hill, tying it to the rest of the palatial compound. The roof is also blue, decorated not with stars but *spikes*. Cruel iron, six feet long, and sharpened to a wicked point. For magnetrons, I suppose, to use against any kind of assault. The rest of the building is the same, covered in Silver weapons. Vines and thorny plants wind up the columns for greenwardens while a pair of wide, still pools hold dark water for nymphs. And of course, there are armed guards at every door, long rifles plain in their hands.

Worse than any guard are the banners.

They flap in the sea breeze, streaming from the walls, turrets, and fishtail columns. They bear not the silver spear of Security but the Burning Crown. Black, white, and red, its points twisting in curls of flame. They stand for Norta, for the kingdom, for *Maven.* For everything we're trying to destroy. And between them, on gilded banners of his own, is Maven. Or at least, his image. He stares out, his father's crown on his head, his mother's eyes glaring. He looks like a young but strong boy, a prince rising to the ultimate occasion. "LONG LIVE THE KING" screams beneath every picture of his sharp, pale face.

Despite the impressive defenses, despite Maven's haunting stare, I can't help but smile. The Center pulses with my own weapon, with electricity. It is more powerful than any magnetron, any greenwarden, any gun. It is everywhere. And it is mine. If only I could use it properly. If only we didn't have to hide.

If. I despise that stupid word.

It hangs in the air, close enough to touch. *What if we can't get in? What if we can't find Ada or Wolliver? What if Shade doesn't come back?* The last thought burns more deeply than the rest. Even though my eyes are sharp, trained on the crowded streets, I can't see my brother anywhere. He should be easy to spot, limping along on his crutch, but he's nowhere to be found.

Panic deepens my senses, taking away a little of the control I worked so hard to cultivate. I have to bite my lip to keep from gasping aloud. *Where is my brother?*

"So now we wait?" Farley says, her voice trembling with dread of her own. Her eyes sweep back and forth, also searching. For my brother. "I don't think even you two can get in there without Shade."

Cal scoffs, too busy examining the Center's defenses to spare a glance for her. "We could get in just fine. It might mean sending the whole place up in smoke. Not exactly the subtle approach."

"No, not at all," I murmur, if only to distract myself. But no matter how hard I try to focus on my feet or Cal's capable hands, I can't stop worrying about Shade. Up until this moment, I never truly doubted he would meet us. He's a *teleporter,* the fastest thing alive, and a few dock thugs shouldn't pose him any threat. That's what I told myself back in the Paltry, when I left him. *When I abandoned him.* He took a bullet for me a few days ago and I threw him to the Seaskulls like a lamb to wolves.

Back in Naercey, I told Shade I didn't

trust his word. I suppose he shouldn't trust mine either.

My fingers stray into my hood, trying to massage the ache from my neck muscles. But it brings me no respite. Because right now we're idling in front of a veritable firing squad, waiting like stupid chickens eyeing a butcher's knife. And while I fear for Shade, I fear for myself too. I cannot be taken. I *will* not.

"The back entrance," I say. It's not a question. Every house has a door, but it also has windows, a hole in the roof, or a broken lock. There is always a way in.

Cal furrows his brow, at a loss for once. A soldier should never be sent to do a thief's job. "We're better off with Shade," he argues. "No one will even know he's in. A few more minutes —"

"We put every newblood at greater risk with every second we waste. Besides, Shade won't have a problem finding us later." I take my first steps off the Port Road and onto a side street. Cal sputters, but follows along. "All he has to do is follow the smoke."

"Smoke?" He blanches.

"A controlled burn," I continue, a plan formulating so fast the words barely have time to pass my lips. "Something *contained.* A fire wall just big enough to hold them

311

back, until we get the names we need. A few nymph grunts shouldn't pose much of a threat to you, and if they do" — I ball my hand, letting a tiny spark spin in my palm — "that's what I'm here for. Farley, I assume you know the records system?"

She doesn't hesitate to nod, her face shining with an odd sort of pride. "Finally," she mutters. "No point in lugging you two around if you're not going to be useful."

Cal's eyes darken into a fearsome glare that reminds me of his dead father. "You know what this will do, don't you?" he warns, as if I'm some kind of child. "Maven will know who did this. He'll know where we are. He'll know what we're doing."

I round on Cal, angry that I must explain. Angry that he doesn't *trust* me to make any kind of decision. "We took Nix more than twelve hours ago. Someone will notice Nix is gone, if they haven't already. It will be *reported.* You think Maven isn't watching every name on Julian's list?" I shake my head, not knowing why I didn't realize sooner. "He'll know what we're doing the moment he hears of Nix's disappearance. It doesn't matter what we do here. After today, no matter what, it will truly be a manhunt. Citywide searches for us, orders to kill on sight. So why not get ahead of the curve?"

He doesn't argue, but that doesn't mean he agrees. Either way, I don't care. Cal doesn't know this side of the world, the gutters and the mud we must throw ourselves into. I do.

"It's time we stop pulling our punches, Cal." Farley joins in.

Again, no answer. He looks dejected, disgusted even. "They're my own people, Mare," he finally whispers. Another man would yell, but Cal is not the type to shout. His whispers usually burn, but I feel only determination. "I won't kill them."

"Silvers," I finish for him. "You won't kill *Silvers.*"

He shakes his head slowly. "I can't."

"And yet you were willing to end Crance not too long ago," I press on, hissing. "He's one of your people too, or he would be if you were king. But I suppose his blood's the wrong color, right?"

"That's —" he sputters, "that's not the same. If he ran, if he was captured, we'd be in such danger. . . ."

The words stick in his throat, trailing away. Because there are simply no words left for him to say. He's a hypocrite, plain and simple, no matter how *fair* he claims to be. His blood is silver and his heart is Silver.

And he will never value another above his own.

Leave, I want to say. The words taste bitter. I can't force them past my lips. As infuriating as his prejudice, his allegiances are, I can't do what should be done. I can't let him go. He is so *wrong* and I can't let him go.

"Then don't kill," I grind out. "But remember that *he* did. My people — and your own. They follow *him* now, and they'll kill us for their new king."

I point one bruised finger back at the street, to the banners bearing Maven's face. Maven, who sacrificed Silvers to the Scarlet Guard, to turn rebels into terrorists and destroy his own enemies in a single swoop. Maven, who murdered everyone at court who truly knew me. Lucas and Lady Blonos and my maids, all dead because I was different. Maven, who helped kill his own father, who tried to execute his brother. Maven, who must be destroyed.

A small part of me fears that Cal will walk away. He could disappear into the city, to find whatever peace still lingers in his heart. But he won't. His anger, while buried deep, is stronger than his own reason. He will have vengeance, just as I will have mine. Even if it costs us everything we hold dear.

"This way." His voice echoes. We have no more time for whispers.

As we round the back corner of the Security Center, my senses reach out, focusing on the security cameras dotting the walls. With a smile, I push against them, shorting out their wiring. One by one, they fall to my wave.

The back door is just as impressively made as the front, albeit smaller. A wide step like a porch, a door grated with curving steel, and only four armed guards. Their rifles are polished to a high sheen, but heavy in their hands. *New recruits.* I note the colored bands on their arms, denoting their houses and abilities. One has no band at all — a lower-class Silver, with no great family, and weaker abilities than the others. The rest are a banshee of House Marinos, a Gliacon shiver, and a Greco strongarm. To my delight, I see no white and black of House Eagrie. No eyes to glimpse the immediate future, to know what we're about to do.

They see us coming, and don't bother to straighten up. Reds are nothing to worry about, not for Silver officers. How wrong they are.

Only when we stop before the steps of the rear door do they notice us. The banshee, little more than a boy with slanted eyes and high cheekbones, spits at our feet.

"Keep moving, Red rats." His voice has a painful, razor edge to it.

Of course, we don't listen. "I would like to lodge a complaint," I say, my voice high and clear, though I keep my face angled to the ground. Heat rises next to me, and out of the corner of my eye, I see Cal's fists clench.

The officers break out in hearty guffaws, exchanging grotesque smiles. The banshee even takes a few steps forward, until he stands over me. "Security doesn't listen to the likes of you. Take it up with the Red Watch." They break out in peals of laughter again. The banshee's hurt my tender ears. "I think they're still *hanging* around" — more disgusting laughs — "in Stark Garden."

Next to me, Farley's hands curl into her jacket, to feel the knife she keeps tucked close. I glare at her, hoping to stop her from stabbing someone before the right moment.

The steel Center door opens, allowing a guard to step out onto the entryway. He mutters to one of the other officers, and I catch the words *broken* and *camera.* But the officer only shrugs, darting to look at the many security cameras dotting the wall above us. He doesn't see anything wrong with them, not that he could.

"Be gone with you," the banshee continues, waving a hand like we're dogs to be dismissed. When we don't move, his eyes narrow into thin, black slits. "Or shall I arrest you all for trespassing?"

He expects us to scurry off. Arrest is as good as execution these days. But we hold our ground. If the banshee wasn't such a cruel idiot, I would feel sorry for him.

"You can try," I say, reaching for my hood.

The shawl falls around my shoulders, flapping like gray wings before crumpling at my feet. It feels good to turn up my gaze, and watch cold recognition draw fear across the banshee's face.

I am not remarkable looking. Brown hair, brown eyes, brown skin. Bruised, bone weary, small, and hungry. Red blood and a red temper. I should not frighten anyone, but the banshee is certainly afraid of me. He knows what power hums beneath my bruises. He knows the lightning girl.

He stumbles, one foot catching on the steps, and falls backward, mouth opening and closing as he summons the strength to scream.

"It's — it's her," the shiver behind him stammers, pointing one shaking finger. It quickly turns to ice. I can't help but smile pointedly, and sparks ball in my hands. Their shocking hiss is a comfort like no other.

Cal compounds the dramatics. He rips away his disguise in a single, smooth motion, revealing the prince they were raised to follow, then told to fear. His bracelet crackles and flame spreads along his shawl, turning it into a blistering, burning flag.

"The prince!" the strongarm gasps. He looks starry-eyed, reluctant to act. After all, until a few days ago, they saw Cal as a legend, not a monster.

The banshee recovers first, reaching for his gun. "Arrest them! Arrest them!" He shrieks, and we duck as one, dodging his sonic blow. It shatters the windows behind us.

Shock makes the officers slow and stupid. The strongarm doesn't dare come close, and fumbles for his holstered pistols, struggling against his own rushing adrenaline. One of them, the officer standing in the open door, has the good sense to run into the safety of the Center. The four remaining are easily dealt with. The banshee doesn't get the chance for another scream, catching an electric bolt instead. The shocks dig into his neck and chest before finding home in his brain. For a split second, I can feel his veins and nerves, splayed like branches in flesh. He drops where he stands, falling into a deep, dark sleep.

A breath of biting cold gets the better of me, and I spin to find a wall of ice shards sailing my way, driven by the shiver. They melt before they reach me, destroyed by a blast of Cal's fire. It quickly turns on the shiver and the strongarm, surrounding them both, trapping them so I can finish the job. Two more shocks knock them out, slamming them to the floor. The last officer, the unknown, tries to flee, pawing at the still open door. Farley grabs him around the neck, but he throws her off, sending her flying. He's a telky, but a weak one, and quickly dispatched. He joins the others on the ground, his muscles twitching slightly from my electric darts. I give the banshee an extra shock, for his malice. His body flops against the steps like a fish from Kilorn's nets.

All of it takes but a moment. The door is still open, swinging slowly on massive hinges. I catch it before the latch locks in place, forcing an arm into the cool, circulated air of the Security Center. Inside, I feel the rush of electricity, in the lights, in the cameras, in my own fingertips. With a single, steadying breath, I shut them all out, plunging the chamber beyond into darkness.

Cal steps carefully over the unconscious bodies of fallen officers, while Farley does her best to kick each one in the ribs. "For the Watch," she snarls, breaking the banshee's nose. Cal stops her before she can do any more damage, sighing as he loops an arm around her shoulder, hoisting her up the steps and through the open back door. With one last glance at the sky, I slip into the Center, and shut the steel firmly behind us.

The dark halls and dead cameras remind me of the Hall of the Sun, of sneaking down to the palace dungeons to save Farley and Kilorn from certain death. But I was almost a princess there. I wore silk, and I had Julian at my back, singing his way through each and every guard, bending their will to our purpose. It was clean, spilling no blood but my own. The Security Center is not like that. I can only hope to keep the casualties to a minimum.

Cal knows where to go, and keeps the lead, but he does nothing more than dodge the officers who try to stop us. For a brute, he's quite graceful, shouldering around blows from strongarms and swifts. He still won't hurt them, and leaves that burden to me. Lightning destroys just as easily as flame, and we leave a trail of bodies in our wake. I tell myself they're only unconscious, but in the heat of battle, I can't be sure. I can't control my surges as easily as I make them, and it's likely I killed one or two. I don't care — and neither does Farley, her long knife plunging in and out of the dark shadows. It drips metallic silver blood by the time we reach our destination, an unremarkable door.

But I feel something remarkable within. A vast machine, pulsing with electricity.

"Here. The records room," Cal says. He keeps his eyes on the door, unable to look back at our carnage. True to his word, he bathes the surrounding hallway in flame, creating a wall of twisting heat to protect us while we work.

We push through the door. I expect mountains of paper, printed lists like the one Julian gave me, but instead I find myself staring at a wall of flashing lights, video screens, and control panels. It pulses, sluggish from my interference with the wiring. Without a thought, I put a hand to the cold metal, calming myself and my ragged breathing. The records machine responds in kind, and kicks into a high whir. One of the screens blinks to life, showing a fuzzy black-and-white display. Text flits across the screen, drawing a gasp from Farley and me. We've never imagined, let alone seen, anything like this.

"Remarkable," Farley breathes, reaching out with a tentative hand. Her fingers brush along the text on-screen, reading slowly. Large letters spell out *Census and Records,* with *Beacon Region, Regent State, Norta* written in smaller type below.

"They didn't have this in Coraunt?" I ask, wondering how she found Nix's location in the village.

She dully shakes her head. "Coraunt barely has a post office, let alone one of these." With a grin, she clicks one of the many buttons beneath the glowing screen. Then another, and another. The screen flashes each time, typing out different questions. She giggles like a child, continuing to click.

I put my hand over hers. "Farley."

"Sorry," she replies. "A little help here, Your Highness?"

Cal doesn't step back from the door, his neck craning back and forth to check for officers. "The blue key. Says *search.*"

I press the button before Farley can. The screen darkens for a moment, before flashing blue. Three options appear, each one inside a flashing white box. *Search by name, search by location, search by blood type.* Hastily, I hit a button marked *select,* choosing the first box.

"Type in the name you want, then hit *proceed.* Hit *printout* when you find what you want, it'll give you a copy," Cal instructs. But a shouting curse draws his gaze away, as an officer makes blistering contact with his fiery barricade. A gunshot blasts, and I pity the stupid guard trying to fight fire with bullets. "Quickly now."

My fingers hover over the keys, hunting down each letter as I type out *Ada Wallace* in frustratingly slow motions. The machine whirs again, the screen flashing three times, before a wall of text appears. It even includes a photograph, the one used on her identification card. I linger on the picture of the newblood, taking in Ada's deep golden skin and soft eyes. She looks sad, even in the tiny image.

Another gunshot echoes, making me jump. I turn my focus on the text, skimming through Ada's personal information. Her birthday and birth location I already know, as well as the blood mutation that marks her as a newblood like me. Farley searches too, her eyes scanning over the words with abandon. "There." I point a finger at what we need, feeling happier than I have in days.

Occupation: Housemaid, employed by Governor Rem Rhambos. Address: Bywater Square, Canal Sector, Harbor Bay.

"I know it," Farley says, jabbing at the *printout* button. The machine spits out paper, copying down the information from Ada's record.

The next name comes even faster from the humming machine. *Wolliver Galt. Occupation: Merchant, employed by Galt Brewery. Address: Battle Garden and Charside Road, Threestone Sector, Harbor Bay.* So Crance wasn't lying about this, at least. I'll have to shake his hand if I ever see him again.

"About done?" Cal shouts from the door, and I hear the strain in his voice. It's only a matter of time until nymphs come running, and his flaming wall crashes down.

"Nearly," I murmur, clicking at the keys again. "This machine isn't just for Harbor Bay, is it?" Cal doesn't respond, too busy maintaining his shield, but I know I'm right. With a grin, I pull the list from my jacket, and thumb to the first page. "Farley, get started on that screen."

She jumps to attention like a rabbit, gleefully clicking until the next panel screen hums to life. We pass the list between each other, typing in name after name, collecting one printout after another. Every name from the Beacon region, all ten of them. The girl from the New Town slums, a seventy-year-old grandmother in Cancorda, twin boys on the Bahrn Islands, and so on. The papers pile on the floor, each one telling me more than Julian's list ever could. I should feel excited, ecstatic at such a breakthrough, but something throttles my happiness. *So many names. So many to save.* And we are moving so slowly. There is no way we'll find them all in time, not like this. Not even with the airjet or the records or all of Farley's underground tunnels. Some will be lost. There is no avoiding it.

The thought disintegrates just like the wall behind me. It explodes inward in a cloud of dust, silhouetting the jagged figure of a man with gray, rocky flesh, hard as a battering ram. *Stoneskin* is all I manage to think before he charges, catching Farley around the waist. Her hand still clutches the line of printouts, ripping the precious paper from the machine. It streams behind her like a white banner of surrender.

"Submit to arrest!" the stoneskin roars, pinning her against the far window. Her head smacks against the glass, cracking it. Her eyes roll.

And then the wall of fire is in the room with us, surrounding Cal as he enters like a mad bull. I snatch the papers from Farley's hand, tucking them away with the list lest they be burned. Cal works quickly, forgetting his oath not to harm, and hauls the stoneskin off her, using his flames to force him back through the hole in the wall. The fire rises, stopping him from coming back. For the time being.

"Done now?" Cal growls, his eyes like living coals.

I nod and turn my gaze on the records machine. It whirs sadly, as if it knows what I'm about to do. With a clenched fist, I overload its circuits, sending a destructive surge shuddering through the machine. Every screen and blinking line explodes in a spray of sparks, erasing exactly what we came for. "Done."

Farley stumbles away from the window, a hand to her head, her lip bleeding, but still inexorably standing. "I think this is the part where we run."

One glance out the window, the natural escape, tells me we're too high up to jump. And the sounds from the hall outside, shouts and marching feet, are just as damning. "Run *where*?"

Cal only grimaces, extending a hand toward the polished wood floor.

"Down."

A fireball explodes at our feet. It digs into the wood, charring the intricate designs and the solid base like a dog chewing through meat. The floor cracks in an instant, collapsing under us, and we fall to the room below, and then the next below that. My knees buckle beneath me, but Cal doesn't let me stumble, one hand holding my collar. Then he drags me, never loosening his grip, pulling us toward another window.

I don't need to be told what to do next.

Our flame and lightning shatter through the thick pane of glass, and we follow, leaping into what I think is thin air. Instead, we land hard, rolling onto one of the stone walkways. Farley follows, her momentum sending her right into a startled guard. Before he can react, she tosses him from the bridge. A sickening smack tells us his fall was not pleasant.

"Keep moving!" Cal growls, hoisting himself to his feet.

In a thunder of feet, we storm across the arched bridge, crossing from the Security Center to the royal palace of Ocean Hill. Smaller than Whitefire, but just as fearsome.

And just as familiar to Cal.

At the end of the walkway, a door starts to open, and I hear the shouts of more guards, more officers. A veritable firing squad. But instead of trying to fight, Cal slams against the door, his hands blazing. And welds it *shut.*

Farley balks, glancing between the blocked door and the walkway behind us. It looks like a trap, worse than a trap. "Cal — ?" she begins, fearful, but he ignores her.

Instead, he extends a hand to me. His eyes are like nothing I've ever seen. Pure flame, pure fire.

"I'm going to throw you," he says, not bothering to sugarcoat a word. Behind him, something shudders against the welded door.

I don't have time to argue, or even ask. My mind spins, poisoned by terror, but I take his wrist, and he grips mine. "Explode when you hit." He trusts me to know what he means.

With a grunt, he heaves, and I'm airborne, falling toward another window. It gleams, and I hope it isn't diamondglass. A split second before I find out, my sparks do as they're told. They obliterate the window in a shriek of glittering glass as I fall through, onto plush, golden carpeting. Stacks of books, a familiar smell of old leather and paper — the musty palace library. Farley slings through the windowpane next. Cal's aim is too perfect, and she lands right on top of me.

"Up, Mare!" she snaps, almost wrenching my arm out of my socket to get me on my feet. Her brain works faster than mine and she reaches the window first, her arms outstretched. I mirror her in a daze, my head spinning.

Above us, on the bridge, guards and officers flood from both ends. In the center, an inferno blazes. For a moment it seems still; then I realize. It's coming at us, leaping, lunging, *falling.*

Cal's flames extinguish a moment before he hits the wall — and misses the window ledge.

"Cal!" I scream, almost diving out myself.

His hand brushes through my own. For a heart-stopping second, I think I'm about to watch him die. Instead, he dangles, his other wrist firm in Farley's grip. She roars, her muscles flexing beneath her sleeves, somehow keeping two hundred pounds of prince from falling.

"Grab him!" she screams. Her knuckles are bone white.

I send a thunderbolt skyward, to the

bridge. To guards and guns all trained on Cal's form splayed out like an easy target. They cower, and pieces of the stone crack. Another, and it will collapse.

I want it to collapse.

"MARE!" Farley shrieks.

I have to reach, I have to pull. His hand finds mine, almost breaking my wrist with the effort. But we get him up as quickly as we can, dragging him over the ledge, and backward. Into disarming silence and a room full of harmless books.

Even Cal seems shocked by the ordeal. He lies for a second, eyes wide, breath heavy. "Thanks," he finally grinds out.

"Later!" Farley snarls. Like with me, she hoists him up. "Get us *out.*"

"Right."

But instead of heading to the ornate library entrance, he sprints across the room, to a wall of bookshelves. He searches for a moment, looking for something. Trying to remember. Then with a grunt, he shoulders a section of shelving until it *slides* sideways, opening onto a narrow, sloping passage.

"In!" he shouts, shoving me through.

My feet fly over the steps, worn by a hundred years of feet. We move in a gentle spiral, angling downward through dim light choked with dust. The walls are thick, old

330

stone, and if anyone's following us, I certainly can't hear them. I try to gauge where we are, but my inner compass spins too quickly. I don't know this place, I don't know where we're going. I can only follow.

The passage seems to dead-end at a stone wall, but before I can attempt to shock my way through, Cal pushes me back. "Easy," he says, laying one hand against a stone a bit more worn than the others. Slowly, he puts an ear to the wall, and listens.

I hear nothing but the blood pounding in my ears and our harried breathing. Cal hears more or, rather, less. His face falls, drawn into a somber expression I can't place. It's not fear, though he has every right to be afraid. If anything, he's oddly calm. He blinks a few times, straining to hear anything beyond the wall. I wonder how many times he's done this, how many times he snuck out of this very palace.

Back then, the guards were there to protect. To serve. Now they want to kill him.

"Stay on my heels," he finally whispers. "Two rights, then left to the gate yard."

Farley grits her teeth. "The gate yard?" She seethes. "You want to make this *easy* for them?"

"The yard is the only way out," he replies. "Ocean Hill's tunnels are closed."

She grimaces, clenching a fist. Her hands are starkly empty, her knife long gone. "Any chance there's an armory between here and there?"

"I wish," Cal hisses. Then he glances at me, at my hands. "We'll have to be enough."

I can only nod. *We've faced worse,* I tell myself.

"Ready?" he whispers.

My jaw tightens. "Ready."

The wall moves on a central axis, revolving smoothly. We press through together, trying to keep our footsteps from echoing in the passage beyond. Like the library, this place is empty and well furnished, dripping in lush, yellow-colored decor. All of it has an air of disuse and neglect, down to the faded golden tapestries. Cal almost lingers, staring at the color, but urges us on.

Two rights. Through another passage and an odd, double-ended closet. Heat radiates off Cal in waves, preparing for the firestorm he must become. I feel the same, the hairs on my arms rising with electricity. It almost crackles on the air.

Voices echo on the other side of the approaching door. Voices and footsteps.

"Immediate left," Cal murmurs. He starts to reach for my hand, but thinks better of it. We can't risk touching each other, not now, when our touch is deadly. "You *run.*"

Cal goes first, and the world beyond *pulses* with an expulsion of fire. It spreads across the massive entrance hall, over marble and rich carpet, until it crawls up the gilt walls. A tongue of flame licks up to a painting overlooking the hall. A giant portrait, newly made. The new king — *Maven.* He smirks like a gargoyle until the fire takes hold, burning at the canvas. The heat is too much, and his carefully drawn lips begin to melt, twisting into a snarl that suits his monstrous soul. The only thing untouched by the flames are two gold banners, dusty silk, hanging from the opposite wall. Who they belong to, I don't know.

The guards waiting for us flee, shouting, their flesh smoking. They're trying not to burn alive. Cal cuts through the fire, his footsteps leaving a safe path for us to follow, and Farley keeps close, sandwiched between us. She covers her mouth, trying not to breath in the smoke.

The officers who remain, nymphs or stoneskins, impervious to flame, are not so immune to me. This time, lightning races, splaying from me in a too-bright webwork of living electricity. I only have enough focus to keep Cal and Farley from the storm. The rest are not so lucky.

I'm a born runner, but my breath stings in my lungs. Each gasp is harder, more painful. I tell myself it's the smoke. But as I vault through the grand entrance of Ocean Hill, the pain doesn't disappear. It only changes.

We're surrounded.

Rows upon rows of officers in black, soldiers in gray, choke the gate yard. All armed, all waiting.

"Submit to arrest, Mare Barrow!" one of the officers shouts. A flowered vine twists around one arm, while the other holds a gun. "Submit to arrest, Tiberias Calore!" He stumbles over Cal's name, still reluctant to address a prince so informally. In any other situation, I would laugh.

Between us, Farley sets her feet. She has no weapon anymore, no shield, and she still refuses to kneel. Her strength is astounding.

"What now?" I whisper, knowing there is no answer.

Cal's eyes dart back and forth, looking for a solution he'll never find. Finally his eyes land on me. They are so empty. And so very alone.

Then a gentle hand closes around my wrist.

The world darkens, and I am squeezing through it, suffocated, confined, trapped for one long moment.

Shade.

I hate the sensation of teleporting, but in this moment, I relish it. Shade is all right. And we're alive. Suddenly, I'm on my knees, staring at the cobblestones of a dank alley far away from the Security Center, Ocean Hill, and the kill zone of officers.

Someone vomits nearby — Farley, judging by the sound. I suppose teleporting and having your head bounced off a window are a bad combination.

"Cal?" I ask the air, already cooling in the afternoon light. A low tremor of fear begins, the first ripple of a cold wave, but he answers from a few feet away.

"I'm here," he says, reaching out to touch my shoulder.

But instead of leaning into his hand, letting his now gentle warmth consume me, I pull away. With a groan, I get to my feet, only to see Shade standing over me. His expression is dark, pulled in anger, and I brace myself for a scolding. *I shouldn't have left him. It was wrong of me to do that.*

"I'm —" I begin the apology, but never get to finish. He crushes me into an embrace, wrapping his arms around my shoulders. I cling to him just as tightly. He trembles a little, still afraid for his little sister. "I'm fine," I tell him, so quietly only he can hear the lie.

"No time for that," Farley spits, forcing herself to her feet. She glances around, still off balance, but gauges our location. "Battle Garden's that way, a few streets east."

Wolliver. "Right." I nod, reaching out to hold her steady. We can't forget our mission here, even after that deadly debacle.

But I keep my eyes on Shade, hoping he knows what lies in my heart. He only shakes his head, dismissing the apology. Not because he won't accept it, but because he's too kind to want it.

"Lead on," he says, turning to Farley. His eyes soften a little, noting her dogged resolve to continue, despite her injuries and her nausea.

Cal is also slow to his feet, unaccustomed to teleportation. He recovers as quickly as he can, following us through the alleyways of the city sector known as Threestone. The smell of smoke clings to him, as does a deeper rage. Silvers died back in the Security Center, men and women who were only following orders. *His orders once.* It can't be an easy thing to stomach, but he must. If he wants to stay with us, with *me.* He must choose his side.

I hope he chooses ours. I hope I never

have to see that empty look in his eyes ever again.

This is a Red sector, relatively safe for the time being, and Farley keeps us to twisting alleys, even pulling us through an empty shop or two to avoid detection. Security officers shout and dart over the main roads, trying to regroup, trying to make sense of what happened at the Center. They're not looking for us here, not yet. They still don't realize what Shade is, how fast and far he can move us.

We huddle against a wall, waiting for an officer to pass us by. He's distracted, like all the others, and Farley keeps us to the shadows.

"I am sorry," I mutter to Shade, knowing I must say the words.

Again, he shakes his head. He even butts me gently with his crutch. "Enough of that. You did what you had to. And look, I'm all right. No harm done."

No harm done. Not to his body, but what about his mind? His heart? I betrayed him, my brother. *Like someone else I know.* I almost spit in anger, hoping to expel the thought that I have anything in common with Maven.

"Where's Crance?" I say, needing to focus on something else.

"I got him away from the Seaskulls; then he went his own way. Ran off like a man on fire." Shade's eyes narrow, remembering. "He buried three Mariners in the tunnels. He's got no place here anymore."

I know the feeling.

"What about you?" He jerks his head, vaguely gesturing in the direction of Ocean Hill. "After all that?"

After almost dying. Again.

"I said I'm okay."

Shade purses his lips, unsatisfied. "Right."

We lapse into a stiff silence, waiting for Farley to move again. She leans heavily against the alley wall, but soldiers on when a crowd of noisy schoolchildren passes ahead. We move again, using them as cover to cross the bigger road before entering another maze of back streets.

Finally we duck under a low arch — or rather, the others duck; I simply walk through. I'm barely to the other side when Shade stops short, his free hand reaching out to stop me from going forward.

"I'm sorry, Mare," he says, and his apology almost knocks me down again.

"*You're* sorry?" I ask, almost laughing at the absurdity. "Sorry for what?"

He doesn't answer, ashamed. A chill that has nothing to do with temperature runs through me as he steps back, allowing me to see past the mouth of the archway.

There's a square beyond, clearly meant for Red use. *Battle Garden.* It's plain but well maintained, with fresh greenery and gray stone statues of warriors all over. The one in the center is the largest, a rifle slung across his back, one dark arm extended into midair.

The statue's hand points east.

A rope dangles from the statue's hand.

A body swings from the rope.

The corpse is not naked, and wears no medallion of the Red Watch. He's young and short, his skin still soft. He was not executed long ago, probably an hour or so. But the square is clear of mourners and guards. No one is here to see him swing.

Even though the sandy hair falls into his eyes, obscuring some of his face, I know exactly who this boy is. I saw him in the records, smiling out from an ID photograph. Now he will never smile again. I knew this would happen. *I knew it.* But that doesn't make the pain, or the failure, any easier.

He is Wolliver Galt, a newblood, reduced to a lifeless corpse.

I weep for the boy I never knew, for the boy I was not fast enough to save.

Sixteen

I try not to remember the faces of the dead. Running for my life makes for an effective distraction, but even the constant threat of annihilation can't block out everything. Some losses are impossible to forget. Walsh, Tristan, and now Wolliver occupy the corners of my mind, catching like deep, gray cobwebs. My existence was their death sentence.

And of course, there are the ones I've killed outright, by choice, with my own two hands. But I don't grieve for them. I can't think about what I've done, not now. Not when we're still in so much danger.

Cal is the first to turn his back on Wolliver's swaying body. He has his own parade of dead faces, and doesn't want to add another ghost to the march. "We need to keep moving."

"No —" Farley leans hard against the wall. She presses a hand to her mouth, gulping in disgust, trying not to throw up again.

"Easy," Shade says, putting a steadying hand on her shoulder. She tries to wave him off, but he stands firm, watching her spit into the garden flowers. "We needed to see this," he adds, burning a righteous glare at Cal and me. "This is what happens when we fail."

His anger is justified. After all, we sparked a firefight in the heart of Harbor Bay, wasting the last hour of Wolliver's life, but I'm too tired to let him berate me.

"This isn't the place for a lesson," I reply. This is a grave, and even speaking here feels wrong. "We should take him down."

Before I can take a step toward Wolliver's corpse, Cal hooks one arm in mine, steering me in the opposite direction. "Nobody touch the body," he growls. He sounds so much like his father it shocks me.

"The body has a name," I snarl when I collect myself. "Just because his blood isn't your color doesn't mean we can leave him like that!"

"I'll get him," Farley grumbles, pushing off her knees.

Shade moves with her. "I'll help."

"Stop! Wolliver Galt had a family, didn't he?" Cal presses on. "Where are they?" He casts his free hand around at the garden, gesturing to the empty trees and shuttered windows looking down on us. Despite the distant echoes of a city marching on toward nightfall, the square is still and quiet. "Certainly his mother wouldn't leave him here alone? Are there no mourners? No officers to spit on his body? Not even a crow to pick his bones? *Why?*"

I know the answer.

A trap.

My grip tightens on Cal's arm, until my nails dig into his hot flesh threatening to burst into flame. Horror to match my own bleeds across Cal's face as he looks, not at me, but into the shadowed alleyway. Out of the corner of my eye, I catch sight of a crown — the one a foolish boy insists on wearing everywhere he goes.

And then, a clicking sound — like a metallic bug snapping its pincers, ready to devour a juicy meal.

"Shade," I whisper, extending my other hand toward my teleporting brother. He'll save us; he'll take us away from all of this.

He doesn't hesitate. He lunges.

But he never reaches me.

I watch in horror as a pair of swifts catch him under either arm, slamming him back against the ground. His head cracks against stone and his eyes roll. Dimly, I hear Farley scream as the swifts speed him away, their bodies blurring. They're at the main archway before I shoot a blast of lightning in their direction, forcing them to turn back. Pain bites up and down my arm, flashing white knives of heat. But there's nothing there but my own sparks, my own strength. It shouldn't hurt at all.

The clicking continues, echoing in my skull, faster with every second. I try to ignore it, try to fight, but my eyes dim. My vision spots, fading in and out with every tick. *What is this sound?* Whatever it is, it's tearing me apart.

Through the haze, I see two fires explode around me. One bright and burning, the other dark, a snake of smoke and flame. Somewhere, Cal roars in pain. *Run,* I think he says. I certainly try.

I end up crawling over the cobblestones, unable to see more than a few inches in front of me. Even that is difficult. *What is this, what is this, what is happening to me?*

Someone grabs me by the arm, their grip biting. I twist without seeing, reaching for where their neck should be. My fingers claw at armor, smoothly paneled and richly carved. "I've got her," says a voice I recognize. *Ptolemus Samos.* I can barely see his face. Black eyes, silver hair, skin the color of the moon.

With a shout, I pull together the strength I can, and slice at him with lightning. I scream as loudly as he does, clutching my arm as fire fills my insides. No, this isn't fire. I know what it is to be burned. This is something else.

A kick catches me in the stomach and I let it roll me. Over and over, until I'm facedown in the dirt of the garden, my face scraped and bleeding. The cool scent is a momentary balm, soothing me enough to let me see again. But when I open my eyes, I want nothing more than to go blind.

Maven crouches in front of me, his head tipped to one side, an inquisitive puppy with a toy. Behind him, battle rages. A very uneven one. With Shade incapacitated, and me in the dirt, only Cal and Farley remain. She has a gun now, but it's little use with Ptolemus deflecting bullets at every turn. At least Cal melts whatever gets close, burning away knives and vines as fast as he can. It can't last, though. They're cornered.

I almost scream. We escape one noose only to find another.

"Look at *me,* please."

Maven shifts, obstructing my view of the scene beyond. But I will not give him the satisfaction of my gaze. I won't look at him, for my own sake. Instead, I focus on the clicking sound, the one no one else seems to hear. It stabs with every passing second.

He grabs my jaw and yanks, forcing me to face him. "So stubborn." He tuts. "One of your most intriguing qualities. Along with this," he adds, drawing a finger through the red blood on my cheek.

Click.

His grip tightens, sending a firework of pain through my jawbone. The clicking makes everything hurt more, hurt deeper. Reluctantly, I meet familiar blue eyes and a pointed, pale face. To my horror, he is exactly as I remember him. Quiet, unassuming, a haunted boy. He is not the Maven of my nightmarish memories, a ghost of blood and shadows. He is real again. I recognize the determination in his eyes. I saw it on the deck of his father's boat, as we sailed downriver to Archeon, leaving the world in our wake. He kissed my lips then and promised that no one would hurt me.

"I said I would find you."

Click.

His hand moves from my jaw to my throat, squeezing. Enough to keep me silent, but not enough to stop me from breathing. His touch *burns*. I gasp, unable to summon enough air to scream.

Maven. You're hurting me. Maven, stop.

He is not his mother. He cannot read my thoughts. My vision spots again, darkening. Pinpoints of black swim before my eyes, expanding and contracting with every awful *click*.

"And I said I would save you."

I expect his grip to tighten. Instead, it remains constant. And his free hand reaches for my collarbone, one blazing palm against my skin. He is scorching me, *branding* me. I try to scream again, and barely get out a whimper.

"I am a man of my word." He tips his head again. "When I want to be."

Click. Click. Click.

My heart tries to match the rhythm, beating at a frenzy I won't survive, threatening to explode.

"Stop —" I manage to choke out, one hand reaching into thin air, wishing for my brother. But it is Maven who takes my hand in his, and that burns too. Every inch of me burns.

"That's enough," I think I hear him say, but not to me. "I said enough!"

His eyes seem to bleed, the last bright spots in my darkening world. Pale blue, streaking across my vision, drawing jagged lines of painful ice. They surround me, caging me. I feel nothing but the burn.

That's the last thing I remember before a white flash of light and sound splits my brain apart. And my entire world is pain.

It's too much of everything, and strangely nothing at all. No bullets, no knives, no fists or fire or strangling green vines. This is not a weapon I've ever faced before — because it's my own. Lightning, electricity, sparks, an overload beyond even my limits. I called up a storm once before in the Bowl of Bones, and it exhausted me. But this, whatever Maven has done, is *killing* me. Pulling me apart, nerve by nerve, splintering bone and ripping muscle. I am being obliterated inside my own skin.

Suddenly I realize — *Is this what they felt? The ones I killed? Is this what it feels like to die by lightning?*

Control. It's what Julian always told me. *Control it.* But this is too much. I am a dam trying to hold back an entire ocean. Even if I could stop what this is, I can't find a way past my own exploding pain. I can't reach out. I can't move. I'm trapped within myself, screaming behind my teeth. *I will be dead soon. And at least this will end.* But it doesn't. The pain stretches on in a constant assault on every sense. Pulsing but never ebbing, changing but never stopping. White spots, brighter than the sun, dance across my vision, until an explosion of red squeezes them out. I try to blink it away, to control *something* in myself, but nothing seems to happen. I wouldn't know if it did.

My skin must be gone by now, scorched away by the surging bolts. Perhaps I'll be given the mercy of bleeding to death. That will be quicker than this white abyss.

Kill me. The words repeat, over and over. It's the only thing I can say, the only thing I want now. All thoughts of newbloods and Maven, my brother and Cal and Kilorn are gone entirely. Even the faces that haunt me, the faces of the dead, have disappeared. Funny, now that I'm dying, my ghosts decide to leave.

I wish they would come back.

I wish I didn't have to die alone.

SEVENTEEN

"Kill me."

The words sear in my mouth, slashing past what must be a throat burned raw from screaming. I expect to taste blood — no, I expect nothing at all. I expect to be dead.

But as my senses return, I realize I am not stripped bare of flesh and bone. I am not even bleeding. I am whole, though I certainly don't feel it. With a burst of willpower, I force open my eyes. But instead of Maven or his executioners, I'm met with familiar green eyes.

"Mare."

Kilorn doesn't give me a chance to catch my breath. His arms circle my shoulders, pressing me into his chest, back into darkness. I can't help but flinch at the contact, remembering the feel of fire and lightning in my bones.

"It's all right," he murmurs. There's something so soothing about the way he speaks, his voice deep and shuddering. And he refuses to let me go, even when I involuntarily shrink away. He knows what my heart wants, even if my frayed nerves can't handle it. "It's over, you're all right. You're back."

For a moment, I don't move, curling my fingers into the folds of his old shirt. I focus on him, so I don't have to feel myself shaking. "Back?" I whisper. "Back where?"

"Let her breathe, Kilorn."

Another hand, so warm it can only be Cal's, takes my arm. He holds on tightly, the pressure careful and controlled, enough for me to focus on. It helps the rest of me swim out of the nightmare, fully returning to the real world. I lean back slowly, away from Kilorn, so I can see exactly what I'm waking up to.

We're underground, judging by the damp, earthy smell, but this isn't another one of Farley's tunnels. We're far out of Harbor Bay, if my electrical sense is any indication. I can't feel a single pulse, meaning we must be well away from the city. This is a safe house, dug right into the ground, camouflaged by forest and design. Red-made, no doubt, probably used by the Scarlet Guard, and everything looks faintly pinkish. The walls and floor are packed dirt, and the slanting roof is sod, reinforced by rusted metal poles. There's no decoration; in fact, there's barely anything in here at all. A few sleeper sacks, my own included, ration packs, a switched-off lantern, and a few crates of supplies from the airjet are all I can see. My Stilts home was a palace compared to this, but I'm not complaining. I sigh in relief, happy to be out of danger and away from my blinding pain.

Kilorn and Cal let me blink around at the sparse room, allowing me to come to my own conclusions. They look haggard with worry, transformed into old men in the span of a few hours. I can't help but stare at their dark-circled eyes and deep frowns, wondering what wounded them in this way. Then I remember. The light slanting in from the narrow windows is red-orange and the air has gone cold. Night is coming. The day is over. And we have lost. Wolliver Galt is dead, a newblood to Maven's slaughter. Ada too, for all I know. I failed them both.

"Where's the jet?" I ask, trying to stand. But they both reach out to stop me, keeping me firmly wrapped into my sleeper. They're surprisingly gentle, as if one touch might break me apart.

Kilorn knows me best, and is the first to note my annoyance. He sits back on his heels, giving me some space. He glances at Cal before begrudgingly nodding his head, allowing the prince to explain.

"We couldn't fly long with you in the . . . state you were in," he says, averting his eyes from my face. "Got a few dozen miles before you set the jet off like an overloaded lightbulb, damn near fried the thing. We had to stagger our flights, and then set out on foot, hide in the woods until you were better."

"Sorry" is all I can think to say, but he waves it off.

"You opened your eyes, Mare. That's all that matters to me," Cal says.

A wave of exhaustion threatens to take me down, and I debate letting it. But then Cal's touch moves from my arm, finding my neck. I jump at the sensation, turning to stare at him with wide, questioning eyes. But he focuses on my skin, on something there. His fingers trace strange, jagged, branching lines on my neck, reaching down my spine. I'm not the only one who notices.

"What is that?" Kilorn growls. His glare would make Queen Elara proud.

My hand joins Cal's, feeling the peculiarity. Ragged streaks, big ones winding down the back of my neck. "I don't know what it is."

"They look like —" Cal hesitates, running a finger down a particularly thick ridge. It shivers my insides. "Scars, Mare. Lightning scars."

I pull out of his touch as quickly as I can and force myself to my feet. To my surprise, I wobble on stupidly weak legs, and Kilorn is there to catch me. "Take it easy," he chides, never letting go of my wrists.

"What happened in Harbor Bay? What did — what did Maven do to me? It was him, wasn't it?" The image of a black crown burns in my mind, deep as a brand. And the new scars are just that. *Brands. His marks on me.* "He killed Wolliver and set a trap for us. And *why* do you look so pink?"

Like always, Kilorn laughs at my anger. But the sound is hollow, forced, more for my benefit than his. "Your eye," he says, brushing a finger over my left cheekbone. "You burst a vessel."

He's right, I realize as I close one eye, then the other. The world is drastically different through the left, tinged red and pink by swirling clouds of what can only be blood. The pain of Maven's torture did this too.

Cal doesn't stand up with the rest of us, and instead leans back on his hands. I suspect he knows my knees are still shaking, and that I'll drop back down soon enough. He has a way of knowing things like that, and it makes me so very angry.

"Yes, Maven slipped into Harbor Bay," he answers, all business. "He didn't make a fuss, so we wouldn't know, and he went for the first newblood he could find."

I hiss at the memory. Wolliver was only eighteen, guilty of nothing but being born different. Guilty of being like *me*.

What could he have been? I wonder, mourning for the soldier we have lost. *What ability did he wield?*

"All Maven had to do was wait," Cal continues, and a muscle in his cheek clenches. "They would've captured us all if not for Shade. He got us out, even with a concussion. It took a few jumps and too many close calls, but he came through."

I exhale slowly, relieved. "Is Farley all right? Shade?" I ask. Cal dips his head, nodding. "And I'm alive."

Kilorn's grip tightens. "How, I don't know."

I raise a hand to my collarbone and the skin beneath my shirt twinges with pain. While the rest of my nightmare, the other horrors inflicted on my body, are gone, Maven's brand is very real.

"It was painful, what it did to you?" Cal asks, causing Kilorn to sneer.

"Her first words in four days were 'kill me,' in case you've forgotten," he snaps, though Cal doesn't flinch. "Of course whatever that machine did was painful."

The clicking sound. "A machine?" I blanch, looking between the two young men. "Wait, *four days*? I've been out for that long?"

Four days asleep. Four days of nothing. Panic chases away all my lingering thoughts of pain, shooting through my veins like icy water. *How many died while I was trapped in my own head? How many hang from trees and statues now?* "Please tell me you haven't been babysitting me all this time. Please tell me you've been doing *something.*"

Kilorn laughs. "I would consider keeping you alive a very big *something.*"

"I mean —"

"I know what you mean," he retorts, finally putting a little distance between us.

With what little dignity I have left, I sit back down on the sleeper and fight the urge to grumble.

"No, Mare, we haven't just been sitting around." Kilorn turns to the wall, leaning against the packed earth so he can see out the window. "We're doing quite a bit."

"They kept hunting." It isn't a question, but Kilorn nods anyways. "Even Nix?"

"The little bull comes in handy," Cal says,

touching the shadow of a bruise on his jaw. He knows Nix's strength firsthand. "And he's quite good at the convincing part. Ada too."

"Ada?" I say, surprised at the mention of what should be another newblood corpse. "Ada Wallace?"

Cal nods. "After Crance slipped the Sea-skulls, he got her out of Harbor Bay. Lifted her right from the governor's mansion before Maven's men stormed the place. They were waiting at the jet when we got there."

As happy as I am to hear of her survival, I can't help but feel a sting of anger. "So you threw her right back to the wolves. Her and Nix both." My fist clenches around the fuzzy warmth of my sleeper, trying to find some comfort. "Nix is a fisherman; Ada's a housemaid. How could you put them in such terrible danger?"

Cal lowers his eyes, shamed by my scolding. But Kilorn chuckles at the window, turning his face into the waning light of sunset. It bathes him in deep red, as if he's been coated in blood. It's just my wounded eye playing tricks, but still the sight gives me chills. His laughter, his usual dismissal of my fears, frighten me most of all.

Even now, the fish boy takes nothing seriously. He'll laugh his way into his grave.

"Something funny to you?"

"You remember that duckling Gisa brought home?" he replies, catching us all off guard. "She was nine maybe, and took it from its mother. Tried to feed it soup —" He cuts himself off, trying to smother another chuckle. "You remember, don't you, Mare?" Despite his smile, his eyes are hard and pressing, trying to make me understand.

"Kilorn," I sigh. "We don't have time for this."

But he continues on undaunted, pacing. "It wasn't long until the mother came. A few hours maybe, until she was circling around the bottom of the house, her other ducklings in tow. Made a real racket, all the quacking and squawking. Bree and Tramy tried to run it off, didn't they?" I remember just as well as Kilorn does. Watching from the porch while my brothers threw rocks at the mother bird. She stood firm, calling to her lost child. And the duckling replied, squirming in Gisa's arms. "Finally, you made Gisa give the little thing back. 'You are not a duck, Gisa,' you said. 'You two don't belong together.' And then you gave the duckling back to its mother, and watched them all scramble away. Ducks in a row, back to the river."

"I'm waiting to hear a point in all this."

"There is one," Cal murmurs, his voice reverberating deep in his chest. He sounds almost surprised.

Kilorn's eyes flicker to the prince, giving him the slightest nod of thanks. "Nix and Ada are not ducklings, and you are certainly not their mother. They can handle themselves." Then he grins crookedly, falling back to his old jokes. "You, on the other hand, look a bit worse for the wear."

"Don't I know it." I try to smile for him, just a little, but something about smiling pulls the skin on my face, which in turn twists my neck and the new scars there. They ache when I speak, and smart terribly under any more strain. *Another thing Maven has taken away.* How happy it must make him, to think I can no longer smile without searing pain. "Farley and Shade are with them, at least?"

The boys nod in unison, and I almost giggle at the sight. They are normally like opposites. Kilorn is lean where Cal is burly. Kilorn is golden-haired and green-eyed while Cal is dark with a gaze like living fire. But here, in the waning light, behind the film of blood clouding my gaze, they start to seem alike.

"Crance too," Cal adds.

I blink, perplexed. "Crance? He's here? He's . . . *with us*?"

"Not like he had anywhere else to go," Cal says.

"And you . . . you trust him?"

Kilorn leans against the wall, stuffing his hands in his pockets. "He saved Ada, and he's helped bring back others in the past few days. Why shouldn't we trust him? Because he's a thief?"

Like me. Like I was. "Point taken." Even so, I can't forget the high cost of misplaced faith. "But we can't be sure, can we?"

"You're not sure of anyone," Kilorn sighs, annoyed. He scuffs his shoe in the dirt, wanting to say more, knowing he shouldn't.

"He's out with Farley now. Not a bad scout," Cal adds in support. Of Kilorn. I'm almost in shock.

"Are you two agreeing on something? What world am I waking up in?"

A true smile splits Cal's face, as well as Kilorn's.

"He's not as bad as you make him out to be," Kilorn says, nodding at the prince.

Cal laughs. A soft noise, tainted by all that came before. "Likewise."

I prod at Cal's shoulder, just to make sure he's solid. "I guess I'm not dreaming."

"Thank my colors, you're not," Cal murmurs, his smile gone again. He runs a hand along his jaw, scratching through a slim beard. He hasn't shaved since Archeon, since the night he watched his father die. "Ada's more useful than the outlaws, if you can believe it."

"I can." A swirl of abilities flashes through my mind, each one more powerful than the last. "What does she do?"

"Nothing I've ever seen before," he admits. His bracelet crackles, throwing off sparks that soon turn into a twisting ball of flame. It idles in his hand a moment, never burning his sleeve, before he lazily tosses it to the small pit dug in the middle of the floor. The fire throws off heat and light, replacing the setting sun. "She's smart, incredibly so. Remembers every word in every book in the governor's library."

And just like that, my vision of another warrior is snuffed out. "Helpful," I bite out. "I'll be sure to ask her to tell us a story later on."

"Told you she wouldn't get it," Kilorn says.

But Cal presses on. "She has perfect memory, perfect intelligence. Every moment of every day, every face she's ever seen, every word she's ever overheard she *remem-*

bers. Every medical journal or history book or map she's ever read, she understands. The same goes for practical lessons, too."

As much as I'd prefer a storm wielder, I can understand the value of a person like this. If only Julian was here. He'd spend day and night studying Ada, trying to understand such a strange ability. "Practical lessons? You mean like Training?"

Something like pride crosses Cal's face. "I'm no instructor, but I'm doing what I can to teach her. She's already a pretty decent shot. And she finished the Blackrun flight manual this morning."

A gasp escapes my lips. "She can fly the jet?"

Cal shrugs, lips curling into a smirk. "She flew the others to Cancorda, and should be back soon. But until then, you should rest."

"I've rested for four days. *You* rest," I fire back, reaching over to shake his shoulder. He doesn't budge under my admittedly weak shove. "You both look like the walking dead."

"Someone had to make sure you kept breathing." Kilorn's tone is light, and another might think him joking, but I know better. "Whatever Maven did to you can't happen again."

The memory of white-hot pain is still too

near for me. I can't help but flinch at the thought of going through it once more. "I agree."

It sobers us all, the thought of what new power Maven holds. Even Kilorn, always twitching or pacing, is still. He glares out the window, at the wall of oncoming night. "Cal, you got any ideas in case she runs into that thing again?"

"If I'm going to get a lecture, I might need some water," I say, suddenly aware of my parched throat. Kilorn all but jumps from his place at the wall, eager to help. Leaving me alone with Cal, and the heat closing in.

"I think it was a sounder device. Modified, of course," Cal says. His eyes stray back to my neck, to the lightning bolt scars marching up and down my spine. With shocking familiarity, he traces them again, as if they hold some clue. The intelligent part of me wants to push him away, to stop the fire prince from examining my brands, but exhaustion and need overrule any other thoughts. His touch is soothing, physically and emotionally. It's proof that someone else is with me. I am not alone in the abyss anymore.

"We dabbled with sounders on the lakes a few years ago. They spit out radio waves, and wreaked havoc with the Lakelander ships. Made it impossible for them to communicate with each other, but it did the same to us. Everyone had to sail blind." His fingers trail lower, following one gnarled branch of scar tissue across my shoulder blade. "I suppose this one throws off electrical waves, or static, in great magnitude. Enough to incapacitate you, to make *you* blind, and turn your lightning against you."

"They built it so quickly. It's only been a few days since the Bowl of Bones," I murmur back. Anything louder than a whisper might shatter this fragile peace.

Cal's hand stills, his palm flat against my bare skin. "Maven turned against you long before the Bowl of Bones."

I know that now. I know it with every bleeding breath. Something releases in me, breaking, bending my back so I can bury my face in my hands. Whatever wall I put up to keep the memories out is steadily crumbling into dust. But I can't let it bury me. I can't let the mistakes I've made bury me. When Cal's warmth wraps around me, his arms around my shoulders, his head tucked against my neck, I lean into him. I let him protect me, though we swore we wouldn't do this back in the cells of Tuck. We are nothing more than distractions for each other, and distractions get you killed. But my hands close over his, our fingers lacing, until our bones are woven together. The fire is dying, flames reduced to embers. But Cal is still here. He will never leave me.

"What did he say to you?" he whispers.

I draw back a little, so he can see. With a shaking hand, I pull on the collar of my shirt, showing him what Maven did. His eyes widen when they land on the brand. A ragged *M* burned into my skin. For a long time, he stares, and I fear his anger might set me on fire again.

"He said he was a man of his word," I tell him. The words are enough to draw his gaze away from my newest scar. "That he would always find me — and save me." I bark out an empty laugh. *The only person Maven has to save me from is himself.*

With gentle hands, Cal pulls my shirt back into place, hiding his brother's mark. "We knew that already. At least now we truly know why."

"Hmm?"

"Maven lies as easily as he breathes, and his mother holds his leash, but not his heart." Cal's eyes widen, imploring me to understand. "He's hunting newbloods not to protect his throne but to hurt you. To find *you.* To make you come back to him." His fist clenches on his thigh. "Maven wants you more than anything else on this earth."

Would that Maven were here now, so I could rip out his horrible, haunting eyes. "Well, he can't have me." I realize the consequences of this, and so does Cal.

"Not even if it stops the killing? Not for the newbloods?"

Tears bite my eyes. "I won't go back. For anyone."

I expect his judgment, but instead he smiles and ducks his head. Ashamed of his own reaction, as I am of mine.

"I thought we would lose you." His words are deliberately chosen, carefully made. So I lean forward, putting a hand on his fist. It's all the assurance he needs to press on. "I thought *I* was going to lose you. So many times."

"But I'm still here," I say.

He takes my neck in his hands like he doesn't believe me. I'm dimly reminded of Maven's grip, but fight the urge to flinch. I don't want Cal to pull away.

I have been running for so long. Since before all this even started. Even back in the Stilts, I was a runner. Avoiding my family, my fate, anything I didn't want to feel. And I am still racing now. From those who would kill me — and those who would love me.

I want so badly to stop. I want to stand still without killing myself or someone else. But that is not possible. I must keep going, I must hurt myself to save myself, hurt others to save others. Hurt Kilorn, hurt Cal, hurt Shade and Farley and Nix and everyone stupid enough to follow me. I'm making them runners too.

"So we fight him." Cal's lips move closer, hot with each word. His grip tightens, like any second someone is going to come and take me from him. "That's what we set out to do, so we do it. We build an army. And we kill him. Him and his mother both."

Killing a king will change nothing. Another will take his place. But it is a start. If we cannot outrun Maven, we must stop him cold. For the newbloods. For Cal. For me.

I am a weapon made of flesh, a sword covered in skin. I was born to kill a king, to end a reign of terror before it can truly begin. Fire and lightning raised Maven up, and fire and lightning will bring him down.

"I won't let him hurt you again."

His breath makes me shiver. A strange sensation, when surrounded with such blazing warmth. "I believe you," I tell him, lying.

Because I am weak, I turn in his arms. Because I am weak, I press my lips to his,

366

searching for something to make me stop running, to make me forget. We are both weak, it seems.

As his hands run over my skin, I feel a different sort of pain. Worse than Maven's machine, deeper than my nerves. It aches like a hollow, like an empty weight. I am a sword, born of lightning, of this fire — and of Maven's. One already betrayed me, and the other might leave at any moment. But I do not fear a broken heart. I do not fear pain.

I cling to Cal, Kilorn, Shade, to saving all the newbloods I can, because I am afraid of waking up to emptiness, to a place where my friends and family are gone and I am nothing but a single bolt of lightning in the blackness of a lonely storm.

If I am a sword, I am a sword made of glass, and I feel myself beginning to shatter.

EIGHTEEN

The thing with heat is, no matter how cold you are, no matter how much you need warmth, it always, eventually, becomes too much. I remember many winters spent with the window cracked open, letting in the blistering cold to combat the fire burning in the family room below. Something about the icy air helped me sleep. And now deep gasps of an autumn breeze help me to calm down, help me forget Cal alone back in the safe house. *I should not have done that,* I think, pressing a hand to my fevered skin. He is not only a distraction I can't afford but a heartbreak waiting to happen. His allegiances are shaky at best. One day he will leave, or die, or betray me like so many others have. One day, he will hurt me.

Overhead, the sun has completely set, painting the sky in darkening streaks of red and orange. *Maybe.* I can't trust the colors I see. I can't trust in much of anything anymore.

The safe house is built into the crest of a hill, in the middle of a large clearing surrounded by forest. It overlooks a winding valley full of trees, lakes, and constant, swirling mist. I grew up in the woods, but this place is as alien to me as Archeon or the Hall of the Sun. There's nothing man-made as far as the eye can see, no echo of a logging village or farm town. Though I suppose there's a runway hidden nearby, if the jet can still be used. We must be deep into the Nortan backcountry, north and inland from Harbor Bay. I don't know the Regent State well, but this looks like the Greatwoods region, dominated by wilderness, rolling green mountains, and a frozen tundra border with the Lakelands. It's sparsely populated, gently governed by the shivers of House Gliacon — and a marvelous place to hide.

"You finished with him?"

Kilorn is little more than a shadow, leaning against the trunk of an oak with sky-splayed branches. There's a water jug forgotten by his feet. I don't need to see his face to know he's upset. I can hear it just fine.

"Don't be unkind." I'm used to ordering him around, but this sounds like a request. As I expected, he ignores me, and keeps rambling.

"I guess all rumors do have a grain of truth. Even the ones that little snit Maven spits out. 'Mare Barrow seduced the prince into killing the king.' It's shocking to know he's half-right." He takes a few prowling steps forward, reminding me very much of an Iral silk creeping in for a final blow. "Because the prince is most certainly bewitched."

"If you keep talking, I'm going to turn you into a battery."

"You should get some new threats," he says, smiling sharply. He's gotten used to my big talk over the years, and I doubt I could scare him with anything, even my lightning. "He's a powerful man, in every form of the word. Don't get me wrong, I'm glad you're holding his reins."

I can't help but scoff aloud, laughing in his face. "Glad? You're jealous, plain and simple. You're not used to *sharing*. And you don't like being useless."

Useless. The word stings. I can tell by the twitch in his neck. But it doesn't stop him from towering over me, his height blocking out the stars winking to life above us.

"The question is, are you under a spell too? Is he using you the same way you're using him?"

"I'm not using anyone." A lie, and we both know it. "And you don't know what you're talking about."

"You're right," he says quietly.

Surprise almost knocks me off my feet. In more than ten years of friendship, I have never heard those words from Kilorn Warren. He's stubborn as a tree stump, too self-assured for his own good, a smarmy bastard most of the time — but now, on this hilltop, he is nothing he ever was. He seems small and dim, a glimmer of my old life steadily flickering into nothing. I clasp my hands together to keep from reaching out and touching him, to prove that Kilorn still exists.

"I don't know what happened to you when you were Mareena. I wasn't there to help you through that. I won't tell you that I understand, or that I'm sorry for you. That's not what you need."

But it's exactly what I want, so I can be angry with him. So I don't have to listen to what he's about to say. Too bad Kilorn knows me better than that.

"The best thing I can do is tell you the truth, or at least, what I *think* is the truth." Though his voice is steady, his shoulders rise and fall with deep, heaving breaths. *He's scared.* "It'll be up to you to believe me or not."

A twitch pulls at my lips, betraying a painful smile. I'm so used to being pushed and pulled, manipulated into thinking and doing by those closest to me. Even Kilorn is guilty of that. But now he's giving me the freedom I've wanted for so long. A choice, small as it may be. He trusts that I have the sense to choose — even if I don't.

"I'm listening."

He starts to say something else, then stops himself. The words stick, refusing to come out. And for a second, his green eyes look strangely wet.

"What, Kilorn?" I sigh.

"What," he echoes, shaking his head. After a long second, something snaps in him. "I know you don't feel the same way I do. About us."

I'm seized by the urge to smash my head against a rock. *Us.* It feels stupid to talk about, a foolish waste of time and energy. But more than that, it's embarrassing and uncomfortable. My cheeks flame red. This is not a conversation I ever wanted to have with him.

"And that's fine," he presses on before I can stop him. "You never saw me the way I see you, not even at home, before all this happened. I thought you might one day, but —" He shrugs his shoulders. "It's just not in you to love me."

When I was Mare Barrow of the Stilts, I thought the same way. I wondered what would happen if I survived conscription, and saw what that future held. A friendly marriage to the fish boy with green eyes, children we could love, a poor stilt home. It seemed like a dream back then, an impossibility. And it still is. It always will be. I do not love Kilorn, not the way he wants me to. I never will.

"Kilorn," I murmur, taking a step toward him. But he takes two back. "Kilorn, you're my best friend, you're like family."

His smile bleeds sadness. "And I will be, until the day I die."

I do not deserve you, Kilorn Warren. "I'm sorry," I choke out, not knowing what else I can say. I don't even know what I'm apologizing for.

"It's not something you can control, Mare," he replies, still standing so far away. "We can't choose who we love. I wish, more than anything, that we could."

I feel cracked open. My skin still runs hot from Cal's embrace, remembering the feel of him only moments ago. But in the deepest part of me, in spite of every fiber of my being, I think beyond the clearing, to ice-colored eyes, an empty promise, and a kiss aboard a boat.

"You can love him all you want, I won't stop you. But for my sake, for your parents, for the rest of us, please don't let him *control* you."

Again, I think of Maven. But Maven is far away, a shadow on the sharp edges of the world. He might be trying to kill me, but he can't control me, not anymore. Kilorn can only mean the other royal brother, the fallen son of House Calore. *Cal.* My shield against the scars and the nightmares. But he's a warrior, not a politician or a criminal. He doesn't have the ability to manipulate anyone, least of all me. It's just not in his nature.

"He's Silver, Mare. You don't know what he's capable of, or what he really wants."

I doubt Cal does either. The exiled prince is even more adrift than I am, without any allegiance or allies beyond a temperamental lightning girl. "He's not what you think he is," I say. "No matter what color his blood may be."

A sneer razors across his face, thin and sharp. "You don't really believe that."

"I don't believe," I say sadly. "I know. And it makes everything harder."

Once, I thought blood was the world entire, the difference between dark and light, an irrevocable, impassable divide. It made the Silvers powerful and cold and brutal, inhuman compared to my Red brethren. They were nothing like us, unable to feel pain or remorse or kindness. But people like Cal, Julian, and even Lucas have shown me how wrong I was. They are just as human, just as full of fear and hope. They are not without their sins, but neither are we. Neither am I.

If only they were the monsters Kilorn believes them to be. If only things were that simple. Quietly, in the deepest part of my heart, I envy Kilorn's narrow anger. I wish I could share in his ignorance. But I've seen and suffered too much for that.

"We're going to kill Maven. And his mother," I add with chilling assurance. *Kill the ghost, kill the shadow.* "If they die, the newbloods will be safe."

"And Cal will be free to reclaim his throne. To make everything as it was."

"That won't happen. No one would let him back on the throne, Red *or* Silver. And from what I can tell, he doesn't want it."

"Really?" I immediately hate the smirk twisting Kilorn's lips. "Whose idea was it? To kill Maven?" When I don't answer, the smirk grows. "That's what I thought."

"Thank you for your honesty, Kilorn."

My gratitude takes him aback, surprising him as much as he surprised me. We have both changed in the past few months, no longer the girl and boy from the Stilts ready to tussle over any topic — and *every* topic. They were children, and they are gone forever.

"I'll keep what you said in mind, of course." My Lessons have never felt so close, helping me know how to dismiss Kilorn without hurting him. As a princess would a servant.

But Kilorn is not so easily cast aside. His eyes narrow into dark green slits, seeing right through my mask of courtesy. He looks so disgusted I expect him to spit. "One day soon you're going to get lost," he breathes. "And I won't be there to lead you back."

I turn my back on my oldest friend. His words sting, and I don't want to hear them, no matter how much sense he makes. His boots crunch over the hard earth as he stalks off, leaving me to stand and stare at the woods. In the distance, an airjet hums, returning to us.

I fear being alone more than anything else. So why do I do this? Why do I push away the people I love? What is so very wrong with me?

I don't know.

And I don't know how to make it stop.

Gathering an army is the easy part. The records from Harbor Bay lead us to new-bloods in towns and villages across the Beacon region, from Cancorda to Taurus to the half-flooded ports of the Bahrn Islands. Because of Julian's list, we expand out, until every part of Norta is within our grasp. Even Delphie, the southernmost city in the kingdom, is just a few hours away by jet.

Every population center, no matter how small, has a new garrison of Silver officers meant to catch us and turn us over to the king. But they can't guard every target at all times, and Maven is not yet strong enough in his reign to kidnap hundreds overnight. We strike randomly, without pattern, and we usually catch them off balance. Sometimes we get lucky, and they don't even know we're there at all. Shade proves his use time and again, as do Ada and Nix. Her abilities help us find our way around city walls — his help us go right through them.

But it always comes down to me. I am always the one to confront each newblood, to explain what they are and what kind of danger they pose to the king. Then they are given a choice, and they always choose to live. They always choose us. We give safe passage to their families, directing the ones left behind to the various sanctuaries and bases operated by the Scarlet Guard. *To Command,* as Farley says, her words more cryptic every time. A few are even sent to Tuck Island, to seek the safety of the Colonel. He might hate newbloods, but Farley assures me he won't turn away true Reds.

The newbloods we find are afraid, some angry, but a few are surprised, usually the children. For the most part, they don't know what they are. But some do, and they are already haunted by the mutations of our blood.

On the outskirts of the city of Haven, we meet Luther Carver. A young boy of eight with wispy black hair, small for his age, the son of a carpenter. We find him in his father's workshop, excused from school to learn the trade. It takes very little convincing to get Mr. Carver to let us in, though he eyes Cal and even Nix with suspicion. And the boy refuses to look me in the eye, his tiny fingers twitching with nerves. He trembles when I speak to him, and insists on calling me lightning girl.

"Your name is on this list because you are special, because you are different," I tell him. "Do you know what I'm talking about?"

The boy shakes his head violently, his long bangs swiping to and fro. But his aptly named father stands like a guardian at his back. Solemnly, slowly, he nods his head.

"It's all right, Luther, it's nothing to be ashamed of." I reach across the table, past intricate designs that are certainly Carver's handiwork. But Luther's fingers ghost away from my touch and he pulls his hands into his lap, squirming out of my reach.

"It's nothing personal," Carver says, putting a soothing hand on his son's shoulder. "Luther's not — he just doesn't want to cause you any harm. It comes and goes — it's getting worse, you see. But you're going to help him, aren't you?" The poor man sounds pained, his voice cracking. My heart goes out to him, and I wonder what my father would be like in such a position. Faced by people who understand your child, who can help — but must take him away from you. "You know why he is this way?"

It's a question I've asked myself many times, a question almost every newblood asks of me. But still I have no answer. "I'm sorry but I don't, sir. We only know that our abilities come from a mutation, something in our blood that can't be explained."

I think of Julian and his books, his research. He never got to teach me about the Divide, the ancient moment when silver blood split from red, only that it happened and resulted in the world now. I suppose a new Divide has begun, in blood like mine. He was studying me before his capture, trying to figure out the answer to this exact question. But he never got the chance.

Cal shifts at my side, and when he rounds the table, I expect to see the intimidating mask he keeps so close. Instead, he smiles kindly, so wide it almost reaches his eyes. Then he bends, kneeling down so he can look Luther in the eye. The boy is transfixed by the sight, overwhelmed not just by the presence of a prince but by his undivided attention.

"Your Highness," he squeaks, even trying to salute. At his back, his father is not so proper, and his brow furrows. Silver princes are not his favorite guests.

Still, Cal's grin deepens, and his eyes remain on the boy. "Please, call me Cal," he says, and extends his hand. Again, Luther pulls away, but Cal doesn't seem to mind. In fact, I'll wager he expected it.

Luther flushes, his cheeks pulsing a dark and lovely red. "Sorry."

"Not at all," Cal replies. "In fact, I used to do the same thing when I was little. A bit younger than you, but then, I had very, very many teachers. I needed them, too," he adds, winking. In spite of his fear, the boy smiles a little. "But you just have your dad, don't you?"

The boy swallows, his tiny throat bobbing. Then he nods.

"I try —" Carver says, again gripping his son's shoulder.

"We understand, sir," I tell him. "More than anyone."

Luther nudges Cal with his shoe, his curiosity overcoming all else. "What could make *you* afraid?"

Before our eyes, Cal's outstretched palm bursts into hot, roiling flame. But it is strangely beautiful, a slow burn of languid, dancing fire. Yellow and red, lazy in movement. If not for the heat, it would seem an artistry instead of a weapon. "I didn't know how to control it," Cal says, letting it play between his fingers. "I was afraid of burning people. My father, my friends, my —" His voice almost sticks. "My little brother. But I learned to make it do as I wished, to keep it from hurting the people I wanted to stay safe. So can you, Luther."

While the boy stares, transfixed, his father

is not so certain. But he is not the first parent we've faced, and I am prepared for his next question. "What you call newbloods? They can do this too? They can — control what they are?"

My own hands web with sparks, each one a twisting purple bolt of perfect light. They disappear into my skin, leaving no trace. "Yes, we can, Mr. Carver."

With surprising speed, the man retrieves a pot from a shelf, and sets it in front of his son. A plant, maybe a fern, sprouts from the dirt within. Any other would be confused, but Luther knows exactly what his father wants. "Go on, boy," he prods, his voice kind and gentle. "Show them what needs fixing."

Before I can bristle at the turn of phrase, Luther holds out one trembling hand. His finger grazes the edge of the fern leaf, careful but sure. Nothing happens.

"It's okay, Luther," Mr. Carver says. "You can let them see."

The boy tries again, his brow furrowing in concentration. This time, he takes the fern by the stem, holding it in his small fist. And slowly, the fern curls beneath his touch, turning black, folding into itself — dying. As we watch, transfixed, Mr. Carver grabs something else from the back shelf and sets it in his son's lap. Leather gloves.

"You take good care of him," he says. His teeth clench, shutting tight against the storm inside his heart. "You promise me that."

Like all true men, he doesn't flinch when I shake his hand.

"I give you my word, Mr. Carver."

Only when we're back at the safe house, which we're starting to call the Notch, do I allow myself a moment alone. To think, to tell myself the lie was well made. I cannot truly promise this boy, or the others like him, will survive what is to come. But I certainly hope he does, and I will do everything I can to make it so.

Even if this boy's terrifying ability is death itself.

The newbloods' families aren't the only ones to flee. The Measures have made life worse than ever before, driving many Reds into the forests and frontiers, seeking a place where they won't be worked to death or hanged for stepping out of line. Some come within a few miles of our camp, winding north toward a border already painted with autumn snow. Kilorn and Farley want to help them, to give them food or medicine, but Cal and I overrule their pleas. No one can know about us, and the Reds marching on are no different, despite their fate. They will keep heading north, until they meet the Lakelander border. Some will be pressed into the legions holding the line. Others might be lucky enough to slip through, to succumb to cold and starvation in the tundra rather than a bullet in the trenches.

My days blend into each other. Recruitment, training, repeat. All that changes is the weather, as winter grows closer. Now when I wake up, long before dawn, the ground is coated in thick frost. Cal has to heat the airjet himself, freeing wheels and gears coated in ice. Most days he comes with us, flying the jet to whatever newblood we've chosen. But sometimes he stays behind, electing to teach rather than fly. Ada replaces him on those days, and is just as good a pilot as he is, having learned with lightning speed and precision. And her knowledge of Norta, of everything from drainage systems to supply routes, is astounding. I can't begin to fathom how her brain can hold so much, and still have room for so much more. She is a wonder to me, just like every newblood we find.

Almost everyone is different, with strange abilities beyond what any known Silver can do, or what I could even imagine. Luther continues his careful attempts to control his ability, shriveling everything from flowers to saplings. Cal thinks he can use his power to heal himself, but we've yet to find out. Another newblood, an old woman who has everyone call her Nanny, seems to be able to change her physical appearance. She gave us all quite a fright when she decided to waltz through the camp disguised as Queen Elara. Despite her age, I hope to use her in recruitment soon enough. She proves herself as best she can in Cal's training, learning to fire a gun and use a knife with the rest. Of course, this all makes for a very noisy campsite, and would certainly draw notice, even deep in the Greatwoods — if not for a woman named Farrah, the first recruit after Ada and Nix, who can manipulate sound itself. She absorbs the explosive blasts of gunfire, smothering each round of bullets so that not even an echo ripples across the valley.

As the newbloods expand their abilities, learning to control them as I did, I begin to hope. Cal excels at teaching, especially with the children. They don't have the same prejudices as the older recruits, and take to following him around the camp even when their training lessons are over. This in turn ingratiates the older newbloods to the exiled prince's presence. It's hard to hate Cal when he has children milling around his ankles, begging for another lesson. Even Nix has stopped glaring at him, though he still refuses to do anything more than grunt in Cal's direction.

I'm not so gifted as the exile, and come to dread the morning and late-afternoon sessions. I want to blame my unease on exhaustion. Half my days are spent recruiting, traveling to the next name on our list, but that's not it at all. I'm simply a poor instructor.

I work closest with a woman named Ketha, whose abilities are more physical and alike to my own. She can't create electricity or any other element, but she can destroy. Like Silver oblivions, she can explode an object, blowing it apart in a concussive cloud of smoke and fire. But while typical oblivions are restricted to things they can actually touch, Ketha has no such limitation.

She waits patiently, eyeing the rock in my hand. I do my best not to shrink from her explosive gaze, knowing full well what it can do. In the short week since we found her, she's graduated from destroying clumps of paper, leaves, even branches, to solid stone. As with the other newbloods, all they need is a chance to reveal their true selves. The abilities respond in kind, like animals finally let out of their cages.

While the others give her training a wide berth, leaving us to the far end of the Notch clearing, I can do no such thing. "Control," I say, and she nods.

I wish I had more to offer her, but my guidance is woefully poor. I myself have only a month of ability training under my belt, much of it from Julian, who wasn't even a proper trainer to begin with. What's more, it's incredibly personal to me, and I find it difficult to explain exactly what I intend to Ketha.

"Control," she repeats.

Her eyes narrow, deepening her focus. Strange, her mud-brown eyes are unremarkable despite the power they hold. Like me, Ketha comes from a river village, and could pass for my much-older sister or aunt. Her tanned skin and gray-tipped hair are firm reminders of our humble, unjust origins. According to her records, she was a schoolteacher.

When I heave the rock skyward, tossing it as far up as I can, I'm reminded of Instructor Arven and Training. He made us hit targets with our abilities, honing our aim and focus. And in the Bowl of Bones, I became his target. He nearly killed me, and yet here I am, copying his methods. It feels wrong — but effective.

The rock pulverizes into dust, as if a tiny bomb went off inside it. Ketha claps for herself, and I force myself to do the same. I wonder if she'll feel differently when her abilities are put to the test, against flesh instead of stone. I suppose I can have Kilorn catch us a rabbit so we can find out.

But he grows more distant with every passing day. He's taken it upon himself to feed the camp, and spends most of his time fishing or hunting. If I were not so preoccupied with my own duties, recruiting and training, I would try and snap him out of it. But I barely have time to sleep, let alone coax Kilorn back into the fold.

By the first snowfall, there are twenty newbloods living at the camp, varying from old maids to twitching young boys. Luckily, the safe house is bigger than I first thought, stretching back into the hill in a maze of chambers and tunnels. A few have shafted windows, but most are dark, and we end up having to steal lanterns as well as newbloods from every place we visit. By the time the first snow falls, the Notch sleeps all twenty-six of us comfortably, with room for more.

Food is plentiful, thanks to Kilorn and Farrah, who turns him into a silent, deadly hunter. Supplies come in with each wave of recruits, ranging from winter clothes to matches and even a bit of salt. Farley and Crance use their criminal ties to get us what we need, but sometimes we resort to good old-fashioned thievery. In a month's time, we are a well-oiled, well-hidden machine.

Maven has not found us, and we keep tabs on him as best we can. Signposts and newspapers make it easy. *The King Visits Delphie, King Maven and Lady Evangeline Review Soldiers at Fort Lencasser, Coronation Tour Continues through the King State.* The headlines pinpoint his location, and we know what each of them means. Dead newbloods in Delphie, in Lencasser, in every place he visits. His so-called coronation tour is just another shroud of secrecy, hiding a parade of executions.

Despite all our abilities and tricks, we are not fast enough to save everyone. For every newblood we discover and bring back to our camp, there are two more hanging from gallows, "missing," or bleeding into gutters. A few bodies show the telltale signs of death by magnetron, skewered or strangled by iron rods. Ptolemus no doubt, though Evangeline might be there too, basking in the glow of a king. She'll be queen soon enough, and will certainly do best to keep Maven close. Once, that would infuriate me, but now I feel nothing but pity for the magnetron girl. Maven is not Cal, and he will kill her if it suits him. Just like the new-bloods, dead to keep his lies alive, to keep us on the run. Dead, because Maven has miscalculated. He believes enough corpses will make me come back.

But I will not.

NINETEEN

After three days of finding nothing but dead newbloods, three days of failure, we travel to Templyn. A quiet town on the road to Delphie, mostly residential, consisting of vast Silver estates and cramped Red row houses along the river. Masters and servants. Templyn is tricky — it has no vast forest, tunnels, or crowded streets to hide in. Usually we'd use Shade to slip inside the walls, but he's not with us today. He twisted his leg yesterday, aggravating a still-healing muscle, and I made him stay behind. Cal is missing too, having elected to teach, leaving Ada to man the Blackrun. She's still there, cozy in her pilot's seat, reading as she always does. I try to not be jumpy, to lead as Cal would, but I feel strangely bare without him and my brother. I've never been without both of them on a recruitment mission, and this is my proving ground. To show the others that I'm not only a weapon to be unleashed but someone willing to fight *with* them.

Luckily, we have a staggering new advantage. A newblood named Harrick, saved from the quarry pits of Orienpratis two weeks ago. This will be his first recruitment, and hopefully uneventful. The man is mousy and twitching, with the wiry muscles of a stonemason. Farley and I make sure to flank him in the cart, quietly watchful in case he decides to dart off. The others with us, Nix across from me and Crance driving the cart, are more preoccupied with the road ahead.

Our cart falls in line with many others, merchants or laborers heading into the town center for work. Crance's hands tighten on the reins of our stolen cart horse, an old, spotty dear with a blind eye and a bad hoof. But he urges her forward, keeping pace with the rest, trying to blend in. The town boundaries loom before us, marked by an open gate flanked by intricate stone columns. A flag is strung between them, a familiar banner of a familiar house. Red and orange stripes, almost bleeding together in the early-morning light. House Lerolan, oblivions, the governors of the Delphie region. I blink at it, remembering the bodies of three dead oblivions, Lerolans all killed in the shooting at the Hall of the Sun. The father, Belicos, murdered by Farley and the Scarlet Guard. And his twin sons, barely more than babies, blown to bits by the explosion that followed. Their dead faces were plastered all over the kingdom, in every broadcast, another rallying flag of Silver propaganda. *The Scarlet Guard kills children. The Scarlet Guard must be destroyed.*

I glance at Farley, wondering if she knows what the flag means, but she focuses on the officers ahead. As does Harrick. His eyes narrow in concentration, and his trembling hands clench. Quietly, I touch his arm, encouraging him. "You can do this," I murmur.

He offers me the smallest smile, and I straighten in assurance. I believe in his ability — he's been practicing whenever he can — but he must believe it himself.

Nix tenses, muscles bulging beneath his shirt. Farley is less obvious, but I know she's itching for the knife in her boot. I will not show the same fear, for Harrick's sake.

Security officers man the gate, eyeballing every person who passes through. Searching their faces and through their wares, not bothering to check their identification cards. These Silvers don't care for what's written on a piece of paper — their orders are to find me and mine, not a farmer straying too far from his village. Soon, our cart is next, and only the sweat on Harrick's upper lip indicates he's doing anything at all.

Crance halts the horse and the cart, stopping at the command of a Security officer. He keeps his eyes down, respectful, beaten, as the officer stares at him. As expected, nothing sets him off. Crance is not a newblood, nor a known associate of ours. Maven will not be hunting him. The officer turns to circle the cart, eyeing the inside. Not one of us dares to move, or even breathe. Harrick is not so skilled that he can mask sound, only sight. Once, the officer's eyes meet mine, and I wonder if Harrick has failed. But after a heart-stopping moment, he moves on, satisfied. *He can't see us.*

Harrick is a newblood of an extraordinary kind. He can create illusions, mirages, make people see what isn't there. And he has hidden us all in plain sight, making us invisible in our *empty* cart.

"Are you transporting air, Red?" the officer says with a hateful grin.

"Collecting shipment, bound for inner Delphie," Crance replies, saying exactly what Ada told him. She spent yesterday studying trade routes. One hour of reading and she's an expert on the imports and exports of Norta. "Spun wool, sir."

But the officer is already walking off, unconcerned. "Move on," he says, waving a gloved hand.

The cart lurches forward and Harrick's hand grips mine, squeezing tightly. I squeeze right back, imploring him to hold on, to keep fighting, to keep up his illusion until we're inside Templyn and clear of the gate.

"One minute more," I whisper. "You're almost there."

We turn off the main road before entering the market, weaving through half-empty side streets lined with humble Red shops and homes. The others search, knowing what we're looking for, while I keep my attentions on Harrick. "Almost there," I say again, hoping I'm right. In a moment or two, his strength will fail, and our illusion will fall away, revealing us all to the street. The people here are Red, but will certainly report a cart suddenly full of the country's most wanted fugitives.

"The left," Nix says gruffly, and Crance obliges. He eases the cart toward a clapboard house with crimson curtains. Despite the sun shining overhead, a candle burns in the window. *Red as the dawn.*

There's an alleyway next to the house, bordered by the Scarlet Guard house and two empty, abandoned homes. Where their occupants are, I don't know, but they probably fled the Measures or were executed for trying. It's cover enough for me. "Now, Harrick," I tell him. He responds with a massive sigh. The protection of his illusion is gone. "Well done."

We waste no time climbing out of the cart and sidling up to the Guard house, using the overhang of the roof to hide as best we can. Farley takes the lead, and knocks three times on the side door. It opens quickly, showing nothing but darkness beyond. Farley enters without hesitation, and we follow.

My eyes adjust quickly to the dark house, and I'm struck by the similarity to my home in the Stilts. Simple, cluttered, only two rooms with knotty plank floors and grimy windows. The lightbulbs overhead are dark, either broken or missing, sold off for food.

"Captain," a voice says. An older woman, her hair steel gray, appears by the window and snuffs out the candle. Her face is lined with age, her hands with scars. And around her wrist, a familiar tattoo. A single red band, just like the one old Will Whistle bore.

As in Harbor Bay, Farley frowns and shakes the woman's hand. "I'm not —"

But the woman waves her off. "According

to the Colonel, but not Command. They have other ideas where you're concerned." *Command.* She notes my interest and bows her head in greeting. "Miss Barrow. I'm Ellie Whistle."

I raise an eyebrow. "Whistle?" I say. "Are you related to —"

Ellie cuts me off before I can finish. "Most likely not. Whistle's a nickname mostly. Means I'm a smuggler. Whistles on the wind, all of us." *Indeed.* Will Whistle and his old wagon were always full of smuggled or stolen goods, many of them things I brought myself. "I'm Scarlet Guard too," she adds.

I knew that, at least. Farley's been in contact with her people over the last few weeks, those not under the command of the Colonel, who would help us and keep our movements quiet.

"Very good," I tell her. "We're here for the Marcher family." Two of them, to be precise. *Tansy and Matrick Marcher, twins judging by their birthdays.* "They'll need to be removed from town, within the hour if possible."

Ellie listens intently, all business. She shifts, and I catch a glimpse of the pistol at her hip. She glances at Farley, and when she nods her head, Ellie does the same. "That I can do."

"Supplies as well," Farley puts in. "We'll

take food if you got it, but winter clothes will be best."

Another nod. "We'll certainly try," Ellie says. "I'll have whatever we can give you ready as fast as possible. Might need an extra pair of hands, though."

"I've got it," Crance offers. His bulk will certainly help speed the process.

I can't believe Ellie's willingness and neither can Farley. We exchange loaded glances as Ellie gets to work, opening cabinets and floorboards in succession, revealing hidden compartments all over the house.

"Thank you for your cooperation," Farley says over her shoulder, quietly suspicious. As am I, watching every move Ellie makes. She's old, but spry, and I wonder if we're truly alone in this house.

"Like I said, I take my orders from Command. And they sent out the word. Help Captain Farley and the lightning girl, no matter the cost," she says, not bothering to look at us.

My eyebrows rise, shocked and pleasantly surprised. "You're going to have to fill me in on this," I mutter to Farley. Again, I'm struck by how organized and deep-rooted the Scarlet Guard seems to be.

"Later," she replies. "The Marcher family?"

While Ellie gives her directions, I move to stand with Harrick and Nix. Though this is Harrick's first recruitment, Nix thinks this is old hat, and rightfully so. I've lost count of how many times he's accompanied me into hostile territory, and for that I'm so grateful.

"Ready, boys?" I ask, flexing my fingers. Nix does his best to look gruff and nonchalant, a veteran of our missions, but I don't miss the flash of fear in Harrick's eyes. "This won't be as hard as coming in. Less people to hide, and the officers aren't bothering to look this time. You've got this."

"Thanks, uh, Mare." He straightens, puffing out his chest, smiling for my benefit. I smile back, even though his voice trembles when he says my name. Most of them don't know what to call me. Mare, Miss Barrow, the lightning girl, some even say *my lady*. The nickname stings, but not so much as the last. No matter what I do, no matter how much I try to be one of them, they see me as something apart. Either a leader or a leper, but always an outsider. Always separated.

Out in the alley, Crance begins loading the cart, not bothering to watch us blink out of existence with the grace of a Silver shadow. But unlike them, Harrick cannot only bend light, creating brightness and darkness — he can conjure anything he wishes. A tree, a horse, another person entirely. Now that we're on the street, he masks us as obscure Reds with dirty faces and hoods. We are unremarkable, even to each other. He tells me this is easier than making us disappear, and a better alternative in the crowd. People won't wonder at bumping into thin air.

Farley leads, following Ellie's directions. We have to cross the market square, past the eyes of many Security officers, but no one gives us pause. My hair blows in the slight wind, sending a curtain of white-blond across my eyes. I almost laugh. Blond hair . . . on *me.*

The Marcher house is small, with a hastily built second floor that looks liable to collapse on top of us. But it has a lovely back garden, overgrown with tangles of vines and bare trees. In the summer, it must look wonderful. We pick through it, doing our best to keep the dead leaves from crunching.

"We're invisible now," Harrick mutters. When I look in his direction, I realize he's gone. I smile, though no one can see it.

Someone reaches the back door before me and knocks. No answer, not even a rustle inside. They could be out for the day, working. Next to me, Farley curses under her breath. "Do we wait?" she breathes. I can't see her, but I see the puffs of breath clouding where her face should be.

"Harrick's not a machine," I say, speaking for him. "We wait inside."

I head for the door, bumping her shoulder, and sink to a knee before the lock. A simple one. I could pick it in my sleep, and it takes no time now. Within seconds, I'm greeted by a familiar, satisfying click.

The door swings back on shrieking hinges and I freeze, waiting for what might be inside. Like Ellie's house, the inside is dark and seemingly abandoned. Still, I give it another moment, listening hard. Nothing moves inside, and I feel no tremors of electricity. Either the Marchers are out of rations, or they don't even have electricity at all. Satisfied, I beckon over my shoulder, but nothing happens. *They can't see you, idiot.*

"Head in," I whisper, and I feel Farley at my back.

Once the door is safely shut again, we burst back into sight. I smile at Harrick, again grateful for his ability and strength, but the smell stops me cold. The air is stale in here, undisturbed, and slightly sour. With a hasty swipe of my hand, I brush half an inch of dust from the kitchen table.

"Maybe they ran. Lots of people have," Nix offers quickly.

Something draws my focus, the tiniest whisper. Not a voice, but a spark. Barely there, so soft I almost missed it. Coming from a basket by the fireplace, covered in a dirty red rag. I drift toward it, drawn by the small beacon.

"I don't like this. We need to regroup at Ellie's. Harrick, pull yourself together and get ready for another illusion," Farley barks as quietly as she can.

My knees scrape the hearthstones as I kneel over the basket. The smell is stronger here. And so is the spark. I should not do this. I know I won't like what I find. *I know it,* but I can't stop myself from pulling back the rag. The fabric is sticky and I tug, revealing what lies beneath. After a numb second, I realize what I'm looking at.

I fall backward, scrambling, gasping, almost screaming. Tears fall faster than I ever thought they could. Farley is the first to my side, her arms surrounding me, holding me steady. "What is it? Mare, what —"

She stops short, choking on the words.

She sees what I see. And so do the others. Nix almost vomits and I'm surprised Harrick doesn't faint.

In the basket is a baby, no more than a few days old. Dead. And not from abandonment or neglect. The rag is dyed in its blood. The message is disgustingly clear. *The Marchers are dead too.*

One tiny fist, clawed with the stiffness of death, holds the tiniest device. *An alarm.*

"Harrick," I hiss through my tears. "Hide us." His mouth falls open, confused, and I grab his leg in desperation. *"Hide us."*

He disappears before my eyes, and not a moment too soon.

Officers appear in the windows, bursting through each door, guns raised, all shouting. "You're surrounded, lightning girl! Submit to arrest!" they roar in succession, as if repeating themselves makes any difference.

Quietly, I ease myself under the kitchen table. I only hope the others have the sense to do the same.

No fewer than twelve officers crowd inside, stomping back and forth. Four break off, heading upstairs, and one pair of boots halts by the baby. The officer's free hand twitches and I know he must be staring at the tiny corpse. After a long moment, he vomits into the fireplace.

"Easy, Myros," one of the others says, pulling him away. "Poor thing," he adds, moving past the baby. "Anything upstairs?"

"Nothing!" another replies, coming back down. "Alarm must've malfunctioned."

"You're sure? The governor will skin us if we're wrong."

"Do *you* see anyone here, sir?"

I almost gasp when the officer drops to a crouch right in front of me. His eyes sweep back and forth beneath the table, searching. I feel a slight pressure on my leg — one of the others. I dare not respond with a nudge of my own, and hold my breath.

"No, I don't," the officer finally says, standing again. "False alarm. Back to your posts."

They leave as quickly as they burst in, but I dare not breathe until their footsteps are long gone. Then I gasp, shaking, as Harrick drops the illusion, and we all blink back into sight.

"Well done." Farley exhales, patting Harrick on the shoulder. Like me, he can barely speak, and has to be helped to his feet.

"I could've taken 'em," Nix grumbles, rolling out from beneath the stairs. He crosses to the door with short strides, one hand already on the knob. "All the same, I don't fancy being here if they come back."

"Mare?" Farley's touch on my arm is gentle, especially for her.

I realize I'm standing over the baby, staring. There were no babies on Julian's list, no children below the age of three. This was not a newblood, not according to our records or any Maven might possess. The child was murdered simply because she was here. For nothing.

With determination, I remove my jacket. I will not leave her like this, with only her own blood for a blanket.

"Mare, don't. They'll know we were here —"

"Let them know."

I pull it across her — and I fight, with everything I have, the urge to lie down beside her and never get back up again. My fingers brush her tiny, cold fist. There is something beneath it. *A note.* Quietly, quickly, I slip it into my pocket before anyone else can see.

When we finally get back to Ada and the jet, I dare to read it. It's dated for yesterday. *Yesterday.* We were so close.

October 22

A crude envelope, I know. But neces-

sary. You must know what you are doing, what you are forcing me to do to
these people. Every body is a message to
you, and to my brother. Surrender to
me, and it will stop. Surrender, and they
will live. I am a man of my word.

Until we meet again,
Maven

We arrive back at the Notch at nightfall. I
cannot eat, I cannot speak, I cannot sleep.
The others discuss what happened in Templyn, but no one dares ask me. My brother
tries but I walk way, deeper into the burrows of our hideaway. I cower in my
cramped hole of a bedroom, convincing
myself I need to be alone for now. On other
nights, I hate this solitary room, being
separated from the others. Now I hate it
even more, but I can't bring myself to join
them. Instead, I wait for everyone to be
asleep before I let myself wander. I take a
blanket, but it does nothing for the cold,
inside and out.

I tell myself it's the autumn chill that
sends me to his room, and not the empty
feeling in my stomach. Not the frozen abyss
that grows with every failure. Not the note
in my pocket, burning a hole right through
me.

Fire dances on the floor, confined to a neat dip ringed by stones. Even in the strange shadows, I can tell he's awake. His eyes look alive with flame, but not angry. Not even confused. With one hand, he pulls back the blankets of his sleeper, and slides to make room for me.

"It's cold in here," I say.

I think he knows what I really mean.

"Farley told me," he murmurs when I settle in. He puts an arm across my waist, gentle and warm, meaning nothing but comfort. The other presses against my back, his palm flat to my scars. *I am here,* it says.

I want to tell him about Maven's offer. But what good would it do? He would only refuse like I have, and have to suffer the shame of that refusal with me. It will only cause him pain, Maven's true goal. And in this, I will not let Maven win. He's already conquered me. He will not conquer Cal.

Somehow, I fall asleep. I do not dream.

TWENTY

From that day on, his bedchamber becomes ours. It is a wordless agreement, giving both of us something to hold on to. We're too tired to do much more than sleep, though I'm sure Kilorn suspects otherwise. He stops talking to me, and ignores Cal altogether. Part of me wants to join the others in the larger sleeping rooms, where the children whisper into the night and Nanny shushes them all. It helps them bond. But I would only frighten them, so I stay with Cal, the one person who doesn't really fear me.

He doesn't keep me awake on purpose, but every night I feel him stir. His nightmares are worse than mine, and I know exactly what he's dreaming of. The moment he severed his father's head from his shoulders. I pretend to sleep through it, knowing he doesn't want to be seen in such a state. But I feel his tears on my cheek. Sometimes

I think they burn me, but I don't wake up with any new scars. At least not the kind that can be seen.

Even though we spend every night together, Cal and I don't talk much. There isn't much to say beyond our duties. I don't tell him about the first note, or the next ones. Though Maven is far away, he still manages to sit between us. I can see him in Cal's eyes, a toad squatting in his brother's head, trying to poison him from the inside out. He's doing the same thing to me, both in the notes and in my memories. I don't know why, but I can't destroy either of them, and I tell no one of their existence.

I should burn them, but I don't.

I find another letter in Corvium, during another recruitment. We knew Maven was on his way to the area, visiting the last major city before the ashlands of the Choke. We thought we could beat him there. Instead, we found the king already gone.

October 31

I expected you at my coronation. It seemed like the kind of thing your Scarlet Guard would love to try to ruin, even though it was quite small. We're still supposed to be mourning Father, and a grand affair would seem disrespectful. Especially with Cal still out there, running around with you and your rabble. A precious few still owe allegiance to him, according to Mother, but don't worry. They are being dealt with. No Silver succession crisis will come and take my brother from your leash. If you could, wish him a happy birthday for me. And assure him it will be his last.

But yours is coming, isn't it? I don't doubt we'll spend it together.

Until we meet again,
Maven

His voice speaks every word, using the ink like knives. For a moment, my stomach churns, threatening to spill my dinner all over the dirt floor. The nausea passes long enough for me to slip out of the sleeper, out of Cal's embrace, to my box of supplies in the corner. Like at home, I keep my trinkets hidden, and two more of Maven's notes are crumpled at the bottom.

Each one bears the same ending. *Until we meet again.*

I feel something like hands around my throat, threatening to squeeze the life from me. Each word tightens the grip, as if ink alone can strangle me. For a second, I fear I might not breathe again. Not because Maven still insists on tormenting me. No, the reason is much worse.

Because I miss him. I miss the boy I thought he was.

The brand he gave me burns with the memory. I wonder if he can feel it too.

Cal stirs in the sleeper behind me, not from a nightmare, but because it's time to wake. Hastily, I shove the notes away, and leave the room before he can open his eyes. I don't want to see his pity, not yet. That will be too much to bear.

"Happy birthday, Cal," I whisper to the empty tunnel hall.

I've forgotten a coat, and the cold of November pricks my skin as I step out of the safe house. The clearing is dark before the dawn, so that I can barely see the eaves of the forest. Ada sits over the low coals of a campfire, perched on a log in a shivering bundle of wool blankets and scarves. She always takes last watch, preferring to wake earlier than the rest of us. Her accelerated brain lets her read the books I bring her and keep an eye on the woods at the same time. Most mornings, she's gained a new skill by the time the rest of us are up and about. Last week alone, she learned Tirax, the language of a strange nation to the southeast, as well as basic surgery. But today, she holds no stolen book, and she is not alone.

Ketha stands over the fire, arms crossed. Her lips move quickly, but I can't hear what she's saying. And Kilorn huddles close to Ada, his feet almost entirely in the coals. As I creep closer, I can see his brow bent in intense focus. Stick in hand, he traces lines in the dirt. *Letters.* Crude, hastily drawn, forming rudimentary words like *boat, gun,* and *home.* The last word is longer than the rest. *Kilorn.* The sight almost brings new tears to my eyes. But they are happy tears, an unfamiliar thing to me. The empty hole inside me seems to shrink, if only a little.

"Tricky, but you're getting it," Ketha says, the corner of her mouth lifting in a half smile. *A teacher indeed.*

Kilorn notices me before I can get much closer, snapping his writing twig with a resounding crack. Without so much as a nod, he gets up from the log and swings his hunting pack over his shoulder. His knife glints at his hip, cold and sharp as the icicles fanging the trees in the woods.

"Kilorn?" Ketha asks, then her eyes fall on me, and my presence answers her question. "Oh."

"It's time to hunt anyways," Ada replies, reaching a hand toward Kilorn's fading form. Despite the warm color of her skin, the tips of her fingers have flushed blue with the cold. But he evades her grasp and she touches nothing but frosty air.

I don't do anything to stop him. Instead, I lean back on my heels, giving him the space he so desperately desires. He draws up the hood of his new coat, obscuring his face as he stalks toward the tree line. Good brown leather and fleece lining, perfect for keeping him warm and hidden. I stole it a week ago in Haven. I didn't think Kilorn would accept such a gift from me, but even he knows the value of warmth.

My company this afternoon doesn't bother just him. Ketha glances at me sidelong, almost blushing. "He asked to learn," she says, almost apologetic. Then she pushes past me, heading back to the warmth and relative comfort of the Notch.

Ada watches her go, her golden eyes bright but sad. She pats the log next to her, gesturing for me to sit. When I do, she tosses one of her blankets across my lap and tucks it around me. "There you are, miss." She was a maid in Harbor Bay, and despite her newfound freedom, old habits haven't worn off yet. She still calls me "miss," though I've asked her to stop many times. "I think they need some kind of distraction."

"It's a good one. No other teacher's ever made it this far with Kilorn. I'll make sure to thank her later." *If she doesn't run away again.* "We all need a little distraction, Ada."

She sighs in agreement. Her lips, full and dark, purse into a bitter, knowing smile. I don't miss her eyes flicker back to the Notch, where half my heart sleeps. And then to the forest, where the rest wanders. "He has Crance with him, and Farrah will join them both soon enough. No bears, either," she adds, squinting at the dark horizon. In daylight, if the mist holds off, we should be able to see the distant mountains. "They've gone quiet for the season by now. Sleeping through the winter."

Bears. At home in the Stilts, we barely had deer, let alone the fabled monsters of the backcountry. The lumberyards, logging teams, and river traffic were enough to drive away any animal bigger than a raccoon, but the Greatwoods region teems with wildlife. Great antlered stags, curious foxes, and the occasional howl of a wolf all haunt the hills and valleys. I've yet to see one of the lumbering bears, but Kilorn and the other hunters spotted one weeks ago. Only Farrah's muffling abilities and Kilorn's good sense to keep downwind kept them safe from its jaws.

"Where did you learn so much about bears?" I ask, if only to fill the air with idle conversation. Ada knows exactly what I'm doing, but humors me anyways.

"Governor Rhambos likes to hunt," she replies with a shrug. "He had an estate outside the city, and his sons filled it with strange beasts for him to kill. Bears, especially. Beautiful creatures, with black fur and keen eyes. They were peaceful enough, if left alone, or attended to by our game warden. Little Rohr, the governor's daughter, wanted a cub for her own, but the bears were killed before any could breed."

I remember Rohr Rhambos. A strongarm who looked like a mouse but could pulverize stone with her own two hands. She competed in Queenstrial so long ago, when I was a maid just like Ada.

"I don't suppose what the governor did could actually be called hunting," Ada continues. Sadness poisons her voice. "He put them in a pit, where he could fight the animals and break their necks. His sons did it too, for their training."

Bears sound like ferocious, fearsome beasts, but Ada's manner tells me otherwise.

Her glazed eyes can only mean she's seen the pit herself, and remembers every second of it. "That's awful."

"You killed one of his sons, you know. Ryker was his name. He was one of your chosen executioners."

I never wanted to know his name. I never asked about the ones I killed in the Bowl of Bones, and no one ever told me. Ryker Rhambos, electrocuted on the sand of the arena, reduced to nothing more than his blackened flesh.

"Beg pardon, miss. I did not mean to upset you." Her calm mask has returned, and with it, the perfect manners of a woman raised as a servant. With her ability, I can only imagine how terrible it must have been, seeing but not speaking, never able to prove her worth or reveal her true self. But it's even worse to think that, unlike me, she can't hide behind the shield of an imperfect mind. She knows and feels so much that it threatens to pull her down. Like me, she must keep running.

"I'm only upset when you call me *that.* Miss, I mean."

"A habit, I'm afraid." She shifts, reaching for something inside her blankets. I hear the distinct sound of crinkling paper, and expect to see another news bulletin detailing Maven's coronation tour. Instead, Ada reveals a very official-looking document, albeit a crumpled one with singed edges. It bears the red sword of the Nortan army. "Shade took this off that officer in Corvium."

"The one I fried." I trace the burned paper, feeling the rough, black material threatening to disintegrate. Strange, this survived where its holder could not. "Preparations," I mutter, deciphering the order. "For relief legions."

She nods. "Ten legions, to replace the nine holding the Choke trenches."

Storm Legion, Hammer Legion, Sword Legion, Shield Legion — their names and numbers are listed plainly. Five thousand Red soldiers in each, with another five hundred Silver officers. They're converging on Corvium before traveling together into the Choke, to relieve the soldiers on the lines. A terrible thing, but not something that interests me.

"Good that we've already checked Corvium" is all I can think to say. "At least we avoided a few thousand Silver officers passing through."

But Ada puts a gentle hand on my arm, her long, able fingers cold even through my sleeve. "Ten to replace nine. Why?"

"A push?" Again, I don't understand why this is my problem. "Maven might want to make a show of it, demonstrate what a warrior he is, to make everyone forget Cal —"

"Not likely. Trench assaults warrant at least fifteen legions, five to guard, ten to march." Her eyes flicker back and forth, as if she can see a battle in her mind's eye. I can't help but raise my eyebrows. As far as I know, we don't have any tactics guides lying around. "The prince is well versed in warfare," she explains. "He's a good teacher."

"Have you shown Cal this?"

Her hesitation is the only answer I need.

"I believe it's a kill order," she murmurs, lowering her eyes. "Nine legions to take up their posts, and the tenth to die."

But this is crazy, even for Maven. "That doesn't make any sense. Why would anyone waste five thousand good soldiers?"

"Their official name is the Dagger Legion." She points to the corresponding word on the paper. Like the others, it contains five thousand Reds, and is heading straight for the trenches. "But Governor Rhambos called them something else. The Little Legion."

"The Little — ?" My brain catches up. Suddenly I'm back on the island of Tuck, in the medical ward, with the Colonel breathing down my neck. He was planning to trade Cal, to use him to save the five thousand children now marching into an early grave. "The new conscripts. The kids."

"Fifteen to seventeen years old. The Dagger is the first of the child legions the king has deemed 'combat ready.' " She doesn't bother to hide her scoff. "Barely two months of training, if that."

I remember what I was like at fifteen. Even though I was still a thief, I was small and silly, more concerned with bothering my sister than with my future. I thought I still had a chance of escaping conscription. Rifles and ash-blown trenches had not yet begun to haunt my dreams.

"They'll be slaughtered."

Ada settles back into her blankets, her face grim. "I believe that's the idea."

I know what she wants, what many would want if they knew about Maven's orders for the child army. The kids about to be sent into the Choke are a consequence of the Measures, a way to punish the kingdom for the Scarlet Guard's insurrection. It feels as if I've sentenced them to death myself, and I don't doubt many would agree. Soon there will be an ocean of blood on my hands, and I have no way of stopping it. Innocent blood, like the baby's in Templyn.

"We can't do anything for them." I drop my gaze, not wanting to see the disappointment in Ada's eyes. "We can't fight whole legions."

"Mare —"

"Can *you* think of a way to help them?" I cut her off, my voice harsh with anger. It cows her into defeated silence. "Then how could I?"

"Of course. You're right. *Miss.*"

The proper title stings, as she meant it to. "I leave you to your watch," I mumble, standing up from the log, march order still in hand. Slowly, I fold it up and tuck it away, deep into a pocket.

Every body is a message to you
Surrender to me, and it will stop.

"We fly for Pitarus in a few hours." Ada already knows our recruitment plans for the day, but telling her again gives me something to do. "Cal's piloting, so give Shade a list of whatever supplies we might need."

"Be mindful," she replies. "The king is in Delphie again, only an hour's flight away."

The thought prickles my scars. *One hour separating me from Maven's torturous manipulations. From his terror machine that turned my own power against me.*

"Delphie? Again?"

Cal walks to us from the mouth of the

420

Notch house, his hair mussed by sleep. But his eyes have never looked so awake. "Why again?"

"I saw a bulletin in Corvium that stated he was visiting with Governor Lerolan," Ada says, confused by Cal's sudden focus. "To share his condolences in person."

"For Belicos and his sons." I met Belicos only once, minutes before his death, but he was kind. He did not deserve the ending I helped give him. Neither did his kin.

But Cal narrows his eyes against the rising sun. He sees something we don't, something even Ada's lists and facts cannot understand. "Maven wouldn't waste time on such a thing, even to keep up appearances. The Lerolans are nothing to him, and he's already killed the newbloods of Delphie — he wouldn't go back without a good reason."

"And that is?" I ask.

His mouth opens, as if he expects the right answer to fall out. Nothing happens, and finally he shakes his head. "I'm not sure."

Because this is not a military maneuver. This is something else, something Cal doesn't understand. He has a talent for war, not intrigue. That is Maven and his mother's domain, and we're hopelessly outgunned on their playing field. The best we can do is challenge them on our own terms, with might, not minds. *But we need more might. And fast.*

"Pitarus," I say aloud, sounding final. "And tell Nanny she's coming."

The old woman has been requesting to help since she came here, and Cal thinks she's ready to do it. Harrick, on the other hand, has not joined us on another recruitment. Not since Templyn. I don't blame him.

I don't need Cal to point out where the Rift region starts. As we pass from the King State, entering into the Prince State, the divide is shockingly clear from our high altitude. The airjet soars over a series of rift valleys, each one bordered by a marching line of mountains. They look almost manmade, forming long gashes like the scrape of fingernails across earth. But these are too big, even for Silvers. This land was made by something more powerful and destructive, thousands of years ago. Autumn bleeds over the land, painting the forest below in varying shades of fire. We're much farther south than the Notch, but I see pockets of snow on the peaks, hiding from the rising sun. Like Greatwoods, the Rift is another wilderness, though its wealth lies in steel and iron, not lumber. Its capital, Pitarus, is the only city in the region, and an industrial nerve center. It sits on a river fork, connecting the steel refineries to the war front, as well as the southern coal towns to the rest of the kingdom. Though the Rift is officially governed by the windweavers of House Laris, it is the ancestral home of House Samos. As the owners of the iron mines and steel factories, they truly control Pitarus and the Rift. If we're lucky, Evangeline might be skulking around, and I'll get to repay her for all her evils.

The nearest rift valley to Pitarus is more than fifteen miles away, but offers good cover to land. This is the bumpiest of all the ruined runways, and I wonder if we've overstepped. But Cal keeps the Blackrun in hand, getting us down safely, if shaken.

Nanny claps her hands, delighted by the flight, her wrinkled face lit by a wide smile. "Is it always this much fun?" she asks, peering at us.

Across from her, Shade pulls a grimace. He still hasn't gotten used to flying, and does his best not to lose his breakfast in her lap.

"We're looking for four newbloods." My voice echoes down the craft, silencing the snapping of buckles and restraints. Shade's feeling better, so he's here again, sitting next to Farley. Then there's Nanny and the new-blood Gareth Baument. This will be his third recruitment in four days, since Cal decided the former horse master would be a welcome addition to our daily missions. Once he worked for Lady Ara Iral herself, maintaining her vast stable of horses at the family estate on the Capital River. At court, everyone called her the Panther for her gleaming black hair and catlike agility. Gareth is less complimentary. He's more likely to call her the Silk Bitch. Luckily, his work for House Iral kept him fit and limber, and his abilities are nothing to scoff at either. When I first questioned him, asking if he could do anything special, I ended up on the ceiling. Gareth manipulated the forces of *gravity* holding me to the earth. If we had been standing in the open, I probably would have ended up in the clouds. But I leave that to Gareth. Besides jettisoning people into the air, he can use his ability to *fly*.

"Gareth will drop Nanny into the city, and she'll enter the Security Center disguised as Lord General Laris." I glance to her, only to find myself staring at a slight older man rather than the woman I've come to know. He nods back at me and flexes his fingers, as if he's never used them before. But I know better. It's Nanny beneath that skin, pretending to be the Silver commander of the Air Fleet. "She'll get us a printout of the four newbloods living in Pitarus and the rest in the Rift region. We'll follow on foot, and Shade will pull us all out."

As usual, Farley is the first out of her seat. "Good luck with that one, Nan," she says, jabbing a finger at Gareth. "If you liked this, you're going to love what he does."

"I don't like that smile, little miss," Nanny says in Laris's voice. Though I've seen her transform before, I'm still not used to the strange sight.

Gareth laughs next to Nanny, helping her from her seat. "Farley flew with me last. Made a real mess of my boots when we touched down."

"I did no such thing," Farley replies, but she stalks down the length of the jet quickly. Probably to hide her flushing face. Shade follows her as he always does, trying to smother his laughter with his hand. She's been ill lately and has done her best to hide it, to everyone's amusement.

Cal and I are the last left on the plane, though I have no cause to wait for him. He goes through the usual motions, twisting knobs and flipping switches that turn off different parts of the jet in rapid succession.

I feel each one sink into electrical death, until the low hum of full batteries is all that remains. The silence pounds in time with my beating heart, and suddenly I can't get off the jet fast enough. Something frightens me about being alone with Cal, at least in daylight. But when night falls, there's no one I'd rather see.

"You should talk to Kilorn."

His voice stops me midstep, frozen halfway down the back ramp.

"I don't want to talk to him."

Heat rises with every moment, as he gets closer and closer to me. "Funny, you're usually such a good liar."

I spin to find myself staring at his chest. The flight suit, pristine when he put it on more than a month ago, now shows distinct signs of wear. Even though he does his best to steer clear of our battles, battle has touched him still.

"I know Kilorn better than you, and nothing I say will snap him out of his little tantrum."

"Do you know he asks to come with us?" His eyes are dark, heavy-lidded. He looks like he does in the moments before he falls asleep. "He asks me every night."

My time at the Notch has made me blunt and easy to read. I don't doubt Cal sees the confusion I feel, or the low currents of jealousy. "He speaks to *you*? He won't talk to me *because* of you, so why on earth would he —"

Suddenly his fingers are under my chin, tilting my head so I can't look away. "It's not me he's mad at. He's not angry because we . . ." And then it's his turn to trail off. "He respects you enough to make your own choices."

"He told me as much."

"But you don't believe him." My silence is answer enough. "I know why you think you can't trust anyone — by my colors, I know. But you can't go through this alone. And don't say you have me, because we both know you don't believe that either." The pain in his voice nearly flattens me. His fingers shake, shivering against me.

Slowly, I pull my face out of his grasp. "I wasn't going to." A half lie. I feel no claim over Cal, and won't let myself trust him, but I can't distance myself from him either. Every time I try, I find myself wandering back.

"He isn't a child, Mare. You don't have to protect him anymore."

To think, all this time, Kilorn has been angry because I want to keep him alive. I almost laugh at the idea. *How dare I do such a thing? How dare I want to keep him safe?* "Then bring him along next time. Let him stumble into a grave." I know he hears the tremor in my voice, but politely pretends to ignore it. "And since when do you care about him?"

I barely hear his answer as I walk away. "I'm not saying this for his sake."

Down on the runway, the others are waiting. Farley busies herself strapping Nanny to Gareth's chest, using a jerry-rigged harness from one of the jet seats, but Shade is staring at his feet. He heard every word, judging by the stern set of his features. He glares at me as we pass, but says nothing. I'll be in for another scolding later, but for now, our focus turns toward Pitarus and hopefully another successful recruitment.

"Arms in, head down," Gareth says, instructing Nanny. Before our eyes, she morphs from the bulky Lord General into her much smaller, thinner self. She tightens the straps accordingly.

"Lighter this way," she explains with a tiny giggle. After long days of serious talk and restless nights, the sight makes me laugh outright. I can't help it, and have to cover my mouth with my hand.

Gareth awkwardly pats the top of her head. "You never cease to amaze, Nan. Feel free to shut your eyes."

She shakes her head. "Had shut eyes my whole life," she says. "Never again."

When I was a child, dreaming of flying like a bird, I never imagined anything like this. Gareth's legs don't bend, his muscles don't tense. He doesn't push off the ground. Instead, his palms flatten, parallel to the runway, and he simply starts to *lift*. I know the gravity around him is loosening, a thread being untied. He rises with Nanny strapped close, faster and faster, until he's merely a speck in the sky. And then the thread tightens, pulling the little dot along the earth, up and down in smooth, rolling arcs. Loose, then tight, until they disappear over the nearest ridge. From down here, it almost looks peaceful, but I doubt I'll ever find out firsthand. The jet is flight enough for me.

Farley is the first to look away from the horizon and return to the task at hand. She gestures to the rising hill above us, crested with red-and-gold trees. "Shall we?"

I march ahead in reply, setting a good pace to get us up and over the ridge. According to our now vast collection of maps, the mining village of Rosen should be on the other side. Or at least, what once was Rosen. A coal fire destroyed the place years ago, forcing Reds and Silvers alike to abandon the valuable, if volatile, mines. According to Ada's readings, it was abandoned overnight, and most likely has a wealth of supplies for us. For now, I intend to pass through, if only to see what we can raid on the way back.

The ashen smell hits me first. It clings to the west side of the slope, strengthening with every step we take down the ridge. Farley, Shade, and I are quick to cover our noses with our scarves, but Cal isn't bothered by the heavy perfume of smoke. *Well, he wouldn't be.* Instead, he sniffs at it, tentative.

"Still burning," he whispers, eyeing the trees. Unlike the other side of the ridge, the oaks and elms here look dead. Their leaves are few, their trunks gray, and not even weeds grow between their gnarled roots. "Somewhere deep."

If Cal wasn't with us, I would be afraid of the lingering coal fire. But even the red heat of the mines is no match for him. The prince could wave off an explosion if he wanted, and so we continue on, pleasantly silent in the dying wood.

Mine shafts dot the hillside, each one hastily boarded up. One breathes smoke, a dull trail of gray clouds lifting into the hazy sky. Farley fights the urge to investigate, but is quick to climb low branches or rocks. She scouts the area with quiet intensity, always on guard. And always within a few feet of Shade, who never takes his eyes off her. I'm quietly reminded of Julian and Sara, two dancers moving to music no one else can hear.

Rosen is the grayest place I've ever seen. Ash coats the entire village like snow, floating on the air in flurries, hugging the buildings in waist-high drifts. It even blots out the sun, surrounding the village in a permanent cloud of haze. I'm reminded of the techie slums of Gray Town, but that foul place still pulsed like a sluggish, blackened heart. This village is long dead, killed by an accident, a spark deep in the mines. Only the main street, a shoddy cross of a few brick storefronts and plank homes, is still standing. The rest has collapsed or burned. I wonder if there's bone dust swirling in the ash we breathe.

"No electricity." I can't feel anything, not even a lightbulb. A cord of tension releases in my chest. Rosen is long gone, and offers us no harm. "Check the windows."

They follow my example, wiping the glass storefronts with already dirty sleeves. I squint into the smallest of the still-standing buildings, barely a closet squashed between a smashed Security outpost and the half-collapsed schoolhouse. When my eyes adjust to the dim light, I realize I'm looking at rows and rows of books. Cluttered onto shelves, thrown into haphazard piles, spilled across the grimy floor. I grin against the glass, dreaming of how many treasures I can bring back for Ada.

A smash splinters through my nerves. I whirl to the sound, only to see Farley standing by a storefront window. She holds a piece of wood, and there's glass at her feet. "They were trapped," she explains, gesturing into the shop.

After a moment, a flock of crows explodes from the broken window. They disappear into the ashen sky, but their cries echo long after they're gone. They sound like children in pain.

"My colors," Cal swears under his breath, shaking his head in her direction.

She only shrugs, smirking. "Did I scare you, Your Highness?"

He opens his mouth to answer, the corners of his mouth pulled in a smile, but someone cuts him off. A voice I don't recognize, coming from a person I've never seen.

"Not yet, Diana Farley." The man seems to materialize out of the ash. His skin, hair, and clothes are just as gray as the dead village. But his eyes are a luminous, horrifying blood red. "Though you will. You all will."

Cal calls on his fire, I on my lighting, and Farley raises her gun in the direction of the gray man. None of these things seem to frighten him. Instead, he takes a step forward, and his crimson gaze finds me.

"Mare Barrow," he sighs, as if my name brings him great pain. His eyes water. "I feel like I already know you."

None of us move, transfixed by the sight of him. I tell myself it's his eyes, or his long gray hair. His appearance is peculiar, even to us. But that's not what keeps me rooted to the spot. Something else has put me on edge, an instinct I don't understand. Though this man looks bent with age, unable to throw a punch let alone brawl with Cal, I can't help but fear him.

"Who are you?" My quavering voice echoes over the empty village.

The gray man tips his head, staring at each of us in turn. With every passing second, his face falls, until I think he might start crying. "The newbloods of Pitarus are dead. The king waits for you there." Before Cal can open his mouth, to ask what we're all thinking, the gray man holds up a hand. "I know because I have seen it, Tiberias.

Just like I saw you coming."

"What do you mean, *saw*?" Farley growls, taking quick steps toward him. Her gun is still tight in her hand, ready to be used. "Tell us!"

"Such a temper, Diana," he chides, side-stepping her with surprisingly quick feet. She blinks, perplexed, and lunges, trying to grab him. Again, he dodges.

"Farley, stop!" I surprise even myself with the order. She sneers at me but obeys, circling around so that she's behind the strange man. "What's your name, sir?"

His smile is just as gray as his hair. "That is of no consequence. My name isn't on your list. I come from beyond your kingdom's borders."

Before I get a chance to ask him how he knows about Julian's list, Farley charges with all her speed, sprinting at the man's back. Though she makes no sound, though he can't see her, he easily steps out of her path. She falls into the ash face-first, cursing, but wastes no time getting to her feet. Now she has her gun aimed at his heart. "You going to dodge this?" she snarls, letting a bullet click into place.

"I won't have to," he replies with a wry smile. "Will I, Miss Barrow?"

Of course. "Farley, leave him be. He's

another newblood."

"You're . . . you're an eye," Cal breathes, taking a few shuffling steps through the ashen street. "You can see the future."

The man scoffs, waving a hand. "An eye sees only what they look for. Their sight is narrower than a blade of grass." Again, he fixes us with his sad, scarlet stare.

"But I see everything."

TWENTY-ONE

Only when we enter the burned-out husk of the Rosen tavern does the gray man speak again, introducing himself as we take seats around a charred table. His name is shockingly simple. *Jon.* And his presence is the most unsettling thing I've ever felt. Every time he looks at me, with eyes the color of blood, I get the sense that he can see right through my skin, to the twisted thing I used to call a heart. But I keep my thoughts to myself, if only to allow Farley more room to air her grievances. She alternates between grumbling and shouting, arguing that we can't trust this strange man who appeared out of the ash. Once or twice, Shade has to calm her down, putting his hands on her arms to still her. Jon sits through it all with a tight smile, staring down her oppositions, only speaking when she finally shuts her mouth.

"The four of you are well known to me,

so there's no need for introductions," he says, holding up a hand in Shade's direction. My brother makes a strangled kind of noise, drawing back a little. "I found you because I knew where you would be. It was nothing to coordinate my journey with yours," Jon adds, turning his gaze on Cal. His face whitens in a flush, but Jon doesn't bother to watch. Instead, he looks to me, and his smile softens a bit. *He'll be a good addition, albeit a creepy one.* "I have no intention of joining you at the Notch, Miss Barrow."

Then it's my turn to swallow my tongue. Before I can recover enough to ask, he answers for me again, and it feels like a cold stab to the belly. "No, I cannot read your thoughts, but I do see what is to come. For instance, what you say next. I figure I'd save us some time."

"Efficient," Farley grinds out. She's the only one of us not transfixed by this man. "Why don't you just tell us what you came to say and be done with it? Better yet, just tell us what's going to happen."

"Your instincts serve you well, Diana," he replies, bowing his gray head. "Your friends, the shifter and the flyer, will return soon. They met resistance at the Pitarus Security Center, and will need medical attention.

437

Nothing Diana cannot accomplish on your jet."

Shade moves to stand from his chair, but Jon waves him back down. "Easy, you have some time yet. The king has no intention to pursue."

"Why not?" Farley raises an eyebrow.

The crimson eyes meet mine, waiting for me to answer. "Gareth can fly, something no known Silver can do. Maven won't want anyone to see that, even his sworn soldiers." Cal nods next to me, knowing his brother as much — or as little — as I do. "He told the kingdom newbloods didn't exist, and he intends to keep it that way."

"One of his many mistakes," Jon muses, his voice dreamy and faraway. He probably is, looking into a future none of us can comprehend. "But you'll find that out soon enough."

I expect Farley to be the one to snarl at more riddles, but Shade beats her to it. He leans forward on his hands, so that he towers over Jon. "Did you come here to show off? Or just to waste our time?"

I can't help but wonder the same thing.

The gray man doesn't flinch, even in the face of my brother's restrained anger. "Indeed I did, Shade. A few more miles and Maven's eyes would see you coming. Or would you have liked to walk into his trap? I confess, I can see action, but not thought, and perhaps you wanted to be imprisoned and executed?" He looks around at us, his tone shockingly cheerful. One side of his mouth lifts, curving his lips into a half smile. "Pitarus would have ended in death, and even worse fates."

Worse fates. Under the table, Cal's hand closes over my own, as if he feels the tremble of dread coiling in my stomach. Without thought, I open my palm to him, letting his fingers find mine. What worse fates were planned for us, I don't even want to ask. "Thank you, Jon." My voice is thick with fear. "For saving us."

"You saved nothing," Cal says quickly, and his grip tightens. "Any decision could have changed what you saw. A misstep in the woods, the beating of a bird's wings. I know how people like you see, and how wrong your predictions can become."

Jon's smile deepens, until it splits his face. That rankles Cal more than anything else, even more than his birth name. "I see farther and clearer than any of the Silver eyes you've ever met. But it will be your choice to hear what I must say. Although, you do come to believe me," he adds, almost winking. "Sometime around your discovery of the jail. Julian Jacos is a friend, is he not?"

Now both our hands are shaking.

"He is," I murmur, eyes wide and hopeful. "He's still alive, isn't he?"

Again, Jon's eyes gloss over. He mutters to himself, words inaudible, and nods occasionally. On the table, his fingers twitch, moving back and forth like a rake through tilled earth. *Pushing and pulling, but at what?*

"Yes, he is alive. But he is scheduled for execution, as is . . ." He pauses, thinking. "Sara Skonos."

The next moments pass strangely, with Jon answering all our questions before we can get them past our lips. "Maven plans to announce their executions, to set another trap for you and yours. They are being held at Corros Prison. It's not abandoned, Tiberias, but rebuilt for Silver imprisonment. Silent Stone in the walls, diamondglass reinforcements, and military guards. No, that's not all for Julian and Sara. There are other dissenters within the cells, imprisoned for questioning the new king or crossing his mother. House Lerolan has been particularly difficult, as well as House Iral. And the newblood prisoners are proving to be just as dangerous as the Silvers."

"Newbloods?" explodes from me, cutting off Jon as he continues, rapid-fire.

"The ones you never found, the ones you assumed to be dead. They were taken to observe, to examine, but Lord Jacos refused to study them. Even after . . . persuasion."

Bile rises in my mouth. Persuasion can only mean torture.

"There are worse things than pain, Miss Barrow," Jon says softly. "The newbloods are now at the mercy of Queen Elara. She intends on using them — with precision." His eyes stray to Cal and they share a glance filled with painful understanding. "They will be weapons against their own, controlled by the queen and her kin, if given enough time. And that is a very, very dark road. You must not allow this to happen." His cracked and dirty nails dig into the table, carving deep grooves into the blackened wood. "You must not."

"What happens if we free Julian and the others?" I lean forward in my chair. "Can you see that?"

If he's lying, I can't tell. "No. I see only the current path, and however far it leads. For example, I see you now, surviving the Pitarus trap, only to die four days on. You wait too long to assault Corros. Oh wait, it's changed now that I've told you." Another strange, sad smile. "Hmm."

"This is nonsense," Cal growls, untangling

his hand from mine. He stands up from the table, slow and deliberate as rolling thunder. "People go crazy listening to predictions like yours, ruined by knowledge of an uncertain future."

"We have no proof but your word," Farley chimes in. For once, she finds herself in agreement with Cal, and it surprises them both. She kicks back her chair, actions fast and violent. "And a few party tricks."

Party tricks. Predicting what we're going to say, reading Farley's attacks before she makes them, those are no such thing. But it's easier to believe Jon is an impossibility. It's why everyone believed Maven's lies about me, about newbloods. They saw my power with their own eyes, and chose to trust what they could understand, rather than what was true. I'll make them pay for their foolishness, but I won't make their mistake. Something about Jon rattles me, and instinct tells me have faith, not in the man, but at least in his visions. What he says is true, though his reason for telling us might be less than honorable.

His maddening smile flags, twisting into a scowl that betrays a quick temper. "I see the crown dripping blood. A storm without thunder. Shadow twisting on a bed of flames." Cal's hand twitches at his side. "I

442

see lakes flooding their shores, swallowing men whole. I see a man with one red eye, his coat blue, his gun smoking —"

Farley beats a fist against the table. "Enough!"

"I believe him." The words taste strange.

I can't trust my own friends, but here I am, allying myself with a cursed stranger. Cal looks at me like I've grown a second head, his eyes screaming out a question he doesn't dare ask aloud. I can only shrug, and avoid the searing weight of Jon's red eyes. They rove over me, examining every inch of the lightning girl. For the first time in ages, I wish for silk and silver armor, to look like the leader I pretend to be. Instead, I shiver in my threadbare sweater, trying to hide the scars and bones beneath. I'm glad he cannot see my brand, but something tells me he knows about it anyway.

Buck up, Mare Barrow. With a great swell of strength, I lift my chin and shift in my chair, effectively turning my back on the others. Jon smiles in the ashen light.

"Where is Corros Prison?"

"Mare —"

"You can drop me off on the way," I shoot back at Cal, not bothering to watch the verbal blow land. "I'm not leaving them to become Elara's puppets. And I won't abandon Julian, not again."

The lines on Jon's face deepen, speaking of many painful decades. He's younger than I thought, hiding youth beneath the wrinkles and the gray hair. How much has he seen, to make him this way? *Everything,* I realize. *Every horrible or wonderful thing that could ever happen. Death, life, and everything in between.*

"You're exactly who I thought you would be," he murmurs, covering my hands with his own. Veins web beneath his skin, blue and purple and full of red blood. The sight of them brings me such comfort. "I'm grateful to have met you."

I offer up a thin but obliging smile, the best I can do. "Where is the prison?"

"They won't let you go alone." Jon glances over my shoulder. "But we both know that, don't we?"

A warm blush rises to my cheeks and I have to nod.

Jon mirrors the action before his gaze shifts, landing on the table. The dreamy look returns and he pulls his hands away. He stands up on wavering feet, still watching something we cannot see. Then he sniffs and pulls up his collar, gesturing for us to do the same.

"Rain," he warns, seconds before a downpour slams into the roof above us. "Pity we must walk."

I feel like a drowned rat by the time we reach the jet, having hiked straight through mud and torrential rain. Jon keeps us at a steady pace, even slowing us once or twice, to "line things up," as he said. A few seconds after the jet comes into view, I realize what he meant. Gareth tumbles out of the sky, a slowing meteor of wet clothes and blood. He touches down fine, and the bundle in his arms, a baby by the looks of it, springs into midair, transforming before our eyes. Nanny's feet hit the ground hard and she stumbles, dropping to one aged knee. Shade jumps to her side, holding her steady, while Farley pulls Gareth's arm over her shoulder. He gladly puts his weight on her, leaning to compensate for a useless leg dripping blood.

"Ambush in Pitarus," he growls, both in anger and pain. "Nanny got away clean, but they surrounded me. Had to upend a city block before I could break off."

Even though Jon assured us there would be no pursuit, I can't help but watch the darkening sky. Every twist of cloud looks like another airjet, but I hear and feel nothing except the distant shivers of thunder.

"They're not coming, Miss Barrow," Jon

says over the rain. His mad smile has returned.

Gareth glances at him, confused, but nods along. "I don't think anyone followed," he says, trailing into a growl of pain.

Farley adjusts her grip on Gareth, taking on almost his entire weight. Even though she helps him toward the jet, her focus is on Jon. "Was the little beast there?"

Gareth nods. "Sentinels were, so the king couldn't have been far."

She curses, but I don't know who she's angrier at. Maven for ambushing our friends, or Jon for being right.

"Leg looks worse than it is," Jon calls over the rain. He points at Gareth as Farley helps him up the ramp and onto the jet. Then his finger waves to Nanny, still crouched against Shade. "She's bone tired and cold. Blankets should do."

"I'm not some old coot to be wrapped up and shut away," Nanny snarls from the ground. She gets to her feet as quickly as she can, burning a glare at Jon. "Let me walk, Shade, or I'll scold you into oblivion."

"Your call, Nanny," Shade mumbles, fighting a smirk as she struts by him. He gives her enough room to move, but is never more than an arm's length away. Nanny proudly stalks into the jet, her head held high and back ramrod straight.

"You did that on purpose," Cal growls as he shoulders past Jon. He doesn't bother to look back, even when Jon barks a laugh at his retreating form.

"And it worked," he says, low enough so that only I can hear.

Trust the vision, not the man. A good lesson to learn. "Cal's got a thing against mind games," I warn, raising one pointed hand. A spark of lightning runs down my finger. The threat is plain as day. "And so do I."

"I don't play games." Jon shrugs, tapping the side of his head. "Even when I was boy. This made it a bit hard to find competition, you see."

"That's not —"

"I know what you meant, Miss Barrow." His placid smile, once unsettling, has become frustrating. I spin on my heel, making for the jet, but after a few quick steps, I realize Jon isn't following.

He stares into the rain, but his eyes are wide and bright. A vision has not taken hold. He's just standing still, enjoying the feel of cold, clean water washing the ash from his skin.

"This is where I leave you."

The pulse of the jet spooling to life echoes in my rib cage, but it feels distant, unimport-

447

ant. I can only stare at Jon. In the dimming light of the rainstorm, he looks like he's fading away. Gray as the ash, gray as the rain, fleeting as both.

"I thought you were going to help us with the prison?" Desperation floods my voice, and I let it. Jon doesn't seem to mind, so I try another tactic. "Maven's hunting for you too. He's killing all of us, and he'll kill you when he gets the chance."

That makes him laugh so hard he doubles. "You think I don't know the moment I die? I do, Miss Barrow, and it will not be at the king's hands."

My teeth gnash together in irritation. *How can he leave? All the others chose to fight. Why won't he?* "You know I can make you come with us."

In the gray downpour, my lightning seems to spark twice as brightly. Purple-white, hissing in the rain, it twists between my fingers and sends shivers of pleasure up my spine.

Again, Jon smiles. "I know you can, and I know you won't. But take heart, Miss Barrow. We will meet again." He tips his head, thinking. "Yes, yes, we will."

I'm only doing what I promised. I'm giving him a choice. Still, it takes all I have not to drag him onto the jet. "We need you, Jon!"

But he's already begun to back away. Every step makes him harder to see. "Trust me when I say you don't! I leave with you these instructions — fly to the outskirts of Siracas, to Little Sword Lake. Protect what you find there, or your imprisoned friends are as good as dead."

Siracas, Little Sword Lake. I repeat the words until they commit to memory.

"Not tomorrow, not tonight, but now. You *must* fly now."

The roar of the jet expands, until the air itself vibrates with strain. "What are we looking for?" I shout over the din, putting up one hand to shield my face from the spinning rain. It stings but I squint through it, if only to see the last silhouette of the gray man.

"You'll know!" comes out of the rain. "And tell Diana, when she doubts. Tell her the answer to her question is *yes.*"

"What question?" But he ticks a finger, almost scolding.

"Attend to your own fate, Mare Barrow."

"And that is?"

"To rise. And rise alone." It echoes like the howl of a wolf. "I see you as you could become, no longer the lightning, but the storm. The storm that will swallow the world entire."

For a split second, it looks like his eyes are glowing. Red against gray, burning through me, to look into every future. His lips curve into that maddening smile, letting his teeth gleam in the silver light. And then he's gone.

When I stomp aboard the jet alone, Cal has the good sense to let me simmer in my anger. Only despair drowns out my rage. *Rise alone. Alone.* I dig my nails into my palm, trying to chase the sadness with pain. *Fates can change.*

Farley is not so tactful as Cal. She looks up from bandaging Gareth's leg, her fingers sticky with scarlet blood, and sneers. "Good, we didn't need the old loon anyways."

"That old loon could've won this war outright." Shade cuffs her lightly on the shoulder, earning a dark glare. "Think of what he can do with his ability."

From the pilot's seat, Cal glowers. "He's done enough." He watches me take the chair next to him, seething all the while. "You really want to storm a secret prison built for people like us?"

"Would you rather let Julian die?" No answer but for a low hiss. "That's what I thought."

"All right, then," he sighs, easing the jet into a crawl. The wheels bump beneath us, rolling over uneven road. "We have to regroup, get a plan together. Anyone who wants to come is welcome, but no kids."

"No kids," I agree. My mind flashes to Luther and the other newblood children back at the Notch. Too young to fight, but not young enough to be spared from Maven's hunt. They won't like being left behind, but I know how Cal cares for them. He won't allow any of them to see the wrong side of a gun.

"Whatever you're talking about, I'm in." Gareth looks at us around Farley, his teeth gritted against the pain in his leg. "Though I'd like to know what it is I'm signing up for."

Scoffing, Nanny swats at him one bony hand. "Just because you're shot in the leg doesn't mean you can stop paying attention. It's a prison break."

"Too right, Nan," Farley agrees. "And a goose chase if you ask me. Going on the word of a madman."

That stills even Nanny's jokes. She fixes me with a stare only a grandmother could summon. "Is that true, Mare?"

"*Madman*'s a bit harsh," Shade mutters, but he doesn't deny what they're all thinking. I'm the only one who believes Jon, and they trust me enough to follow that faith.

451

"He was right about Pitarus, and everything else he said. Why would he lie about the jail?"

Rise and rise alone.

"He didn't lie!"

My shout silences them all, until there's only the rumble of jet engines. They rise to a familiar dull roar that shudders through the craft, and soon the pavement beneath us falls away. Rain spatters against the windows, making it impossible to see, but Cal's too good to let us drop. After a few moments, we burst through the gunmetal clouds and into bright midday sun. It's like throwing off an iron weight.

"Take us to Little Sword Lake," I murmur. "Jon said we would find something there, something that will help."

I expect more arguments, but no one dares cross me. It's not wise to annoy a lightning girl when you're flying in a metal tube.

Thunder rolls beneath us, in the clouds below, a harbinger of the lightning churning in the rainstorm. Great bolts strike the land, and I feel each one as an extension of myself. Fluid but sharp as glass, burning through everything in their way. The Little Sword is not far, on the northern edge of the storm, and it reflects the steadily clearing sky like a mirror. Cal circles once, high enough and deep enough in the clouds to hide our presence, before he spots a runway half-buried in the forested hills around the lake. When we touch down, I all but leap from my seat, though I have no idea what I'm looking for.

Shade is close behind me as I sprint down the jet ramp, eager to get to the lake. It's a mile north, if memory serves, and I let my inner compass take hold. But I barely make it to the tree line before a familiar sound stops me cold.

The click of a gun.

TWENTY-TWO

She's holding the pistol wrong. Even I know that. It's too big for her, made of shimmering black metal, with a barrel nearly a foot long. Better suited to a trained soldier rather than a shivering, slight teenage girl. *A soldier,* I realize with cold clarity. *A Silver.* It's the same kind of gun a Sentinel shot me with, so long ago in the cells deep beneath the Hall of the Sun. The bullet felt like a blow from a hammer and went straight through my spine. I would've died if not for Julian and a blood healer under his control. In spite of my ability, I raise my hands, palms open in surrender. I'm the lightning girl, but I'm not bulletproof. But she takes this as a threat instead of submission, and tenses, her finger itching too close to the trigger.

"Don't move," she hisses, daring to take another step toward me. Her skin, the dark, rich color of blackwood bark, offers her perfect camouflage in the forest. And yet, I see the red bloom beneath, and the tiny scarlet veins webbing the whites of each eye. I gasp to myself. *She's Red.* "Don't bleeding think about it."

"I won't," I tell her, tipping my head. "But I can't speak for him."

Her brows furrow in confusion. She doesn't have time to be afraid. Shade appears behind her, solidifying out of thin air, and wraps her up in an expert military hold. The gun falls from her grasp, and I snatch it before it can hit the rocky ground. She fights, snarling, but with Shade's arms firmly locked behind her head, she can't do much more than sink to her knees. He follows, keeping her firmly in hand, his mouth set in a grim line. A scrawny girl is no match for him.

The gun feels foreign in my hand. It's not my chosen form of weapon — I've never even shot one before. I almost laugh at that. To come so far without even firing a gun.

"Get your Silver hands off me!" she growls, struggling against Shade's grip. She's not strong, but slippery, with long, lean muscles. Keeping her still is like holding on to an eel. "I won't go back, I won't! You'll have to kill me!"

Sparks crackle in my empty hand, while

the other still clutches the gun. The sight of my lightning freezes her immediately. Only her eyes move, widening in fear.

Her tongue darts out, wetting dry and cracked lips. "Knew I recognized you."

Cal's heat outruns his body, enveloping me in a pocket of warmth moments before he skids to my side. His fingertips burn blue with fear, but his flames recede at the sight of the girl.

"I got you a present," I mutter, pressing the gun into his hand. He glares at it, seeing exactly what I saw.

"How did you get this?" he asks, dropping to a crouch so he can look her in the eye. His manner, cold and firm, takes me back to the last time I watched him interrogate someone. The memory of Farley's screams and frozen blood still turns my stomach. When she doesn't answer, he tightens, a coil of hard muscle. "*This* gun? How?!"

"I took it!" she rages back, squirming. Her joints crack with the action.

I wince with her, and lock eyes with my brother. "Let her be, Shade. I think we can handle this fine."

He nods, glad to let go of the wriggling teenager, and releases her. She pitches forward, but catches herself before eating dirt. She skirts away from Cal's attempt to help. "Don't touch me, Lordy." She looks liable to bite, her teeth bared and gleaming.

"Lordy?" he mutters under his breath, now just as confused as the girl.

Above her, Shade narrows his eyes in realization. "Lordy. High lords — Silvers. It's slum slang," he explains for our benefit. "What Town are you from?" he asks her, his tone much kinder than Cal's. It takes her off guard, and she glances at him, her black eyes darting in fear. But she keeps looking back at me, transfixed by the thin spindles of sparks between my fingers.

"New Town," she finally replies. "They took me from New Town."

Now it's my turn to bend, so I can look at her fully. She seems like my opposite, long and lean where I am short, her braided hair a gleaming oil black while mine fades from brown to splinters of gray. She's younger than me; I can see it in her face. Maybe fifteen or sixteen, but her eyes speak of weariness beyond her short years. Her fingers are long and crooked, probably broken by machinery too many times to count. If she's from the New Town slum, she's a techie, doomed to work the factories and assembly lines of a city born in smoke. There are tattoos on her neck, but nothing so superfluous as Crance's anchor. *Numbers,*

I realize. *NT-ARSM-188907.* Big and blocky, two inches high, wrapping halfway around her throat.

"Not pretty, is it, lightning girl?" she sneers, noting my gaze. Disdain drips from her words like venom from fangs. "But you don't like to bother with ugly things."

Her tone grates, and I'm tempted to show her exactly how ugly I can be. Instead, I hearken back to my court training and do what so many did to me. I smirk in her face, laughing quietly. I hold the cards here, and she needs to know it. Her expression sours, annoyed by my reaction.

"You took this from a Silver?" Cal presses on, gesturing to the gun. His disbelief is plain for all to hear. "Who helped you?"

"No one helped. You should know that firsthand," she throws back. "Had to do it all myself. Guard Eagrie didn't see me coming."

"What?" Only my lessons with Lady Blonos keep me from gasping outright. A soldier of House Eagrie. The House of Eyes. Any one of them can see the immediate future, like lesser versions of Jon. It's almost impossible for a Silver to attack them without them knowing, let alone a Red girl. *Impossible.*

She only shrugs. "Thought Silvers were

supposed to be tough, but she was nothing. And fighting was better than waiting around in my cell. For whatever they had planned."

Cell.

I fall back on my heels, leveled by understanding. "You escaped from Corros Prison."

Her eyes fly to mine, and her lower lip quivers. It's the only indication of the fear coursing beneath her enraged exterior.

Cal's hand finds my elbow, steadying me. "What's your name?" he asks, his tone taking on a gentler edge. He treats her like a spooked animal, and that provokes her like nothing else.

She stands quickly, fists clenched, making the veins stand out in arms scarred by years of factory work. Her eyes narrow, and for a moment, I think she might bolt. Instead, she digs her feet into the dirt and straightens her spine with pride.

"My name is Cameron Cole, and if you don't mind, I'm going to be on my way."

She's taller than me, as graceful and elegant as any lady of court. My head barely reaches her chin when I draw myself up to my full height, but the flicker of fear is still in her. She knows exactly who and what I am.

"Cameron Cole," I repeat. Julian's list

floods my thoughts, her name and information with it. And then, the records from Harbor Bay, more detailed than Julian's findings. I feel quite like Ada when I spit back what I remember, my words quick and sure. "Born January third, 305, in New Town. Occupation: Apprentice mechanic, indentured by Assembly and Repair, Small Manufacturing Sector. Address: Unit Forty-Eight, Block Twelve, Residence Sector, New Town. Blood type: Not applicable. Gene mutation, strain unknown." Her mouth falls open, letting loose a tiny gasp. "Does that sound right?"

She can barely nod her head in agreement. Her whisper is even weaker. "Yes."

Shade whistles under his breath. "Damn, Jon," he murmurs, shaking his head. I nod at him, agreeing. What he sent us to find wasn't an *it* at all, but a *who.*

"You're a newblood, Cameron. Just like Shade and me. Red-blooded, with Silver abilities. That's why they locked you up in Corros, and that's why you were able to escape. Whatever ability you have set you free, so you could find us." I take a step toward her, meaning to embrace my new-blood sister, but she darts away from my touch.

"I didn't escape to find *you,*" she spits.

I smile as best I can for her, trying to put her at ease. After so many recruits, the words come out easy. I know exactly what to say, and exactly how she'll respond. It's always the same. "You don't have to come, of course, but you'll die alone. King Maven *will* find you again —"

Another step back, shocking me. She sneers, shaking her head. "The only place I'm going is the Choke, and not you or your lightning can stop me."

"The Choke?" I exclaim, perplexed.

Next to me, Cal tries his best to be civil. His best isn't very good.

"Idiocy," he snaps. "The Choke has more Silvers than you know, each one instructed to arrest or kill you on sight. If you're *lucky*, they'll take you back to prison."

The side of her mouth twitches. "The Choke has my twin brother and five thousand others like him marching right into a grave. They'd have me too if it weren't for whatever it is that put me in prison. You might be all right with abandoning your own, but I'm *not*."

Her breath comes hard and harsh. I almost see the scales tipping back and forth in her head, weighing her options. She's easy to read, wearing her thoughts and emotions plainly in every twitch of her face. I don't

461

flinch when she runs, sprinting into the trees. We don't follow, and I feel Shade and Cal watching me, waiting for what to do next.

I told myself I would give everyone a choice. I let Jon go, even though we needed him. But something tells me we need Cameron even more, and that the young girl can't be trusted, not with a decision this monumental. She doesn't know how important she is, no matter her ability. She got out of Corros somehow, and she's going to get us back in.

"Grab her," I whisper. It feels wrong.

Shade disappears with a grim nod. Deep in the woods, Cameron screams.

I had to trade seats with Farley, letting her take my pilot's chair so I can sit across from Cameron and keep an eye on her. She's firmly strapped in, with her hands bound in a spare safety belt. That, paired with our current altitude, should be enough to keep her from bolting again. But I'm not willing to take such a chance. For all I know, she can fly or survive a fall from an airjet. As much as I want to use the journey back to the Notch to catch up on much-needed sleep, I keep my eyes open, meeting her glare with as much fire as I can muster. *She chose wrong,* I tell myself every time the guilt creeps up. *We need her, and she's worth too much to lose.*

Nanny babbles at her side, regaling her with tales of the Notch as well as her own life story. I half expect her to pull out the weathered photographs of her grand-children, as she always does, but Cameron stands firm where none of us could. Even the kindly old woman cannot get through to the scowling girl, who stays silent and staring at her feet.

"What's your ability, dear? Superhuman rudeness?" she finally scoffs, fed up with being ignored.

That gets Cameron to at least turn her head, wrenching her eyes off the floor. She opens her mouth to sneer back, but instead of an old woman, she finds herself staring at her own face. "Stop the line!" she curses, letting loose more of her slum slang. Her eyes widen and her bound hands squirm, trying to get free. "Is anyone else seeing this?"

I chuckle darkly to myself, not bothering to hide my smirk. Leave it to Nanny to scare the girl into speaking. "Nanny can shift her appearance," I tell her. "Gareth manipulates gravity." He waves from his makeshift stretcher fixed to the side of the plane. "And

463

you already know about the rest."

"I'm useless," Farley chirps from her seat. A blade flicks back and forth in her hands, betraying exactly how wrong she is.

Cameron snorts, her eyes following the knife as it flashes. "Just like me." There isn't a shred of pity in her voice, only fact.

"Not true." I pat Julian's journal at my side. "You got past an eye, in case you've forgotten."

"Well, that's all I've ever done, or will ever do." The straps around her arms twist, but hold firm. "You grabbed a nobody, lighting girl. You don't want to waste your time on me."

Coming from anyone else, it might sound sad, but Cameron is smarter than that. She thinks I don't see what she's doing. But no matter what she says, no matter how useless she tries to make herself seem, I won't believe it. Her name is on the list, and that's no mistake. Maybe she doesn't know what she is yet, but we will certainly find out. I'm not blind either. Even while I hold her challenging stare, letting her think she has me fooled, I'm aware of her deeper game. Her able fingers, trained on a factory floor, work at her bindings with slow but sure efficiency. If I don't keep an eye on her, it won't be long until she twists out of her restraints.

"You know Corros better than any of us." As I speak, Nanny morphs back to her usual self. "That's enough for me."

"You got a mind reader here then? 'Cause that's the only way you're getting a bleeding word out of me." I half expect her to spit at my feet.

Despite my best efforts, I find myself losing my patience. "You're either useless or you're resistant. Pick one." She raises an eyebrow, surprised by my tone. "If you're going to lie, you might as well do it properly."

The corner of her mouth twitches, betraying a wicked grin. "Forgot you know all about that."

I hate children.

"Don't act so high-and-mighty," she presses on, throwing words like daggers. Besides her voice, the drone of the jet fills the air. The others are listening intently, Cal most of all. I expect to feel heat rise at any moment. "You're no lordy lady now, no matter how many of us you try to order around. Bedding a princeling doesn't make you queen of the heap."

Lights flicker over her head, the only indication of my anger. Out of the corner of my eye, I see Cal tighten his grip on the jet controls. Like me, he's doing his best to keep calm and reasonable. But this bitch insists on making it so difficult. *Why couldn't Jon send us a map instead?*

"Cameron, you're going to tell us how you escaped that prison." Lady Blonos would be proud of my composure. "You're going to tell us what it looks like, where the cells are, where the guards are, where they keep the Silvers, the newbloods, and everything else your remember, down to the last *bleeding* nail. Is that clear?"

She flicks one of her many braids over her shoulder. It's the only thing she can move without straining against her many belts and straps. "What's in it for me, then?"

"Innocence." I heave a breath. "You keep running your mouth and you leave all those prisoners to their fate." Jon's words float back to me, a haunting echo of a warning. "To die, or face worse. I'm saving you from the guilt of that." *A guilt I know too well.*

There's a slow pressure at my shoulder — Shade. Leaning into me, letting me know he's there. A brother in blood and arms, another to share in victory, and blame.

But instead of agreeing, as any rational person should, Cameron looks even angrier than before. Her face darkens, a thundercloud of emotion. "Can't believe you've got the stones to say that. You, who abandoned so many after you sentenced them to the trenches."

Cal's had enough. He slams a fist onto the arm of his chair. It echoes bluntly. "That wasn't her order —"

"But it was your fault. You and your stupid band of ratty red rags." She tosses a glare at Farley, cutting off any retort she might throw. "Gambling with *our* families, *our* lives, while you ran and hid in the woods. And now you think you're some kind of hero, flying around saving everyone you think is *special,* who's worth the lightning girl's precious time. I bet you walk right through the slums and the poor villages. I bet you don't even see what you've done to us." The blood rises with her anger, coloring her cheeks in a dark, lurid flush. I can't do much more than stare. "Newbloods, silverbloods, redbloods, it's all the same, all over again. Some who are special, some who are better than the rest, and the ones who still have nothing at all."

Sickness rolls in my belly, a foreboding wave of dread. "What do you mean?"

"*Division.* Favoring one over the other. You're on the hunt for people like you, to protect them, to train them, to make them fight your war. Not because they want to, but because *you* need them. What about those kids going to fight? You don't care about them at all. You'd trade them all for another walking, whining spark plug."

The lights flicker again, faster than before. I feel every revolution of the jet engines, despite their blinding speed. The sensation is maddening. "I'm trying to save people from Maven. He's going to turn newbloods into weapons, which will end in *more* death, *more* blood —"

"You're doing exactly what *they* did." She points her bound hands at Cal. They shake with anger. I know the feeling, and try to hide the tremors of rage in my own fingers.

"Mare." Cal's warning falls on deaf ears, drowned out by my thundering pulse.

Cameron spits venom. She's enjoying this. "An age ago, when the Silvers were new. When they were few, hunted by the people who thought they were too different."

My hands grip the edge of my seat, digging into something solid. *Control.* Now the jet whines in my ear, a screech to split bone.

We bounce in the air, and Gareth yelps, clutching at his leg. "Cameron, stop!" Farley shouts, her hands flying to her belts. They unsnap in rapid succession. "If you don't shut yourself up, I will!"

But Cameron only has eyes, and anger, for me. "Look where that road led," she growls, leaning as far as her straps will allow. Before I know it, I'm on my feet, my balance unsteady as the jet sways. I can barely hear her over the metallic shrieks bouncing around my skull. Her hands are out of her bindings, unfastening her belts with striking precision. She jumps up to stand, snarling into my face. "A hundred years from now a newblood king will sit the throne you built him on the skulls of children."

Something tears inside me. It's the barrier between human and animal, between sense and madness. Suddenly I've forgotten the jet, the altitude, and everyone else relying on my weakening control. I can think only of *educating* this brat, of showing exactly who and what we're trying to save. When my fist collides with her jaw, I expect to see sparks spread over her skin, dragging her down to the floor.

There's nothing but my bruised knuckles.

She stares, just as surprised as me. All around us, the flickering lights return to normal and the jet levels out. The whine in my head abruptly cuts off, as if a blanket of silence has fallen over my senses. It hits like a punch in the gut, dropping me to one knee.

Shade has my arm in a second, clutching

with brotherly concern. "Are you okay? What's wrong?"

In the cockpit, Cal glances between me and his control panel, his head whipping back and forth. "Stabilized," he mutters, though I'm anything but. "Mare —"

"Not me." A cold sweat breaks across my brow, and I fight the sudden urge to be sick. My breath comes in short pants, like the air is being pressed from my lungs. Something is smothering me. "Her."

She takes a step back, too shocked to lie. Her mouth falls open in fear. "I didn't do anything. I didn't, I bleeding swear it."

"You didn't mean to, Cameron." That might surprise her most of all. "Just calm yourself, just — just stop —" I can't breathe, I really can't breathe. My grip tightens on Shade, nails digging in. Panic spikes through my nerves, alone without my lightning.

He takes my full weight on his bad shoulder, ignoring the slight twinge of pain. At least Shade is smart enough to know what I'm trying to say. "You're silencing her, Cameron. You're shutting her abilities down, you're shutting *her* down."

"I can't — how?" Her dark eyes are full of terror.

My vision spots, but I see Cal blunder past. Cameron flinches away from him, as any person in their right mind would, but Cal knows what to do. He's coached the children, and me, through similar episodes of superhuman chaos.

"Let go," he says, firm and steady. No coddling, but no anger. "Breathe, in through the nose, out through the mouth. Let go of what you're holding."

Please let go. Please let go. My breath comes in gasps, each one shallower than the last.

"Let her go, Cameron."

It's as if a boulder has been placed on my chest, and is pressing me to death, squeezing out any semblance of myself.

"Let her go."

"I'm trying!"

"Easy."

"I'm trying." Her voice is softer, more controlled. "I'm trying."

Cal nods, his motions smooth as rolling waves. "That's it. That's it."

Another gasp, but this time the air sears into my lungs. I can breathe again. My senses are dull, but returning. They increase with every strengthening beat of my heart.

"That's it," Cal says again, looking over his shoulder. His eyes find mine, and a thread of tension releases between us. "That's it."

I don't hold his gaze long. I have to look at Cameron, at her fear. She squeezes her eyes shut and furrows her brow in concentration. A single tear escapes, trailing down her cheek, and her hands massage the tattoo at her neck. She is only fifteen. She doesn't deserve this. She shouldn't have to be so afraid of herself.

"I'm all right," I force out, and her eyes snap open.

Before she slams shut the walls to her heart, relief flashes across her face. It doesn't last long. "This doesn't change how I feel, Barrow."

If I could stand, I would. But my muscles still tremble with weakness. "You want to do this to someone else? To your brother when you find him?"

There it is. The bargain we must make. She knows it too.

"You get us into Corros, and we'll make sure you know how to use your ability. We'll make you the deadliest person in the world."

I fear I will regret those words.

TWENTY-THREE

My voice echoes strangely in the wide entrance chamber of the safe house. The storm from the Rift has caught up with us, and a heavy mix of snow and freezing rain howls on the other side of the dirt wall. Cold comes with it, but Cal does his best to chase it away. The inhabitants of the Notch huddle together, trying to warm themselves over the campfire he kindled on the floor. Every eye catches the firelight, becoming too many red and orange jewels. They flicker with every twist of flame, always staring at me. Fifteen pairs in all. In addition to Cameron, Cal, Farley, and my brother, the adults of the Notch have come to hear what I have to say. Sitting next to Ada are Ketha, Harrick, and Nix. Fletcher, a skin healer immune to pain, extends his pale hands too close to the fire. Gareth pulls him back before his skin can burn. There's also Darmian, invulnerable as Nix, and Lory from the rocky islands of Kentosport. Even Kilorn graces us with his presence, sitting firmly between his hunting partners, Crance and Farrah.

Thankfully there are no children present. They will have no part in this, and continue on in whatever safety I can give. Nanny keeps them in their room, amusing them with her transformations, while anyone over sixteen listens to me explain everything we learned on the way to Pitarus. They sit in rapt attention, faces pulled in shock or fear or determination.

"Jon said four days would be too long. So we must do it in three."

Three days to storm a prison, three days to plan. I had more than a month of hard training with the Silvers, and years before that on the streets of the Stilts. Cal is a soldier from birth, Shade spent more than a year in the army, and Farley is a captain in her own right, though she has no abilities of her own. But the others? As I look on the collected strength of the Notch, my resolve wavers. If only we had more time. Ada, Gareth, and Nix are our best chances, having abilities best suited to a raid, not to mention the most time training at the Notch. The others are powerful — Ketha can obliterate an object with the blink of an eye

474

— but woefully inexperienced. They've been here for a few days or weeks at most, coming from gutters and forgotten villages where they were nothing and no one. Sending them to fight will be like putting a child behind the wheel of a transport. They'll be a danger to everyone, especially themselves.

Everyone knows it's foolish, an impossibility, but no one says so. Even Cameron has the good sense to keep her mouth shut. She glares into the fire, refusing to look up. I can't watch her for long. She makes me too angry, and too sad. She's exactly what I was trying to avoid.

Farley finds her voice first. "Even *if* that Jon character spoke true about his abilities, there's no proof what he told us isn't a lie." She leans forward, cutting a sharp silhouette against the pit of fire. "He could be an agent of Maven's. He said Elara was going to start controlling newbloods — what if she was controlling him? Using him to lure us? He said Maven would set a trap. Maybe this is it?"

With a sinking feeling, I see a few nod along with her. Crance, Farrah, and Fletcher. I expect Kilorn to side with his hunting crew, but he keeps still and silent. Like Cameron, he won't look at me.

Warmth breaks against me on all sides.

From the fire ahead, and Cal behind, leaning against the dirt wall. He radiates like a
furnace, but is quiet as the grave. He knows
better than to speak. Many here tolerate him
only because of me, or the children, or both.
I cannot rely on him to win soldiers. I must
do that myself.

"I believe him." The words feel so foreign
in my mouth, but they are stone solid. These
people insist on treating me like a leader, so
I will act like one. And I'll convince them to
follow. "I'm going to Corros, trap or not.
The newbloods there face two fates — to
die, or be used by the puppeteer everyone
calls the queen. Both are unacceptable."

Murmurs of agreement roll through the
ones I'm trying to win over. Gareth leads
them, bobbing his head in a show of loyalty.
He saw Jon with his own eyes, and needs
no more convincing than I do.

"I won't make anyone go. Like before, you
all have a choice in this." Cameron shakes
her head slightly, but says nothing. Shade
keeps close to her, always within arm's
reach, in case she decides to do something
else stupid. "It will not be easy, but it is not
impossible."

If I say it enough, I might start to believe
it myself.

"How's that?" Crance pipes up. "If I heard

476

you right, that prison was built to keep people like you shut up. It's not just bars and locked doors you'll have to get through. There'll be eyes at every gate, a fleet of Silver officers, an armory, cameras, Silent Stone, and that's only if you're lucky, lightning girl."

Next to him, Fletcher swallows thickly. He might not be able to feel pain, but the pale, fleshy man can certainly feel fear. "And what if you're not?"

"Ask her." I tip my head toward Cameron. "She escaped."

Gasps ripple through the crowd as if they were the surface of a pond. Now I'm not the one they're staring at, and it feels good to relax a little. In contrast, Cameron tightens, her long limbs seeming to fold inward, shielding her from their many eyes.

Even Kilorn looks up, but not at Cameron. His gaze trails past her, finding me as I lean back against the wall. And all my relief washes away, replaced by a twist of some emotion I can't place. Not fear, not anger. No, this is something else. *Longing.* In the shifting firelight, with the storm outside, I can pretend we're a boy and girl huddled beneath a stilt house, seeking refuge from autumn's howl. Would that someone could control the span of time,

477

and bring me back to those days. I would hold on to them jealously, instead of whining about the cold and hunger. Now I'm just as cold, just as hungry, but no blanket can warm me, no food can sate me. Nothing will ever be the same. It's my own fault. And Kilorn followed me into this nightmare.

"Does she speak?" Crance sneers when he gets tired of waiting for Cameron to open her mouth.

Farley chuckles. "Too much for my taste. Go on, Cole, tell us everything you remember."

I expect Cameron to snap again, maybe even bite Farley on the nose, but an audience calms her temper. She sees my trick, but that doesn't stop it from working. There are too many hopeful eyes, too many willing to step in harm's way. She can't ignore them now.

"It's past Delphie," she sighs. Her eyes cloud with painful memory. "Somewhere near the Wash, so close you can almost smell the radiation."

The Wash forms the southern border of Norta, a natural divide from Piedmont and the Silver princes that reign there. Like Naercey, the Wash is a land of ruin, too far gone for Silvers to reclaim. Not even the Scarlet Guard dares walk there, where radiation is not a deception, and the smoke of a thousand years still lingers.

"They kept us isolated," Cameron continues. "One to each cell, and many didn't have enough strength to do anything other than lie on their cots. Something about that place made the others sick."

"Silent Stone." I answer her unasked question, because I remember the same feeling all too well. Twice I've been in such a cell, and twice it leached my strength away.

"Not much light, not much food." She shifts on her seat, eyes narrowed against the flames. "Couldn't talk much either. Guards didn't like us speaking, and they were always on patrol. Sometimes Sentinels came and took people away. Some were too weak to walk and had to be dragged along. I don't think the block was full, though. I saw lots of empty cells in there." Her breath catches. "More every bleeding day."

"Describe it, the structure," Farley says. She nudges Harrick and I understand her line of thinking.

"We were in our own block, the new-bloods taken out of the Beacon region. It was a big square, with four flights of cells lining the walls. There were catwalks connecting the different levels, all tangled, and the magnetrons pulled them back at night.

Same with the cells, if they had to open them. Magnetrons all over," she curses, and I don't blame her for her anger. There were no men like Lucas Samos in the prison, no kind magnetrons like the one who died for me in Archeon. "No windows, but there was a skylight in the ceiling. Small, but enough to let us see the sun for a few minutes."

"Like this?" Harrick asks, and rubs his hands together. Before our eyes, one of his illusions appears above the campfire, an image turning slowly. A box made of faint green lines. As my eyes adjust to what I'm seeing, I realize it's a rough, three-dimensional outline of Cameron's prison block.

She stares at it, eyes flickering over every inch of the illusion. "Wider," she murmurs, and Harrick's fingers jump. The illusion responds. "Two more catwalks. Four gates on the top level, one in each wall."

Harrick does as he's told, manipulating the image until she's satisfied. He almost smiles. This is easy for him, a simple game, like drawing. We stare at the rough picture in silence, each one of us trying to puzzle out a way in.

"A pit," Farrah moans, dropping her head in her hands. Indeed, the prison block looks just like a square, sharp hole.

Ada is less gloomy, and more interested in dissecting as much of the prison as she can. "Where do the gates lead?"

With a sigh, Cameron's shoulders slump. "More blocks. How many total, I don't know. I got through three in a line before I was out."

The illusion changes, adding blocks onto the sides of Cameron's. The sight feels like a punch in the gut. So many cells, so many gates. So many places for us to stumble and fall. *But Cameron escaped. Cameron, who has no training and no idea how much she can do.*

"You said there were Silvers in the prison." Cal speaks for the first time since we began the meeting, and his mood is dark indeed. He won't step into the circle of firelight. For a moment, he looks the shadow Maven always claimed to be. "Where?"

A barking, angry laugh, harsh as stone against steel, escapes from Nix. He jabs an accusing finger in the air, stabbing. "Why? You want to let your friends out of their cages? Send them back to their mansions and tea parties? Bah, let them rot!" He waves a veined hand in Cal's direction, and his laughter turns cold as the autumn storm. "You should leave this one behind, Mare. Better yet, send him away. He's got no mind to protect anything but his own."

My mouth moves faster than my brain, but this time, they're in agreement. "Every single one of you knows that's a lie. Cal has bled for us all, and protected each of us, not to mention trained most of you. If he's asking about the other Silvers in Corros, he has a reason, and it is *not* to free them."

"Actually —"

I spin, eyes wide, and surprise echoes over the room. "You *do* want to free them?"

"Think about it. They're locked up because they defied Maven, or Elara, or both. My brother came to the throne under strange circumstances, and many, *many,* will not believe the lie his mother tells. Some are smart enough to lie low, to bide their time, but others are not. Their court schemes end in a cell. And of course, there are those like my uncle Julian, who taught Mare what she was. He aided the Scarlet Guard, saved Kilorn and Farley from execution, and his blood is blinding silver. He's in that prison too, with others who believe in an equality beyond the colors of blood. They're not our enemies, not right now," he replies. He uncrosses his arms, gesturing madly, trying to make us understand what the soldier in him sees. "If we set them all loose on Corros, it'll be chaos. They'll attack the guards and do everything they can to get out. It's a better distraction than any of us can give."

Even Nix deflates, cowed by the quick and decisive suggestion. Though he hates Cal, blaming him for the death of his daughters, he can't deny this is a good plan. Perhaps the best we might come up with.

"Besides," Cal adds, retreating back into the shadow. This time, his words are meant only for me. "Julian and Sara will be with the Silvers, not the newbloods."

Oh. In my haste, I'd actually forgotten, somehow, that their blood was not the same color as mine. That they are Silver too.

Cal presses on, trying to explain. "Remember what they are, and how they feel. They are not the only ones who see the ruin in this world."

Not the only ones. Logic tells me he must be right. After all, in my own limited time with Silvers, I met Julian, Cal, Sara, and Lucas, four Silvers who were not so cruel as I believed them to be. There must be more. Like the newbloods of Norta, Maven is eliminating them, throwing both dissenters and political opponents into jail to waste away and be forgotten.

Cameron worries at her lip, teeth flashing. "The Silver blocks are the same as ours, staggered in like a patchwork. One Silver, one newblood, Silver, newblood, and so on."

"Checkered," Cal mutters, nodding along. "Keep them separated from each other. Easier to control, easier to fight. And your escape?"

"They walked us once a week, to keep us from dying. Some guard laughed about it, said the cells would kill us if they didn't let us out a bit. The rest could hardly shuffle along, let alone fight, but not me. The cells didn't make me sick."

"Because they don't affect you," Ada says, her voice controlled and even and gently correct. She sounds so much like Julian it makes me jump. For a blistering second, I'm back in his classroom full of books, and I'm the one being examined. "Your silencing abilities are so strong that the normal measures don't work. A canceling effect, I think. One form of silence against another."

Cameron just shrugs, uninterested. "Sure."

"So you slipped away on the walk," Cal mutters, more to himself than anyone else. He's thinking this through, putting himself in Cameron's position, imagining the prison as she escaped, so he can figure out a way to break in. "The eyes couldn't see what you planned to do, so they couldn't stop you. They guarded the gates, yes?"

She bobs her head in agreement. "One watched every cell block. Took his gun, put my head down, and ran."

Crance lets out a low whistle, impressed by her boldness. But Cal is not so blinded, and pushes further. "What about the gates themselves? Only a magnetron can open them."

At that, Cameron cracks a brittle smile. "Seems Silvers are no longer stupid enough to leave command of every cell and gate to a handful of metal manipulators. There's a key switch, to open the doors in case you don't have a magnetron around — or to shut them with stone sliders, if one decides not to play nice."

This is my doing, I realize. *I used Lucas against the cells in the Hall of the Sun. Maven is taking steps to make sure another can't do the same.*

Cal cuts a glance at me, thinking exactly the same thing. "And you have the key?"

She shakes her head, gesturing instead to her neck. The tattoo there is black, darker even than her skin. It marks her as a techie, a slave to the factories and smoke. "I'm a mechanic." She waggles her crooked fingers. "Switches got gears and wires. Only an idiot needs a key to get those working right."

Cameron might be a pain, but she's certainly useful. Even I have to admit that.

"I was conscripted, even though we had jobs in New Town," she continues, dropping her tone.

"The prison, Cameron," I tell her. "We have to focus —"

"Everyone works there, and it used to be we couldn't join the army, even if we wanted." She speaks over me, her voice stronger and louder. To compete would devolve into a shouting match. "The Measures changed that. There was a lottery. One in twenty, for everyone between fifteen and seventeen. My brother and I were both chosen. Long odds, right?"

"Less than a three percent chance," Ada whispers.

"They separated us, me to the Beacon Legion out of Fort Patriot, and Morrey to the Dagger Legion. That's what they did with anyone who made trouble, who even looked at an officer wrong. The Dagger Legion is a death sentence, you know. Five thousand kids who had the spine to fight, and they're going to end up in a mass grave."

My teeth grate together. The memory of the military orders burns sharp and bright in my mind.

"It's a death march after they leave Corvium, a slaughter. Right through the trenches and into the heart of the Choke. They sent Morrey there because he tried to hug our mother one last time."

My tenuous hold on command strains. I see it in every face, as my newbloods digest Cameron's words. Ada is worst of all. She stares at me, never blinking. It's not a harsh look, but a blank one. She's doing her best to keep judgment from clouding her eyes, but it's not working. The fire rages in the center of the floor, turning the whites of her eyes gold and red and glaring.

"There are newbloods in that prison, and Silvers too." Cameron knows she has them in her hand, and tightens her grip. "But there are five thousand children, five thousand Red boys and girls, about to disappear forever. Do you let them die? Do you follow her" — she tosses her head in my direction — "and her pet prince?"

Cal's fingers twitch too close to mine and I pull away. *Not here.* They all know we share a bedchamber, and who knows what else they assume. But I will not give Cameron any more ammunition than what she already has.

"She says you have a choice, but she doesn't know the meaning of the word. I was taken here, just like the legionnaire took me, like the Sentinels took me a few days later. The lightning girl does not give people choices."

She expects me to fight the accusation, but I hold my tongue. It feels like defeat, and she knows it well. Behind her eyes, the gears have already begun to turn. She hurt me before, and she can do it again. *So why does she stay? She could silence us and march out of here. Why stay?*

"Mare saves people."

Kilorn's voice sounds different, older. The longing ache in my chest returns.

"Mare saved every one of you from prison or death. She risked herself every time she walked into your cities. She's not perfect, but she's not a monster, not by any measure. Trust me," he adds, still refusing to look at me. "I have seen monsters. And so will you, if we leave newbloods to the mercy of the queen. Then she'll make you kill each other, until there's nothing left of what you are, and no one alive to remember what you were."

Mercy, I almost scoff. *Elara has none.*

I don't expect Kilorn's words to have much weight, but I'm dead wrong. The rest look on him with respect and attention. It's not the same way they look at me. No, their eyes are always tinged with fear. I'm a general to them, a leader, but Kilorn is their brother. They love him like they never could Cal or even me. They listen.

And just like that, Cameron's victory is snatched away.

"We'll turn that prison into dust," Nix rumbles, putting a hand on Kilorn's shoulder. His grip is too tight, but Kilorn doesn't flinch. "I'll go."

"And me."

"And me."

"Me too."

The voices echo in my head. More than I could have hoped for volunteer. There's Gareth, Nix, Ada, the explosive Ketha, the other invulnerable wrecker Darmian, Lory with her superior senses, and, of course, Nanny has already pledged to come along. The silent ones, Crance, Farrah, Fletcher, and the illusionist Harrick, fidget in their seats.

"Good." I step forward again, fixing them all with the strongest look I can muster. "We'll need the rest of you here, to keep the kids from burning the forest down. And to protect them, if something happens."

Something. Another raid, an all-out attack, what could become a slaughter of the ones I've tried so hard to save. But staying behind is less dangerous than going to Corros, and they exhale sighs of quiet relief. Cameron watches them relax, her face twisted in envy. She would stay with them if she could, but then who would train her? Who would teach her how to control her abilities — and use them? *Not Cal, and certainly not me.* She doesn't like the price, but she'll pay it.

I try to look at the other volunteers in turn, hoping to see determination or focus. Instead, I find fear, doubt, and, worst of all, regret. Already, before we've even begun. What I would give now for Farley's wasted Scarlet Guard, or even the Colonel's Lakeland soldiers. At least they have some shred of belief in their cause, if not themselves. *I must believe enough for all of us. I must put up my mask again, and be the lightning girl they need. Mare can wait.*

Dimly, I wonder if I'll ever get the chance to be Mare again.

"I'll need you to walk me through this again," Cal says, gesturing between Cameron and the spinning illusion of Corros Prison. "The rest of you, eat well and train as best as you can. When the storm lets up, I want to see you all back in the yard."

The others snap to attention, unable to disobey. As I learned to speak like a princess, Cal has always known how to speak like a general. He commands. It's what he's good at, it's what he was *meant* for. And now that he has a mission, a set objective beyond recruiting and hiding, all else fades away. Even me. Like the others, I leave him to his muttered plans. His bronze eyes glow against the faint light of the illusion, as if it has bewitched him. Harrick stays behind, dutifully keeping his illusion alive.

I don't follow the newbloods deeper into the Notch, to the tunnels and holes where they can practice without hurting each other. Instead, I face the storm and step outside, letting a cold blast of freezing rain hit me head-on. Cal's warmth is quickly snuffed out, abandoned behind me.

I am the lightning girl.

The clouds are dark above, swirling with the weight of rain and snow. A nymph would find them easy to manipulate, as would a Silver storm. When I was Mareena, I lied and said my mother was a storm of House Nolle. She could influence the weather as I can control electricity. And in the Bowl of Bones, I called bolts of lightning out of the sky, shattering the purple shield above me, protecting Cal and me from Maven's soldiers as they closed in. It weakened me, but I am stronger now. I must be stronger now.

My eyes narrow against the rain, ignoring the sting of each freezing drop. It soaks through my thick winter coat, chilling my fingers and toes. But they do not numb. I feel everything I must, from the pulsing web beneath my skin to the thing beyond the clouds, beating slowly like a black heart. It intensifies the more I focus on it, and it seems to bleed. Fingers of static spin from the maelstrom I cannot see, until they tangle into the low rain clouds. The hairs on the back of my neck rise as another storm takes shape, crackling with energy. A lightning storm. I clench a fist, tightening my grip on what I've created, hoping it resounds.

The first clap of thunder is soft, barely a rumble. A weak bolt follows, touching down in the valley, briefly visible through the mist of snow and rain. The next one is stronger, veining purple and white. I gasp at the sight, both in pride and exhaustion. Every blast of lightning feels brilliant inside me, but drains as much power as it holds.

"You've got no aim."

Kilorn leans against the opening to the Notch, careful to keep as dry as he can beneath a lip of roof. Away from the fire he looks harder and thinner than ever, though he eats as well as he did in the Stilts. Long hunts and constant anger have taken their toll.

"Guess it's for the best, if you insist on practicing with *that* so close to home," he adds, pointing at the valley. In the distance, a tall pine smokes. "But if you plan on improving, do us all a favor and take a hike."

"Are you talking to me now?" I huff, trying to hide how out of breath I am. I squint, glaring at the smoking tree. A weak bolt slices down a hundred yards away, well past where I'm aiming.

A year ago, Kilorn would've laughed at my efforts and teased me until I fought back. But his mind has matured like his body. His childish ways are disappearing. Once I hated them. Now I mourn them.

He draws up the hood of his sweater, hiding his poorly cut hair. He refused to let Farley shear him into her buzzed style, so Nix tried his hand, leaving Kilorn with an uneven curtain of tawny locks. "Are you letting me go to Corros?" he finally asks.

"You volunteered."

The grin that splits his face is as white as the snow falling around us. I wish he didn't want this so badly. I wish he would listen, and stay behind. But Cal says Kilorn will trust me to make my own decisions. So I must let him make his own.

"Thank you for speaking up for me in there," I continue, meaning every word.

He tips his head, shoving his hair out of his eyes. He picks at the earthen wall behind him and forces an uninterested shrug. "You think you would've learned how to convince people after all those Silver lessons. But then, you are pretty stupid."

Our laughter melds together, a sound I recognize from days gone by. In that moment, we're different from who we are now, but the same as we've always been.

We haven't talked in weeks, and I didn't realize how much I missed him. For a moment, I debate blurting out everything, but fight the painful urge. It hurts to hold back, to not tell him about Maven's notes, or the dead faces I see every night, or how Cal's nightmares keep him awake. I want to tell him everything. He knows Mare as no one else does, as I know the fisher boy Kilorn. *But those people are gone. Those people* must *be gone. They cannot survive in a world like this.* I need to be someone else, someone who doesn't rely on anything but her own strength. He makes it too easy to slip back into Mare, and forget the person I need to be.

Silence lingers, soft as the clouds of our breath in the cold air.

"If you die, I'll kill you."

He smiles sadly. "Likewise."

TWENTY-FOUR

Strangely, I get more sleep in the next three days than I have in weeks. Tough drilling in the yard paired with long planning sessions run us all ragged. Our recruitment trips stop entirely. I do not miss them. Every single mission was a gasp of either relief or horror, and they were both a ruin on me. Too many bodies on the gallows, too many children choosing to leave their mothers, too many torn away from the life they knew. For better or worse, I did it to them all. But now that the jet is grounded, and my time spent poring over maps and floor plans, I feel another kind of shame. I've abandoned the ones still out there, just like Cameron said I abandoned the children of the Little Legion. How many more babies and children will die?

But I am only one person, one little girl who can no longer smile. I hide her from the rest, behind my mask of lightning. But she remains, frantic, wide-eyed, afraid. I push her away in every waking moment, but still she haunts me. She never leaves.

Everyone sleeps hard, even Cal, who makes sure everyone gets as much rest as they can after training. While Kilorn is talking again, allowing himself back into the fold, Cal pulls away more and more as the hours tick by. It's like he has no room left in his head for conversation. Corros has already entrapped him. He wakes before I do, to jot down more ideas, more lists, scribbling over every scrap of paper we can scrounge together. Ada is his greatest asset, and she memorizes everything so intently I fear her eyes might burn holes in the maps. Cameron is never far away. Despite Cal's orders, she looks more exhausted by the minute. Dark circles round her eyes, and she leans or sits whenever she can. But she doesn't complain, at least in front of the others.

Today, our last day before the raid, she's in a particularly foul mood. She takes it out on her training targets. Namely, Lory and me.

"Enough," Lory hisses through gritted teeth. She falls to a knee, waving her hand in Cameron's direction. The teenager clenches a fist but lets go, her ability falling away, pulling back the stifling curtain of silence. "You're supposed to knock out my sense, not *me,*" Lory adds, fighting back to her feet. Though she's from frigid Kentosport, a craggy, half-forgotten harbor town already assaulted by snow and sea storms, she pulls her coat closer around her. Cameron's silence doesn't only take away your blood-born weapons, it shuts you down entirely. Your pulse slows, your eyes darken, and your temperature drops. It unsettles something in your bones.

"Sorry." Cameron has taken to speaking in as few words as possible. A welcome change from her blustering speeches. "No good at this."

Lory snaps back in kind. "Well, you better get good, and fast. We leave tonight, Cole, and you're not just coming to play tour guide."

It's not like me to end fights. Instigate them, yes, watch them, definitely, but stop them? Still, we have no time for arguing. "Lory, enough. Cameron, once more." Mareena's court voice does me well here, and both stop to listen. "Block her sense. Make her *normal.* Control *what she is.*"

A muscle twitches in Cameron's cheek, but she doesn't voice her opposition. For all her complaining, she knows this is something she must do. If not for us, then for herself. Learning to control her ability is the best thing she can do, and it is our bargain. I train her, she takes us to Corros.

Lory is not so agreeable. "You're next, Barrow," she grumbles to me. Her far-north accent is sharp and unforgiving, just like Lory and the harsh place she came from. "Cole, if you make me sick again, I'll gut you in your sleep."

Somehow, that gets a crinkle of a smile out of Cameron. "You can try," she replies, stretching out her long, crooked fingers. "Let me know when you feel it."

I watch, waiting for some sign. But like Cameron, Lory's abilities are a bit harder to see. Her so-called sense ability means everything she hears, sees, touches, smells, tastes is incredibly heightened. She can see as far as a hawk, hear twigs snapping a mile away, even track like a hound. If only she liked to hunt. But Lory is more inclined to guard the camp, watching the woods with her superior sight and hearing.

"Easy," I coach. Cameron's brow creases in concentration, and I understand. It's one thing to let loose, to drop the walls of the dam inside and simply let everything spill out. That's easier than keeping hold, reining yourself in, being steady and firm and controlled. "It's yours, Cameron. You own it. It answers to *you.*"

Something flickers in her eyes. Not her usual anger. *Pride.* I understand that too. For girls like us, who had nothing, expected nothing, it's intoxicating to know there is something of our own, something no one else can claim or take away.

To my left, Lory blinks, squinting. "It's going," she says. "I can barely hear across the camp."

Still far. Her ability remains. "A bit more, Cameron."

Cameron does as I tell her, throwing out her other hand. Her fingers twitch in time with what must be her pulse, shaping what she feels into what she wants it to be. "Now?" she bites out and Lory tips her head.

"What?" she calls, squinting harder. *She can barely see or hear.*

"This is your constant." Without thinking, I reach over, putting my palms against Cameron's shoulders. "This is what you aim for. Soon it'll be as easy as flipping a switch, too familiar to forget. It'll be instant."

"Soon?" she says, turning her head. "We fly tonight."

Without thought, I force her to look back at Lory, my fingers pushing her jaw. "Forget

500

about that. See how long you can hold without hurting her."

"Full blind!" Lory shouts, her voice too loud. *Full deaf, too, I think.*

"Whatever you're doing, it's working," I tell Cameron. "You don't need to say what it is, but just know, this is your trigger." Months ago, Julian told me the same thing, to find the trigger that released my sparks in the Spiral Garden. I know now that letting go is what gives me strength, and it seems Cameron has found whatever enables hers. "Remember how this feels."

Despite the cold, a bead of sweat rolls down Cameron's neck and disappears into her collar. She grits her teeth, jaw clenching to keep back a grunt of frustration.

"It will get easier," I continue, dropping my hands back to her shoulders. Her muscles feel tense beneath my fingers, wiry and taut like cords drawn too tight. While her ability wreaks havoc on Lory's senses, it weakens Cameron as well. *If only we had more time. One more week, or even one more day.*

At least Cameron doesn't have to hold back once we get to Corros. Inside the prison, I want her to inflict as much pain as she can. With her temper and her history in the cells, silencing guards shouldn't be too difficult, and she'll carve us a clear path through rock and flesh. But what happens when the wrong person gets in her way? A newblood she doesn't recognize? Cal? *Me?* Her ability might be the most powerful I've ever seen or felt, and I certainly don't want to be her victim again. Just the thought makes my skin crawl. Deep in my bones, my sparks respond, bursting into my nerves. I have to push them back, using my own lessons to keep the lightning quiet and far away. Even though it obeys, fading into the dull hum I barely notice anymore, the sparks curl with power. Despite my constant worry and stress, my ability seems to have grown. It is stronger than before, healthy and alive. *At least some part of me is,* I think. Because beneath the lightning, another element lingers.

The cold never leaves. It never ends, and it feels worse than any burden. The cold is hollow, and it eats at my insides. It spreads like rot, like sickness, and one day I fear it will leave me empty, a shell of the lightning girl, the breathing corpse of Mare Barrow.

In her blindness, Lory's eyes roll, searching vainly through Cameron's blanket of darkness. "Starting to feel it again," she says loudly. The hiss of her words betrays her pain. Though she's tough as the salty rocks she was raised on, even Lory can't keep quiet against Cameron's weapons. "Getting worse."

"Release."

After a moment too long for my liking, Cameron's arms drop, and her body relaxes. She seems to shrink, and Lory falls to a knee again. Her hands massage her temples and she blinks rapidly, letting her senses return.

"Ow," she mutters, angling a smirk at Cameron.

But the techie girl has no smile in return. She turns sharply on her heel, braids swaying with the motion, until she faces me fully. Or, I should say, she faces the top of my head. I see anger in her, the familiar kind. It will serve her well tonight.

"Yes?"

"I'm done for the day," she snaps, teeth blinding white.

I can't help but fold my arms, drawing my spine up as straight as I can. I feel very much like Lady Blonos when I glare at her. "You're done in two hours, Cameron, and you should wish it was more. We need every second we can get —"

"I said, I am *done,*" she repeats. For a girl of fifteen, she can be disarmingly stern. The muscles of her long neck gleam with sweat, and her breath comes hard. But she fights the urge to pant, trying to face me on even terms. *Trying to seem like an equal.* "I'm tired, I'm hungry, and I'm about to be marched to a battle I don't want to fight, *again.* And I'll be damned if I die with an empty stomach."

Behind her, Lory watches us with wide, unblinking eyes. I know what Cal would do. *Insubordination,* he calls this, and it cannot be tolerated. I should push Cameron harder, make her run a lap around the clearing, maybe see if she can bring down a bird with the pressure of her ability. Cal would make it clear — *she is not in charge.* Cal knows soldiers, but this girl is not one of his troops. She will not bend to my will, or his. She's spent too long obeying the whistles of a shift change, the schedules handed down through generations of enslaved factory workers. She has tasted freedom, and will not submit to any order she doesn't want to follow. And though she protests every moment of her time here, she stays. Even with her ability, she stays.

I will not thank her for that, but I will let her eat. Quietly, I step aside.

"Thirty minutes' rest, then come back."

Her eyes spark with anger, and the familiar sight almost makes me smile. I can't help but admire the girl. One day, we might even be friends.

She doesn't agree, but she doesn't argue either, and stalks away from our corner of the clearing. The others in the yard watch her go, their eyes following her as she defies the lightning girl, but I don't care a bit for what they might think. I'm not their captain, I'm not their queen. I'm not better or worse than any of them, and it's time they started to see me as I am. Another newblood, another fighter, and nothing more.

"Kilorn's got some rabbit," Lory says, if only to break the silence. She sniffs at the air and licks her lips in a manner that would make Lady Blonos screech. "Juicy ones too."

"Go on, then," I mutter, waving my hand to the cook fire on the other side of the clearing. She doesn't need to be told twice.

"Cal's in a mood, by the way," she adds as she flounces past. "Or at least, he keeps cursing and kicking things."

One glance tells me Cal is not outside. For a second, I'm surprised, then I remember. Lory hears almost everything, if she stops to listen. "I'll see to him," I tell her, and set a quick pace. She tries to follow, then thinks better of it, and lets me rush on ahead. I don't bother to hide my concern — Cal is not quick to anger, and planning calms him, makes him *happy* even. So whatever has him in a twist has me worried too, far more than I should be on the eve of our raid.

The Notch is all but empty, with everyone outside training. Even the children have gone to watch their elders learn to brawl, shoot, and control their abilities. I'm glad they're not underfoot, pulling at my hands, pestering me with silly questions about their hero, the exiled prince. I don't have the patience for children like Cal does.

As I round a corner, I almost run headfirst into my brother, coming from the direction of the bedchambers. Farley follows him, smirking to herself, but it disappears the second she spots me.

Oh.

"Mare," she mutters in greeting. She doesn't stop and marches past.

Shade tries to do the same, but I put out an arm to stop him cold.

"Can I help you with something?" he asks. His lips twitch, fighting a losing battle against a wretched, playful grin.

I try to look cross with him, if only to keep up appearances. "You're supposed to be training."

"Worried I'm not getting enough exercise?

I assure you, Mare," he says, winking, "we are."

It makes sense. Farley and Shade have been inseparable for a long while. Still, I gasp aloud, and swat his arm. "Shade Barrow!"

"Oh, come on, everyone knows. Not my fault you didn't figure it out."

"You could've *told* me," I sputter, grasping for something to scold him over.

He only shrugs, still grinning. "Like you tell me all about Cal?"

"That's —" *Different,* I want to say. We're not sneaking off in the middle of the day, or even doing much of anything at night. But Shade holds up a hand, stopping me.

"If it's all the same to you, I really *don't* want to know," he says. "And if you'll excuse me, I think I have some training to do, as you so kindly pointed out."

He retreats, palms outward, like a man surrendering a battle. I let him go, dismissing him with a wave while I fight a smile of my own. A tiny blossom of happiness sparks in my chest, a foreign feeling in so many days of despair. I protect it as I would a candle flame, trying to keep it alive and alight. But the sight of Cal quickly snuffs it out.

He's in our room, seated on an upturned

crate, with a familiar paper spread across his knees. It's the back of one of the Colonel's maps, now covered in painstakingly drawn lines. A map of Corros Prison, or at least as much of it as Cameron could remember. I expect to see the edges of the paper smoking, but he keeps his fire contained to the charred dip in the floor. It casts a dancing red light that must be hard to read by, but Cal squints through it. In the corner of the room, my pack lies undisturbed, full of Maven's haunting notes.

Slowly, I pull up another crate, and sink down beside him. He doesn't seem to notice, but I know he must. Nothing escapes his soldier's sense. When my shoulder bumps his, he doesn't raise his eyes from the map, but his hand slips to my leg, drawing me into his warmth. He doesn't loosen his grip, and I don't push him away. I never truly can.

"What's wrong now?" I ask, laying my head on his shoulder. *So I can see the map better,* I tell myself.

"Besides Maven, his mother, the fact that I *hate* rabbit, and the layout of this hellhole of a prison? Nothing at all, thanks for asking."

I want to laugh, but I can barely muster a smile. It's not like him to joke, not at times like this. I leave poor taste like that to Kilorn.

"Cameron's doing better, if that helps any."

"Really?" His voice reverberates in his chest, thrumming into me. "Is that why you're here and not training her anymore?"

"She needs to eat, Cal. She's not a block of Silent Stone."

He hisses, still glaring at the outline of Corros. "Don't remind me."

"It's in the cells alone, Cal, not the rest of the prison," I remind him. Hopefully he hears me, and pulls himself together long enough to get out of this strange mood. "We'll be fine as long as no one locks us in."

"Let Kilorn know." To my chagrin, he chuckles at his own joke, sounding very much like a schoolboy instead of the soldier we need. What's more, he tightens his grip on my knee. Not enough to hurt, but enough to make his thoughts clear.

"Cal?" I push at his hand, swiping it away like a spider. "What's the matter with you?"

Finally, he snaps his head up and looks at me. He's still smiling, but there isn't a shred of laughter in his eyes. Something dark draws across them, turning him into someone I don't recognize at all. Even in the

Bowl of Bones, before his own brother sentenced him to death, Cal did not look like this. He was afraid, distraught, a wretch instead of a prince, but he was still Cal. I could trust that frightened person. But this? This laughing boy with wandering hands and hopeless eyes? *Who is he?*

"Do you want a list?" he replies, grinning wider, and something in me snaps. I hit him hard, one balled fist to his shoulder. He's huge, but he doesn't fight the momentum of my blow, and lets it knock him backward, catching me off guard. I fall with him, and we land on the earthen floor. His head thumps back, a hollow noise, and he grumbles in pain. When he tries to get up, I push, holding him firmly beneath me.

"You're not getting up until you pull yourself together."

To my surprise, he only shrugs. He even *winks.* "Not much of an incentive."

"Ugh." Once, the noble ladies of Norta would have fainted if Prince Tiberias winked at them. It only turns my stomach, and I punch him again, this time in the gut. At least he has the good sense to keep his mouth shut, and his eyes blissfully wink-free. "Now tell me what your problem is."

What began as a smile twists into a frown, and he lays his head back. His brow furrows. He contemplates the ceiling. *Better than acting like a fool.*

"Cal, there are eleven people coming with us to Corros. Eleven."

His jaw clenches. He knows what I'm getting at. *Eleven who will die if we don't pull this off, and countless more in Corros if we leave them alone.*

"I'm scared too." My voice quivers more than I want it to. "I don't want to let them down, or get them hurt."

Again, his hand finds my leg. But his touch is not urgent, not pressing. It's simply a reminder. *I am here.*

"But most of all" — my breath catches, hanging on a sharp edge of truth — "I'm afraid for me. I'm afraid of the sounder, of feeling like that again. I'm afraid of what Elara will do if she gets to me. I know I'm more valuable than most, because of what I've done and what I *can* do. My name and face have as much power as my lightning, and that makes me important. It makes me a better prize." *It makes me alone.* "And I *hate* thinking this way, but I still do."

What began as Cal's breakdown has become mine. One dark night I spilled my secrets to him, on a road thick with summer heat. I was the girl who tried to steal his money then. Now, winter looms, and

I'm the girl who stole his life.

The worst of my confessions lingers, rattling my brain like a bird in a cage. It knocks against my teeth, begging to be free. "I miss him," I whisper, unable to hold Cal's gaze. "I miss who I thought he was."

The hand on my leg balls into a fist, and heat spreads from it. *Anger.* Cal's easy to read, and it's a welcome respite after so long in a den of lying wolves.

"I miss him too."

My eyes snap back to his, startled beyond belief.

"I don't know what will make it easier to forget him. To think that he wasn't always this way, that his mother poisoned him. Or that he was simply born a monster."

"No one is born a monster." *But I wish some people were. It would make it easier to hate them, to kill them, to forget their dead faces.* "Even Maven."

Without thinking, I lay down, my heart against his. They beat in time, mirroring our joined memories of a boy with a quick tongue and blue eyes. Clever, forgotten, compassionate. We will never see that boy again. "We have to let him go," I murmur against his neck. "Even if it means killing him."

"If he's at Corros —"

"I can do it, Cal. If you can't."

He's quiet for what feels like an eternity, but can't be more than a minute. Still, I almost fall asleep. His warmth is more inviting than the finest bed in any palace. "If he's at Corros, I'm going to lose control," he finally says. "I'm going to go after him with everything I have, him and Elara both. She'll use my anger, and she'll turn it on you. She'll make me kill you, like she made me —"

My fingers find his lips, stopping him from saying the words. They cause him so much pain. In that instant, I glimpse a man with no drive but vengeance, and no heart but the one I broke for him. Another monster, waiting to take true form.

"I won't let that happen," I tell him, pushing away our deepest fears.

He doesn't believe me. I see it in the darkness of his eyes. The emptiness, the one I saw in Ocean Hill, threatens to return.

"We are not going to die, Cal. We've come too far for that."

His laugh is hollow, aching. He pushes my hands away gently, but never lets go of my wrist. "Do you know how many people I love are dead?"

I know he feels the thrum of my pulse, and I'm too close to mask the pain I feel for him. He almost sneers at my pity.

"All gone. All murdered. By *her.*" *Queen Elara.* "She kills them, and then she erases them."

Another would assume he's thinking about his father, or even the brother he thought Maven was. But I know better. "Coriane," I murmur, speaking the name of his mother. Julian's sister. The Singer Queen. Cal doesn't remember her, but he can certainly mourn her.

"That's why Ocean Hill was my favorite. It was hers. Father gave it to her."

I blink, trying to remember past the nightmare that was the Harbor Bay palace. Trying to remember what it looked like while we were fighting for our lives. Dimly, slowly, I remember the colors that dominated the insides. Gold. Yellow. Like old paper, like Julian's robes. The color of House Jacos.

It's why he looked so sad, why he couldn't burn the banners. Her banners.

I don't know what it's like to be an orphan. I've always had a mother and father. It's a blessing I never understood until they were taken away from me. It feels wrong to miss them in this moment, knowing they are safe while Cal's parents are dead and gone. And now, more than ever, I hate the cold inside me, and my selfish fear at being left alone. Of the two of us, Cal is lonelier than I'll ever be.

But we cannot stay in our thoughts and memories. We cannot linger in this moment.

"Tell me about the prison," I press on, forcing a new topic. I will pull Cal out of this slump even if it kills me.

The strength of his sigh heaves his whole body, but he's grateful for the distraction. "It's a pit. A fortress protected by ingenious design. The gates are on the top level, with the cells beneath, and magnetron catwalks connecting everything. A flick of the wrist will drop us forty feet, and put us at the bottom of a barrel. They'll massacre us and anyone we let out."

"What about the Silver prisoners? You don't think they'll put up much of a fight?"

"Not after weeks in silent cells. They'll be an obstacle, but not much. And it'll make their escape slow."

"You're . . . going to let them escape?"

His silence is answer enough.

"They might turn on us down there, or come after us later."

"I'm no politician, but I think a prison break will give my brother more than a few headaches, especially if the runaway prisoners happen to be his political enemies."

I shake my head.

"You don't like it?"

"I don't trust it."

"There's a surprise," he says dryly. One of his fingers loops at my neck, tracing the scars his brother's device gave me. "Brute force is not going to win this for you, Mare. No matter how many newbloods you collect. Silvers still outnumber you, and they still have the advantage."

The soldier advocating for a different kind of fight. How ironic.

"I hope you know what you're doing."

He shrugs beneath me. "Political intricacies aren't exactly my strong suit," he says. "But I'll give it a shot."

"Even if it means civil war?"

Months ago, Cal told me what rebellion would be. A war on both sides, in each color of blood. Red against Red, Silver against Silver, and everything in between. He told me he would not risk his father's legacy for a war like that, even if the war was just. Silence falls again, and Cal refuses to answer. I suppose he doesn't know where he stands anymore. Not a rebel, not a prince, not sure of anything except the fire in his bones.

"We might be outnumbered, but that doesn't stack the odds against us," I say.

Stronger than both. That's what Julian wrote to me, when he discovered what I was. Julian, who I may, to my great surprise, very well see again. "Newbloods have abilities no Silver can plan for, not even you."

"What are you getting at?"

"You're going into to this like you're leading your troops, with abilities you understand and have trained with."

"And?"

"And I'd like to see what happens when a guard tries to shoot Nix or a magnetron drops Gareth."

It takes Cal a second to realize what I'm saying. Nix is invulnerable, stronger than a stoneskin. And Gareth, who can manipulate gravity, will not be falling anywhere anytime soon. We don't have an army, but we certainly have soldiers, and abilities the Silver guards don't know how to fight. When it dawns on him, Cal grips the sides of my face, pulling me upward. He plants a firm, fiery kiss that is far too short for my liking.

"You're a genius," he mutters, and springs to his feet. "Get back to Cameron, get everyone ready." He grabs the map in one hand, almost mad with intensity. The same crooked smile returns, but this time I don't hate it. "This might actually work."

TWENTY-FIVE

The Notch flickers behind me, and I watch in awe as my home of the last few months disappears with a single sweep of Harrick's hand. The hill remains, as does the clearing, but any sign of our camp wipes away like sand from a flat stone. We can't even hear the children who were standing there a moment ago, waving good-bye, their voices echoing in the night. Farrah muffles them all and, together with Harrick, drops a curtain of protection around the youngest newbloods. No one has ever come close to finding us, but the added defense gives me more comfort than I care to admit. Most of the others let out victorious whoops, as if the act of disguising the Notch alone is cause for celebration. To my annoyance, Kilorn leads the cheer, whistling hard. But I don't scold him, not now when we're finally back on speaking terms. Instead, I offer a forced smile, my teeth gritted painfully together. It keeps back the words I wish I could say — *Save your energy.*

Shade is just as quiet as I am, and falls in next to me. He doesn't look back at the now empty clearing, and keeps his eyes forward, to the dark, cold woods and the task ahead of us. His limp is almost entirely gone and he sets a quick pace that I eagerly follow, drawing the rest along with us. The hike to the airjet is not long. I try to take in every second of it. The cold night air bites at my exposed face, but the sky is blissfully clear. No snow, no storms — *yet.* For a storm is certainly coming, whether by my hand or someone else's. And I have no idea who will survive to see the dawn.

Shade murmurs something I don't hear, putting one hand on my shoulder. Two of his fingers are crooked, still healing from when we recruited Nanny in Cancorda. A strongarm managed to get a grip on Shade, and crushed the first fingers on his left hand before he could jump away. Farley patched him up, of course, but the sight still makes me cringe. It reminds me of Gisa, another Barrow broken to pay for my deeds.

"This is worth the cost," he says again, his voice louder than before. "We're doing the right thing."

I know that. As afraid as I am for myself

and those closest to me, I know that Corros is the right choice. Even without Jon's assurance, I believe in our path. How could we not? Newbloods cannot be left to Elara's whispering, to be killed or made into hollow, soulless shells to follow her orders. This is what we must do to stop a more horrible world than the one we live in now.

Still, Shade's assurance is a warm blanket of comfort. "Thank you," I mutter back, putting a hand over his.

He smiles in reply, a crescent of white to reflect the waning moon. In the darkness, he looks so much like our father. Without age, without the wheelchair, without the burdens of a life come undone. But they share the same intelligence, the same slanting suspicion that kept them both alive on the war front, and now keeps Shade alive on a very different battlefield. He pats me on the cheek, a familiar gesture that makes me feel like a child, but I don't dislike it. It's a reminder of the blood we share. Not in mutation, but birth. Something deeper and stronger than any ability.

On my right, Cal marches on, and I pretend not to feel his gaze. I know he's thinking about his own brother and his own bonds of blood now torn apart. And behind him is Kilorn, clutching his hunting rifle, scanning the woods for any and all shadows. For all their differences, the two boys share a startling connection. They are both orphans, both abandoned, with no one but me to anchor them.

Time passes too quickly for my taste. It seems like we're on the Blackrun and soaring through the air in moments. Every second moves faster than the last as we hurtle toward the dark cliff before us all. *This is worth the cost,* I tell myself, repeating Shade's words over and over. I must keep calm, for the jet. I must not look afraid, for the others. But my heart thrums in my chest, so loud I fear everyone can hear it.

To combat the harried beat, I press myself against the flight helmet in my lap, curling my arms around the smooth, cool shape. I stare at the polished metal, examining my reflection. The girl I see is both familiar and foreign, Mare, Mareena, the lightning girl, the Red Queen, and no one at all. She does not look afraid. She looks carved of stone, with severe features, hair braided tight to her head, and a tangle of scars on her neck. She is not seventeen, but ageless, Silver but not, Red but not, human — but *not.* A banner of the Scarlet Guard, a face on a wanted poster, a prince's downfall, a thief . . . a

521

killer. A doll who can take any form but her own.

The extra flight suits from the jet stores are black and silver, providing us with a ragtag kind of uniform that will also serve as our disguises. The others fuss over their suits, making adjustments where they must to fit into them. As always, Kilorn fiddles with his collar, trying to loosen the stiff fabric a little. Nix's barely zips over his belly, and looks liable to rip open at any moment. In contrast, Nanny is practically swimming in hers but doesn't bother to roll her sleeves or pant legs like I have to. She'll take a different form when the jet lands, a form that turns my stomach and makes my heart race with too many emotions to count.

Luckily, the Blackrun was built for transport, and holds all eleven of us with room to spare. I expect the extra weight to slow us down, but judging by the control panel, we're cruising along at the same speed as always. Maybe even a little faster. Cal pushes the craft as best as he can, keeping us out of the moonlight and safely hidden in the autumn clouds rolling along the Nortan coast.

He glares out the window, eyes flitting between the clouds and the many blinking instruments before him. I still don't understand what any of them mean, despite my many weeks sitting next to him in the cockpit. I was a poor student in the Stilts and that has not changed. I simply don't have a mind like he does. I know only shortcuts, how to cheat, how to lie, how to steal, and I know how to see what people hide. And right now, Cal is certainly hiding something. I would be afraid of anyone else's secrets, but I know what Cal keeps close cannot hurt me. He's trying to bury his own weakness, his own fear. He was raised to believe in strength and power and nothing else. To falter was the ultimate mistake. I told him before that I was afraid too, but a few whispered words are not enough to break years of belief. Just like me, Cal puts up a mask, and he won't even let me see behind it.

It's for the best, the practical side of me thinks. The other part, the one that cares too much for the exiled prince, worries terribly. I know the physical danger of this mission, but the emotional never crossed my mind until this afternoon. What will Cal become in Corros? Will he leave the same way he went in? *Will he leave at all?*

Farley checks our cache of weapons for the twelfth time. Shade tries to help and she bats him away, but there's little force behind the action. Once, I catch a smirk pass between them, and she finally allows him to count out bullets from a packet marked *Corvium.* Another stolen shipment, Crance's doing most likely. Together with Farley's contacts, he managed to smuggle us more guns, blades, and various other weapons than I could have imagined possible. Everyone will be armed, with their ability and whatever else they choose. I myself want nothing but my lightning, but the others are more eager, claiming daggers or pistols or, in Nix's case, the brutal, collapsible spear he's favored these past few weeks. He hugs it close, running his fingers along the sharpened steel with abandon. Another would have cut himself open by now, but Nix's flesh is tougher than most. The other invulnerable newblood, Darmian, follows his lead and lays a thick, cleaver-like blade across his knobbly knees. The edge gleams, begging to cut through bone.

As I watch, Cameron shakily takes a small knife, careful to keep it sheathed. She spent the last three days honing her ability, not her knife work, and the dagger is a last resort, one I hope she doesn't have to utilize. She catches my eye, her expression pained, and for a moment I fear she might snap at me or, worse, see through my mask.

Instead, she nods in grim acknowledgment.

I nod back, extending the invisible hand of friendship between us. But her gaze hardens and she looks away sharply. Her meaning is clear. *We are allies but not friends.*

"Not long now," Cal says, nudging me on the arm so that I turn around. *Too soon,* my mind screams, though I know we're right on schedule.

"This will work." My voice shakes, and thankfully he's the only one to hear it. He doesn't poke at my weakness, letting it fester. "This will work." Even weaker this time.

"Who has the advantage?" he asks.

The words shock, sting, and soothe in succession. Instructor Arven asked the same thing in Training, when he paired his students against each other in battles for blood and pride. He asked it again in the Bowl of Bones, before a Rhambos strongarm skewered him like a fat, foul pig. I hated the man, but that doesn't mean I didn't learn anything from him.

We have surprise; we have Cameron; we have Shade and Gareth and Nanny and five other newbloods no Silver could possibly plan for. We have Cal, a military genius.

And we have cause. We have the Red dawn at our backs, begging to rise.

"*We* have the advantage."

Cal's grin is just as forced as mine, but it warms me anyway. "That's my girl."

Again, his words bring forth roiling, conflicting emotion.

A click and a hiss of static from the radio wipe all thoughts of Cal from my mind. I turn my gaze on Nanny, who nods in reply. Before my eyes, her body changes, transforming from an old woman into a boy with ice-blue eyes, black hair, and no soul. *Maven.* Her clothes shift with her appearance, replacing the flight suit with a pristine, black dress uniform, complete with a row of gleaming medals and a bloodred cape. A crown nestles in the black curls, and I have to fight the urge to toss it from the jet.

The others watch in rapt attention, amazed by the sight of the false king, but I feel only hatred, and the smallest twinge of regret. Nanny's kindness bleeds through the disguise, turning Maven's lips into a soft smile I recognize far too well. For a single, painful moment, I'm looking at the boy I thought he was, and not the monster he turned out to be.

"Good," I force out, my voice thick with emotion. Only Kilorn seems to notice, and wrenches his gaze away from Nanny. I barely shake my head at him, telling him not to worry. We have more important things to dwell on.

"Corros Air, this is Fleet Prime," Cal says into the radio. On other flights, he did his best to sound bored, uninterested in the mandatory call-ins to different bases, but now he's all business. After all, we're pretending to be the king's own transport, what is known as Fleet Prime, a craft above all scrutiny. And Cal knows firsthand what this particular call-in is supposed to sound like. "The Throne approaches."

No complicated call sign, no requesting permission to land. Nothing but stern authority, and any operator on the other end would be hard-pressed to deny him. As expected, the responding voice stammers.

"R-r-r-received, Fleet Prime," a man says. His deep, rasping voice does nothing to hide his unease. "Your pardon, but we were not expecting His Royal Highness until tomorrow afternoon?"

Tomorrow. The fourth day, when Jon said we would die — and he was right. Maven would bring an army of guards with him, from Sentinels to deadly warriors like Ptolemus and Evangeline. We would be no match for them.

I wave a hand behind me, gesturing, but Nanny's already there. Her closeness in

527

Maven's form makes my skin prickle.

"The king follows no schedule but his own," she says into the radio, her cheeks flushed silver. Her tone isn't sharp enough, but the voice is unmistakable. "And I will not explain myself to a glorified doorman."

A crash on the other end of the radio can only be the operator falling out of his seat. "Yes — yes, of course, Your Highness."

Behind us, someone snorts into his sleeve. Probably Kilorn.

Cal offers Nanny a nod, before taking the radio mouthpiece back. I see the same pain in him, the one I feel too deeply. "We will be landing in ten minutes. Prepare Corros for the king's arrival."

"I'll see to it personal —"

But Cal switches off the radio before the operator can finish, and allows himself a single, relieved smile. Again, the others cheer, celebrating a nonexistent victory. Yes, the obstacle is hurdled, but many more will follow. All of them are below us, on the gray-green fields that edge the Wash wastelands, hiding the prison that might be our doom.

A tinge of daylight bleeds on the eastern horizon, but the sky above is still a deep, drowning blue when the Blackrun lands on the smooth Corros runway. This is not a military base crowded with jet squadrons and hangars, but it's still a Silver facility, and a palpable air of danger hangs over everything. I slide the flight helmet over my head, hiding my face. Cal and the others follow suit, donning their own helmets and slapping the face shields into place. To an outsider, we must look frightening. All in black, masked, accompanying the young, ruthless king to his prison. Hopefully the guards will look right past us, more concerned with the king's presence than his companions'.

I can't sit any longer, and get out of my chair as fast as I can. The safety belts dangle in my wake, jingling together. I do what I must, what I wish I didn't have to, and take Nanny by the arm. *She even feels like Maven.*

"Look through people," I tell her, my voice muffled by the helmet. "Smile without kindness. No small talk, no court talk. Act as if you have a million secrets, and you're the only one important enough to know them all."

She nods, taking this all in stride. After all, Cal and I have both instructed her on how to pass as Maven. This is merely a reminder, a last glance at the book before the test. "I'm not a fool," she replies coldly, and I almost punch her in the jaw. *She is not Maven* rings in my head, louder than a bell.

"I think you've got it," Kilorn says as he stands. He grabs my arm, pulling me slightly away. "Mare nearly killed you."

"Everyone ready?" Farley shouts from the rear of the jet. Her hand hovers next to the ramp release, eager to press it.

"Form up!" Cal barks, sounding a bit too much like a drill sergeant. But we respond, falling into the ordered lines he taught us, with Nanny at the head. He takes her side, falling into the role of her most lethal bodyguard.

"Let's make some bad decisions," Farley says. I can almost hear her smiling as she pushes the release.

A hiss — then gears turn, wires pulse, and the back of the jet yawns open to greet the last morning some of us will ever see.

A dozen soldiers wait a respectable distance from the Blackrun, their formation tight and practiced. At the sight of the newblood masquerading as their king, they snap into stiff, perfect salutes. One hand to the heart, one knee to the ground. The world looks darker behind the shield of my flight helmet, but it doesn't hide the clouded gray of their military uniforms, or the squat, unassuming compound behind them. No bronze gates, no diamondglass walls — there aren't even windows. Just a single, flat brick of concrete stretching out into the abandoned fields of this wasteland. *Corros Prison.* I allow myself one glance back at the craft and the runway stretching into the distance where shadows and radiation dance. I can just see a pair of airjets idling in the gloom, their metal bellies full and round. Prison planes, used to transport the captured. And if all goes to plan, they'll see action again soon.

We approach Corros in silence, trying to march in step. Cal flanks Nanny, one fist permanently clenched at his side, while I trail just behind, with Cameron on my left and Shade on the right. Farley and Kilorn keep to the center of the formation, never letting go of their guns. The air itself seems electrified, coursing with danger.

It is not death I fear, not anymore. I've faced dying too many times to be afraid of it. But the prison itself, the thought of being captured, forced into chains, turned into the Queen's mindless puppet — *that* I cannot bear. I would rather die a hundred times than face such a fate. So would any of us.

"Your Highness," one of the soldiers says,

daring to look up at the person he believes to be king. The badge on his breast, three crossed swords in red metal, mark him as a captain. The bars on his shoulders, bright red and blue, can only be his house colors. *House Iral.* "Welcome to Corros Prison."

As instructed, Nanny looks straight through him, waving one pale hand in dismissal. That should be enough to convince anyone of her supposed identity. But as the soldiers stand, the captain's eyes flick over us, noting our own uniforms — and the lack of Sentinels accompanying the royal sovereign. He hesitates on Cal, one razored glance focusing on his helmet. He says nothing, however, and his soldiers fall into formation next to us, their footsteps echoing with ours. *Haven, Osanos, Provos, Macanthos, Eagrie* — I note the familiar colors on a few uniforms. The last, House Eagrie, the House of Eyes, is our first target. I tug on Cameron's sleeve, nodding gently toward the bearded blond man with darting eyes and white-and-black stripes on his shoulder.

She inclines her head, and her fists ball at her sides in quiet concentration. The raid has begun.

The captain takes Nanny's other side, stepping in front of me so smoothly I barely notice. *A silk.* He has the same tanned skin, gleaming black hair, and angled features of Sonya Iral and her grandmother, the sleekly dangerous Panther. I can only hope the captain is not so talented at intrigue as she is, or else this is going to be much more difficult than expected.

"Your specifications are nearly completed, Your Highness," he says. There's a prickling air to his words. "Every cell block is individually sealed, as instructed, and the next shipment of Silent Stone arrives tomorrow with the new unit of guards."

"Good," Nanny replies, sounding uninterested. Her pace quickens a little, and the captain adjusts in kind, keeping up with her. Cal does the same, and we follow. It looks like a chase.

While the Security Center of Harbor Bay was a beautiful structure, a vision of carved stone and sparkling glass, Corros is as gray and hopeless as the waste around it. Only the entrance, a single, black-iron door set flush against the wall, breaks the monotony of the prison. No hinges, no lock or handle — the door looks like an abyss, like a gaping mouth. But I feel electricity, bleeding around the edges, originating from a small square panel set next to it. *The key switch.* Just like Cameron said. The key itself dangles from a black chain at Iral's neck, but he doesn't pull it loose.

There are cameras too, beady little eyes trained on the door. They don't bother me in the slightest. I care more about the silk captain and his soldiers, who have us surrounded, and keep us marching forward.

"I'm afraid I don't know you, Pilot, or the rest of you for that matter," the captain prods, leaning so he can see past Nanny and fix Cal with a flint-eyed stare. "Would you identify yourself?"

I clench my fist to keep my fingers from shaking. Cal does no such thing, and barely turns his head, reluctant to even acknowledge the prison captain. "Pilot suits me fine, Captain Iral."

Iral bristles, as expected. "The Corros facility is under my command and my protection, *Pilot*. If you think I'm going to let you inside without —"

"Without what, Captain?" Every word out of Nanny's mouth cuts like a knife, slicing through the deepest parts of me. The captain stops cold and flushes silver, swallowing an ill-advised retort. "Last I checked, Corros belongs to Norta. And who does Norta belong to?"

"I am only doing my job, Your Highness," he sputters, but the battle is already lost. He puts a hand to his heart again, saluting.

"The queen charged me with defense of this prison, and I only wish to obey her commands, as well as yours."

Nanny nods. "Then I *command* you to open the door."

He bows his head, giving way. One of his soldiers, an older woman with a severe, silver braid and square jaw, steps forward, laying one hand on the iron door. I don't need the black-and-silver stripes on her shoulder to know she's of House Samos. The iron shifts beneath her magnetron touch, splintering into jagged pieces that retract with sharp efficiency. A blast of cold air hits us head-on, smelling faintly of damp and something sour. *Blood.* But the entrance hall beyond is made of stark, blinding-white tiles, each one without a hint of stain. Nanny is the first to step inside, and we follow.

Next to me, Cameron trembles, and I nudge her softly. I would hold her hand if I could. I can only imagine how terrible this must be — I would tear myself apart before returning to Archeon. And yet, she returns to her own prison for me.

The entrance is strangely empty. No pictures of Maven, no banners. This place has no one to impress, and needs no decoration. There are only whirring cameras.

Captain Iral's soldiers quickly retake their posts, flanking each of the four doors around us. The one behind, the black, shuts with the earsplitting screech of metal sliding against metal. The doors to the left and right are painted silver, and gleam in the harsh prison light. The one ahead, the one we must pass through, is a sickening bloodred.

But Iral stops short, gesturing to one of the silver doors. "I assume you'd like to see Her Highness, the queen?"

I am very glad for our helmets, or else the captain would see horror on every single face. *Elara is here.* My stomach flips at the thought of facing her, and I'm almost sick inside my helmet. Even Nanny pales and her voice sticks, despite her best efforts. I feel Kilorn at my back, inches from me. He is silent, but I hear his meaning all the same. *Run. Run. Run.* But running is not something I can do anymore.

"Her Highness is here?" Cal bites out. For a second, I'm afraid he's forgotten himself. "Still?" he adds, the afterthought of a lie. But suspicion flares in the captain all the same. I see it like an explosion in his eyes.

Blessed Nanny laughs aloud, her forced chuckle cold and detached. "Mother has always done as she likes, you know this," she says to Cal, scolding him. "But I am here on other business, Captain. No need to bother her."

The captain offers up an obliging smile. It pulls at his face like a sneer, twisting his fine features into something ugly. "Very well, sir."

Kilorn taps my arm, his touch urgent. He sees what I see. *The captain no longer believes us.* Turning, I take Cameron by the elbow, and squeeze. Her next signal. Under my touch, her muscles tighten. She's pouring everything she has into blocking Eagrie's ability, to keep him from seeing what's coming. Confusion crosses his face, but he shakes it off, trying to focus on us. He doesn't understand what's happening to him.

"And what have you come here to do?" Iral presses on, still wearing his pointed, demon grin. He takes one languid step toward us. It will be his last. "Remove your helmets, if you please."

"No," I tell him.

With an easy breath, I take hold of the cameras pointed down at all of us. As Iral opens his mouth to shout, I exhale, and the cameras explode into a twist of sparks like fireworks. The lights go next, flashing on and off, plunging us into pitch-black and striking brightness in succession. We are prepared for this. The soldiers of Corros are not.

Flame races along the tile, casting strange, dancing light across the white. It bars every door, jumping up to the ceiling, effectively locking the soldiers in with us and the flickering darkness. The Osanos soldier, a nymph, hastily leaches moisture from the air, but not enough to combat Cal's crackling fire. A stoneskin rushes at me, his flesh turning to rock before my eyes, but he hits the wall known as Nix Marsten. Darmian joins in, and the two invulnerable newbloods set to taking the soldier apart. The others fare just as well. Ketha obliterates the Provos telky, planting an explosion in his heart that rips him from the inside out. The Haven soldier does her best to combat my darkness, using her ability to collapse the shadows, pooling them into a black mist that suddenly erupts with blinding, brilliant light. Even our helmets do nothing to stop the glare, and I have to shut my eyes. When I open them, the Haven is on the ground, with a deep gash in her neck. She coughs silver blood onto the tile, and my brother stands over her, knife in hand. Behind him, Eagrie drops to his knees, clutching his head and screaming.

"I can't see!" he weeps, tearing at his own eyes. Blood joins his painful tears. "I can't see anything, what's happening?! What is this?! What are you?!" he shouts to no one.

Cameron is the first to pull off her helmet. She has never killed a man before, not even in her escape. I see it all over her face, in the horror twisting through her. But she doesn't let go. Out of bravery or malice, I can't say. Her silence takes hold, until the man on the ground stops crying, stops clawing, stops breathing. He dies with his eyes wide open, staring at nothing, blind and deaf in his last moments. It must feel like being buried alive.

It's over in a minute or so. Twelve Silver soldiers dead on the tile, some burned, some electrocuted, some shot, some with their heads bashed in. Ketha's kills are the messiest. An entire wall is splattered with her handiwork, and she pants noisily, trying not to look at what she's done. Her explosive ability is gruesome at best.

Only Lory is wounded, having taken on the magnetron with Gareth. She got a shard of metal in the arm, but nothing too bad. Farley is the first to her side, and pulls out the makeshift blade, letting it clatter to the floor. Lory doesn't so much as grunt in pain.

"We forgot bandages," Farley mutters,

putting one hand over the bleeding cut.

"*You* forgot bandages," Ada replies, pulling a small swatch of white fabric from inside her suit. She expertly ties it around Lory's arm. It stains in an instant.

Kilorn chuckles to himself, the only one to enjoy a joke at a time like this. To my relief, he looks perfectly all right, focusing on reloading his gun. The barrel smokes, and there are at least two bodies riddled with his bullets. Anyone else would think him unaffected, but I know better. Despite the laughter, Kilorn finds no joy in this bloody work.

Neither does Cal. He bends over the dead Captain Iral, gingerly taking the black key from his neck. *I won't kill them,* he told me once, before we stormed the Security Center of Harbor Bay. He broke his own promise, and it's wounded him more deeply than any battle.

"Nanny," he mutters, unable to look away from Iral. With shaking fingers, he closes the captain's eyes forever. Behind him, Nanny focuses on Iral's face, staring at him. It only takes a moment before her features match his own, and I breathe a small sigh of relief. Even a fake Maven is nearly too much for me to bear.

A hiss of static crackles at Iral's belt. His

radio — the command center attempting contact. "Captain Iral! Captain, what's going on down there? We lost visual."

"Just a malfunction," Nanny replies with Iral's voice. "Might spread, might not."

"Received, Captain."

Cameron tears her eyes away from the dead Eagrie. She lays a hand on the red door.

"This way," she says, almost inaudible over the drip of blood and the sighs of the dying.

I feel the prison's command center like a nerve, pulsing, controlling all the cameras in the facility. It pulls at me, dragging me through the sharp turns of its hallways. The corridors are white tile, just like the entrance, but not so clean. If I look closely, I can see blood between the tiles, turned brown by time. Someone tried to wash away whatever happened, but they weren't thorough enough. *Red blood is so hard to clean up.* I see the queen in this, in whatever nightmares she's concocted deep in the bowels of Corros.

She's here somewhere, continuing her frightening work. She might even be coming for us now, alerted to a disturbance. *I hope she is. I hope she turns the corner right now, so I can kill her.*

But instead of Queen Elara, we round the bend to find another door with a large *D* on it and no lock. Cameron runs to it, her knife in hand, and gets to work prying at the switch panel. It comes loose in a second, and her fingers plunge into the wiring.

"We have to go through here to get to command," she says, jerking her head at the door. "There are two magnetron guards inside. Be ready."

Cal quietly clears his throat, dangling the key in front of her. "Oh," she grumbles, flushing, and takes it from his hand. With a scowl, she jams it into the corresponding slot on the switch. "Tell me when."

"Gareth," Cal begins, but he's already stepped forward, bracing himself against the metal door. Nanny takes his side, still disguised as Captain Iral. They both know what they must do.

The others are not so sure. Ketha looks on the edge of tears, her hands twitching up and down her arms, as if she's afraid she's lost a limb. Farley reaches out, only to be batted away. My heart sinks when I realize I don't know how to comfort Ketha. Does she need a hug or a slap?

"Watch our backs," I bark at her, electing what I hope is the happy medium. She shivers, glaring at me. Her braid has come undone, and she tugs at the strands of dark hair. Slowly, she nods, turning on the spot to watch the empty corridor behind us. Her sniffles echo off the tile.

"No more," she murmurs. But she holds her ground. Darmian and Nix take her side, more in a show of solidarity than strength. At least they'll make a very good wall when the guards realize what's happening up here. *Which should be soon.*

Cal knows the urgency as well as I do. "Now," he says, and flattens himself against the wall with the rest of us.

The key turns. I feel the electricity jump in the switch and flood the door's mechanism. It flies open, screeching back into the wall to reveal a cavernous cell block. In stark contrast to the white tile corridors, the cells are gray, cold, and dirty. Water drips somewhere, and the air is sickly damp. Four levels of cells reach down into the gloom, one stacked on top of the other, with no landings or stairs connecting the sets. Four cameras, one in each corner of the ceiling, watch over all. I shut them off with ease. The only light is a harsh, flickering yellow, though the small skylight above has gone blue, betraying the rising sun. Standing beneath it, on a single catwalk made of gleaming, reflective metal, are two magnetrons in gray uniforms. Both of them spin at the sound of approach.

"What are you — ?" the first says, taking a single step toward us. He has Samos colors on his uniform. He freezes at the sight of Nanny, standing at Gareth's shoulder. "Captain Iral, sir." With a wave of his hand, the Samos magnetron officer raises flat sheets of metal from the block floor, constructing a new section of catwalk before our eyes. It connects to his, allowing Gareth and Nanny to walk forward.

"Fresh blood?" The other officer chuckles, nodding at Gareth with a sly grin. "What legion are you out of?"

Nanny cuts in before Gareth can answer. "Open the cells. It's time for a walk."

To our chagrin, the officers exchanged confused glances. "We just walked them yesterday, they're not due for —"

"Orders are orders, and I have mine," Nanny replies. She raises Iral's key, dangling it in open threat. "Open the cells."

"So it's true? The king's back again?" Samos asks, shaking his head. "No wonder everyone's in an uproar back at command. Got to look sharp for the crown, I guess, especially with his mother still skulking around."

"She's a strange one, the queen," the other

says, scratching his chin. "Don't know what she does in the Well, don't want to know either."

"The *cells,*" Nanny repeats, her voice hard.

"All right, sir," the first magnetron grumbles. He elbows the other and they turn together, facing the dozens of cells rising from floor to ceiling. Many are empty, but some hold shadows languishing under the crush of Silent Stone. Newblood prisoners, about to be let loose.

More catwalk clangs into place, the sound like a giant hammer beating a wall of aluminum. They line the cells, creating walkways around the perimeter of the block, while more sheets twist and fold into steps to connect the levels. For a moment, I'm seized by a sense of wonder. I've only seen magnetrons in battle, using their abilities to kill and destroy. Never to create. It's not hard to imagine them designing airjets and luxurious transports, curving jagged iron into smooth arcs of razor-thin beauty. Or even the metal dresses Evangeline was so fond of. Even now, I admit they were magnificent, though the girl wearing them was a monster. But when the bars of every cell yawn open, causing the people inside to stir, I forget all my wonder and amazement.

These magnetrons are jailers, killers, forcing innocent people to suffer and die behind bars for whatever feeble reason Maven gives them. They are following orders, yes, but *choosing* to follow them all the same.

"Come on, out you go."

"On your feet, time to take the dogs for a walk."

The magnetron officers move in rapid succession, trotting to the first set of cells. They bodily drag newbloods from their cots, tossing the ones who can't get up fast enough out onto the catwalk. A little girl lands dangerously close to the edge, almost falling. She looks so much like Gisa I take a step forward, and Kilorn has to yank me back. "Not yet," he growls in my ear.

Not yet. My hands clench, itching to let loose on the two officers as they get closer and closer to the door. They haven't seen us yet, but they certainly will.

Cal is the first to remove his helmet. Samos stops short, as if shot. He blinks once, not believing his eyes. Before he can react, his feet leave the ground, and he hurtles toward the ceiling. The other follows suit as his tenuous hold on gravity releases. Gareth bounces them both, smacking them against the concrete ceiling with sickening, final crunches of bone.

We flood into the cell block, moving as one, as fast as we can. I reach the fallen girl first, hauling her to her feet. She wheezes, her small body shivering. But the pressure of Silent Stone has fallen away, and some color returns to her pale, clammy cheeks.

I remove my own mask.

"The lightning girl," she murmurs, touching my face. It breaks my heart.

Part of me wants to pick her up and run, to take her away from all this. But our task is far from over, and I cannot leave. Even for the little girl. So I put her down on shaky legs, and pull my hand gently from her grasp.

"Follow us as best you can. Fight as best you can!" I shout to the block. I make sure to lean over the edge of the catwalk, so everyone can hear and see me. Far below, the few prisoners still alive in the low cells have already begun the climb up the metal steps. "We are leaving this prison tonight, together, and alive!"

By now, I should know better than to lie. But a lie is what they need to carry on, and if my deceit saves even one of them, it is worth the cost to my soul.

TWENTY-SIX

Blind cameras can protect us for only so long — and that time has apparently run out. It starts with explosions back in the corridor. I hear Ketha screaming with every blast, frightened by what she's done and what she continues to do to flesh and bone. Each ragged cry shocks through the cell block, stilling the already slow newbloods.

"Keep moving!" Farley barks. Her manic energy is gone, replaced by stern authority. "Follow Ada, follow Ada!" She herds them like sheep, bodily pulling many of them up the stairs. Shade is more helpful, jumping the oldest and sickest up from the lowest levels, though it disorients most of them. Kilorn keeps them from stumbling off the catwalk, his long limbs coming in handy.

Ada waves her arms, directing the newbloods to the door next to her. It has a big, black *C* on it. "With me," she shouts. Her eyes flicker over everything and everyone, counting. I have to push many of them toward her, though they're inexplicably drawn to me. At least the little girl gets the message. She toddles over to Ada and clings to her leg, trying to hide from the noise. Everything echoes horribly in the block, transformed into beast-like howls by the concrete walls and metal plating. Gunshots ring out next, followed by Nix's unmistakable laughter. But he won't be laughing long, if this assault keeps up.

Now comes the part I dread the most, the part I fought hardest against. But Cal was clear — *we must split up.* Cover more ground, free more prisoners, and, most important, get them out safely. So I move through the throng of newbloods, fighting the tide, with Cameron next to me. She tosses the key over her shoulder, and Kilorn catches it deftly. He watches us go, not daring to blink. This might be the last time he ever sees me, and we both know it.

Cal follows behind me. I feel his warmth from yards away. He burns the catwalk behind us, letting it melt, cutting us off from the others. When we reach the opposite door, the one marked "COMMAND," Cameron gets to work on the switch panel. I can do nothing but stare, glancing between Kilorn and my brother, memorizing their faces. Ketha, Nix, and Darmian run back into the block, sprinting from the onslaught they can no longer hold back. Bullets follow, pinging off metal and Nix's flesh. Again, the world slows, and I wish it would stop entirely. I wish Jon were here, to tell me what to do, to tell me I made the right choices. To tell me who dies.

A hot, almost scalding hand takes my cheek, forcibly turning me away from the rest. "Focus," Cal says, glaring into my eyes. "Mare, you're going to have to forget them right now. Trust what you're doing."

I can barely nod. I can barely speak. "Yes."

Behind us, the cell block empties. Ahead, the switch sparks. The door slides open.

Cal pushes us both through, and I land hard on another tile floor. My body reacts before my mind can, and lightning sparks to life all around me. It shatters my thoughts of Kilorn and Shade, until all that remains are the command center across the hall and what I must do.

Just like Cameron said, it's a triangular room of impenetrable, rippled diamond-glass, filled with control panels, monitoring screens, six bustling soldiers, and the same metal doors as the cells. Three in all, one set in each wall. I run to the first, expecting it to open, expecting the command soldiers inside to rise to the occasion. To my surprise, they keep to their chairs and stations, watching me with wide, fearful eyes. I bang one fist on the door, enjoying the pain that shoots through my hand. "Open up!" I scream, like that can do anything. Instead, the soldier closest to me flinches, jumping back from the wall. He too has a captain's badge.

"Don't!" he commands, holding out a hand to still his fellow officers.

Overhead, a siren screams to life.

"If that's the way they want it," Cal mutters, moving to the other door.

A slam makes me jump, and I turn to see great granite blocks slide into place, replacing the metal door we just came through. Cameron smirks at the control panel, even patting it fondly. "That should buy us a few minutes." She gets to her feet, knees cracking. Her face sours at the sight of the command center. "Bleeding fools are scared," she growls, and makes a very rude hand gesture more suited to the alleys of the Stilts. "Can we reach them through the glass?"

In reply, I turn my gaze on the monitoring screens. They explode in rapid succession, showering the soldiers in a spray of sparks and broken glass. The siren screeches to a low whine, then cuts out. Every piece of metal inside the command room jumps with electricity, frying like eggs in a pan, making the soldiers cluster in the center of the room. One of them collapses, clutching his head in a gesture I now recognize. His body rocks in time with Cameron's clenching fist, fighting wave after wave of suffocating ability. Blood drips from his ears, nose, and mouth. It isn't long before he chokes on it.

"Cameron!" Cal barks, but she pretends not to hear him.

"Julian Jacos!" I shout, banging on the glass again. "Sara Skonos! Where are they?"

Another soldier drops, howling.

"Cameron!"

She shows no signs of stopping. Not that she should. These people imprisoned her, tortured her, starved her, and would have killed her. Revenge is her right.

My own lightning intensifies, bouncing inside the glass box, forcing the soldiers to cower from its purple-white wrath. Each bolt crackles and spits, blasting closer and closer to their flesh.

"Mare, *stop it* —" Cal continues shouting, but I barely hear him.

"Julian Jacos! Sara Sko—"

The captain, now scrambling across the

floor, throws himself at the wall in front of me. "Block G!" he screams, slapping his palm on the glass a few inches from my face. "They're in Block G! Through that door!"

"That's it, come on!" Cal growls. Inside the command module, the captain's eyes flicker to his fallen prince.

Cameron laughs, high and clear. "You want to leave them alive? Do you know what they've done to us? To everyone here, your Silvers included?"

"Please, *please,* we were following orders, *the king's orders* —" the captain pleads, ducking to avoid another arc of lightning. Behind him, Cameron's second victim curls into himself, succumbing to her silence. Tears cling to his lashes in crystal drops. "Your Highness, I beg for mercy, *your* mercy —"

I think of the little girl in the cells. Her eyes were bloodshot, and I could feel her ribs through her clothes. I think of Gisa and her broken hand. The bled baby in Templyn. Innocent children. I think of everything that's happened to me since this fateful summer, when a dead fisherman began all this trouble. *No, it wasn't his fault. It was theirs. Their laws, their conscription, their doom for every single one of us. They did this.*

They have brought this ending upon them-selves. Even now, when it is Cameron and me destroying them, they beg for *Cal's* mercy. They beg to a Silver king, and spit upon Red queens.

I see the prince through the rippled glass. It distorts his face, and he looks so much like Maven. "Mare," Cal whispers, if only to himself.

But his whispers cannot stop me now. I feel something new inside myself, familiar but strange. A power that comes not from blood but choice. From who I have become, and not what I was born as. I turn from Cal's warped image. I know I look just as twisted.

I bare my teeth in a snarl.

"Lightning has no mercy."

Once, I watched my brothers burn ants with a bit of glass. This is similar — and worse.

While the individually sealed cell blocks make it difficult, almost impossible, for prisoners to escape, they also make it that much harder for the guards to communicate with each other. Confusion is as effective as lightning or flame. Guards are loath to leave their posts, especially with rumors of the king around, and we find four buzzing magnetrons arguing in Block G.

"You heard the siren, something's wrong —"

"Probably a drill, showing off for the little king —"

"I can't get command on the radio."

"You heard them before, cameras are malfunctioning, the radios are going too. Might be the queen messing around again, bloody witch."

I spear a bolt through one of them to get their attention. "Wrong witch."

Before the metal catwalk can drop beneath me, I grab onto the bars to the left of the door, holding fast. Cal goes to the right, and the bars turn red beneath his flaming touch, melting straight through. Cameron stays in the doorway, a light sheen of sweat across her brow, but she shows no signs of slowing down. One of the magnetrons topples from his retracting perch, clutching his head as he falls three levels to the concrete floor. It knocks him out cold. Two left.

A hailstorm of jagged metal screams at me, each piece a tiny dagger meant to kill. Before they can, I let go, sliding down the bars, until my feet hit the slight ledge of the cell below. "Cal, a little help!" I shout, dodging another blast. I answer it with my own, but the magnetron dips, stepping into what should be midair. Instead, his metal moves with him, allowing him to seemingly run through the open atrium.

To my chagrin, Cal ignores me, and pries away the melted bar of the cell. His back spikes with flame, protecting himself from any weapon the other magnetron can throw at him. I can barely see him through the twists of fire, but I see enough. He's horribly angry, and it's no mystery why. He hates me for killing those Silvers — for doing what he can't. I never thought I'd see the day when Cal, the soldier, the warrior, would fear to act. Now he focuses on opening as many cells as he can, ignoring my pleas for help, forcing me to fight alone.

"Cameron, drop him!" I yell, glancing up at my unlikely ally.

"With pleasure," she snarls, extending a hand to the magnetron attacking me. He stumbles, but doesn't fall. *She's weakening.*

I scramble along the cells, toes almost slipping, fingers straining with every passing second. I'm a runner, not a climber, and I almost can't fight this way. *Almost.* A sharp, diamond-shaped razor grazes my cheek, opening a wound across my face. Another cuts my palm. When I grab the next bar, my grip is weak, slipping through my own blood. I fall the last six or seven feet, landing hard in the bowels of the block. For a second, I can't breathe, and I open my eyes to see a gigantic spike whistling at my head. I roll, dodging the killing blow. Another and another rain down, and I have to zigzag across the floor to stay alive. "Cal!" I shout again, more angry than afraid.

The next spike melts before it reaches me, but the iron globs splatter too close, burning across my back. A scream escapes me as the fabric of my suit melts into my scars. It's nearly the worst pain I've ever felt, second only to the sounder and the excruciating coma that followed. My knees slam into the ground, sending jolts of agony up my legs.

Pain, it seems, is another one of my triggers.

The skylight high above us shatters, and a bolt of lightning explodes down to me. For a split second, it's like a purple tree has grown up from the sublevel, branching and veining through the open atrium of Block G. It catches one of the magnetrons, and she doesn't even have time to scream. The other, the last guard, is all but finished, reduced to cowering on his last sheet of metal, curled up against Cameron's hammering will.

"Julian!" I shout once the air clears. "Sara!"

Cal jumps down at the other end of the floor, his hands cupped around his mouth. He refuses to look at me, searching the cells instead. "Uncle Julian!" he roars.

"I'll just wait up here," Cameron says, watching us from the open doorway at the top level. Her legs dangle. She even has the gall to whistle, eyeing the last magnetron as he moans.

Block G is just as dank as the newblood D, and, thanks to me, half-destroyed. A hole smokes in the center of the floor, the only remnants of my massive bolt. From what I can see, the bottom cells are almost pitch-black, but they're all full. A few prisoners have stumbled to their bars, coming to look at the commotion. *How many faces will I recognize?* But they're too drawn, too gaunt, their skin almost blue with fear, hunger, and cold. I doubt I'd recognize even Cal after a few weeks down here. I expected more for the Silvers, but I guess political prisoners are just as dangerous as secret, mutated ones.

"Here," a voice croaks.

I nearly trip over a magnetron body, running even though the burns on my back protest with every step. Cal meets me there, his hands on fire, ready to melt the bars, to save his uncle, to make amends for some of his sins.

The man in the cell looks weak, as old and frail as his beloved books. His skin has gone white, his remaining hair thin, and the lines on his face have multiplied and deepened. I think he's even missing teeth. But there's no mistaking his familiar brown eyes and the spark of intelligence still burning deep inside. *Julian.*

I can't get to him fast enough, and hover almost too close to the melting metal. *Julian. Julian. Julian. My teacher, my friend.* The first bar buckles and Cal wrenches it away, creating a space big enough for me to slip through. I barely notice the suffocating pressure of Silent Stone and focus instead on pulling Julian to his feet. He feels brittle, as if his bones might snap, and for a moment, I wonder if he'll get out of this alive. Then his grip on me tightens and his brow furrows in concentration.

"Bring me to that guard," he growls, betraying some of his old spirit. "And get Sara out."

"Of course. We're here for her too." I put his arm over my shoulder, helping him walk. Though he's much taller than me, he feels shockingly light. "We're here for everyone."

When we get him outside the cell, Julian stumbles, but keeps his footing. "Cal," he mutters, reaching for his nephew. He takes his face in his hands and studies the exiled prince like he would an old book. "Things were done, weren't they?"

"Yes, they were," Cal growls. He doesn't look my way.

The cells changed what Julian looks like, but not who he is. He nods in understanding, looking very solemn. It comforts Cal in no small way. "Such thoughts have no place here and now. But after."

"After," Cal repeats. Finally, he turns his blazing eyes on me. I feel burned by them. "After."

"Come, Mare, help me to that festering lump." Julian points to the guard on the floor, unconscious but still living. "Let's see if I'm not totally useless."

I do as I'm told, acting as Julian's crutch as he limps to the fallen officer. Meanwhile, Cal gets to work on Sara's cell, located across the floor from Julian. Within sight and earshot, but too far away to touch. Another small torture that they had to withstand.

I've seen Julian do this before, but never with such effort or pain. His fingers shake as he pries open one of the officer's eyes,

560

and he swallows many times, trying to call forth the voice that he needs. *The song.*

"It's all right, Julian, we can find another way —"

"Another way will get us killed, Mare. Have I taught you nothing at all?"

Despite the situation, I have to smile. I fight the urge to hug him, and try to hide my grin.

Finally, Julian exhales, eyes half-shut. Veins stand out in his neck. Then his eyes snap open, wide and clear. "Wake," he says in a voice more beautiful than sunset. Beneath us, the officer does as he's told, his other eye drifting open. "Open the cells. All of them." A twisting shriek echoes up and down the block as the bars of every single cell bow open in unison. "Build the stairs and walks. Connect everything." *Clang. Clang. Clang.* Every shred of metal, the daggers, the electrocuted shards, even the melted drops, flatten and reform, banging together in succession. "Walk with us." Julian's voice quivers in the last order, but the magnetron obeys, if a little slowly.

"You're lucky you came today, Mare," Julian says as I help him straighten. "They walked us yesterday. We are not so weak as we usually are."

I debate telling Julian about Jon, his ability, his advice. Julian will love hearing about him. *After,* I tell myself. *After.*

For the first time, I have hope.

There will be an after.

Chaos descends on Corros. Gunfire echoes in every corridor, behind every door. The ragged band of Silvers follows us weakly, but a few have the strength to complain. I don't trust them at all, and almost walk backward to keep watch. Many branch off, slipping around corners, eager to be rid of this place. Others go deeper into the prison, looking for revenge. A few stay with us, their eyes downcast, ashamed to follow the lightning girl. But still they follow. And they fight as best they can. It's like dropping a stone in a still pond. The ripples start small, but they certainly grow. Each block falls more easily than the last, until the magnetrons inside must run from us. The Silvers kill more than I do, falling on their betrayers like hungry wolves. But even this cannot last. When a Lerolan oblivion blasts away a stone barrier, opening Block J to us, the debris falls not down — but up. And before I understand what's happening, I'm being sucked into a whirlwind of smoke, shards, and unearthly whispers.

Cameron grabs at my hand, but she slips

from my grasp, disappearing into what must be mist. *A nymph.* I can't see anything but shadows and gloomy yellow light, each one like a distant, hazy sun. Before I can fall into such oblivion, I reach out, grabbing for anything. My cut hand closes on a cold, limp leg, stopping me with a bone-rattling jolt. "Cal!" I shout, but the howl swallows up my voice.

Grunting, I pull myself up the leg. It must belong to a corpse, because it isn't moving. Cold fear tears at my mind, reaching with icy, sharp fingers. I almost let go, not wanting to see the face that belongs to this body. It could be anyone. It could be everyone.

It's wrong to feel relieved, but I do. I don't recognize the man tangled in the bars of his cell, one leg wrapped, the other still dangling. He's certainly a prisoner, but I don't know him, and I won't mourn him. My back feels nearly split open by scars and burns, and for a second, I allow myself to lean back against the bars. The gravity in this block has shifted. Gareth is here, which means Kilorn, Shade, and Farley are not far behind. They're supposed to be on the other side of the prison, emptying the far cell blocks — something has forced them in. Or trapped them entirely.

Before I can call out, I'm falling again, as

the block seems to spin. But it's not the cells that are moving. It's gravity itself. "Gareth, stop!" I shout into the void. No one answers. At least, no one I want to hear.

Little lightning girl.

Her voice almost splits my skull in two.

Queen Elara.

This time, I wish for the sounder device. I wish for something to kill me, to give me the safety of death. I am still falling. Perhaps that will do it. Maybe I'll die before she wriggles into my brain, and turns me loose on everything and everyone I care about. But I feel the tendrils in my mind, already taking hold. My fingers twitch at her command, and sparks jump between them. *No. Please no.*

I hit the other side of the block hard, probably breaking my arm, but I feel no pain. She takes it away.

With one last ragged scream, I do what I must, and use the last drops of my own free will to slip between the twisted bars beneath me, into the prison of Silent Stone. It shatters my ability — and hers. The sparks die, her control breaks, and blinding pain sears through my left arm and up into my shoulder. I laugh through my tears. How fitting. She built this prison to hurt me and the other newbloods. Now, it's the only thing stopping her from doing just that.

Now, it is my last sanctuary.

From my place on the back wall of the cell — I guess it's the floor now — I watch the mist dance. The gunfire slows, either because bullets are running low or it's impossible to aim in such terrible visibility. A curling snake of flame blazes by, and I expcct to see Cal follow, but his shape never appears. I call for him anyway. "Cal!" But my voice is weak. The Stone that saved me is taking hold. It presses like a weight against my neck.

She doesn't take long to find me. Her boots edge the bars of my cage, and for a second, I think I must be hallucinating. This is not the glittering, glorious queen I remember. Gone are her dresses and jewels, replaced by a neat, navy-blue uniform with white detailing. Even her hair, usually perfectly curled and braided, has been slicked back into a simple bun. When I see gray at her temples, I laugh again.

"The first time we met, you were in a cell just like this," she muses, stooping so she can see me better. "Bars did not stop me then, and they will not stop me now."

"Come in, then," I tell her, spitting blood. *Definitely missing a tooth.*

"Still the same girl you were. I thought

the world would change you, but instead"
— she tips her head, smiling like a cat —
"you changed a little bit of the world. If you
give me your hand, you can change even
more."

I can barely breathe through my laughter.
"How stupid do you think I am?" *Keep her
talking. Keep her distracted. Someone will see
her soon, someone must.*

"Have it your way then," she sighs, standing. She gestures to someone I can't see.
Guards, I realize, with a hollow, sinking
resignation. Her hand reappears with a
pistol, her finger already on the trigger. "I
would have liked to be in your head once
again. You have such lovely delusions."

A small victory, I think, shutting my eyes.
She will never have the lightning, and she
will never have me. *A victory indeed.*

Again, I feel myself falling.

But instead of the bullet, the bars smack
against my face. I open my eyes in time to
see Elara sailing away from me, the gun
spilling from her hand, a look of terrible
anger twisting her beautiful face. Her guards
scatter with her, disappearing into the yel-
lowed clouds. And someone grabs my good
arm, pulling me to him.

"C'mon, Mare, I can't get you through on
my own," Shade says, trying to ease me

through the bars. Breathless, I squeeze, pulling as much of myself as I can through. I guess it's enough, because suddenly the world shrinks, the mist disappears, and I open my eyes to see blinding, white tile.

I almost collapse with joy. When I see Sara sprinting toward me, her hands outstretched, with Kilorn and Julian on her heels, I really do. Someone else catches me, someone warm. He turns me on my side and I hiss when my arm catches a bit of the pressure.

"Arm first, then burns, then scars," Cal says, all business. I can't help but moan when Sara touches me, and a blissful numbing spreads through my arm. Something cool hits my back, healing the burns, which were certainly infected. But before the healing can spread to my ugly, gnarled scars, I'm pulled to my feet and out of Sara's control.

The door at the end of the corridor explodes outward, broken apart by rapidly growing twists of tree trunk. The mist follows, spinning toward us at great speed. The shadows come last. I know who they belong to.

Cal throws a blast of fire at the oncoming branches, burning them back, but the charred embers simply join the roaring whirlwind. "Cameron?" I yell, craning my head to look for the one person who can stop Elara. But she's nowhere to be found.

"She's already out, now *go,*" Kilorn yells at me, pushing me ahead.

I know I'm what Elara wants. Not only for my ability but for my face. If she can control me, she can use me as a mouthpiece again, to lie to the country, to do as she says. That's why I run faster than the others. I have always been the fast one. When I look back over my shoulder, I'm yards ahead, and what I see chills me.

Cal has to forcibly pull Julian along, not because he's weak, but because he keeps trying to stop. He wants to face her. He wants to pit his voice against her mind, against her whispers. To avenge a dead sister, a wounded love, a broken and torn-apart pride. But Cal won't lose the last piece of family he has left, and all but drags Julian away. Sara keeps close to Julian's side, one hand in his, unable to scream in fear.

Then I turn the corner. And I hit something. No, *someone.*

Another woman, another person I never wanted to see again.

Ara, the Panther, the head of House Iral, glares at me with eyes black as coal. Her fingers are still tinged gray-blue by Silent

Stone and her clothes are tattered rags. But her strength is already returning, evidenced by the pure steel in her gaze. No way around but through. I raise my lightning to kill her, another one who knew I was different all along.

She reacts before I can, grabbing my shoulders with agility no human should possess. But instead of breaking my neck or slitting my throat, she tosses me sideways, and something ruffles my hair. A curved, spinning blade, sharp as a razor, big as a dinner plate, flies past my face, centimeters from my nose. I hit the ground, gasping in shock, clutching at the head I almost lost. And above me, Ara Iral stands her ground, dodging every blade that sails over us. They're coming from the opposite end of the hall, where another person from the past stands, forming metal disks from the plates of his familiar scale armor.

"Didn't your father ever teach you respect for your elders?" Ara crows at Ptolemus, stepping neatly under another blade. The next one she pulls out of the air, and tosses it back at him. An impressive but useless trick, as he waves it off with a curled smirk. "Well, Red, aren't you going to do something?" she adds, toeing my leg.

I stare at her, stunned for a moment. Then

I clamber to my feet, forcing myself to stand. A little bit of my terror disappears. "With pleasure, my lady."

At the end of the corridor, Ptolemus's grin widens. "Now to finish what my sister started in the arena," he growls.

"What your sister *ran from,*" I call back, directing a bolt at his head. He throws himself sideways, against the wall, and in the time it takes him to recover, Ara closes the distance between them and leaps, kicking off the tile wall. Using the momentum, she breaks Ptolemus's jaw with her elbow.

I follow and, judging by the pounding footsteps behind me, I'm not the only one.

Fire and lightning. Mist and wind. Metal rain, curling darkness, explosions like tiny stars. And bullets, always bullets, close behind. We move forward through the battle storm, praying for an end to this prison, following the map we all did our best to memorize. It should be here, no here, no here. In the mist and shadows, it's easy to get lost. And then there's Gareth, always spinning the bounds of gravity, sometimes doing more harm than good. When we finally find the entrance hall, the room with red and silver and black doors, I'm bruised all over again, and my strength is fading fast. I don't even want to think about the others,

Julian and Sara, who could barely walk earlier. *We need to get in the open. To the sky. To the lightning that can save us all.*

Outside, the sun has risen. Ara and Ptolemus continue their visceral dance as the Wash looms, a gray haze on the horizon. I only have eyes for the Blackrun and the other jet idling on the runway. A crowd swarms around the crafts, newblood and Silver alike, boarding everything within reach. Some disappear into the fields, hoping to escape on foot.

"Shade, get him to the jet," I yell, grabbing Cal by the collar as we run. Before he can protest, Shade does as instructed, and jumps him a hundred yards away. I can always count on Shade to understand; Cal is one of our only two pilots. He cannot die here, not when we're so close to getting away. We need him to fly, and fly well. A split second later, Shade returns, wrapping his arms around Julian and Sara. They disappear with him, and I breathe a small sigh of relief.

I call on everything I have left, down to the deepness of my bones. It makes me slow, makes me weak, taking my will, and turning it into something stronger. To my delight, the sky darkens.

Kilorn stops next to me, his rifle tucked

against his shoulder. He shoots with precision, picking off our pursuers one by one. Many men step in front of the queen, protecting her, whether by their own volition or hers. She'll be within range soon, of both my ability — and her own. I have only one chance.

It happens in slow motion. I glance at the two Silvers locked in battle between me and the jets. A long, thin blade, like a giant needle, cuts through Ara's neck, spilling a silver fountain. Ptolemus spins with the momentum, directing it through her, at me. I move to duck, expecting what I think is the worst.

I can't possibly see what's coming.

Only one person could. *Jon.* He walked away from all this. He let this happen. He didn't want to warn us. He didn't care.

Shade appears in front of me, intending to take me away from all this. Instead, he gets a cruel, gleaming needle through his heart. He doesn't realize what's happening. He doesn't feel any pain. He dies before his knees hit the ground.

I don't remember anything else until we're in the air. My face runs with tears but I can't wipe them away. I stare at my hands, painted in both colors of blood.

Twenty-Seven

This is not the Blackrun.

Instead, Cal pilots a massive cargo jet, built to carry heavy transports or machinery. Now the cargo bay holds over three hundred escaped prisoners, many injured, all shell-shocked. Most are newbloods, but there are also Silvers among them, keeping to themselves, biding their time. For today at least, they all look the same, cloaked in rags, exhaustion, and hunger. I don't want to go down to them, so I stick to the upper level of the jet. At least it's quiet in this section, separated from the bay by a narrow stairwell, and from the cockpit by a closed door. I can't make myself move past the two bodies at my feet. One lies beneath a white sheet, stained only by the blossom of red blood over his pierced heart. Farley kneels over him, frozen, a hand under the sheet to clutch my brother's cold, dead fingers. The other corpse I refuse to cover.

Elara looks ugly in death. Lightning twisted her muscles, pulling her mouth into a sneer even she couldn't muster while alive. Her simple uniform is cooked to her skin, and her ash-blond hair is almost gone, burned away until only stringy patches remain. The other bodies, her guards, were just as deformed. We left them rotting on the runway. But the queen is still unmistakable. Everyone will know this corpse. I'll make sure of it.

"You should go lie down."

The body unsettles Kilorn, that much is clear. I don't know why. We should be dancing on her bones. "Let Sara check you out."

"Tell Cal to change course."

He blinks at me, perplexed. "Change course? What are you talking about? We're going back to the Notch, back home —"

Home. I scoff at such a childish word. "We're going back to Tuck. Tell him, please."

"Mare."

"Please."

He doesn't move. "Have you gone crazy? Do you remember what happened back there, what the Colonel will do to you if you come back?"

Crazy. I wish. I wish my mind would snap from the torture my life has become. That would be such a relief, to simply go mad.

"He can certainly try. But there are too many of us now, even for him. And when he sees what I bring him, I doubt he'll refuse us this time."

"The body?" he breathes, visibly shaking. *It's not the corpse scaring him,* I realize quietly. *It's me.* "You're going to show him the body?"

"I'm going to show everyone." Again, firmer. "Tell Cal to change course. *He* will understand."

The jab stings Kilorn, but I don't care. He hardens, drawing back to do as I tell him. The cockpit door shuts behind him, but I barely notice. I'm preoccupied with more important things than petty insults. Who is he to question my orders? He's no one. A fish boy with only good luck and my foolishness to protect him. Not like Shade, a teleporter, a newblood, a great man. *How can he be dead?* And he is not the only one. No, there are certainly others left to make the prison their tomb. We'll only know when we land, and can see who else escaped on the Blackrun. And we *will* be landing on the island compound, not trekking to some lonely, backwoods cave.

"Did your seer tell you about this?" The first words Farley's spoken since we left Corros. She hasn't wept yet, but her voice sounds hoarse, as if she spent the last few days screaming. Her eyes are horrible, ringed with red, the irises a vivid blue.

"That fool, Jon, who told us to do this?" she continues, turning to face me. "Did he tell you Shade would die? *Did he?* I suppose that was an easy price for the lightning girl to pay, so long as it meant more newbloods for you to control. More soldiers in a war you have no idea how to fight. One measly brother for more followers to kiss your feet. Not a bad trade, was it? Especially with the queen thrown in. Who cares about a dead man no one knows, when you could have *her* corpse?"

My slap sends her back a step, more in surprise than pain. She catches the sheet as she falls, pulling it sideways, revealing my brother's pale face. At least his eyes are closed. He could be only sleeping. I move to tug the sheet back into place — I can't look at him long — but she hits me with her shoulder, using her considerable height to drive me into the wall.

The cockpit door bangs open, and the two boys rush out, drawn by the noise. In an instant, Cal takes Farley down, tapping the back of her knee so she stumbles. Kilorn is less fancy, simply wrapping both his arms around me, hoisting me clean off the ground.

"He was my brother!" I yell at her.

She screams her response. "He was *far more than that!*"

Her words trigger a memory.

When she doubts. Jon told me to tell her something. *When she doubts.* And Farley certainly doubts now.

"Jon did tell me something," I say, trying to push off Kilorn. "Something for you to hear."

She lunges, reaching, and Cal pushes her back down again. He gets an elbow to the face for the trouble, but doesn't relinquish his firm hold on her shoulders. She isn't going anywhere, yet she continues to struggle.

Farley, you never know when to quit. I used to admire you for it. Now I only pity you.

"He told me the answer to your question."

It stops her short, her breath coming in tiny, frightened puffs. She stares, wide-eyed. I can almost hear her heart beating.

"He said *yes.*"

I don't know what that means, but it levels her. She slumps, falling on her hands, and bows her head behind a short curtain of blond hair. I see the tears anyway. *She isn't going to fight anymore.*

Cal knows it too, and backs away from

her shaking form. He almost trips on Elara's deformed arm, and shies away from it, flinching. "Give her space," he murmurs, and seizes me by the arm in a bruising grip. He all but drags me away, despite my protests.

I don't want to leave her. Not Farley, but Elara. Despite her wounds, her burns, and her glassy eyes, I don't trust her corpse to stay dead. A foolish worry, but I feel it all the same.

"By my colors, what's the matter with you?" he snarls, slamming the cockpit door behind us, shutting out Farley's low sobs and Kilorn's scowl. "You know what Shade was to her —"

"You know what he was to me," I reply. Being civil isn't at the top of my list, but I try. My voice quivers anyway. *My closest brother. I lost him before, and now again. This time he isn't coming back. There's no coming back.* "You don't see me screaming at people."

"You're right. You just kill them."

Breath hisses between my teeth. *Is that what this is about?* I almost laugh at him. "At least one of us can."

I expect a screaming match at the very least. What I get is worse. Cal takes a step back, bumping against the instrument panel, trying to put as much distance as he can between us. Usually I'm the one to pull away, but not anymore. Something breaks behind his eyes, betraying the wounds he hides beneath his flaming skin. "What happened to you, Mare?" he whispers.

What hasn't happened to me? A single day without worry, that's what. All to prepare me for this, for the fate I bought myself with the mutations of my blood — and the many mistakes I've chosen to make, Cal included. "My brother just died, Cal."

But he shakes his head, never looking away from me. His gaze burns. "You killed those men in the command center, you and Cameron, while they *begged.* Shade wasn't dead then. Don't blame this on him."

"They were Silver —"

"*I* am Silver."

"*I* am Red. Don't act like you haven't killed hundreds of us."

"Not for me, not the way you kill. I was a soldier following orders, obeying my king. And they were just as innocent as I was when my father was alive."

Tears prick my eyes, begging to be spilled. Faces swim before me, murdered soldiers and officers, too many to count. "Why are you saying this to me?" I whisper. "I did what I had to, to stay alive, to save people

— to save you, you stupid, stubborn prince of *nothing*. You of all people should know the burden I carry. How *dare* you try to make me feel guiltier than I already do?"

"She wanted to turn you into a monster." He nods toward the door, and the twisted body behind it. "I'm just trying to make sure that doesn't happen."

"Elara is dead." The words taste sweet as wine. *She's gone, she can't hurt me.* "She can't control anyone anymore."

"But still, you feel no remorse for the dead. You do whatever you can to forget them. You abandoned your family without a word. You can't control yourself. Half the time you run away from leadership, and the other half you act like some untouchable martyr, crowned in guilt, the only person who's really giving herself to the cause. Look around you, Mare Barrow. Shade's not the only one who died in Corros. You are not the only one to make sacrifices. Farley betrayed her father. You forced Cameron to join us against her will, you chose to ignore everything but Julian's list, and now you want to abandon the kids back at the Notch. For what? To step on the Colonel's neck? To take a throne? To kill anyone who looks at you the wrong way?"

I feel like a child being scolded, unable to

speak, to argue, to do anything but keep from crying. It takes everything to keep my sparks contained.

"And you still hold on to Maven, a person who doesn't exist."

He might as well put a hand around my throat and squeeze. "You looked through my things?"

"I'm not blind. I watched you take the notes off the bodies. I thought you'd rip them up. But when you didn't — I suppose I wanted to see what you were going to do. Burn them, throw them away, send them back dipped in Silver blood — but not keep them. Not read them while I slept next to you."

"You said you missed him too. You said so," I whisper. I have to refrain from stamping my foot like a frustrated child.

"He's my brother. I miss him in a *very* different way."

Something sharp scrapes my wrist, and I realize I'm scratching myself in my misery, creating a physical pain to mask the agony inside. He watches, conflicted.

"Every single thing I did, you stood behind me," I say. "If I'm turning into a monster, then so are you."

He drops his gaze. "Love blinds."

"If this is your idea of love —"

"I don't know if you love anyone at all," he snaps, "if you see anything out there but tools and weapons. People to manipulate and control, to sacrifice."

There is no possible defense to such an accusation. How can I prove him wrong? How can I make him see what I've done, what I'm trying to do, what I've become to keep everyone I care about safe! How badly I've failed. How terrible I feel. How the scars and memories ache. How deeply he's wounded me with such words. I cannot prove my love for him, or Kilorn, or my family. I cannot put such feelings into words, nor should I have to.

So I don't.

"After the Archeon bombing, Farley and the Scarlet Guard used a Silver news broadcast to claim responsibility." I speak slowly, methodic and calm in my explanation. It's the only thing keeping me sane. "I'm going to do the same now, with the queen's body. I'm going to show every single person in this kingdom the woman I killed, and the people she kept locked up, newblood and Silver. I am finished letting Maven control this game by spouting his lies to the kingdom. What we've done isn't enough to bring him down. We need to let the country do it for us."

Cal's mouth gapes open. "Civil war?"

"House against house, Silver against Silver. Only Reds will stand united. And we will win because of it. Norta will fall, and we will rise, Red as the dawn." A simple, costly, lethal plan on both sides. But a step we must take. *They forced us down this road long ago. I am only doing what must be done.* "You can collect the Notch children after we land in Tuck. But I need the Colonel, and I need his resources to get this in motion. Do you understand that?"

He barely nods.

"And after, well, I will go north, to the Choke, to the ones I've so willingly abandoned. You can do as you like, Your Highness."

"Mare." He grazes my arm and I flinch away, almost hitting the wall.

"Don't touch me anymore."

The words sound like a slamming door. I suppose they are.

Tuck is quiet and disgustingly bright. No clouds, no wind, just brisk autumn and sunlight. Shade shouldn't have died on such a beautiful day, but he did. Too many did.

I am the first to step down from the cargo plane, with two covered stretchers close behind. Kilorn and Farley hover by one, each of them resting a hand on Shade. But the other stretcher is what I care about now. The men holding her up seem afraid of her body, just like I was. The last few hours of quiet reflection, staring at Elara's cold corpse, have been a strange comfort. She is not going to wake up. Just like Cal will never speak to me again, not after everything we said to each other. I don't know where he is in the line, or if he's even coming down at all. I tell myself not to worry. Thinking about him is a waste.

I have to shield my eyes to see the Colonel's blockade across the runway. He perches atop a medical transport, surrounded by nurses in white shifts. Ada must have radioed ahead to tell him we would sorely need help. Her Blackrun is already here, the only dark shadow in sight. When the first of the prisoners hit the runway behind me, the familiar black ramp descends from the other jet. Fewer than I thought get out, following Ada. She begins the brisk march toward the wall of armed Lakelanders, stoic Guardsmen, and curious onlookers. Quietly, I curse myself. My family will be back there, waiting to see their children, but they'll find only one of us.

You don't care about your family. Maybe Cal was right, because I certainly forget them more than any sane person should.

"That's far enough, Miss Barrow," the Colonel barks, holding up a hand. I do as he asks, halting five yards away. From this close, I can see the guns pointed at us, but more important, the men behind the bullets. They're alert, but not on edge. They have no kill orders, not yet. "Have you come to return what you've stolen?"

I force a laugh, putting us both at ease. "I come with a gift, Colonel."

The corner of his mouth lifts. "Is that what you call these" — he searches for the right word to describe the ragged folk following me — "people?"

"They were prisoners until this morning, at a secret facility called Corros. Jailed by the command of King Maven, left to be experimented on, tortured, and murdered." I glance behind me, expecting to see broken hearts and minds. Instead, I see unflagging pride. The little girl, the one who almost fell off the catwalk, looks close to tears, but her tiny fists clench at her sides. She won't cry. "They are newbloods like me." Behind the girl, a protective teenager with too-pale skin and orange hair stands like her guard. "And Silvers too, Colonel."

He reacts as I expect him to. "You *fool,* you brought Silvers here?!" he shouts, panicking. "Ready guns!"

The line of Lakelanders, two deep, and probably about twenty wide, does as he commands. Their guns click in unison, sliding bullets into chambers. Ready to fire. Behind me, the prisoners flinch, drawing back. But no one begs. They are done begging.

"Hollow threats." I fight the urge to smile.

His hand flies to the pistol at his hip. "Don't try me."

"I know your orders, Colonel, and they are not to kill the lightning girl. Command wants me alive, don't they?" I remember Ellie Whistle, one of many Guardsmen instructed to help me in my endeavors. She was no match for the Colonel, but the Colonel is no match for Command, whoever they may be.

The Colonel loses some of his edge, but doesn't back down.

"Bring her forward," I snap, looking to the stretchers. The two men do as I say as quickly as they can. They lay Elara's stretcher at my feet. The guns follow their every shaking step. I feel the crosshairs even now, on my heart, my brain, over every inch.

"Your gift, Colonel." I toe the stretcher, nudging the body beneath the white sheet. "Don't you want to see it?"

His good eye flashes, almost too quick to discern. It finds Farley in the crowd, and the crease in his brow disappears a little. With a sickening jolt, I realize why. *He thought I killed her.*

"Who is it, Barrow? The prince? Have you murdered the best bargaining chip you had?"

"Hardly," a voice calls from the crowd. Cal.

I don't turn to look at him, electing to focus on the Colonel instead. He holds my gaze, never wavering. Slowly, one hand raised, the other reaching, I pull away the sheet, laying her out for everyone to see. Her limbs have gone stiff. Her fingers are especially twisted, and bits of bone show through the flesh of her right hand. The gunmen are the first to react, lowering their weapons a little. One or two even gasp, covering their mouths to stifle the sound. The Colonel is completely silent and still, content to stare. After a long moment, he blinks.

"Is that who I think it is?" he says hoarsely.

I nod. "Elara of House Merandus, Queen of Norta. Mother to the king. Killed by newbloods and Silvers, in the prison she built for them." That explanation should stay his hand for the moment.

His red eye gleams. "What do you plan to do with this?"

"The king and this country deserve a chance to say good-bye to her, don't you think?"

The Colonel looks just like Farley when he smiles.

"Again," Colonel Farley barks, moving back into position.

"My name is Mare Barrow," I tell the camera, trying not to sound foolish. After all, this is the sixth time I've introduced myself in the last ten minutes. "I was born in the Stilts, a village in the Capital River Valley. My blood is Red, but because of this" — I stretch out my hands, allowing two balls of sparks to rise — "I was brought to the court of King Tiberias the Sixth, and given a new name, a new life, and made into a lie. They called me Mareena Titanos, and told the world I was Silver born. I am not." Flinching, I draw the knife across my palm, over already torn flesh. My blood winks like rubies in the harsh light of the empty hangar. "King Maven told you this was a trick." Sparks dance through the gash. "It is not. And neither are the others like me, all of you born Red with strange, Silver abilities. The king knows you exist, and he is hunting you down. I tell you now, run. Find me. Find the Scarlet Guard."

Next to me, the Colonel straightens proudly. He wears a red scarf around his face, as if his bleeding eye wasn't identification enough. But I'm not complaining. He's agreed to take in the newbloods, having seen the error of his ways. He now knows the value — and the strength — of people like me. He can't afford to make enemies of us too.

"Unlike the Silver kings, we see no division between ourselves and other Reds. We will fight for you, and we will die for you, if it means a new world. Put down the ax, the shovel, the needle, the broom. Pick up the gun. Join us. Fight. Rise, Red as the dawn."

The next part turns my stomach, and I want to scrub my skin with acid. When my fingers knot in her frayed hair, holding her head up to face the decrepit, sputtering camera, I'm fighting tears. As much as I hate her, I hate this more. It feels against nature, against anything good I might have left inside myself. I've already lost Cal — thrown him away — but now I feel I'm losing my soul. And yet I speak the words I must. I believe in them, and they help a little.

"Fight, and win. This is Elara, Queen of

Norta, and we have killed her. This war is not impossible, and with you, it can be won for good."

I hold my position, trying my best not to blink. Tears will fall if I do. I think of anything but the corpse in my hands. "Even now, Guardsmen are leaving their strongholds to wait for anyone to answer our call."

"Arm yourselves, my brothers and sisters," the Colonel says, stepping forward. "You outnumber your masters, and they know it. They fear it. They fear *you,* and what you will become. Look to the Whistles in the woods. They will lead you home."

After six attempts, we finally finish in perfect unison. "Rise, Red as the dawn."

"As for the Silvers of Norta." I speak quickly, tightening my grip on Elara. "Your king and queen have lied to you — and betrayed you. The Scarlet Guard liberated a prison this morning, and inside we found Red and Silvers both. Missing members of House Iral, Lerolan, Skonos, Jacos, and more. Wrongfully imprisoned, tortured with Silent Stone, left to die for nonexistent crimes. They are with us now, and they are alive. Your lost ones live. Rise to help them. Rise to avenge the ones we could not save. Rise, and join us. For your king is a monster." I glare deep into the camera, knowing he will see this. "Maven is a *monster.*"

The Colonel gapes at me, affronted. The camera stops. He tears away his scarf in his anger. "What are you doing, Barrow?"

I stare back at him. "I'm making your life a whole lot easier. Divide and conquer, Colonel." I point to the crew working the camera, not bothering to remember their names. "You go to the Silver barracks, get some film of them. Don't show the guards. Mark my words. This will set the country on fire, and even Maven won't be able to put it out."

They don't need to speak to show they agree. I turn on my heel. "I'm done."

The Colonel follows me, dogging my steps even when I push my way out of the hangar. "Barrow, I didn't say we were finished —" he growls, but when I stop short, so does he. I don't need lightning to frighten people. Not anymore.

"Make me turn around, Colonel." I extend my arm, daring him to pull. Daring him to test me. "Go on."

Once, this man put Cal in a cell. He leads who knows how many soldiers, and killed however many more men. I don't know how many battles he's seen, or how many times he's cheated death.

He has no right to be afraid of a girl like

me, but he is. I returned to Tuck his equal, *better* than his equal, and he knows it.

I spin to face him slowly, and only because it now suits me to do so. "What changed you, Colonel? Because I know it wasn't your own good sense, or even the orders of your Command."

After a long, drawn-out moment, he nods. "Follow me. They've been asking to meet you."

TWENTY-EIGHT

Tuck seems smaller than I remember, with the three hundred from Corros as well as the Colonel's own reinforcements clustering all over the island. He leads me past them all, setting a pace I must struggle to match. Many of the new soldiers are Lakelanders, smuggled from the far north like the guns and food streaming in from the docks, but there are a good number of Nortans as well. Farmers, servants, deserters, even some tattooed techies drill in the open space between barracks. Many have come over the last few months. They are the first of many outrunning the Measures, and more will certainly follow. I would smile at the thought, but smiling comes too hard these days. It hurts my scars and my head. Back on the runway, a familiar jet roars, and the Blackrun climbs into the sky. Headed for the Notch, I'll bet, with Cal at the controls. All the better. I don't need him skulking around, watching and judging my every move.

Barracks 1. Last time I entered in secret. Now I enter in broad daylight, with the Colonel at my side. We walk through the narrow passages of the underwater bunker, and his Lakelanders step aside to let me pass every juncture. I'm acutely aware of this place — once I was its prisoner — but I no longer fear anything down here. We follow the piping in the ceiling, toward the pulsing heart of the barracks and the entire island. The control room is small, but crowded, filled with screens, radio equipment, and maps on every flat surface. I expect to see Farley barking orders, but she's nowhere to be found. Instead, there's a healthy mix of Lakelander blue and Guard red. Two men are different, wearing thick, faded green uniforms with black detailing. I have no idea what country or kingdom they stand for.

"Clear the room," the Colonel murmurs. He has no reason to shout; they obey him quickly.

Except for the pair in green. I get the feeling they've been waiting for this. They move in strange unison, turning toward us in perfect sync. Both wear badges on their uniforms, a white circle with a dark green triangle inside. The same marks I saw on smuggled crates the last time I was here.

The men are twins, the unsettling kind. Identical, but somehow more than that. Both have curly black hair, tight like a cap, mud-colored eyes, brown skin, and immaculate beards. A scar is the only difference between them — one has a jagged line on the right cheek, the other the left. *To distinguish them.* With a cold shudder, I realize they even blink at the same time.

"Miss Barrow, a pleasure to meet you at last." Right Scar extends his hand, but I'm loath to take it. He doesn't seem to mind, and presses on. "My name is Rash, and my brother —"

"Tahir, at your service," the other cuts in. They bow their heads gracefully, again in startling unison. "We have traveled far to find you and yours. And waited —"

"— for what feels like even longer," Rash finishes for him. He eyes the Colonel, and I catch a flicker of distaste deep in his eyes. "We bring you a message, and an offer."

"From whom?" I feel breathless, almost dizzy. Surely these men are newbloods — their bond is not a natural one — and they are neither Nortan nor Lakelander. *Traveled far,* they said. *From where?*

They speak in melodic chorus. "The Free

Republic of Montfort."

Suddenly I wish Julian were at my side, to help me remember his lessons, and the maps he kept so close. Montfort, a mountain nation, so far away it could be the other side of the world. But Julian told me it was like Piedmont to the south, ruled by a collection of princes, all of them Silver. "I don't understand."

"Neither did Colonel Farley —" says Tahir.

Rash cuts in. "— for the Republic is well guarded, hidden by mountains —"

"— snows —"

"— walls —"

"— and by design."

This is very annoying.

"My apologies," Rash adds, noting my discomfort. "Our mutation links our brains. It can be quite —"

"Unsettling," I finish for him, drawing a smile from them both. But the Colonel continues to scowl, his red eye gleaming. "So you're newbloods too? Like me?"

A double nod. "In Montfort, we are called the Ardents, but it differs from nation to nation. No one can agree on what to call the Red-and-Silver ones," Tahir says. "There are many of us, all over this world. Some in the open, as in the Republic, or hidden, as

596

it is in your country." He turns his gaze on the Colonel, speaking with two meanings. "But our bonds run deeper than the borders of nations. We protect our own, for no one else will. Montfort has been hiding for twenty years, building our republic from the ashes of brutal oppression. I believe you understand that." I do indeed. I don't even care that I'm grinning, despite the pain it causes. "But we are not hiding now. We have an army and a fleet of our own, and they will not be idle any longer. Not while kingdoms like Norta, the Lakelands, and all the rest still stand. Not while Reds die, and Ardents face even worse fates."

Ah. So the Colonel accepts us not out of goodness or even necessity, but fear. Another player has joined the game, one he does not understand. They share an enemy at least, that much is clear. *Silvers. People like Maven. We share an enemy too.* But a chill goes through me, one I cannot ignore. *Cal is Silver, Julian is Silver. What do they think of them?* Like the Colonel, I must sit back and see what these people truly want.

"Premier Davidson, the leader of the Republic, sent us as ambassadors, to extend a hand of friendship to the Scarlet Guard," Rash says, his own hand twitching on his thigh. "Colonel Farley willingly accepted this alliance two weeks ago, as have his superiors, the Red Generals of Command."

Command. Farley's cryptic words seem so close now. She never explained what she meant, but now I begin to see a little more of the Guard. I have never heard of the Red Generals, but I keep my face still. They don't know how much — or how little — I am told. Judging by the way the twins are talking, they think me a leader too, with control over the Scarlet Guard. *I barely have control over myself.*

"We've allied with similar groups and sub-sects in nations across the continent, form-ing a complex network like spokes of a wheel. The Republic is the hub." Rash's eyes bore into mine. "We offer safe passage, to any of the Ardents here, to a country that will not only protect you but offer you freedom. They need not fight; they need only live, and live free. That is our offer."

My heart beats wildly. *You need only live.* How many times have I wished for such a thing? *Too many to count.* Even back in the Stilts, when I thought I was painfully nor-mal, when I was nothing. I only wanted to live. The Stilts taught me the value, and the rarity, of an ordinary life. But it also taught me something else, a more valuable lesson. *Everything has its price.*

"And what do you ask in return?" I murmur, not wanting to hear his answer.

Rash and Tahir exchange loaded glances, their eyes narrowing in silent communication. I don't doubt the brothers can speak to each other without words, whispering like Elara once did. "Premier Davidson requests that *you* escort them," they say together.

A "request." There is no such thing.

"You are a firebrand in your own right, and will be of great help to the coming war." *They need not fight.* I should've known that wouldn't apply to me. "You will have your own unit, your own handpicked Ardents at your side —"

A newblood king will sit the throne you built him.

Cameron said that to me a few days ago, when I forced her to join us. Now I know exactly how she felt, and how horribly true her words could be.

"But only Ardents?" I reply, moving steadily to my feet. "Only newbloods? Tell me, what is it truly like in your Republic? Have you simply traded Silver masters for new ones?"

The brothers stay seated, watching me with keen eyes. "You misunderstand," says Tahir. He taps the scar below his left eye. "We are like you, Mare Barrow. We have suffered for what we are, and simply wish for no one else to meet this fate. We offer sanctuary for our kind. You especially."

Liars, both of them. They offer nothing but another stage for me to stand on and perform.

"I'm fine where I am." I look to the Colonel, focusing on his good eye. He's not scowling anymore. "I won't run away, not now. There are things that must be handled here. Red problems that you need not bother with. You may take any newblood who wants to go with you, but not me. And if you try to make me do anything against my will, I'll fry you both. I don't care what color your blood is or how free you claim to be. Tell your leader I can't be bought with promises."

"And what of action?" Rash offers, raising one manicured eyebrow. "Would that sway you to the leader's side?"

I've walked this road before. I've had my fill of kings, no matter what they're called. But spitting on the twins will get me nowhere, so I shrug instead. "Show me action and we'll see." Chuckling, I turn to go. "Bring me Maven Calore's head and your leader can use me as a footstool."

Tahir's response chills my blood. "You killed the she-wolf. It should be nothing at all to kill the pup."

I exit the control room at a brisk march.

"Strange, Miss Barrow."

"What?" I growl, snarling to face the Colonel. He can't even let me walk out of this barracks in peace. His open expression takes me aback, displaying something like understanding. He is the last person I expect to *understand.*

"You came here with so many more followers, but you lost the ones you left with." He raises an eyebrow, leaning against the cold, damp wall of the passage. "The village boy, your prince, and my daughter all seem to be avoiding you. And of course, your brother —" One quick step forward stops him short, frightening him into silence. "My condolences," he murmurs after a long moment. "It's never easy to lose a family member."

I remember the photograph in his quarters. He had another daughter, and a wife, two people who aren't here now. "We all need some time," I tell him, hoping that's enough.

"Don't give them too much. It's not good to let them dwell on your sins."

I can't find the heart to argue, because he's right. I lashed out at the people closest to me, and showed them the monster beneath my skin.

"And what about this Red problem you mentioned?" he continues. "Anything I should know about?"

Back on the jet, I told Cal I was going north. Half of me said it out of anger, to prove something to him. The other half said it because it is the right thing to do. Because I've ignored things for far too long.

"A few days ago we intercepted a march order. The first of the child legions is being sent to the Choke." My breath hitches, remembering what Ada said. "They're going to be massacred, ordered to march out past the trenches, right into the kill zone. Five thousand of them, slaughtered."

"Newbloods?" the Colonel prods.

I shake my head. "Not that I know of."

He settles a hand on his pistol, draws up his spine, and spits at the floor. "Well, Command did order me to help you. I think it's time we did something useful together."

The infirmary is quiet, a good place to wait. Sara was allowed to leave the barracks designated for Silver use, and she made quick work of anyone injured. Now the beds are empty but for one. I lie on my side, staring at the long window in front of me. The deceivingly blue sky has faded into steel gray. Another storm maybe, or perhaps my eyes have darkened. I simply cannot see any more sunlight today. The sheets are soft, worn by too many washings, and I fight the urge to pull them up and over my head. As if that could stop the memories from coming, each one breaking hard as an iron wave. Shade's last moment, his eyes wide, one hand reaching for me, before the blood burst from his chest. He was coming back to save me, and it got him killed. I feel like I did so many months ago, when I hid in the woods, unable to face Gisa and her broken hand. Now I can't stand the thought of returning to my family and seeing the hole Shade left behind. They are certainly wondering where I am, the girl who cost them a son. But it is not a Barrow that finds me here.

"Shall I come back later, or have you finished feeling sorry for yourself?"

I sit up sharply, only to see Julian standing at the foot of my bed. His color has returned, as have his missing teeth, courtesy of Sara. But for the mismatched clothes, leftovers from the Tuck stores, he looks like his old self again. I expect a smile, maybe even a thank-you, but not a scolding. Not from him.

"Can a girl get a moment's peace around here?" I huff, falling back against the thin pillow.

"By my reckoning, you've been hiding for the better part of an hour. I think that's more than a moment, Mare." The old teacher is trying his best to be kind. It isn't working.

"If you must know, I'm waiting on the Colonel. We have an operation to plan, and he's rounding up volunteers as we speak." *So there.* But Julian isn't that easily deterred.

"And you decided taking a nap was a better use of your time than, say, addressing the other newbloods, maybe calming down a bunch of very jumpy Silvers, getting some medical attention, or even speaking with your own grieving family?"

"I have not missed your lectures, Julian."

"You lie well, Mare," he says, smiling.

He closes the distance between us almost too quickly, coming to sit beside me. He smells clean, fresh from a shower. This close, I can see how thin he's become, and the hollow emptiness of his eyes. *Even Sara cannot heal minds.* "And a lecture needs a listener. You are certainly *not* listening to me anymore." He lowers his voice and tips my face, making me look at him. I'm tired enough to let him. "Or anyone, for that matter. Not even Cal."

"Are you going to yell at me too?"

He smiles sadly. "Have I ever?"

"No," I whisper, wishing I didn't have to. "No, you haven't."

"And I'm not about to start now. I have only come to tell you what you need to hear. I will not *make* you listen, I will not *make* you obey. I leave you the choice. As it should be."

"Okay."

"I told you once that anyone can betray anyone. I know you remember." *Oh, do I remember.* "And I say it again. Anyone, *anything,* can betray anyone. Even your own heart."

"Julian —"

"No one is born evil, just like no one is born alone. They *become* that way, through choice and circumstance. The latter you cannot control, but the former . . . Mare, I am very afraid for you. Things have been done to you, things no person should suffer. You've seen horrible things, done horrible things, and they will change you. I'm so afraid for what you could be, if given the wrong chance."

So am I.

I let my hand close around his. The connection is calming enough, but weak. Our bond is strained at best, and I don't know how to fix it. "I will try, Julian," I murmur. "I will try."

In the back of my mind, I wonder. Will Julian tell tales of me one day? When I have become something wretched, someone like Elara, with nothing and no one to love her? Will I simply be the girl who tried? *No. I cannot think that way. I will not. I am Mare Barrow. I am strong enough.* I've done things, terrible things, and I don't deserve forgiveness for them. But I see it in Julian's eyes all the same. And it fills me with such hope. I will not become a monster, no matter what I must do in the days ahead. I will not lose who I am, even if it kills me.

"Now, do you need me to walk you to your family's bunk, or can you find the way?"

I can't help but snort. "Do *you* even *know* the way?"

"It's not polite to question your elders, lightning girl."

"I had a teacher once who told me to question everything."

His eyes twinkle and he puffs out his weak chest proudly. "Your teacher was a smart man."

I notice his eyes lingering, and the light in

them goes out. He stares at my exposed collarbone, at the brand there. I debate covering it up, but decide not to move. I won't hide the *M* burned into me, not from him.

"Sara can fix that," he murmurs. "Shall I get her?"

On shaky legs, I stand. There are many scars I want her to heal, but not this one. "No." *Let it be a reminder to us all.*

Arm in arm, we leave the empty infirmary. It echoes with our footsteps, a white room steadily fading to gray. Outside, a shade has been drawn across the world. Winter waits on our doorstep — it will knock soon. But I like the cold air. It wakes me up.

As we cross the central yard, heading for Barracks 3, I take note of the compound. A few familiar faces mix in with the various groups, some training, others transporting goods or simply milling around. I spot Ada sliding beneath a broken transport, an instruction manual in hand. Lory kneels next to her, sifting through a pile of tools. A few yards away, Darmian falls in with a troop of Guardsmen, joining them on a jog. They're the only ones from the Notch I see, and it turns my stomach. *Cameron, Nix, Nanny, Gareth, Ketha, where are they?* I feel quite sick, but swallow the sensation. I only have the strength to mourn the person I know for sure is dead.

Julian is not permitted to enter Barracks 3. He informs me of this with a tight-lipped smile, his words dripping disdain. There's no way to enforce the order, but he obeys it all the same. "I'm just trying to be a 'good' Silver," he says dryly. "The Colonel's already been *kind* enough to let us out of our barracks. I would hate to betray his trust."

"I'll come find you after." I squeeze his shoulder. "It must be getting pretty bad in there."

Julian only shrugs. "Sara is taking her time healing — we don't want too many over-powered, underfed, and angry Silvers in an enclosed space. And they know what you did for them. They have no reason to make a fuss — yet." *Yet.* A simple but effective warning. The Colonel doesn't know how to handle so many Silver refugees, and will certainly misstep soon.

"I'll do my best," I sigh, and add quelling a possible riot to my growing to-do list. *Don't cry in front of Mom, apologize to Farley, figure out how to save five thousand children, nanny a bunch of Silvers, put my head through a wall.* Seems doable.

The barracks is as I remember, full of labyrinthine twists and turns. I get lost once or twice, but finally I find the door with the purple scarf tied to the doorknob. It's firmly shut, and I have to knock.

Bree opens the door. His face is red from crying, and that almost does me in right then and there. "Took you long enough," he growls, stepping back so I can enter. I flinch at his harsh tone, but don't retaliate. Instead, I put a hand on his arm. He cringes, but doesn't pull away.

"I'm sorry," I tell him. And then, louder, to the rest of the room, "I'm sorry I didn't come sooner."

Gisa and Tramy sit on mismatched chairs. Mom curls up on one of the beds, with Dad and his chair firmly planted next to her. While she turns away, hiding her face in a pillow, he looks straight at me.

"You had things to do," Dad says. Gruff as always, but more insulting than he's ever been. I deserve it. "We understand."

"I should've been here." I move farther into the room. How can I feel lost in such a small space? "I brought his body back."

"We've seen it," Bree snaps, taking a seat on the bunk opposite Mom. It sags under his enormous weight. "One little blast of a needle, and he's gone."

"I remember," I murmur before I can stop myself.

Gisa twitches in her chair, her thin legs

drawn up beneath herself. She flexes her bad hand, distracting herself. "Do you know who killed him?"

"Ptolemus Samos. A magnetron." Back in the arena, Cal could've killed the wretched man. But he was merciful. And his mercy killed my brother.

"I know that name," Tramy says, just to have something to fill the tense air. "He was one of your executioners. Couldn't get you, but he got Shade." It sounds like an accusation. I have to look down, examining my shoes instead of the hurt in his eyes.

"Did you get him back at least?" Bree gets to his feet again, unable to keep still. He towers over me, trying to look intimidating. He forgets that I'm not scared of brute force anymore. "Did you?"

"I killed a lot of people." My voice breaks, but I soldier on. "I don't even know how many, I just know the queen was one of them."

On the bed, Mom pulls up, finally deciding to look at me. Her eyes swim with tears. "The queen?" she whispers, breathless.

"We have her body as well," I say, almost too eager. Talking about her corpse is easier than grieving for my brother. So I tell them about the broadcast, what we hope to do.

The horrible thing should go out tonight,

during the evening news bulletins. They're mandatory now, an addition to the Measures, forcing every person in the kingdom to eat lies and propaganda with their dinner. A youthful, eager king, another victory in the trenches, and the like, but not tomorrow. Instead, Norta will see their dead queen. And the world will hear our call to arms. Bree paces, grinning madly at the thought of civil war, and Tramy follows, as he always does. They jabber between each other, already dreaming of marching into Archeon together, and planting our red flag on the ruins of Whitefire Palace. Gisa is less enthusiastic.

"I guess you won't be here for long," she says, forlorn. "They'll need you back on the mainland, recruiting again."

"No, I won't be recruiting, at least not for a while."

I can't stand the hope that sparks in them, especially Mom. I almost don't tell them at all, but last time I left so suddenly. I won't do that to them again. "I'm going to the Choke, and soon."

Dad roars so loudly I expect him to fall out of his wheelchair. "You will *not*! Not while I still draw breath!" He wheezes to emphasize his point. "No child of mine will ever return to that place. *Ever*. And don't

611

you dare tell me I can't stop you, because believe me, I can and I *will*."

Once, the Choke took Dad's leg and a lung. He gave so much to that place. And now, I guess he thinks he's going to lose me to it too. "I'm sure you would, Dad." I try to humor him. That usually works.

But this time he waves me off, wheeling up to me so fast his leg bumps my shin. He glares like a demon, one quivering finger pointed at my face. "Give me your word, Mare Barrow."

"You know I can't do that." And I tell him why. Five thousand children, five thousand sons and daughters. Cameron was right all along. The divisions of blood are still very real, and they can't be tolerated any longer.

"Let someone else go," he growls, trying his best not to fall apart. I never wished to see my father cry, and now I wish I could forget the sight. "The Colonel, that prince, *someone* else can do it." He clutches my arm like a man at sea.

"Daniel." Mom's voice is soft, soothing, a single white cloud in an empty sky. "Let her go."

When I pry his hand from my wrist, I realize I'm crying too.

"We'll go with her."

Bree barely gets the words out before I

can tell him no. Dad's face purples, his sadness giving way to anger. "Do you want me to die of a heart attack?" he snarls, spinning to face my oldest brother.

"She's never been to the Choke, she doesn't know what it's like up there," Tramy pipes in. "We do. Spent almost a decade between us on the trench lines."

I shake my head, putting out a hand to stop him before Dad really does lose it. "The Colonel's coming, he's seen the Choke too, there's no need —"

"Maybe from the Lakelander side." Bree's already at his trunk, going through his things. *Looking for what to bring.* "But the Nortan trenches are a different design. He'll be turned around in seconds."

It's probably the smartest thing I've ever heard Bree say. He's not known for his brain, but then again, he survived almost five years on the lines. That's four years longer than most. It can't be luck. I realize instead, this is bravery from both of them, more than I can possibly know. Once I thought about how much of my life my older brothers missed — but I've done the same. They are not as I remember. They are warriors as much as I am.

My silence is all they need to start packing. I wish I could tell them not to come.

They would listen if I truly meant it. But I can't. I need them, just like I needed Shade.

I only hope I won't lead another brother into the grave.

After a long moment, I realize I'm shaking. So I climb into bed next to my mother, and I let her hold me for a long while. I do my best not to cry. My best is not enough.

TWENTY-NINE

The mess hall is crowded, but not for a meal. The Colonel put out the call for a "top-priority operation" only an hour ago, and the room bursts with his handpicked men as well as volunteers. The Lakelanders are quiet, well trained, and stoic. The Guardsmen are much rowdier, though Farley is anything but. She's been reinstated as a captain, but shows no sign of noticing. She sits in silence, absently twisting a red scarf around her hands. When I enter the mess, flanked by my brothers, the noise dies away, and every eye watches me. Except Farley. She doesn't look up at all. Lory and Darmian actually clap as I walk across the room, making me blush. Ada joins in, and then, to my delight, Nanny stands up next to her, as does Cameron. *They made it.* I exhale a little, trying to feel relieved. But there's still no sign of Nix, Gareth, or Ketha. *They could have chosen not to come.*

They must be sick of danger by now. That's what I tell myself as I sit down next to Farley. Bree and Tramy follow, taking the seats directly behind me, like bodyguards.

We are not the last to arrive. Harrick slips in, having just arrived from the Notch, and shoots me a curt nod. He holds the door open, allowing Kilorn to enter. My heartbeat doubles when Cal follows, trailing at his heels, with Julian and Sara behind him. My entrance was quiet — this is the opposite. At the sight of three Silvers, many jump to their feet, mostly Lakelanders. In the din, it's hard to hear their shouts, but the meaning is clear. *We do not want you here.*

Cal and I lock eyes through the commotion, if only for a second. He turns away first, finding a seat at the back of the room. Julian and Sara stick close to his side, ignoring the jeers, while Kilorn picks his way to the front. He drags a chair with him, and plops down beside me. He gives me a casual nod, as if we're just sitting down to lunch.

"So what's all this about?" he says, his voice loud enough to be heard over the noise.

I stare at my friend, perplexed. The last time I saw him, he was prying me off Farley, and looked disgusted with my existence.

Now he's all but smiling. He even pulls an apple from his jacket and offers me first bite. Shaky but sure, I take the gift.

"You weren't yourself," he whispers in my ear. He pulls the apple away again, taking a bite. "Forget about it. But go off the rails like that again and we'll have to settle this Stilts-style. Yeah?"

My scars twinge as I smile. "Yeah." And lower, so only he can hear me. "Thank you."

For a second, he stills, strangely thoughtful. Then he waves a hand, smirking. "Please, I've seen you way worse than that." A comforting lie, but I let him tell it anyway "Now, what's this top-priority business? Your idea or the Colonel's?"

As if on cue, the Colonel enters the mess, his hands stretched wide, asking for silence. "Mine," I murmur, as the complaints fade away.

"Quiet," he barks, his voice like a whip crack. The Lakelanders obey at once, taking their seats in practiced motion. His glare is enough to shut up the other dissenters. He points to the back of the room — to Cal, Julian, and Sara. "Those three are Silver, yes, but proven allies to the cause. They have my permission to be here. You will treat them as you would any ally, any brother or sister at arms."

It silences them all. For now.

"You're here because you've volunteered for an operation without knowing what it is. That's true bravery, and I commend you all for it," he continues, taking his place at the front of the hall. I get the sense he's done this before. In this setting, the cropped hair and red eye give him an air of authority, as does his commanding voice. "As you know, the lowered conscription age has resulted in younger soldiers, down to the age of fifteen. At present, one such legion is on their way to the war front. Five thousand strong, all with only two months of training." An angry murmur goes through the crowd. "We owe our gratitude to Mare Barrow and her team for giving us this information."

I can't help but flinch. *My team.* They belonged to Farley or even Cal, but not to me. "Miss Barrow is also the first to volunteer to stop this tragedy before it happens."

Kilorn's neck cracks, he turns so quickly. He widens his green eyes, and I can't tell if he's angry or impressed. Maybe a little bit of both.

"They've been nicknamed the Little Legion," I say, forcing myself to my feet so I can address the crowd properly. They stare at me, expectant, every eye like a knife. Lady Blonos's lessons will serve me well now.

"According to our information, the children will be sent directly into the Choke, past the trench lines. The king wants them dead, to scare our people into silence, and he'll succeed if we don't do something. I propose a two-pronged operation, led by Colonel Farley and myself. I will infiltrate the legion outside Corvium, using soldiers who can pass for fifteen, in order to separate the Silver officers from the children. We will then proceed directly into the Choke." I do my best to keep my eyes on the back wall, but they keep trailing back to Cal. This time, I'm the one who has to look away.

"That's suicide!" someone shouts.

The Colonel moves to my side, shaking his head. "My own unit will be waiting in the north, on the Lakelander trench line. I have contacts within that army, and I can buy Miss Barrow enough time to get across. Once she reaches me, we'll retreat to Lake Eris. Two grain freighters should be enough to ferry us across, and from there, we enter the disputed lands."

"Ludicrous."

I don't need to look up to know Cal is standing. He's flushed, fists clenched, annoyed at such a foolish plan. I almost smile at the sight.

"One hundred years and no Nortan army

has ever crossed the Choke. *Ever.* You think you can do it with a bunch of kids?" He turns on me, imploring. "You'd have better luck turning them back to Corvium, hiding in the woods, anything other than crossing a damned kill zone."

The Colonel takes this all in stride. "How long since you entered the trenches, Your Highness?"

Cal doesn't falter. "Six months ago."

"Six months ago, the Lakelanders had nine legions on the line, to match Nortan numbers. As of today, they have two. The Choke is open, and your brother does not realize it."

"A trap? Or a diversion, then?" Cal sputters, puzzling out what this could mean.

The Colonel nods. "The Lakelanders plan to push across Lake Tarion, while your armies are busy defending a stretch of waste no one wants. Miss Barrow could walk across blindfolded and not get a scratch."

"And that's exactly what I intend to do." Slowly, surely, I steel my heart. I hope I look brave, because I certainly don't feel it. "Who's coming with me?"

Kilorn is the first to stand, as I knew he would be. Many more follow — Cameron, Ada, Nanny, Darmian, even Harrick. But not Farley. She sits rooted, letting her lieutenants stand in her place. The scarf is wound too tight around her wrist, turning her hand faintly blue.

I try not to look at him. I certainly try.

At the back of the room, the exiled prince gets to his feet. He holds my gaze, as if his eyes alone could set me on fire. *A waste.* There is nothing in me left to burn.

The graves in Tuck's cemetery are new, marked by freshly turned earth and a few woven bits of sea grass. Collected rocks stand in for headstones, each one painstakingly carved by loved ones. When we lower Shade's plank coffin into the ground, all of us Barrows standing around the hole, I realize we are lucky. We have a body to bury, at the very least. But there are so many other graves marking nothing but earth. Their names are carved too. Nix, Ketha, and Gareth. Their bodies abandoned but not forgotten. According to Ada, they never got on the Blackrun or the cargo jet. They died in Corros, along with forty-two others by her impeccable count. But three hundred survived. Three hundred, traded for forty-five. *A good deal,* I tell myself. *An easy bargain.* The words sting, even in my head.

Farley clutches herself against the cold wind but refuses to wear a coat. The Colonel is here too, standing a respectful distance away. He's here not for Shade but his grieving daughter, though he makes no move to comfort her. To my surprise, Gisa takes her side, worming one arm around the captain's waist. When Farley lets her, the shock almost knocks me over. I didn't know the two ever met, but they're so familiar. Somehow, beneath my grief, I manage to feel a bit of jealousy. No one tries to comfort me, not even Kilorn. Shade's funeral is too much for him to bear and he sits on the rise above, far away enough so that no one can see him cry. His head dips every once in a while, unable to watch when Bree and Tramy begin to shovel dirt into the grave.

We don't say anything. It's too hard. The whistling air goes straight through me, and I wish for warmth. I wish for comfortable heat. But Cal is not here. My brother is dead, and Cal cannot find it in his stubborn heart to watch us bury him.

Mom shovels the last bit of dirt, her eyes dry. She has no more tears left to give. We have that in common at least.

Shade Barrow, his headstone reads. The letters look clawed, written by some feral beast instead of my parents. It feels wrong to bury him here. He should be at home, by the river, in the woods he loved so well. Not here, on a barren island, surrounded by dunes and concrete, with nothing but empty sky to keep him company. This was not a fate he deserved. *Jon knew this would happen. Jon* let it *happen.* A darker thought takes hold. *Perhaps this is another trade, another bargain. Perhaps this was the best fate he would ever face.* My smartest, most caring sibling, who would always come to save me, who always knew what to say. *How could this be his end? How is this fair?*

I know better than most that nothing in this world is fair.

My vision blurs. I stare at the packed earth for who knows how long, until it's just me and Farley left in the cemetery. When I look up, she's staring at me, a storm raging between anger and sorrow. The wind ruffles her hair. It's grown longer over the past few months, nearly reaching her chin. She shoves it away so violently I fear she might tear her scalp.

"I'm not going with you." She forces out the words.

I can only nod. "You've done enough for us, more than enough. I understand."

At that she scoffs. "You don't. I couldn't care less about protecting myself, not now." Her eyes trail back to the grave. A single tear escapes, but she doesn't notice. "The answer to my question," she murmurs, not thinking about me anymore. Then she shakes her head and steps closer. "It wasn't much of a question anyway. I knew, deep down. I think Shade did too. He is — *was* — very perceptive. Not like you."

"I'm sorry for everyone you've lost," I say, blunter than I wish to be. "I'm sorry —"

She only waves a hand, dismissing the apology. She doesn't even care to ask how I know. "Shade, my mother, my sister. And my father. He might be alive, but I lost him too."

I remember the worry on the Colonel's face, the brief glint of concern when we returned to Tuck. He was afraid for his daughter. "I wouldn't be so sure. No real father could ever be truly lost to the child he loves."

The wind blows a curtain of hair across her face, almost hiding the look of shock flashing in her eyes. Shock — and hope. One hand splays across her stomach, strangely gentle. The other pats my shoulder. "I hope you make it out of this alive, lightning girl. You're not entirely awful."

It might be the nicest thing she's ever said to me.

Then she turns, never to look back. When I leave a few minutes later, neither do I.

There's no time to mourn Shade or the others properly. For the second time in twenty-four hours, I must board the Blackrun, forget my heart, and prepare to fight. It was Cal's idea to wait until evening, to leave the island while our hijacked broadcast crosses the nation. By the time Maven's dogs come hunting for us, we'll already be in the air and on our way to the hidden airfield outside Corvium. The Colonel will continue north, using the cover of night to cross the lakes and circle around. By morning, if the plan holds, we'll both be in charge of our own legions, one on each side of the border. And then we march.

The last time I left my parents, there was no warning. Somehow, that was easier than this. Saying good-bye to them is so hard I almost run to the Blackrun and its familiar safety. But I force myself to hug them both, to give them whatever small comfort I can, even if it might be a lie.

"I'll keep them safe," I whisper, tucking my head against Mom's shoulder. Her fingers run through my hair, braiding it quickly. The gray ends have spread, almost reaching to my shoulders. "Bree and Tramy."

"And you," she whispers back. "Protect

yourself too, Mare. Please."

I nod against her, not wanting to move.

Dad's hand finds my wrist, giving it a gentle tug. Despite his outburst earlier, he's the one to remind me I must go. His eyes linger over my shoulder, at the Blackrun behind us. The others have already boarded, leaving only the Barrows on the runway. I suppose they want to give me some semblance of privacy, though I have no use for such a thing. I've spent the last few months living in a hole, and before that, a palace crawling with cameras and guards. I don't care about spectators.

"For you," Gisa blurts, holding out her good hand. She dangles a scrap of black silk. It feels cool and slick in my hand, like woven oil. "From before."

Red and gold flowers decorate the fabric, embroidered with the skill of a master. "I remember," I murmur, running a finger over the impossible perfection. She sewed this so long ago, the night before an officer broke her hand. It is unfinished, just like her old fate. Just like Shade. Shaking, I tie it around my wrist. "Thank you, Gisa."

I reach into my pocket. "And I have something for you, my girl."

A trinket, cheaply made. The single earring matches the winter ocean around us.

Her breath catches as she takes it. Tears quickly follow, but I can't watch them. I turn away from them all and board the Blackrun. The ramp closes behind me, and by the time my heart stops racing, we're in the sky, soaring high above the sea.

My soldiers are few compared to the many following the Colonel into the Lakelands. After all, I could only take people who looked young enough to play the part of the Little Legion, and preferably those who had served, who knew how to act like soldiers. Eighteen Guardsmen fit the bill, and have joined us in the sky. Kilorn sits with them, doing his best to acclimatize them to our close-knit group. Ada isn't with us, and neither are Darmian and Harrick. Unable to pass for teenagers, they went with the Colonel, to aid our cause however they can. Nanny is not so restricted, despite her advanced age. Her appearance flickers, fluttering between different iterations of young faces. Of course Cameron has joined us — this was truly her idea in the first place, and she all but bounces with adrenaline. She's thinking of her brother, the one she lost to the legion. I find myself envying her. She still has a chance to save him.

Cal and my brothers will be the hardest to disguise. Bree has a young face, but he's larger than any fifteen-year-old should be. Tramy is too tall, Cal too recognizable. But their value lies in not their appearance or even their strength but their knowledge of the trench lines. Without them, we'll have no one to navigate such a maze, and enter the nightmare wasteland of the Choke. I've only seen the Choke in photographs, news bulletins, and my dreams. After my ability was discovered, I thought I'd never have to go there. I thought I escaped that fate. How wrong I am.

"Three hours to Corvium," Cal barks, not looking up from his instruments. The seat next to him is conspicuously empty, reserved for me. But I won't join him, not after he abandoned me to face Shade's funeral alone.

"Rise, Red as the dawn." The Guardsmen speak in unison, banging the butts of their guns on the floor. It takes us all by surprise, though Cal does his best not to react. Still, I see distaste pull at the corner of his mouth. *I'm not part of your revolution,* he said once. *Well, you sure look like it, Your Highness.*

"Rise, Red as the dawn," I say, quiet but sure.

Cal scowls openly, glaring out the window. The expression makes him look like his father, and I think of who he could have been. A thoughtful warrior prince, married to the viper Evangeline. Maven said he would not have lived past the coronation night, but I don't truly believe that. Metal is forged in flame, not the other way around. He would have lived, and ruled. To do what though, I cannot say. Once, I thought I knew Cal's heart, but now I realize that is impossible. No heart can ever be truly understood. Not even your own.

Time passes in suffocating silence. Within the jet, we are still, but on the ground, things are in motion. My message blares on video screens all over the kingdom.

I wish I were in Archeon, standing in the middle of the commercial sector, watching the world as it changes. Will the Silvers react as I hope? Will they see Maven's betrayal for what it is? Or will they look away?

"Fires in Corvium."

Cal leans against the cockpit glass, his mouth agape. "In the city center, and the River Town slums." He runs a hand through his hair, at a loss. "Rioting."

My heart leaps, then plunges. *War has begun. And we have no idea what the cost may be.*

The rest of the jet erupts in cheers, clapping, and too many handshakes to stomach.

I almost stumble out of my seat, my feet tripping over themselves. I never trip. Never. But I barely make it to the back of the plane in one piece. I feel dizzy and sick, ready to lose the dinner I never ate all over the wall. One hand finds the metal, letting the coolness calm me. It works a little, but my head still spins. *You wanted this. You waited for this. You made this happen. This is the bargain. This is the trade.*

The control I've worked so hard to maintain starts to splinter. I feel every pulse of the jet, every turn of the engines. It veins in my head, a map of white and purple, too bright to stand.

"Mare?" Kilorn stands from his seat. He takes a step toward me, one hand outstretched. He looks like Shade did in his last moments.

"I'm fine," I lie.

It's like ringing a bell. Cal turns in his seat, finding me in an instant. He crosses the jet with strong, deliberate steps, boots slamming on the metal floor. The others let him pass, too afraid to stop the prince of fire. I share no such fear, and turn my back to him. He spins me around, not bothering to be gentle.

"Calm down," he snaps. He has no time for temper tantrums. I'm seized by the urge to shove him away, but I understand what he's trying to do. I nod, trying to agree, trying to do as he says. It stills him a little. "Mare, calm down," he says again, this time just for me, soft as I remember. But for the pulse of the jet, we could be back at the Notch, in our room, in our cot, wrapped up in our dreams. "Mare."

The alarm sounds seconds before the tail of the plane explodes.

The force knocks me on my back, so hard I see stars. I taste blood, and I feel blazing heat. If not for Cal, the fire would incinerate me. Instead, it licks at his arms and back, harmless as a mother's touch. It recedes as quickly as it grows, pushed back by Cal's power, containing itself to embers. But even he can't rebuild the back of a jet — or keep us from falling out of the sky. The noise threatens to split my head, roaring like a train, screaming with the voice of a thousand banshee shrieks. I hold on to whatever I can, metal or flesh.

When my vision clears, I see black sky and bronze eyes. We hold on to each other, two children trapped in a falling star. All around us, the Blackrun peels apart, piece by piece, each tear another bloodcurdling screech. With every passing second, more of the jet disappears, until only thin bars of metal remain. It's freezing cold, hard to breath, and impossible to move anything of my own volition. I cling to the bar beneath me, holding on with all I have left. Through slitted eyes, I watch the dark ground below, getting closer with every terrifying second. A shadow darts past. It has an electric heart and gleaming wings. *Snapdragon.*

My stomach plummets with the remnants of the Blackrun. I can't even summon the strength to scream. But the others certainly do. I hear them all, shouting, pleading, begging for mercy from gravity's pull. The structure shudders all around, accompanied by a familiar clang. Metal, slamming together. *Re-forming.* With a gasp, I realize what's happening to us.

The jet is no longer a jet. It is a cage, a steel trap.

A tomb.

If I could speak, I would tell Cal that I'm sorry, that I love him, that I need him. But the wind and the drop steal my breath away. I have no more words. His touch is achingly familiar, one hand at my neck, imploring me to look at him. Like me, he can't speak. But I hear his apology all the same, and he understands mine. We see nothing but each other. Not the lights of Corvium on the horizon, the ground rising up to meet us, or the fate we're about to find. There is nothing but his eyes. Even in darkness, they glow.

The wind is too strong, tearing at my hair and skin. My mother's braid comes undone, the last vestige of her pulled away. I wonder who will tell her how I died, if anyone will even know the end we met. What a death for Maven to dream up. This must be his idea — to kill us together, and give us time to realize what is coming.

When the cage stops short, I scream.

There is stiff grass beneath my dangling arms, just kissing the tips of my fingers. *How?* I wonder, pulling away. It's hard to find balance, and I fall. The cage rocks with my motion, like a swing hanging from a tree.

"Don't move," Cal growls, putting a hand to the back of my neck. The other clutches a steel bar, and it glows red in his fist.

I follow his gaze, looking across the forest clearing to the people standing in a wide circle around us. Their silver hair is hard to mistake. Magnetrons of House Samos. They stretch out their arms, moving in unison, and the cage lowers slowly. It drops the last inch, earning yelps from us all.

"Loose."

The voice feels like a lightning bolt. I throw off Cal's grip and vault to my feet, sprinting to the edge of the cage. Before I can hit the side, the bars drop, and my momentum carries me too far. I stumble, hitting the half-frozen grass, skidding on my knees. Someone kicks me in the face, sending me sprawling in the mud. I shoot a jagged spark in their direction, but my attacker is too fast. A tree splinters instead, toppling over with a splitting crack.

The strongarm's knee hits my back, pinning me so forcefully he knocks the air from my lungs. Strange-feeling fingers, coated in plastic, maybe gloves, close around my throat. I claw at his grip, sparking, but it doesn't seem to work. He lifts me without any effort at all, forcing me to scramble on my toes to keep from strangling myself. I try to scream, but it's useless. Panic knifes through me and my eyes widen, searching for a way out of this. Instead, I see only my friends, still confined by the cage, pulling at the bars in vain.

The metal shrieks again, twisting and curling, each bar becoming its own prison. Through one bruised eye, I watch metallic snakes lock around Cal, Kilorn, and the others, binding their wrists, and ankles, and necks. Even Bree, big as a bear, has no defense against the coiling rods. Cameron fights as best she can, silencing one magnetron after another. But there are too many.

When one falls, another takes their place. Only Cal can truly resist, burning through every bar that comes close. But he's just fallen out of the sky. He's disoriented at best, and bleeding from a cut above the eye. One bar cracks him across the back of the head, knocking him out cold. His eyelids flutter, and I will him to wake. Instead, the silver vines wrap around him, tightening with every passing second. The one at his throat is worst of all, digging in deep, enough to strangle.

"Stop!" I choke out, turning toward the voice. Now I fight with my own meager muscles, trying to break the strongarm's grip the old-fashioned way. Nothing could be more fruitless. "Stop!"

"You are in no position to bargain, Mare."

Maven is coy, keeping to the darkness, to his shadows. I watch his silhouette approach, noting the spiky crown on his head. When he steps into the starlight, I feel a brief twinge of satisfaction. His face does not match his confident drawl. There are bruise-like circles beneath his eyes, and a sheen of sweat coats his forehead. His mother's death has taken its toll.

The hands around my throat loosen a little, allowing me to speak. But I still dangle, my toes slipping in cold grass and icy mud.

No bargain, no trade. "He's your brother," I say, not bothering to think. *Maven doesn't care about that at all.*

"And?" He raises one dark eyebrow.

On the ground, Kilorn squirms against his restraints. They tighten in response, and he gasps, wheezing. Next to him, Cal's eyelids flutter. He's coming around — and then Maven will certainly kill him. I have no time, no time at all. I would give anything to keep these two alive, anything.

With one last explosion of rage, fear, and desperation, I let myself loose. I killed Elara Merandus. I should be able to kill her son and his soldiers. But the strongarm is ready for me, and squeezes. His gloves hold, protecting his skin from my lightning, doing exactly what they were made for. I gasp against his grip, trying to call to the sky above. But my vision spots, and a sluggish pulse sounds in my ears. He will choke me dead before the clouds can gather. And the others will die with me.

I will do anything to keep him alive. To keep him with me. To not be alone.

My lightning has never looked so weak or forlorn. The sparks fade slowly, like the beat of a dying heart. "I have something to trade," I whisper hoarsely.

"Oh?" Maven takes another step. His presence makes my skin crawl. "Do tell."

Again, my collar loosens. But the strongarm digs a thumb against the vein in my throat, an open threat.

"I'll fight you to the last," I say. "We all will, and we'll die doing it. We might even take you with us, just like your mother."

Maven's eyelids flicker, the only indication of his pain. "You will be punished for that, mark my words."

The thumb responds in kind, pressing further, probably leaving a spectacular bruise. But this is not the punishment Maven speaks of, not by a long shot. What he has in store for us will be much, much worse.

The bars around Cal's wrists redden, glowing with heat. His slitted eyes reflect the starlight, watching me with bated breath. I wish I could tell him to lie still, to let me do what I have to do. To let me save him as he saved me so many times.

At his side, Kilorn stills. He knows me better than anyone, and understands my expression plainly. Slowly, his jaw tightens, and he shakes his head from side to side.

"Let them go, let them live," I whisper. The strongarm's hands feel like chains, and I picture them crawling over every inch, winding like iron serpents.

"Mare, I don't know if you understand the definition of the word *trade,*" Maven sneers, pressing further. "You must give *me* something."

I won't go back to him for anyone. I told Cal that once, after I survived the sounder device, and he realized what this was all about.

Surrender, Maven's note said, begging me to return.

"We won't fight. *I* won't fight." When the strongarm drops me, my walls disintegrate. I lower my head, unable to look up. It feels like bowing. *This is my bargain.* "Let the rest go — and I will be your prisoner. I will surrender. I will return."

I focus on my hands in the grass. The coldness of the frost is familiar. It calls to my heart, and the hole that grows there. Maven's hand is warm beneath my chin, burning with a sickly heat. Daring to touch me is a stark message. He does not fear the lightning girl, or at least he wants to seem that way. He forces me to look at him, and I see nothing of the boy he once was. There is only darkness.

"Mare, no! Don't be an idiot!" I barely hear Kilorn, pleading now. The whining in my head is so loud, so painful. Not the hiss of electricity, but something else, inside me. My own nerves, screaming in protest. But at the same time, I feel a sick and twisted relief. So many sacrifices have been made for me, for my choices. It's only fair that I take my turn, and accept the punishment fate has in store.

Maven reads me well, searching for a lie that doesn't exist. And I do the same. Despite his posturing, he *is* afraid of what I've done, of the lightning girl's words and the affect they have. He came here to kill me, to put me in the ground. Now he's found a greater prize. And I've given it to him willingly. He is a betrayer by nature, but this is a bargain he wants to uphold. I see it in his eyes; I heard it in his notes. He wants *me,* and will do anything to hold my leash again.

Kilorn squirms against his restraints, but it's no use at all. "Cal, do something!" he shouts, lashing out at the body next to him. Their bonds clang together in a hollow echo. "Don't let her!"

I can't look at him. I want him to remember me differently. On my feet, in control. Not like this.

"Do we have a deal?" I am reduced to a beggar, pleading with Maven to put me back in his gilded cage. "Are you a man of your word?"

Above me, Maven smiles as I quote him. His teeth gleam.

The others are shouting now, shaking in their bonds. I hear none of it. My mind has closed to all but the trade I am ready to make. I suppose Jon saw this coming.

Maven's hand moves from my chin to my throat. His grip tightens. Softer than the strongarm, but so much more painful.

"We have a deal."

EPILOGUE

Days pass. At least, I think they're days. I spend most of my time in dull blindness, subject to the sounder. It doesn't hurt so much anymore. My jailors have perfected the so-called dosage, using it to keep me unconscious, but not in skull-splitting pain. Every time I come out of it, my vision spotting to show men in white robes, they turn the dial, and the device clicks again. The insect burrows in my brain, clicking, always clicking. Sometimes I feel pulled, but never enough to fully wake. Sometimes, I hear Maven's voice. Then the white prison turns black and red, both colors too strong to stand.

This time when I come around, nothing clicks. The world is too bright, and slightly blurry, but I don't fall back under. I truly wake up.

My chains are clear, probably plastic or even diamondglass. They bind my wrists and ankles, too tight for comfort, but loose enough to allow circulation. The manacles are the worst part, sharp and grating against the sensitive flesh. Worn wounds, shallow and stinging, ooze blood. The red seems to bite in contrast to my pale shift dress, and no one bothers to wipe it away. Now that Maven can't hide what I am, he must show it for all the world, for whatever twisting scheme he has now. The chains clink, and I realize I'm in an armored transport, a moving one. This must be used for prisoners, because there are no windows, and the walls have rings. My chains are hooked to one, swaying slightly.

Across from me are the two men in white, both bald as eggs. They bear a striking resemblance to Instructor Arven. His brothers or cousins, most likely. That explains the stifling sensation and my difficulty breathing. These men are silencing my ability, holding me hostage in my own skin. Strange, that they need chains too. Without my lightning, I'm just a seventeen-year-old girl, almost eighteen now. I can't help but smile. I'll spend my birthday a prisoner of my own volition. This time last year, I thought I'd be marching to the war front. Now I'm heading who knows where, locked into a rolling transport with two men who would very much like to kill me. Not much of an upgrade.

And I guess Maven was right. He warned me we would spend my next birthday together. It seems he *is* a man of his word.

"What day is it?" I ask, but neither responds. They don't even blink. Their focus on me, on silencing what I am, is perfect and unbreakable.

Outside, a strange, dull roar begins to grow. I can't place it, and don't want to waste energy trying. I'm sure I'll find out soon enough.

I'm not wrong. After a few more minutes, the transport eases to a stop, and the rear door is wrenched open. The roar is a crowd, an eager one. For a terrifying second, I wonder if I'm being sent back to the Bowl of Bones, to the arena where Maven tried to have me killed. *He must want to finish the job.* Someone unlatches my chains, yanking, pulling me forward. I almost fall out of the transport, but one of the Arven silencers catches me at the last moment. Not out of kindness but necessity. I must look dangerous, like the lightning girl of old. No one cares about a weak prisoner. No one jeers at a sniveling coward. They want to see a conqueror brought lower, a living trophy. For that is what I am now.

I willingly stepped into this cage.

I always do.

My body quivers when I realize where I am.

The Bridge of Archeon. Once, I watched it crumble and burn, but the symbol of power and strength is rebuilt. And I must walk across it, my feet cut and bare, my chains and captors close at hand. I stare at the ground, unable to look up. I don't want to see the faces of so many people, so many cameras. I can't let them see me break. That is what Maven wants, and I will never give it to him.

I thought it would be easy to be put on parade — after all, I'm used to it by now. But this is so much worse than before. The tremors of relief I felt in the forest clearing are gone now, giving way to dread. Every eye crawls over me, looking for the cracks in my famous face. They find many. I try not to listen to their shouting, and for a few seconds, I succeed. Then I realize what most of them are saying, and the horrible things they hold up for me to see. *Names. Photographs. All the Silvers dead or missing.* I had a hand in all their fates. They scream at me, throwing words more harmful than any object.

By the time I reach the far end of the

Bridge and the crowded Caesar's Square, the tears come too fast and hard to stop. Everyone sees. With every step, my body tightens. I reach for what I cannot have, for the ability that cannot save me. I can barely breathe, as if the noose is already tight around my neck. *What have I done?*

There are many gathered on the steps of Whitefire Palace, eager to see my downfall. The nobles and generals are all in mourning black, this time for the queen. Evangeline's own gown is hard to ignore, midnight spikes of crystal, glinting as she moves.

One person alone wears gray, the only color that suits him. *Jon.* Somehow, he stands with the rest of them and watches my approach. His eyes, bloodred, hold an apology I will never accept. *I should have never let him go.* I curse to myself.

Once, he said I would rise alone. Now I know he was lying. For I have certainly fallen.

The front of the platform is empty, raised above all else. A good place for an execution, if Maven is so inclined. He sits there, waiting, seated on a throne I don't recognize.

My jailers pull me toward him, forcing me to approach the king. I wonder if he'll murder me in front of everyone, and paint the steps of his palace with my blood. I flinch as he stands. We face each other as betrothed people would, stark and alone before a crowd of faces. But this is not a wedding. This might be my funeral, my ending.

Something glints in his grip. *His father's sword? An executioner's blade?* I feel shivering cold as he clamps the something around my neck. *A collar.* Jeweled, gilded, sharp-edged, a beautiful thing of horrors. My blurred tears make it hard to see, until I'm sure of nothing but the black-armored king before me, and the brand scalding my collarbone.

There's a chain attached to the collar. A leash. *I am nothing more than a dog.* He holds it tightly in his fist, and I expect him to drag me from the platform. Instead, he stands firm.

He tugs smartly, testing the chain in hand, making me stumble toward him. The points of the collar dig in. I almost choke.

"You put her body on display." His lips brush my ear as he forces the words through clenched teeth. Pain hums in his voice. "I'll do the same to you."

His expression is unreadable, but his meaning is clear. With one hand, he points at his feet. His fingers are whiter than I

remember.
    I do as he says.
    I kneel.

ACKNOWLEDGMENTS

Before I thank any one person, I would like to thank the leftover pizza I'm currently eating. It's really good.

As with the last time around, I owe thanks to so many people, and I'm going to do my best to include them all here. First and foremost, to my parents, Heather and Louis, who continue their disgusting level of support. I honestly could not have done this, and continue to do this, without you both. And, of course, my baby brother, Andrew, who is somehow now an adult. When that happened, I don't know, but I'm so proud of you and so excited to see you continue to grow up. So much love and thanks to my grandparents — George and Barbara, Mary and Frank — I treasure you all and miss two of you so much. And to the rest of the extended family, aunts, uncles, cousins, etc., thank you for your support and friendship. Special thanks and congratulations to Michelle, who is an author herself on the publishing road.

Last year's acknowledgments ran very long, so I'm going to try to be a bit less wordy this time around. Thank you to all my friends on both coasts. Sorry for being weird. A sincere thank-you to Morgan and Jen, who tolerate and sometimes encourage my nonsense.

Thank you so much to the team at Benderspink, who continue to make great strides in the battle to bring *Red Queen* to the movie theater, not to mention keeping my own screenwriting career afloat. Christopher Cosmos, Daniel Vang, the Jakes, JC, David, and all the interns and their coverage. And, of course, thank you to Gennifer Hutchinson and Sara Scott, as well. I can't wait to see where we go from here. Finally, to my lawyer, Steve Younger, who always has my back no matter what.

I could write pages thanking the team at New Leaf Literary, but I'll spare you and summarize: they are, without question, the best. Top to bottom, side to side, every single person at my agency is outrageously talented and I thank my lucky stars I landed with them. To Jo, Pouya, Danielle, Jackie, Jaida, Jess, Kathleen, and Dave — thank you for existing and condescending to deal with me. To Suzie, I say it all the time, but only because it's true: You are wonderful and unparalleled and the reason I can do what I do.

In case my gushing wasn't quite gross enough, I'm going to continue. I truly consider the success of *Red Queen* to be a minor miracle, which I guess makes the people at HarperTeen saints. First and foremost, Kari Sutherland, my first editor, my first and only offer, who believed in my manuscript and made it so. To my other gem of an editor, Kristen Pettit, a shepherd in great clothes with an even greater sense of story. Thank you for your continued work and perseverance in shaping my clay ideas into lovely story sculptures. And also to Elizabeth Lynch(pin), you work so hard and tolerate me so well. The rest of the Harper team is no different: Kate Jackson (even if your food blog haunts me), Susan Katz, Suzanne Murphy, Jen Klonsky, wizards all. In marketing, the tireless Elizabeth Ward, Kara Brammer, actual celebrity superstar Margot Wood, and the rest of Epic Reads. *Red Queen* would never have made such a splash without any of you. To Gina, my lovely publicist, who makes it possible to see even more lovely readers. In managing editorial and production, my gratitude to

Alexandra Alexo, Lillian Sun, Stephanie Evans, Erica Ferguson, Gwen Morton, and Josh Weiss. If not for you, *Red Queen* and *Glass Sword* would be an incoherent lump. In sales, Andrea Pappenheimer, Kerry Moynagh, Kathy Faber, Susan Yeager, and Jen Wygand. And a shout-out to Kaitlin Loss, who helps coordinate with my international publishers. Last, but in no way least, the design team, who I think might be actual magical beings? Seriously, have you seen my covers? There's no way humans made those. But thank you for the art and I am on to you: Sarah Kaufman, Alison Donalty, Barb Fitzsimmons, and Toby & Pete.

Having now been published and officially in the living world of literature, I realize how expansive it is — and how scary it can be. Thank you so much to all the people who've made my transition from baby author to published author so smooth and easy. To the bloggers, vloggers, tweeters, readers, carrier pigeon-ers who continue to push *Red Queen* and now *Glass Sword,* thank you, thank you, thank you. To the fellow writers who are nothing but support, I'm so grateful for your friendship. I'd name names, but there's too many of you, and honestly it feels like bragging to call you guys my friends. And once again, to Emma

Theriault, who is greedy for *RQ,* generous with notes, and always willing to chat.

As is tradition, I will also thank a few things that are not people. Well, the first is a collection of people. To the New England Patriots. Last year I thanked you and you won the Super Bowl. Let's keep that tradition going. Free Brady. To Wikipedia, the National Park Service, Scotland, Target, San Diego Comic-Con, the changing of the seasons, cashmere scarves, my excellent new printer, globes, coffee with too much cream, my Delta points, and brunch. And to my personal inspirations: Tolkien, Rowling, Martin, Spielberg, Lucas, Jackson, Bay. Yes, I said Michael Bay, get out of my face.

Nearly there. These are repeats, but they're important, so if you've made it this far, you might as well read on. To Morgan. To Suzie. And again to my parents. This starts and ends with you.